THE SOUND OF SILENCE

ESME CARMICHAEL

YOUR MAP AWAITS!

Thank you for reading *The Sound of Silence!*

Have you signed up to my newsletter? You'll receive exclusive stories, a gorgeous map of the New World, and get first dibs on all my future releases. Scan the QR code below:

For those who never stop Protecting

1

WINTER

Slave. Aristocrat. Rebel.

Words floated around in my head, each one telling a different story. What story fit me best? The Slave who'd spent her life running from Mason? The Aristocrat who'd spent her life succumbing to him? Or the Rebel who was going to fight him, to *kill* him?

Standing before Mikael Ashworth, I pondered each of these words—each of my many lives—as the train rocked gently back and forth. So much had changed in so little time. So many lives had been destroyed by the same organisation that vowed to free the New World from Mason's tyranny. The same organisation that promised to save me from that monster forever.

So why didn't I believe it?

"That's impossible," I said, sneering around the words. "Mason can't be killed; he's immortal." I turned sharply to Campbell, the sight of him breathing still shocking me. "You stabbed him through the heart, for Odin's sake!"

"Yes, for many years, that was true," a firm, enunciated, and rather high-pitched voice arose from around the metal table. A man, dressed in a long robe decorated with gold trim, stood below a swaying lightbulb, the light bouncing off his flawless bald head. He had a round face and eyes that spilled calculations. Out of everyone in that room, he stuck out like a sore thumb. Definitely an Aristocrat.

"What do you mean, *was?*" I asked, eyes narrowing.

The room descended into silence. I flicked my diamond eyes to each of them, focusing on Mikael Ashworth for the longest of all. "How do you expect to kill a man who's invincible?"

Ashworth crossed skinny arms over a narrow chest, scrutinising me. Those dark brown eyes dropped to my belly, only to flick back up to meet my gaze.

"First things first," he said unkindly. "We need to ask you a few questions."

Another man stepped into the light. Incredibly tall, with dark skin and a trimmed black beard, he sported a pair of thick, black-rimmed glasses. One lens was cracked directly down the middle. "We need to know if you're pregnant," he said.

A bitter laugh escaped my lungs. "No, I'm not."

"How can you be sure?"

"I am." Anya came to my side, her long copper hair glinting in the dim light. "I gave her emergency contraception."

"Did you take it?"

Hands curled into fists at my sides. "Yes."

"What type?"

Anya delved into the pocket of her oversized leather jacket and picked out a small glass bottle full of those white pills. She threw it at the bearded man, who caught it with one hand and studied the label.

"Yep, that'll do it," he said, and threw the bottle back to Anya.

The entire room expelled a long sigh of relief.

My knuckles whitened. "What's going on? Why are you so determined to find out if I'm pregnant or not?"

A cautious exchange of stares. Each one pinned me down, one writhing limb at a time.

The bald Aristocrat stepped forward. "Alira, how much do you know?"

"Nothing."

"Hm. Yes, well, I suppose the key thing you need to understand is that you must not become pregnant, under any circumstances."

"Why?" I glared as memories of my lost babies echoed in my head. "After everything you people put me through, you can at least tell me *why*."

"Because he's mortal," Campbell breathed from the outskirts. "Because he's fucking mortal..."

Air sped out of my lungs, unable to cling to it. This supposed truth, the one that—for some reason—seemed to cause Campbell the most pain of all, was just so absurd that it couldn't *possibly* be real... I refused to believe it.

"I've seen bullet holes in his coat," I said, barely holding back my snarl. "He's survived explosions."

"Yes, he has. While you were pregnant."

Something hard and cold sank in my empty belly, writhing against a sore truth.

"You see, my dear," the bald Aristocrat began, "your species is flawless. They have one job: to Destroy, and to Protect. Mason, quite obviously, is the Destroyer. But you are the Protector: Mason's exact opposite.

"You both create a child. It's your only purpose and certain *devices* initiate this. The music forces you both to its will, one way or another, and Mason is immortal while you are simply reborn each time you die. A different body and memories, of course, but the same soul—"

The same soul. With a falling heart, I thought about my predecessors. All those *Aliras* killed by knife, bullet, or the frigid New World air. I thought about all those lost lives, and then my soul—shaped into its irregular form by each stab, each undeserving bullet. I glanced at Campbell and imagined myself in a soaked cot, wrapped in a cold, damp blanket. On a rainy night, many years ago, I stared into the empty black snout of his worn revolver—

I hastily pushed aside the visions, fighting the rush of painful nausea.

Oblivious to my turmoil, the bald Aristocrat continued, "That is the fate of the Protector. Doomed to switch from one body to another until you finally give the Destroyer a son. It seems rather final, doesn't it?"

Yes, it did seem final, and I felt tired. Ever so tired.

Ashworth took a slow step forward. "But there's a loophole, a way to break the cycle."

In the corner of my eye, Campbell sniffed back tears. "I'm so sorry, girl..."

"Miscarriage," I whispered, tears prickling my eyes. *That's* the loophole?"

The bald man nodded. "Yes, my dear, I'm afraid it is. If you miscarry, by accident or design, the cycle is disrupted. Mason is unable to heal, and you both become vulnerable. Ultimately, there are only two ways for the cycle to resume. Impregnation, or death."

It made so much sense now: *why* Mason wanted to try again; *why* the Free People tried so hard to take away my child.

"You didn't know, did you? That I was pregnant again?" Questions tumbled from the rusted, frosted ceiling. "The explosion in Bolton Square... W-was that meant to kill him?"

"Yes," Ashworth said, marching towards the map covered with small tokens, evidently swiped from a chessboard. "We had no idea you'd be there. We assumed we'd just kill Mason but realised our mistake when the bastard didn't die, so we needed to get you the hell out of that Palace, at any cost. Now, more than ever, you need to be kept safe."

"*Safe?*" My bitter tongue caressed the word, finding cruel mockery between the vowels. "There's no such thing as *safe*."

Ashworth scowled, taking angry steps closer. "Then would you like me to send you back there? Should I throw you to the ruins of your grand Palace?"

The shadow man smiled, the swaying lightbulb gleaming against yellowed teeth. "Or we could just kill you."

"No, *no!* You are *not* touching her!" Campbell rushed forwards and stabbed a sharp finger in the air.

The shadow man produced a low, raspy chuckle. "A little late to protect her now, wouldn't you say, Campbell?"

Campbell lurched forward with murderous intent. "You dare touch her and I'll cut your damn throat, Carter!"

Ashworth jumped in and pushed Campbell back with a firm hand on his shoulder.

"Gentlemen," the bald Aristocrat interjected, lifting his hands to calm the room. "This is an uneasy alliance at the best of times. Do try to stay focussed."

Carter chuckled to himself as Campbell shook off Ashworth's hand with hushed profanities.

"No, Ben," Ashworth eventually said. "We kill her and another Alira will be born. Then Mason is returned to his full strength, and all Free People will be dead within the year. No, she *has* to live."

"Whatever you say, Ashworth," Ben Carter grumbled.

Ben Carter.

"You're Mike the Mulch," I realised.

"It's Ben Carter to you, sweetheart." He mocked the Aristocratic accent and turned to the bald man. "After all, such nicknames don't do well in the presence of these *dignified* men. Not that you can really call yourself a *man* anymore, hey Theo?"

"*Theodore*, please." The bald man smiled tightly. "I have not come this far for my name to be slandered with such colloquialism."

"Fellas, can we get back to the point?" The woman spoke this time. The shadows left little to be distinguished, but she was clearly a refined beauty with thick locks of pure ebony.

"Yes, Isla's right," Ashworth said. "Time is not on our side. Minutes are wasted as we sit around deciding what to do with her."

"Agreed." Theodore's attention fixated on me. "Ultimately, the choice is up to you, dear. Will you help us?"

Would I? Would I help *them:* the Free People, the Rebels, the terrorist organisation that had destroyed me twice already?

The pain of miscarriage shot through me, mocking its inevitable finality. Anger was simmering, just below the ball of despair that tried to flush up against my gullet. A few months ago, I'd have thrown their offer in their faces —likely followed by a knife, or maybe a bullet.

But now... Memories of Mason lingered, still so new and raw: the experiences we had shared, the twisted happiness that once plagued my gullible heart... Those memories had been defiled the moment Mason pinned me over that dressing table, and I *hated* him for that.

I hated him more than I hated Ashworth.

"Yes," I replied. "I'll help you."

"Good." Theodore formed another tight smile and headed for the door. It was more of a shuffle than a walk—like a man who had his ankles tied together. "I'm sure you understand we need the opinion of another to fully gauge your devotion to the cause."

"My *devotion?*" I felt mildly insulted.

"Why, my dear, you can't expect us to take your word at face value. There have been many reports of you cavorting about Maelstrom, after all."

"Nothing beats a spot of tea after a good fuck, hey?" Ben Carter snarled.

I charged forward, a chipped nail stabbing the air as Campbell held me back by both shoulders. "You have *no* idea what Mason did to me in that place, so don't you dare judge me for trying to make my life a little easier!"

Campbell whispered soothing words into my ear, but I just wasn't in the mood. Shaking his arm off heated skin, I clutched my throbbing temple and attempted to stave my fury. The familiar urge to *destroy* slowly crawled up my gullet. I shuddered and swallowed it down, only to have Carter drive it up again.

"I'm sure you understand that you being an Aristocrat is a liability to us, girl."

I glared at him. "The Aristocratic life was the shit-hole you threw me to in the first place, *mate*."

"I think you'll find Joe Matheson was the guilty party."

"And why did he do that, hm? Didn't just wake up one morning and decide to sell Campbell's name to Mason, did he? No, it was because *you* blackmailed him into being his mule!"

"It's a shame he got caught then, wasn't it?"

Fury. Unmitigated fury rose like vomit in my throat. Screams pressed against the corners of my mouth, all the agony of those past twenty-four hours—those past two weeks, those *twenty-one months*—finally erupting.

Anya stormed forwards, pushing Campbell out of the way, and grasped my head within her clammy hands.

"Look at me, honey," she said softly, those bright blue eyes so wide and pleading. "*Breathe...* That's it, don't let it get to you..."

Eventually, Anya's words percolated through the wall of fire. Her voice soothed me, cooling my boiling blood until I felt the burn of panic inside my lungs. With gasping breaths, I wiped the last of my anger away as Ben Carter stood.

"Yes," he spat, marching towards me. "You're definitely Mason's fucking mate."

Beneath the flickering light, I caught a brief glimpse of his face. Such a hard face, broad and muscular, sculpted from the ice itself. A large scar ran from his temple to his chin, cutting through his nose and clouding what would have been a cerulean blue eye. A truly horrific-looking man.

As soon as the light touched his features, he stormed completely from the room.

"I apologise for him," Isla said with a sigh. "He's a bastard at the best of times."

"Why is he helping you?" I asked, scowling. "He's a drug lord. His insanity is famous in all five Territories."

"Six," Ashworth added. "Lightlands, remember?"

Oh, of course. The Aurora Territory. Mason had created it for me, to cheer me up after Erksow Castle.

That strange ache returned. Like some damned, persistent heartburn.

"Regardless, the Mulch Gang is helping us simply because we share a common enemy. We couldn't have stormed the Palace if it weren't for the combined efforts of his men as well as ours."

"It's a wonder his men didn't kill me where I stood," I muttered bitterly to the air.

"That's a sore spot. Don't bring it up."

Great. I'd been saved from Mason and thrown to thirsty Rebels, desperate to gulp my blood. After everything I'd done, I couldn't say I blamed them.

Mason's anger viciously plucked the violin's strings inside my head. I grimaced at the growing ache, but deflated as the music waned into something a little more bearable.

Mason would also kill me, if given the chance. Or make me wish for death, at least. The thought pushed a shuddering sigh past my lips.

Theodore reappeared, looking ever so pleased with himself. A tall man lingered in his shadow, his slick hair not quite as neat as normal.

"Bentley?"

His nod was his only greeting. A thick rod of steel shot down his spine as Rebel Commanders formed an interrogatory huddle.

Theodore stepped forwards. "Bentley, thank you for joining us at this ungodly hour. I hope you have recovered from the events of the last few hours?"

"Yes, Sir."

"We're not *Sirs* here, Bentley," Ashworth snapped. "You're not a Slave anymore."

"Apologies; force of habit."

"We just have a few questions; they won't take long." As Theodore began, Anya squeezed my hand. I returned the gesture, my palm sweating. "You were at the Palace for the entirety of Alira's imprisonment, yes?"

"That is correct," Bentley replied, puffing out his chest like some proud peacock. "First when she was using the alias *Maya Doe*, then as her true identity."

Maya Doe. Even the name sent shivers down my spine.

"You must have witnessed a whole manner of terrible things. Tell us, in your personal opinion, are you surprised that Alira has agreed to join the Free People's Rebellion?"

"No, I am not surprised at all that she seeks revenge for all she has suffered."

"You have no doubts of her loyalty? Nothing you can recall that would make you question her devotion to our cause?"

Tendrils of fear slithered up my spine. They worked their scheming way through my muscles, causing an uncomfortable sickness that settled deep in my nervous stomach. I recalled the shared kisses between Mason and me, enraptured with each other's company as Bentley stood against the Dining Room wall. Or the times Mason had placed a gentle hand upon my pregnant belly, feeling its immature roundness between the morning news articles. Bentley must have remembered the smiles, the laughs, the happiness in two sets of diamond eyes that twinkled like stars in the night...

"No," Bentley replied, loud and firm. "Nothing at all."

A subtle exhale of air—the first of many—as I inwardly praised Bentley for his deception. He was certainly a better liar than me. I needed to remember that.

Bentley's disclosure had pleased the Rebels, Ashworth especially, who finally viewed me with something akin to respect.

"Good," he said. "Thank you for your help on this matter, Bentley. It is appreciated."

With a swift nod, Bentley left the compartment. I stared at each hole in his matted jumper for as long as I could, until the door closed behind him.

"Well," Ashworth continued. "Now we have assurances of your loyalty, we can begin."

"Begin what?"

From the shadows in the corner of the compartment, Ashworth returned with a worn revolver and a hunting knife, polished to perfection.

"Follow us, Alira. There's someone we'd like you to see."

2

———————

Emilia Eynesbury lay on a rickety old bed beneath layers of thin, moth-eaten sheets. Her breathing strained, her skin wrinkled and withered, grey eyes perusing the scene with startling clarity—and plenty of distaste. Oh yes, still very much alive and kicking.

Those hard, stony eyes softened as I rushed towards her and clamped her cold hand within my own.

"Emilia, oh Gods, are you alright?"

"Of course I am, darling!" She clicked her tongue at me. "It'll take more these ruffians to part me from this world."

Those *ruffians*—comprising Ashworth, Theodore, and Campbell—almost completely dominated the small carriage that housed nothing more than the bed and a small chest. Thick, musty air, riddled with dust and mould, did little for Emilia's degrading lungs.

"C-can't you move her someplace else?" I asked Ashworth, who looked down his long, sharp nose at me. "She's ill, for Freya's sake!"

"She's not got long left. No point in moving her now."

Emilia patted me on the arm. "It's alright, darling. These old bones are far too fragile for any further relocation."

I observed each tuft of grey, shrivelled hair upon her balding head, and a painful lump arose in my throat. The headscarf was long gone, no doubt burned away with the rest of her possessions. All she had left were some pearl earrings and the lime green nightgown. It barely covered her chest.

It was cruel for such a proud and glamorous woman to spend her last few hours inhaling mould spores, without her precious headscarf, interrogated by people who only wanted her dead. Her only comforts were Orzo and Heidi, plain-clothed and sitting patiently by her side. Orzo had an open leather case in his lap, boasting the glass syringes nestled inside.

As the train rocked gently from side to side, Ashworth stepped forward. His sharp features shone beneath the light. "Ms. Eynesbury, we need to know where Sebastian Svellec is hiding."

A mucus-filled laugh rattled around her lungs, followed by a cough and a splutter. Heidi leant forwards with a small glass of water, supporting Emilia's head as she sipped.

"Thank you, my dear," she said, as Heidi eased her back down to the stained, misshapen pillow. Stone-cold eyes return to Ashworth. "And why, may I ask, should I do that?"

"You need morphine. You know this cancer isn't going to let you out kindly."

"And who's going to give it to me? That drug lord? Ha! Don't piss on my funeral parade, Ashworth!"

Theodore stepped forwards. "Surely you realise that such medicine will make your passing tenfold more comfortable."

"How typical of you, Theodore, to meet your Maker with such cowardice. Unlike you, I fully intend to leave this world exactly how I entered it: screaming like a banshee!"

"Oh, how exceptionally droll of you, Emilia," Theodore retorted, hands concealed within his robe. "Do give my regards to your Maker, when you eventually depart us."

"Your father would be ashamed," Emilia scowled. "Cooped up in here, helping the likes of these...*people*. My, Harold Addington would turn in his grave!"

"As you know well, my father was more interested in other little boys, rather than his own. Rather fortunate, now that I recall such things."

Emilia pulled her attention away with a grimace and fixed on Campbell.

"And you, Mr. Anders..." She shook her head in disgust. "What the hell do you think you're doing? Didn't you lose enough last time?"

"This isn't like last time, Emilia," Campbell said, shaking his head softly from side to side. "Now we have a chance to kill him."

"The *only* thing you're going to kill is Alira's chance for a blissful existence. Do you even comprehend the type of danger you've put her in?"

"*Danger?*" Campbell snarled, rounding his shoulders like a wolf going in for the kill. "Mason *raped* her, *tortured* her! Do tell me what a danger *I* am!"

"Campbell," Emilia whispered. "Send her back."

I met Emilia's pleading expression with stubborn resolve. "Emilia, I'm not going back."

"Alira," she said, gripping my hand with a firm squeeze. "I will not see your eyes gouged out because of the reckless whims of Rebels with a death wish. Go back to him, apologise—tell him you're sorry! Please, darling, before he grows angry."

"He's already pretty fucking angry, Emilia!"

"Now I will not hear those sorts of profanities whilst I'm on my deathbed."

A small, miserable chuckle escaped me. I sniffed my tears away and snapped, "Emilia, I'm not having his child. Not now, not *ever*."

My heart ached at the thought, and the crippling *longing* that survived beneath mounds of rage and revenge.

Emilia clicked her tongue. "Don't be so childish. Spread your legs for five minutes and you'll have nine months to recover from past mishaps."

My face twisted with shocked disgust. "You don't get it, do you?"

"I do, darling, trust me," she said, stony eyes melting. "But you have to see the bigger picture. This... *Rebellion* is going to rot well before Mason does, and you will have to answer for your idiocy."

"Do you think Alira has a choice, Ms Eynesbury?" Ashworth sneered, with his arms firmly crossed. "She's staying here whether she likes it or not."

Theodore's thin lips twisted with clear triumph. "Although, Mikael's threats are somewhat redundant, given Alira has already agreed to help us."

Emilia turned to me with widening eyes, gripping my hand with white-knuckle force. "Reconsider," she breathed. "I know he's hurt you, but think about the consequences of what you're doing!"

I remained silent, too exhausted to reply. Mason's anger whacked his violin against the inside of my skull, breaking into thousands of tiny splinters that dug into my eyeballs.

"Where's Sebastian?" I asked weakly.

Emilia huffed bitterly to the mouldy ceiling and ripped her hand from mine.

"Stupid girl," she hissed, tears in her eyes.

Ashworth released a tiresome sigh. "Ms Eynesbury, time is in short supply. It's late, we're all tired—help us out here! Tell us where Sebastian Svellec is, and you have my word that you'll get all the morphine you need."

I observed Emilia, usually so flamboyant, and saw the fragile rigidity hanging to each muscle, the subtle clench and release of each limb as pain flared inside her bones.

"Keep your damn morphine," she said. She tried to sit up, to spit more profanities in Ashworth's face, but quickly collapsed with a dreadful, gasping cough.

"Heidi, get Zackery," Campbell said. Heidi rushed from the room, strands of golden hair rippling across her red jumper.

Mason's dressing gown was a similar shade to that jumper. It was so soft.

Just as Emilia's face was losing colour, Zackery rushed into the room with a small leather bag.

"Okay, Emilia, just try to breathe normally..." He took out a stethoscope and listened to her failing lungs. Next, he pressed two fingers against her pulse. A hopeless look over his shoulder made Ashworth's face fall.

"Emilia, it doesn't have to be like this. Tell me what I need to know and let us ease your pain!"

Emilia coughed up a large bubble of blood. It fell to her bare chest, pooled in each little groove between her exposed ribs, and trickled into the thin mattress.

"She's too weak," Zackery said. Bottles clinked as he dived into his leather bag. "Let me try to stabilise her, then you can ask your questions."

* * *

We left the carriage as Emilia's coughs resounded in the metallic space. I cringed at the noise—it sounded so final.

"How long does she have?" I asked the group of men, huddled together with their expressions grave and concerned.

"Not long," Theodore replied. "The disease is in its final stages."

"Can't you give her something? To help her?"

"We've already offered medicine in exchange for Sebastian's where-abouts. If the stubborn wench refuses to cooperate, then it's her decision." Theodore puffed his shoulders, accentuating his rotund middle. "Now, if you'll excuse me."

Gold robes shimmered as he shuffled into the adjoining carriage.

"Why do you need Sebastian?" I asked once the door had clicked shut.

"He's the key to information that we desperately need."

"What kind?"

Ashworth raised his sharp nose to me. "Why you're the End of Everything."

The familiar pile of unanswered questions grew taller, spreading out its branches like some ever-evolving tree.

"I thought you knew." I turned to Campbell. He always seemed to know it all.

"I know a lot of things, girl," Campbell said. "But not everything."

"The general belief is that Mason's hold over this world will be irrefutable. That is correct, for he'll be forever immortal should you bear him a son, but..." Ashworth shook his head, a frown forming deep ruts across a forehead riddled with black coal smuts. "This other rumour: that you'd destroy the world, that Mason's child will be the doom of us all? Nah, I don't believe that at all."

"Svenja Svellec knew everything, but she was incredibly secretive." Campbell scratched his chin through dense stubble. "She told us only about your souls—about Mason's immortality—and yet downright refused to relay anything more."

My nose scrunched. "Why? Why hide such things?"

"Because she's a power-hungry witch," Ashworth grumbled to himself. "She only ever told us the bare minimum so she'd always have the upper hand."

"Mason's hold over this world is at its weakest," Campbell said, meeting my confused gaze. "Only now can we strike, but we need to ensure there are no surprises."

I hummed around a deepening frown. "But Svenja's dead; Mason killed her. All that knowledge died with her, surely?"

Campbell smiled. "It'll take a lot more than Mason to kill Svenja Svellec, I assure you."

Svenja Svellec's *alive?* No, I didn't believe that. Mason abhorred the woman, and I had absolutely no doubt he *did* slice her throat.

"But..." My brow scrunched. "Mason *said* he'd killed her. Why would he lie about that?"

Campbell ignored my question and rubbed his smile away with his palm. "If we find Sebastian, we'll find Svenja. We need to get to him as soon as possible."

"So long as Emilia Eynesbury doesn't die on us," Ashworth muttered beneath his breath.

The air became heavy, the dull swaying of the train accentuating the claustrophobia. It was musty and cold. Unforgiving.

Still, through the metal walls and flickering lightbulbs, resolve shone as bright as ever. These people were determined, relentless, and all too fearless. Could I be described as any of those words? No, not at the moment at least. My predicament was still too new, too real.

Yet, the continued urge for knowledge was one I knew all too well. Besides, I disliked Sebastian Svellec as much as the next Rebel on that train.

"Jury's Alpine." Attention flocked to me. I cleared my throat and said, "That's where Sebastian told me he was. Whether he's there now, I have no idea. It's somewhere on the Glasslands-Woodlands border, at any rate."

The look Campbell gave me was nothing less than proud. His eyes sparkled, his lips curling into a tender smile.

"Much appreciated," Ashworth said. If he was surprised, he was too preoccupied to notice. He rushed from that compartment on a clear mission, barking demands through the metal structure until his sonorous voice disappeared entirely.

Finally, Campbell and I were left alone. Awkwardness threatened.

"Come on, girl." Smiling, he nodded to the door. "I owe you a drink."

* * *

The sun was rising. It peeked above the trees, spreading bloody fingers across the land.

Our continued ascent north only emphasised the *Shortest Day*, and the wintry blackness that the sleepy sun's power did little to alleviate.

We had crossed into the Woodlands, where trees spurt in great waves from the ground. Smothered with snow, they merged into the red horizon, blanketing the rolling hills that quickly burst into rugged mountains.

Campbell and I perched upon the edge of a compartment. The door opened wide to boast the beautiful, speeding view. I cradled my steaming cup of spiced wine and inhaled its comforting scent: earthy notes of cinnamon and nutmeg, the sweet tang of blackberries. Its warm aroma was a welcome contrast to the fresh, bitter air that smelled of pine and fresh snowfall.

In this quiescence, I regaled the story of Maya Doe. Of how I was first bought by Emilia, then sold to Mason. How I had met Joe Matheson, discovered my true purpose in this frozen world, and how the depraved actions of one Masonian Captain revealed my true identity. My fingers ached to caress the scar on my eyebrow, time and experience doing little to repair the seams Jayson had cut that night.

"Jeez, I'm so sorry, girl," Campbell said, visibly pained by my tale. "When I offered you into Slavery, I stupidly thought you'd be safe from Mason. I didn't consider that others might take an interest."

"The Fjordlands are brutal," I said with a sigh. "Slaves are there to make their Masters happy, however possible. Mason took great pleasure in reminding me about that."

"It wasn't right," Campbell said, his black hair streaked with silver that flickered in the cold breeze. "It was always possible that Mason would find you, but never in a thousand Ragnaröks did I believe it would be like that. You didn't deserve that, girl."

I shrugged a lazy shoulder, the cold air numbing the lingering ache behind my eyes.

Mason's music fluctuated in intensity, battling his insatiable anger with his insistent, almost desperate desire to sleep. Still no silence. Sleep remained elusive to him.

I sighed, chestnut waves rippling in the breeze. "Montgomery's dead. Mason killed him as soon as he attacked me. Shame really, I would've liked to have killed him myself."

Perhaps it would have been revenge for what happened afterwards—not for me, but for Tia. Poor Tia. I stared solemnly at the outside world, wishing Tia was drinking spiced wine by my side, her glorious curls bouncing upon her shoulders as she laughed at her freedom.

"We should have got you out months ago," Campbell grumbled to himself.

I met the anger behind his stare. "Why didn't you?"

"We didn't have the numbers. Ben Carter's association to the Rebellion is only recent, and we needed his help to infiltrate the Palace."

Visions of that horrific, scarred face lingered in my memories. Despite his role in storming Mason's Palace, he didn't seem remotely interested in my welfare. "Why is Mike the Mulch helping you anyway?"

Campbell sighed, expelling his evident frustration. "He wants the Ice Territory. He wants it as an independent state, free of Mason's dictatorship."

My eyebrows shot up to my hairline. "That's an incredibly large ask."

Campbell bobbed those bushy eyebrows. "Course it is. But ever since Erinton's Cavern was destroyed, Mason's gradually been losing control of the Ice Territory. Now, the Mulch Gang walks all over it—much to Mason's chagrin. He's increased Masonian patrols up there, but he hasn't reclaimed any land and all it's done is piss off Carter. Now, Carter's on a mission to kill the bastard entirely."

"I'm sure the feeling is mutual."

"Ha, exactly." Campbell returned my gentle amusement. "Nah, Ben Carter's methods are rather extreme and he's a mean old bastard, make no mistake. But he has more firepower in the Icelands than all the Free People in all the other Territories. At the end of the day, we need him a lot more than he needs us."

I nibbled at the raised scar on my lip. "Is he trustworthy?"

"You should know by now that no one's trustworthy." Campbell's lips curled upwards ever so slightly. "But stay on his good side, and you'll be okay."

I'd spent the last twenty-one months remaining on the *good side* of evil people. For the most part, I had succeeded. A few times, I did not.

The scars on my wrists shone, now free of the bracelet's disguise. I stared at them, contemplating their existence. Campbell followed my gaze, and a muscle pounded in his jaw.

"How did you get those?" There was a tone in his voice that suggested he did not want to know the answer. Good—I didn't want to tell him either.

I pulled down the sleeve of my coat, hiding them. "Doesn't matter," I mumbled.

A long pause. "Did Mason do it?"

For a long time, I watched my breath float towards the compartment door. It was always whipped away by the speeding air. "Yes," I replied.

"May..." Campbell seemed reluctant. "May I ask you something?"

"Depends on what the question is," I carefully replied.

"Elliot Trevelyan..." His throat bobbed with a large swallow. "What happened to him?"

Anger—*rage*—swarmed around my body as Campbell's shoulders dropped with a loud thud. That name—I'd never forget that name, or the satisfying way his head decorated the wall of Mason's Gun Room.

I straightened my spine. "I put a bullet in his brain."

Campbell closed his eyes. "Jeez, girl..."

The dam burst, spilling *months* of grief. "You don't have any comprehension of what he did to me. Or what *you*, Ashworth, and the rest of the Rebels did to me, for that matter."

"I was against it," he whispered, trying to catch my eye. He wanted me to see his regret. "I need you to know that I was fully against that—"

"It doesn't matter," I said, focussing on the warmth of the tankard so my hands wouldn't clench. I wished my stomach was that calm, for it boiled with a thousand unresolved memories that were eager—oh, so *fucking* eager—to spit in Campbell's face. "You're no better than a bunch of terrorists."

"*Terrorists?*" Campbell's face instantly reddened as silver lined his eyes. "Your *mate* is the goddamned terrorist around here, girl!"

"Mason's an evil, sadistic man—I don't deny that at all." I refused to back down and matched Campbell's infuriated glare. "And yet, despite everything he's done, Mason *never* strapped his Masonians with bombs and threw them into innocent crowds!"

"No, he just destroys entire towns, slaughters men, women, and children by the *billions!* He's a mass murderer, a serial rapist, a genoci—"

I jolted back, that horrible *R*-word ripping the air from my chest. "You don't need to tell me what he is. I was at the other end of his cruelty for *months*. I know exactly what he is."

Yes, I knew what he was, yet I once craved his touch, the sound of his voice, the gentle stroke of his finger down my cheek. Yes, Mason was a monster. So, what did that make me?

The more generous side of my personality reminded me that I was a victim. A damaged, torn woman, looking for any comfort she could find. I liked that explanation. It agreed better with my conscience.

"I don't want to argue with you, girl," Campbell said, casting his glacial-blue eyes to the bleeding horizon.

"I don't want that either," I said with a large sigh. And it was true. My heart had been beaten so much, I didn't want a pointless fight to deepen those scars. So, I wiped away the painful memories from my chapped cheeks. "I've missed you, Campbell," I admitted.

His face softened, those icy eyes melting. "I've missed you too, so damn much. And for what it's worth, I'm so sorry for the part I played."

Tears itched. Bitter tears, acidic and corrosive, as I realised some scars on my heart would never disappear. I didn't want them to.

I met Campbell's teary stare with staunch defiance. "I'm sorry too, but I can't accept your apology, Campbell. Yes, I'll help you kill Mason. I'll help you create a New World free from his tyranny. But despite how happy I am to see you again—and I *am* happy about that, Campbell—I can never forget the lives this Rebellion stole from me, and I sure as Hel can never forgive them for that."

I can never forgive you.

"I know," Campbell whispered. He stared at the mountains, unable to look at me. "I don't expect you to."

An uncomfortable silence bloated the air between us. I watched the world speed by, absorbed in the trees and the snow stained with the same red flush as the sky. My mind wandered, however unwillingly, to everything I had endured over the past year. It all started when Jason Montgomery attacked me, and Mason discovered who I really was.

What would have happened if I had remained Maya Doe for a little while longer? Would I have succeeded with my grand race for freedom? I recalled the small knapsack hidden beneath my rickety bed, full of blankets and pickled vegetables. Would I have escaped? Made it to the trees before the dogs ripped me apart?

No matter the tune fate sang, Maya Doe would have died. One way or another, she was just another tragedy of Mason's cruel regime.

I sniffed back the memories, determined to keep them hidden as Zackary arrived in our little compartment. His head was bowed, his cracked glasses slipping down his nose.

"Emilia is on her way out," he said, a solemn look in his eye. "The time has come for you to say your farewells."

* * *

Heidi Ice-Dancer wiped a tear from her cheek as she exited Emilia's compartment. Small dots of moisture dripped from her chin and onto her jumper full of holes, a grey t-shirt peeking from underneath. Still, as her honey-brown eyes went large and glassy, she managed a smile.

I hugged her close, inhaling the cigarette smoke etched into her hair.

I asked if she was alright, the Herdinese words rolling effortlessly off my tongue. She nodded her head, albeit slowly, and forced another smile.

Heidi and Orzo had said their goodbyes to Emilia. I was the last, the chosen one to see her out, into the next world.

Taking a deep breath, I entered Emilia's compartment.

She was lying on the same stained mattress, her bald head dry and flaky, her eyes closed and sunk deep into her skull. Large clots of blood dotted the blanket that covered her, her breaths ragged, and her once sumptuous nightdress splattered with crusty pools of red. It was almost like her iron exterior had started to rust in the damp air.

It was a travesty to see her like this. My heart ached at the sight.

Slowly, I inhaled my courage and knelt beside a hand that lay open, relaxed, and soft by her side. I took it firmly, embracing it with my cold fingers, and gently pressed my lips against the chapped skin.

Emilia's eyes opened, dull and delicate, incredibly shiny.

"Alira," she said, barely above a whisper. "I'm afraid my time has come."

"Who knows..." I forced a smile. "You've proven Grant wrong before. Perhaps you'll fool this doctor as well."

"If I have some fight left in me, it's bloody hard to find." Those thin, bloodless lips formed a small smile. "I'm ready to go now, darling. I'm content."

"I-I can ask them for something," I said, my voice cracking. "Something to make it easier?"

"I'm in no pain now. I can't feel anything below my navel, as a matter of fact."

I laughed in spite of myself, and her, and this entire situation. She was just so nonchalant, even as Death breathed down her neck. That woman's resolve was something to be admired, to be paraded. Not to be shunned behind the closed door of a damp train carriage, surrounded by her enemies. My spiteful laugh malformed into a miserable grimace.

"I'm so sorry, Emilia," I said, the words painful to utter. "I'm sorry you have to die like this, in this place, surrounded by these people."

"Don't you dare be sorry," she said, with a feeble squeeze of my hand. "It's not your fault that we're here, any more than it is mine. Those Rebels took you, whether you wanted it or not."

"I did want it," I admitted, in barely a whisper. "I wanted to escape that Palace so badly..."

I stared at her skin, translucent and hanging from her bones. Death had already taken a hold of her, absorbing her life force as the seconds wore on. Perhaps, if I stayed with her long enough, she would turn transparent and disappear entirely.

"What Mason did to you is unforgivable," she said, those eyes growing larger, shinier. "My God, I could have killed him when I found out."

"So, you do understand?"

"Of course I understand. That doesn't mean what you're doing now is right."

"I can't go back there," I said, bubbles catching in my throat, tears clinging to my eyelashes. I leant in close, afraid the metal walls had ears. "It's not about babies, Emilia. It was the betrayal, the fact that he forced me when he *knew* I didn't want to, even when I *begged* him to stop. That's the worst part. For him to actively hurt me like that, after all we'd shared, after I'd given him everything and was *happy* about it."

"And that's why you have to go back," Emilia said between her audible breaths. "If you ever want the chance to be happy again, you need to go back, and quickly. Each second you remain here will do nothing but add resentment. Hate is an easy emotion to accrue in your situation."

I scoffed beneath my breath. "And what situation might that be?"

Emilia closed her eyes, her long, skinny limbs flexing beneath the blankets. When they reopened, her pupils dilated into black, desperate voids. "Alira, don't make him hurt you again. Don't make him take your child away, to replace you with another simply because you're emotionally fraught."

"I'm not emotionally fraught! Emilia, I *hate* him!"

A long pause. A terrible, weighted pause.

"No, you don't," she whispered.

Dampness and mould encroached upon my nostrils, settling on a belly that was suddenly so tight and nauseous. Words tickled my tongue, that *resentment* ached at the back of my throat. Yet no retort came. I remained silent. Shell-shocked.

Alone.

Emilia's breath quickened as she struggled against Death's grip. I perched on the side of the bed, squeezing her hand.

And then, as Emilia's gasping breaths lessened and her throat closed upon itself, I saw the fear behind those stony eyes.

"It's okay, Emilia..." I whispered, cupping her cheek.

Did she hear me? Those eyes stared blindly above, lost in their own images, their own dreams. A single tear trickled down my cheek, across my trembling lower lip.

I stayed with her as breaths disappeared into the mattress. As her lungs deflated, and her skin cooled. Her eyes still stared at the mould on the ceiling. I closed those lids, protecting the intensity of that stony stare.

Silence. *Finally,* there was silence.

Mason had submitted to his sleep. If I listened hard enough, I might have detected the concerned chatter from the next room.

But I did not want to listen hard. I wanted the silence. I wanted to hear my own raging heartbeat, to feel the strange ache that still lingered there. It was a miserable ache. A sad ache.

Another tear trickled down my cheek. It dripped onto Emilia's papery skin as I placed a final kiss upon her forehead.

"Goodbye, Emilia," I whispered, slipping my hand from hers.

3

Sleep eluded me.

Every time I closed my eyes, Emilia's corpse glared back at me, thrown from the train like some leftover piece of meat. I had screamed at Ashworth and Campbell, to demand they give her a proper burial. They refused, simply asking why Emilia Eynesbury would receive something not even their own brethren had the pleasure of. After all, bodies of Rebels littered all forests, ripped apart by scavenging wolves and bears, snow leopards, and white foxes. Why would the body of a captured Aristocrat be treated any different?

I was still stewing over this as Anya slept in small cot next to me. The exhaustion of the past twenty-four hours had finally captured her, clawing its way into her body and dragging her into an instant sleep. I envied her.

I closed my eyes and saw the tufts of white upon Emilia's dry head, the flakes of dry skin merging into the snow that had probably covered her by now. Had she been ripped apart by animals already? Had a lonesome bear stumbled upon her carcass?

I sat up, ripping the images from my mind.

Mason would likely realise something had happened. The misery of Emilia's death was still so fresh that when he'd awake, he'd hear my mournful piano inside his head and ponder over what caused it. Would he realise that I was mourning for Emilia? Would he understand that I had shed countless tears for her?

I stared solemnly at the metal walls, trying my best to find some calm. But it remained forever hiding. In the end, I could take no more.

Throwing the chequered scarf around my neck, I exited the carriage and wandered through the train. I avoided the mess of sleeping people, holding my breath through the ripe stench of sweaty bodies. It was quieter at the end of the train. Above the lingering bitterness of gun grease, the air was fresh enough for a long, laboured sigh.

I opened the carriage door and inhaled the frigid air. Mountains towered around us, specks of snow whipped up from the tracks, illuminated by a sky dancing with ethereal colours. Musical threat disintegrated beneath the roaring of the train, and I sank into that distraction, allowing myself to finally —*finally*—relax.

Sleep remained elusive.

But as I watched the sunrise bleed across the snow-smothered landscape, I admitted that sleep could wait. The world was just too beautiful to ignore.

Which was why, not long after the sun awoke, I was rather perturbed by Campbell's sudden presence.

"C'mon, girl," he said, wiping his nose on his sleeve. "Ashworth wants a word with you."

Ashworth carefully studied his map, fists clenched and pressed upon the table. Isla remained by his side, her gorgeous ebony hair glinting in the light from the swinging bulbs. Some years older than me, she was an elegant beauty with soft features, a small mouth, and large eyes that glowed a deep and powerful green—like jade. If anything, her colouring would have reminded me of Verity Ulster. Her eyes played a different chord though: kinder, more mellow.

Theodore remained too dignified to lean over the table and stood as though with a poker down his spine. His intelligent eyes surveyed the scene with sharp precision.

I felt immediately relieved that Ben Carter was absent, yet the combined stares of the remaining Rebel Commanders still caused gooseflesh to race up my arms.

"What do you want?" I asked, alternating concerned stares between them all.

"We have a request," Ashworth said with an unsettling grin that sank straight to my stomach.

"Oh yes?" I mumbled. "What did you have in mind?"

Before me, Ashworth's grin widened. "You're going to get in contact with Mason."

Air shot out of me. I deflated with its absence, shoulders slouched, my knees feeling detached from my body and yet somehow still holding my stunned, icy body upright. "You bloody what?"

Ashworth hid his amusement behind thin, dry lips.

Campbell's expression, unlike Ashworth's, contained genuine concern. Even defeat. "Emilia Eynesbury's death is a blow to Mason."

"It was to me too," I choked.

"I know, girl," he said gently. "And your music must be screaming inside Mason's head. Sooner or later, he'll put the pieces together, and then we'll be in deep shit."

My spine grew tight and rigid. "So how do I fit in?"

"You're going to explain that Emilia's death was natural, that she succumbed to the disease and was not, in *any* way, harmed by the Free People."

I remembered them withholding Emilia's precious morphine and a harsh, doubtful laugh escaped my lungs. "Do you really think that's going to change anything?"

"Perhaps..." Ashworth sighed. "Or perhaps not. Either way, we're going to try. We can't afford to have innocent people die over a misunderstanding."

A misunderstanding. Yes, that was a good word for it. It was a *misunderstanding* that I was Maya Doe. A *misunderstanding* that I originally thought Mason wanted to kill me. Emilia's death, and the circumstances surrounding it, was not a *misunderstanding*.

"This is ridiculous," I said as my legs carried me—aimlessly—around the room. "And what sort of *misunderstanding* will happen when *I* contact him, huh? He thinks I'm your prisoner, and you forcing me to explain the grizzly details of Emilia's death ain't going to help matters!"

Isla sighed, her arms tightly crossed. "She's right. Having Alira explain Eynesbury's death may just cause more trouble."

Ashworth chewed on his tongue, thinking. "Alira, give us a minute, would you?" he asked, but it was a terrible disguise for the order it really was. Shaking my head at the audacity of it all, I returned to the previous compartment and let the cold air dull the anger in my veins.

"Is it good news or bad?" I whispered when Campbell reappeared.

"A little bit of both," he replied, before leading me back to the group.

I stood before them with my head held high, my arms tightly across my breasts—as if to quieten my thundering heartbeat.

"Well then?" I pressed when the silence became heavy.

"A letter will still be written," Ashworth said. "I will personally hand it to a trusted courier, who will deliver it to Mason at the Barracks, but a prisoner won't be writing it."

Relief spread through me, powerful and exhausting.

"You will instead write is as our ally," Theodore said, puffing up his shoulders.

I remained staring, unable to breathe. Even my anxiety was shocked into the numbness that trickled through my limbs.

"I-I'm sorry?"

"You're right, writing this letter—while he believes you're our prisoner—is just going to piss him right off. But if you tell him outright that you're working with us, that his precious mate is trying to kill him..." Ashworth's bitter comment did not agree with the smile on his face. "Well, that's a reaction I would very much like to see."

"Alira," Isla said, as she saw my terror. "As you say, Mason currently believes you're our prisoner, and that puts us in a very dangerous position."

"So, you'd sooner put *me* in a dangerous position? That's alright for you? You lose, and you die—life is over for you! I'll have to continue on, to deal with Mason's fury until the end of time because he *can't* kill me!" My stare turned nasty. "Mason's going to be fucking pissed and yet *I* don't have the luxury of dying, and he'll make me realise that too!"

"Girl," Campbell said, coming to my side. "Whatever happens, I assure you that Mason will never hurt you again. If this Rebellion fails, we all die. *All of us.*"

There was a knowing look behind his eyes. The look of a lone bullet, straight through the temple. Or a bottle of poison slipped into a tankard of mead. Maybe all it would take was a bash on the head. A flash of pain—a glorious white light—and then I'd be with my parents and Emilia, watching Mason's cruelty from behind that heavenly veil.

No, I solemnly realised, *I'll never go behind the aurora.* Instead of being reunited with my Pa, my soul would be thrust down into a new body. I'd have new parents, an entirely new life. A new chance for Mason to find me. *Again.*

Regardless of my *future,* Campbell would ensure my current *incarnation* would die with the rest of the Free People. If such a time came, I'd doubt he'd even think twice about it. He'd already killed me once, after all, beneath those rainy skies in Gainstorn. I wrapped my arms around myself, suddenly very cold.

Theodore shuffled to the table and placed a piece of paper and pen upon it. It was a delicate movement, as though the metal structure would buckle under the weight. I certainly was, for the pen shook in my trembling hand once Campbell had curled my fingers around it.

"I assume you can use one of those?" Isla asked delicately. Unable to speak, I nodded. "Good. This is what you shall write."

* * *

LIFE ON TRAIN tracks moved in perpetual motion. Even when Ashworth jumped off to deliver my shaky, handwritten letter to the courier, the train did not stop moving. It remained plodding along, swaying back and forth at a more subdued pace. After his brief conversation, Ashworth hopped back on a little further down the line of carriages. A frantic wave from Campbell and the train sped up once more.

Soon, we headed towards the Glasslands. Towards Jury's Alpine, or wherever it was. Nobody expected Sebastian to be there, of course, but there might be clues regarding his current whereabouts. The priority now was to find Sebastian Svellec, wherever he might be, and to interrogate and kill him. They still believed Svenja was alive—*somehow*—and Sebastian was the only key to her whereabouts. I bit back my doubts and continued doing what I was told—I was too tired to do anything else.

Two weeks passed before my letter reached Mason's hands. His music exploded with such terrible intensity. *Hatred, betrayal, misery…*

All these emotions—a myriad of intense feelings—burst through my skull with a ferocity that made me scream.

Anya found me writhing on the floor, blood pouring from my nose, ears, and eyes. She rushed to find Zackary, leaving Heidi to hold my hand and cry, saying everything was going to be okay…

The sweet prick of a needle in my arm was a welcome, liberating saviour. When I eventually awoke—with Anya and Heidi bedside me—the music had dulled into a miserable ache. Still angry, though it allowed me space to think and ponder over my idiotic actions.

I knew writing that letter was a mistake.

The next few weeks crawled on. Mountains grew steeper, and the threat of avalanches constantly lingered. Occasionally, the train was forced to dodge half-buried tracks littered with bits of uprooted trees. These diversions added days to our journey yet were the preferred option, lest Masonians stumble upon a bunch of Rebels clearing tracks for a motionless, trapped train.

"Rebellions are all about patience," Campbell said to me, after I dejectedly asked why we couldn't just shovel away the snow. "But it'll get better," he added when he saw my shoulders droop. "Spring will be upon us soon, melting the snow with it."

Spring. Was it almost Spring already?

Three weeks after Mason received my letter, and many diversions later, the first breath of sunlight illuminated the tracks just outside Jury's Alpine.

The train remained moving slowly as Ashworth, Campbell, and the others went to clear the town, find Sebastian, and to kill any lingering Masonian. I was ordered to stay behind—for my own safety, apparently— and wait with bated breath for any news. With Anya on one side and Heidi on the other, silence encompassed us like an old friend. Very little could be heard through the thick mess of trees. Not even a single gunshot.

I had yet to decide if that was a blessing or not.

Orzo stood at the open door, the sunlight punching through the trees. His acne scars created bare pits in a patchy beard that glowed a deep ruby in the morning light. "Hey up," he remarked, gathering the gun leaning against the door. "Someone's coming."

I perked up, my fingers itching for a gun. I expected to see Masonians surrounding us, their hands clenched around revolvers, their eyes spitting brutality—

"It's Isla," Anya said, with narrowing eyes. I followed her gaze towards the mess of black hair, fluttering delicately in the cold breeze.

"You think they've found him, then?" I asked.

No one answered.

Goggles covered her eyes, yet I still felt their green stare. "Come on," she said, curling a gloved hand around the handlebar at the edge of the compartment door. "Place is deserted."

My heart sank. "No Sebastian?"

"Not a whiff."

Guilt grew, my stomach shrivelling with the knowledge that I'd brought them here for nothing. "Jeez, I'm sorry, Isla."

Visibly affronted, Isla just clicked her tongue. "Nonsense—it was the best lead we've had in ages. Could still be, as Campbell wants you to take a look around."

"Why?"

"You might be able to tell us where the old guy went. Besides, the place is quite ostentatious. It's worth a look."

Ostentatious was a suitable adjective. As Jury's Alpine peeked through the trees, it struck me as a horrid blemish on an otherwise pristine landscape. Nothing more than a small, Aristocratic hub, surrounded by mountainous peaks and curling glaciers. Each thundering creak foretold movements buried deep in the turquoise ice. Those creaks and cracks continued as my boots sank into the snow, a hunting rifle in my hands that weighed heavy with familiarity. It reminded me of a life so long ago.

"Are you sure there aren't any Masonians around here?" I asked.

"If there were, they would've attacked long ago. We've been tearing the place apart for the last hour, and surely Sebastian wouldn't want his prized collection destroyed?"

I exhaled a long sigh of milky mist. "No, I suppose not."

Punching through the last barrier of trees, I realised that Jury's Alpine wasn't a town at all. A lonely, giant mansion of pristine marble shone like a pearly jewel against the dirty white. At its front, a stained-glass window observed an enormous set of double doors, forced open to reveal the grandeur inside.

The window created a circle of speckled colour on a marble floor streaked with gold, leading to a large staircase that curled around the room and disappeared into the upper levels. A plethora of rooms spread from this grand hallway, like tributaries from a river: dining rooms, drawing rooms, sitting rooms—a whole manner of useless rooms that just existed to boast wealth.

Display cabinets and paintings littered the walls, bursting with expensive relics, jewellery, and gold statues. Those relics were being piled into sacks, the protective glass broken and strewn across the floor.

Rebels infested the building, smearing mud across the marble as dirty footprints stained bearskin rugs. Nothing but ants, scurrying beneath the painted ceiling that surrounded dull, cracked chandeliers.

One little ant rushed towards me, the faded black of Campbell's leather jacket appearing tenfold darker against the bright marble.

"This place could be a fucking museum," he grumbled once within earshot.

"No sign of Sebastian, I take it?"

"No, bastard's not been here for a while by the looks of things."

"Sorry," I said again, for I cared more about Campbell's opinions rather than Isla's. "I've led you here for nothing."

"Oh, don't be silly." Campbell slammed the thought upon my shoulder. "You did good bringing us here. We can sell a lot of these artefacts for a lot of ammunition."

"You, or the Mulch Gang?" I added, noticing Ben Carter's scarred face as he smashed another display cabinet with a crowbar. The glass shattered into thousands of tiny pieces, crunching beneath his boot.

Following my gaze, Campbell sighed heavily. "We're on the same side, as crazy as that is to believe. Anything the Gang has, we essentially have too. If only by association."

I remained unconvinced.

"Take a look around," Campbell said, patting me on the shoulder again.

"We'll be here for a while yet. See if you can find anything that could be important." After a friendly smile, he raced up those stairs with his weapons swinging from his hips.

Doubt spread its traitorous fingers across my skin. Some days, it was still hard to accept that Campbell was alive. Harder still to realise that I was now a Rebel. Officially too, now that Mason had read that letter.

I shivered, then rubbed my hands up and down my arms, trying to induce warmth as I wandered the rooms.

Most had already been ransacked. Only bits of furniture remained, the wooden structures broken, splintered, and littered across the floor. Most paintings had been graffitied, harsh curses and crude illustrations sprawled across those superior, painted eyes. The few ornaments that had dodged sticky Rebel fingers remained shattered and without purpose.

I kicked a piece of broken pottery. It clanked sadly against the marble, resonating into my heart. I wished art held more value to the Rebels. It deserved better than to be marred with angry red paint, then scattered as tiny pieces across the floor.

Like a rising flood, I had the urge to take a paintbrush against the paper, to spread colour across its bare, white skin. All my paintings were destroyed with the rest of Mason's Palace. A pang of sadness bloomed as I thought of their smouldering ashes.

A library appeared, of all things, each wall stacked with books of various literary achievement. I fingered a few of these books, blowing dust off their leather bindings. The books themselves were in good condition, the writing legible and the pages free from damp. I hid a few in the knapsack hung over my shoulder, next to my hunting rifle. Yes, those long train journeys needed a book or two. Perhaps I could teach Heidi to read English?

Besides, why shouldn't I take the books? The *Last Day* had already passed and these books were my birthday present. A way to stamp out the last birthday I endured with far nicer memories.

I hastily shook the thought away and continued my exploration, my bag of books pulling on my shoulders.

I arrived at an office, albeit not nearly as large or as impressive as Mason's. My eyes skimmed the desk—neat, tidy, and bare of all except a few pens and a calligraphy set. A bookcase proudly stood beside it, nestled between a bearskin rug and a fireplace bordered with black enamel. On the far side of the room, directly beneath a large window that overlooked the curling structure of the glacier below, a large document was spread across a table. Curious, I traced a delicate hand upon its surface.

Its edges were frayed, as though incredibly old, yet the ink remained legible in various shades of black. Most had faded, yet one word stood out like a slither of black night on a sea of stars: *Alira*. Recently added.

A line stretched out from my name, merging into another's: *Mason*. Another line flowed up, more faded than the last. It met two names, also linked by a line: *William, Arabella*.

More names jumped out, the first spawning from William.

Barclay, Hickman, Henry, Oliver...

They were each linked to female names: *Penelope, Juliane, Ebony, Sasha...*

More names emerged, spreading to the tip of the document. Fourteen male names in total, each *connected* to fourteen female ones. A Family Tree.

At the top, only one name remained: *Grayson*. He was linked to *Tara*.

The top of the line. The Head of the Family. The Conductor of them all.

I knew Mason had a family but... William, Grayson, the *Line*—what did this all mean? I needed more time to think about this, so I carefully folded up the document and hid it between my books.

The next room beckoned, joined to the study. Musical potential jumped out at me. Violins, violas, cellos, flutes, clarinets, harps... They spread their musical fingers into every corner of the room, beckoning me. One musical instrument shouted so loudly inside my soul, my legs barely held their strength.

Sebastian's piano was a large beast, and unnecessarily pretentious. Doused in gold, carved with stags—it was an elaborate, highly boastful piece of musical instrumentation that did not sit well with my Herder roots.

The sadistic music hadn't reappeared in my head yet, but those keys still grasped me, pulling me in with the promise of chords and melodies.

I dropped the knapsack to my side, followed by the rifle. Ammunition jingled in my pockets as I sat upon the stool.

Black and white keys shouted at me, their skins so shiny and beckoning. The cushioned seat, soft against my buttocks, caressed me in a field of plump, red velvet. My foot positioned itself upon the pedal, my heel pivoting upon the wood.

Fingers poised, palms sweating, I held my breath.

Hands fell.

Music jumped around the room, caressing the constant, dull ache in my head and replacing it with such profound, musical ecstasy that tears itched my eyes. The music enraptured me, filling and embracing me with familiarity. Chords reverberated inside my very bones, pulling me further and further into the song that quivered the dust in the air.

The song neared its end. Life flowed into my muscles, my skin flushed with comforting warmth...

The final note echoed across the room. Such sweet silence. Hands hovering above the keys, trembling in the wake of this musical climax.

Slowly, as a large, relieved sigh filled my lungs, I lowered the key lid. I turned. A crowd of Rebels stared back at me.

They littered the periphery of the room and gathered around the entrance, owning the space between each instrument. Amongst the crowd, Campbell and Ben Carter stared at me with their expressions unreadable.

"Take this," I said, patting the piano's gold skin. "Unless you want me to be a screaming, inconsolable heap in a few weeks, I'm going to need to play it."

* * *

MOVING the piano was more laborious than it should have been. Branches and twigs scratched and marred its golden skin, already muddied by Rebel hands. I accepted their flood of groans and curses with a clenched jaw, but I had explained the music's sadism to Campbell and he agreed it would be necessary in the weeks to come.

Had Mason played his violin yet?

Three great heaves and six men finally lifted the piano into the slow-moving train. It screeched against the metal floor, unhappy about being manhandled into its final position. No doubt it would be out of tune, given its reluctance to be moved.

Rebels emptied the compartment, following the promise of a well-deserved drink, and left me alone with the golden beast. And Anya, of course.

"Why did Sebastian have this?" she asked, wiping away the specks of mud from its golden skin. "He hardly seemed like a musical guy."

"The Family, I think." When Anya's quizzical stare found me, I gathered the document I'd hidden in my knapsack and spread it out on the floor. Anya's eyes widened as she read each name portrayed by faded ink.

"This is his Line, isn't it?"

"Yes." I pointed to the name directly above Mason's. "Arabella is Mason's mother."

Anya's finger traced the horizontal line connected to Arabella. "Do you think she was William's mate?"

"I think all these women were. All of them, paired for eternity with an evil man." I shook my head, the reality of my heritage suddenly becoming clear. "Each one is *connected* to their mates, hence these lines."

"And they each had a child..." The train quickly gained speed and specks of snow stuck to the document. Anya wiped them away before the ink could run. "All sons too."

"Firstborns," I said, then met Anya's stare. "Mason said that all Firstborns are boys. I think Mason is Arabella's Firstborn."

"What does it mean to be a Firstborn?" Anya paused for a moment, chewing on her rosy lip. "That they have diamond eyes perhaps? That their stares can kill?"

"Maybe." Another sigh as I considered options. "But I'm certain those instruments in Jury's Alpine are the ones the Family use."

"So, it's not just a violin and a piano?"

"You heard what Theodore said a few weeks back: how the music forces us together. So we must all hear it, and why not have a different instrument each time?" My finger traced up the lines, to the man at the top of the tree. "But the music had to start somewhere, and I bet it was with this man: Grayson."

"A Family Orchestra, with its own Conductor." Anya shook her head with a grimace. "God, all those poor women forced to endure and stop the music inside their heads. And you, of course."

"I've had it easy so far."

"Alira..."

"No, it's true," I said, meeting her scolding frown. "The worst Mason ever did to me—physically, I mean—was the day he gave me these..." I gestured to the scars on my wrists, flicking in and out of the sunlight as it fought against the cloak of trees. "That was because I lost control that night at the dinner party."

"Yes, I remember."

"Can you imagine what he would've done to me if I tried to kill our son?" I visibly shivered at the thought. "Arabella tried to kill Mason—several times —and Gods only know how William punished her for that."

"You think they're all like Mason?"

"I don't see how they can't be." I licked my lips, feeling the scar's raised skin. "Mason's the Destroyer—that's obvious. But I'm... I'm the *Protector*."

"What's your point?"

I stared at Anya, at each fleck of blue inside eyes that just popped colour and compassion. "There's a reason we hear the music. If I'm the Protector, then my very existence doesn't agree with what Mason does, what he *is*... We need the music to force us together, one way or another." I stared at the Family Tree, scanning each line, each faded swirl of ink, and could feel those musical claws inside my soul, edging me towards the destiny it desperately wanted. "So, that's why they hear music too."

"Because they're each a Destroyer and a Protector."

"Exactly." I threw my fingers in my hair, parting the greasy strands. "I think all Firstborns are Destroyers..." I whispered the words, as if their very presence was damning.

I pulled Anya's attention by folding the document away and hiding it between the pages of a book.

"We're missing something," Anya said, scowling at the ruts in the floor. "Whether or not the music forces you together, it still doesn't explain *why* Mason wants a child in the first place."

I frowned at her. "He wants his immortality back."

"Exactly, he wants it *back*," Anya said, sitting on her heels. "He was immortal before you miscarried, remember? So why did he spend all those years—all that effort—looking for you and your predecessors when he already had his immortality? Surely, if he wanted ultimate control, he wouldn't care about a child and would've just left you out there to live, die—*whatever...*" Anya collapsed onto her buttocks, crossing her legs as frustration lined her features. "And where are his ancestors? If they each sired a First-born, then they'd be immortal—so where are they? You said yourself that Mason was *born*, so he didn't just pop into existence. His parents must still be alive and then he's..."

Anya trailed off, lost in her own thoughts.

"What is it?" I whispered.

For a moment, she remained still. Then those glorious eyes flicked up. Sunlight illuminated Anya Whittaker with stubborn resolve.

"We need to find Sebastian Svellec," she said. "Once and for all, we need to know why you're the End of Everything."

4

———

A few days after Jury's Alpine, Mikael Ashworth received a visitor. No doubt relaying news about Sebastian. At that moment, bathed in freedom, I couldn't care less.

I leant far out of the train, my hair rippling in the cold breeze. It was glorious, to feel such freedom upon my skin. To gawk at the mountains as they towered on either side. Smothered with thick snow, the trees did their very best to punch through. Some trees were swallowed completely, with only the very tips gasping for breath. Others remained tall with their emerald needles—a delicious contrast against the pure, virgin white. If I stretched out far enough, I could touch those leaves. Snow tickled my fingers, rippling to the ground in waves.

A loud knock on the door and Campbell march in, his eyes shadowed with concern.

And anger. Brimming, unrelenting anger.

"Come on, girl," he said, his voice low and even. "There's something you need to see."

* * *

38

ASHWORTH WAS HUNCHED over the metallic table when I arrived, squeezing one of the map's tokens in a fist pressed to closed lips. The air in that room was stagnant, old. As though all oxygen had been sucked from it. In its place was an odour of fear, regret, and maybe a little determination.

"What's happened?" I asked. Most remained dwelling in their own thoughts. All except Ben Carter, that is, who examined me with an ugly smirk that I did my very best to ignore.

"A courier delivered a letter today," Theodore said.

"The man who got on the train?"

"The very same."

I shrugged. "So? What's this letter?"

Ashworth stood to his full height and released the token from his crushing grip. It hit the metallic table with a high-pitched little clank. "It's a reply," he said.

Fear worked its way through me, rendering my speech useless. I coughed into my elbow. "And?" I eventually pressed.

A large sigh escaped Ashworth's thin lips. Then he turned to Isla, and the letter poised between two elegant fingers. A ghost of neat black calligraphy shone through the paper, below the golden emblem of a stag. Embossed antlers stretched the entire width of the page.

Isla took a deep breath.

"My Dearest Alira.

I thank you for informing me of Emilia's untimely demise, and I do so note that she died of natural causes.

In light of this newfound trust between us, I invite you—and your Rebel Commanders, whom you now hold in such high regards—to a parley at Giant's Respite. Said parley will commence exactly four weeks from the date of this letter, on the Seventeenth Day of the Second Month, *as the sun reaches its peak. I hope you will attend.*

Mikael Ashworth, I now write directly to you. I strongly implore you to observe this meeting, for I hold in my possession something of high value to you. It is in your best interests to see exactly what I have to offer.

I look forward to seeing you, Alira, and all the Commanders of the Free People's Rebellion."

No need to relay the signature, for Mason's voice spoke loudly throughout. It was a warning, as well as an invitation. Be at Giant's Respite, or else.

"How long until the meeting?" I asked, my throat dry. I craved mead.

"Ten days," Ashworth responded, arms folded across his narrow chest.

"Can we make it in time?"

"Yes."

I sucked the scar on my lip, shuffling my weight from one foot to the other. "Are we?"

"I believe Mason's letter was pretty damn clear, don't you?" Ben Carter's voice, soaked in hostility, echoed nastily around the compartment. "Ashworth, I told you that letter was a liability. You should never have sent it."

"He would have tried to meet with us regardless," Campbell grumbled, marching to Ashworth's side. "He knows we have Alira, and he will do everything in his power to get her back. It was only a matter of time before he suggested a parley."

Panic festered. "You can't send me back! No, not after everything, you can't send me back to him!"

"My dear, that would never happen," Theodore said, somewhat pitying. "Whatever the reason for Mason's proposed parley, I can guarantee that we would never trade nor sell you."

"Can't let him have any more babies, can we?" Carter's raspy voice hissed in my ear.

"Then what are we going to do?"

Ashworth thought for a moment, lost in his own indecision. His shoulders hunched and I practically heard the debate inside his head.

In the end, there was only option left to us.

"We're going to Giant's Respite. Full speed."

* * *

GIANT'S RESPITE WAS NAMED SO because of a legend.

In the early days, when Herders created stories to tell their children, there spoke of a giant who had swam across the Endless Sea. The coast of the northern Woodlands beckoned from the horizon, yet he was tired from his long journey. He collapsed onto the wide, black-sanded beach, cold waves lapping at his ankles and large towers of stone erupting from the waves behind him. Directly ahead, the base of Legless Glacier lay: a wide expanse of ice that fell down the subtle slopes of the Giant's Spine—a thin, jagged range of mountains that encroached from the southern Glasslands. To his left, the black sand merged into a forest. To his right lay a stone cliff face, decorated with caves and hexagonal pillars of dark grey rock: a chandelier of geology that fell into the seething cauldron of the sea.

I stared at one of these caves—my boots sinking into that same black sand, the cold wind biting at my skin—and wondered if the giant was still in there. He'd made his home in one of those caves, or so legend said. Perhaps he lay sleeping, listening to the crashing of the waves, sucking the slimy green moss from the walls.

The scent of salt and seaweed brightened the air—an uplifting odour, strangely pleasant. It matched those thundering waves, hurdling towards us from a calamitous grey sea speckled with ice bergs. Those stone pillars and stacks still dotted the bay, their black and green skin continually brutalised by the clawing white of those crashing waters.

A dull sky, smothered with clouds, weighed upon the beach. Snow fell in tiring motions. Small drops, almost miniscule. Barely noticeable. The noon sun tried to punch through, but those clouds hid everything, dousing the world in ominous grey light. Despite this, those navy coats shone like sapphires against the black sand. A group of men approached from the far side of the beach. Three Masonians, one General. Another man was there too, a brown sack flung over his head, his gait shaky and unequal. A different man led this troop, his navy coat flowing gently in the cold breeze, his diamond eyes easily puncturing the dim light.

It came as no surprise that Mason chose Giant's Respite as a parley location. The beach was flat, the bay was large. No snipers could hide in the undergrowth, no assassin could wait patiently at the periphery. We were exposed, bare for our adversary to clearly assess.

A shaky breath escaped my pursed lips, fists clenched tightly at my side. With every ounce of control, I willed my music to remain silent. Mason could not know my fear. I would not give him the pleasure.

"You doing alright there, girl?" Campbell asked, his gaze still fixed ahead, his limbs stiff and rigid.

I did not answer.

"Remind me again why we're doing this, Ashworth," Isla snapped, her ebony hair flowing behind her, kept away from her face by those black goggles pushed up against her hairline.

"Because we don't have a choice," Ashworth replied, hands nestled in his coat pockets.

"Really? We could have turned the train the other way." Isla rolled her eyes. "You utter moron."

"If Mason claims to have something we need, that can't be ignored."

Isla huffed beneath her breath. "I can't believe you're making me stand here and be civil to him."

A dark silence ensued, only punctured by the crashing waves edging up the beach and sinking between the smooth particles of black sand.

"He killed my parents too, Isla," Ashworth said. "Trust me, I don't want to be here anymore than you do."

"Your parents had it easy compared to mine." Isla's soft tone was nearly carried away by the wind.

"Let's not compare sad stories this afternoon," Theodore interjected, a large scarf wrapped around his neck, his bald head protected by a woollen hat. "Perhaps it is best that Mason does not see us squabbling like children."

Ben Carter smirked. "Easy for you to say when you've got no balls to protect."

Theodore gritted his teeth, yet ultimately ignored him.

Out of everyone, Theodore and Ben Carter remained the most immobile, the most unbreakable to Mason's steady advance. They stood tall, rods of pure steel down their spines, their hands concealed within pockets or large, gaping sleeves.

Silence descended as Mason and the rest of his party stood a little more than two metres ahead of us. Those diamond eyes studied each of us in turn. From Campbell, to me, then to Ashworth. A smile inched across his lips, decorating his handsome face with a duplicitous warmth he had practised to perfection.

"Gentlemen." He nodded to Isla and me. "And Ladies."

I studied the neat precision of his uniform, stitched with elegance and devoid of his usual weapons—a peculiarity that we all shared. My gaze roamed further, across a defined jaw to a face that was clean-shaven, and up to those diamond eyes, sparkling intensely. His inky black hair rippled in the cold wind.

"Mason," Ashworth replied, standing tall. "I can't say it's a pleasure to meet you."

"Mikael Ashworth, I presume." His Aristocratic nod was the exact opposite of courteous. "Interesting company you keep. Drug lords, disgraced Aristocrats, traitors…"

"The company I keep is of none of your concern."

"I strongly disagree." Those eyes briefly flicked to me, then focussed on Campbell.

An exchange of hating glares ensued before Isla snapped, "We'd appreciate if you'd get to the point of this meeting. The sooner that happens, the sooner we can all be on our merry way."

Mason's attention flocked to her. His cold gaze roamed across her slim body, then up to her face, where those jade eyes were so penetrating against the dim light.

He narrowed his eyes. "Have we met before?"

A harsh, bitter laugh erupted from Isla's lungs. She shifted her weight from one foot to another, sand encroaching up her boot.

"Not me, no," she said, lifting her head in a proud display of defiance.

"Isla," Ashworth mumbled to his side.

Isla's face twisted into a grimace. "You knew my parents."

"Did I?" Mason's sneer grew contemptuous. "Please, my dear, remind me."

"Isla," Ashworth said, a little louder.

But her blood brimmed with newfound aggression as she grew taller with every second. "My name is *Isla Dagger.*"

Realisation flooded Mason's handsome features, twisting them into cruel amusement.

"Is it really? Now that *is* an interesting development." He took a step closer, his pounding footsteps muffled by the sand. "Ah, I see the resemblance now. Not with Harrison Dagger, but your mother—ah yes, the resemblance is most striking." Hands clasped behind his back, he leant closer with a smirk. "Would you like to know what I did to her?"

Ashworth grabbed Isla's shoulder and dragged her behind him. It was unclear who he was protecting, for Isla's strangled expression was pure wrath.

Mason grinned. "I wouldn't worry, my dear. Depending on the outcome of this meeting, you could likely experience something similar before your time is up."

"We are not here to exchange threats," Campbell said loudly so his voice penetrated the crashing waves. "Tell us what you want."

Mason attention slid to him. "Such impatience, Campbell. But yes, I agree that time is ticking on." Mason puffed up his shoulders. "I am here to offer you a deal. One that will benefit all parties involved."

I scoffed beneath my breath, highly doubting that.

"And what deal, dare I ask, would the Destroyer of the Old World have for us?" Theodore asked, raising wispy eyebrows. "Forgive me, but I hardly believe any deal from you would do well in our favour."

"You'd be surprised, Mr Addington," Mason replied, that cruel amusement persisting. "I'm sure you remember just how generous I can be, given the circumstances."

"Generosity is not in your repertoire," Theodore shot back.

Mason's attention switched to Ben Carter, who had his shoulders slouched and was so inherently disinterested in the entire situation. That cerulean eye surveyed the scene, matched only by the scarred one, shining as dimly as the dirty white sky above.

"You want the Ice Territory," Mason said simply, as a matter of undeniable fact. "I am willing you give you that Territory, completely. I will remove all my forces from it, and they shall never set foot in it again. It will be yours for the taking."

"And in return?" Ben Carter asked, carefully.

Mason's diamond eyes flicked to me, a smirk decorating his lips.

"My mate," he replied. Cold fear sank into my anxious belly, like rocks to an empty riverbed. "Give me Alira, and I shall give you the Ice Territory."

"And how does such a trade benefit the Free People?" Theodore asked with narrowing eyes.

"Because I shall let all Rebels, all Free People, live out their days in the Ice

Territory. I will not pursue or seek to punish. You will all live free and grow to a grand old age without the fear of retribution."

The commanders exchanged glances, secretly weighing his words.

Mason's smile grew wide. "It really is an offer you cannot refuse," he said.

My eyes darted around the area, gauging how far I could run, which direction was closest to freedom. Indeed, it was an incredibly generous offer. How much did Ashworth value his Rebellion over the combined lives of all the people who followed him?

Ashworth stared to the grey sky, his dirty blonde hair stroking his forehead. "Tell me, Mason, how do we know you're telling us the truth? Why, we could give you Alira right now, and you could cut us all down at first opportunity."

Mason's stare darkened. "The thought has occurred to me."

"So why should we believe anything you say?"

"Because I daresay I respect you, Ashworth. You, and your people."

"Respect?" Ashworth practically spat the word away, unwilling to be anywhere near it. "If you respected us, you wouldn't be slaughtering us!"

"And yet, I have granted you amnesty. A chance for you all to live, to grow old together, to die peacefully in your beds surrounded by your children."

Waves crashed upon the shore. A low rumble followed, the sea turning into thunder as it rolled upon the black.

Ashworth glanced at Campbell. Only for a second. A split, knowing second.

"That is a very generous offer, my Lord Mason," Ashworth said, his thin lips twisting. "But why should we settle with the Ice Territory?"

Confusion washed upon Mason's face. One could practically see the cogs turning in his brain, wondering if he'd heard correctly.

"You're mortal, you're able to be killed," Ashworth said, still smiling. "So, why should we settle with the Ice Territory when we can kill you and liberate the entirety of the New World?"

Mason's stare turned nasty. "Do you know what I'm offering you, *boy?*"

"Yes, I know alright, and you're desperate." A delicate, winning smile as a fresh shadow descended upon Mason's eyes, brimming with angry colour. "You know you're vulnerable. You know that we know you're vulnerable. I think, for the first time in your life, the thought terrifies you. You're trying to find a way out, a way to brush us all away, to not have to worry about us until you have Alira and regain your immortality. And, when that happens, you'll come to the Ice Territory and destroy every last one of us."

"I will destroy you whether I am immortal or not."

"Yes," Ashworth said, taking a brave step forward. The tails of his scruffy brown coat fluttered in the wind. "You'll certainly try."

Violin notes pounded inside my head, each quivering string vibrating at the centre of my skull. I bit my tongue, grimacing around the ache, determined to hide the evidence of a Connection that still terrified me.

"Well then," Mason said, his fists clenched. I stared at each scar upon those whitening knuckles, already feeling the pain they would produce. "It appears we have reached an impasse."

"It does indeed." Ashworth grinned, his boyish charm radiating. Perhaps that was why Mason was so angry: because Ashworth was still very much a boy. Immature, inexperienced. All too arrogant, all too celebratory for a victory he had not yet gained, even more ignorant to the consequences of failure. "Forgive us, but we really must be going. Things to do, and all of that jazz."

"There is one more thing I would like to address, before this parley is up." The violin notes halted inside my head; a lingering pause of emotion as Mason stared directly at me. "I would like to speak to you, Alira. Alone, if you'd be so kind."

The cold seeped into my coat, freezing my limbs until they were dull and heavy, completely immobile.

"Absolutely not!" Campbell shouted, grabbing my wrist with crushing force.

Mason's stare slid to Campbell. "Fathering her again? So soon, after you so readily abandoned her?"

Campbell's grip tightened around my wrist, bruising the protruding bones. "She is not yours anymore, Mason."

"She's always been mine. She always will be."

Campbell inched forward. A subtle movement, but one filled with resounding hatred.

Ashworth halted the motion with a palm against Campbell's chest. "No, Mason," he said. "I will not allow you to speak with her.

Mason huffed to himself, his anger bubbling like a pot of water, placed above a raging fire fanned by the wind. "Then let me persuade you."

He gestured to the hooded man. General Alden brought him forward, that ugly scar down his cheek made small by the one decorating Ben Carter.

Mason ripped the sack from the man's head. Chocolate-brown hair ruffled in the wind, sticking to the scabbed skin on a forehead riddled with dirt. Gaunt cheeks framed a face painted with painful colour, yet those seafoam-green eyes shone gloriously.

"Joe," I whispered.

Joe Matheson took a careful look at his surroundings, then to me. Pure pain was etched across his bruised features. Apologetic eyes shone brightly, his mouth still trying to say the words the black muzzle prevented. Alden kicked his knee, halting those strained muffles. He collapsed to the sand, his limbs lacking the energy to survive any more assaults.

"An incredibly difficult man to find." Mason smiled proudly. "It took a great deal of effort on my part, and far too many months. Alas, it was worth it. Joe Matheson is a whirlwind of information. I'd very much consider having a conversation with him, if I were you."

"Joe Matheson is a traitor," Campbell said through gritted teeth, looking down to his former friend like a starving polar bear would a faltering seal pup.

"Yes, he is—to us both." Mason's smile turned triumphant. "In fact, I can think of no fouler way for him to spend the rest of his meagre days than under the roof of the Free People. A little poetic justice, wouldn't you say, Campbell?"

The grip on my wrist grew so tight, my fingers numbed.

"We have too many mouths to feed as it is," Ashworth said, before Campbell could respond.

"Well, that is a shame." Mason wandered behind Joe, and seafoam eyes sparkled with terror as his hands slinked around Joe's gaunt cheeks. "It seems Mr Matheson has lost his usefulness."

Muscles tensed. The snap of Joe's neck hung upon the air, ready to punch through the breaking waves—

"Wait!" The word was out of my mouth before I could stop it. Eyes flocked to me, yet I stared at Joe's fearful face—at my *friend.*

I met Mason's gaze. "I'll talk to you," I whispered.

Mason instantly released Joe, who crumbled to the black sand like some deflated balloon.

"What're you doing, girl?" Campbell hissed beneath his breath. I ripped my hand away and massaged life into numb fingers.

I saved Joe because he was my friend, but the Rebels didn't need—or want—to know that.

Mason just stared at me, the corner of his mouth tilted upwards, ever so slightly. Of course, he already knew Joe was my friend—that was why he threatened him in the first place. *Bastard.*

I raised knowing eyebrows to Campbell's evident disapproval. "Don't you think we ought'a know exactly what Joe told him? I'll be fine, just t-take Joe and let me get this over with."

Campbell stomped forwards and plucked Joe Matheson's abused form from the wet, black sand. He shivered profusely, his rags doing little to alleviate the immense chill, yet he still sent a sad stare of thanks in my direction. A slight tilt of my head in response, before Campbell, Joe, and the rest settled a little way behind me.

Mason nodded to his own party, who gave us a similar amount of privacy. Far enough away to stay out of earshot. Close enough to rush forwards, should violence return.

So, there I was. Face to face with Mason. I inhaled the chilly air into my lungs, wishing to swim into that grey, calamitous sea. To be far away from him, far away from that beach.

"Alira." His voice was so low, so rich... "I'm going to give you a choice. You come with me, right now, and we can forget this ever happened. We can return to how things were, how they should be."

A huff of bitter laughter escaped my throat. Mason's brow lowered at my reaction, shadowing diamond eyes that were scrutinising me intently.

"It's the only time I will offer such clemency, the *only* way this will end well for you. I know the Rebels did not give you a choice in this. They took you, kidnapped you. I understand the difficult position they've put you in and I respect the choices you've made because of that. But now I'm offering you a way out. A way for us to put this all behind us, to move on. Please,

Alira," he said, that rare tenderness showing. I swallowed hard, through the hard lump at my throat. "Please, come with me."

"Why?"

The word hung heavily in the air. It stunned Mason, ripping away his retorts, all the usual words that donned his silver tongue. It licked the scar upon my lip and then more scars ached, positioned around my body. I rubbed the ones upon my wrists, for they were the most painful.

"Why would I go back to you? I know what awaits me."

"I'm giving you my word. I will not punish you for this treachery if you simply come with me. Now, *today*."

"Do you know what disgusts me the most, out of everything you're saying?" A long lock of hair flew across my face. I captured it, locking it behind an ear donned with those seven golden rings. "You don't even consider it a punishment. You don't consider it a crime, or an act of perversion. To you, it's a necessity. Heck, you enjoy it—how could you not? You'd be getting what you want, as always. You don't care that I don't want to. You don't care when I scream or beg you to stop. All that matters to you is your immortality: the child you'll force upon me as soon as we're alone."

Tears licked my eyeballs, the moisture fluttering in the wind. "That's what hurts most of all. Not what happened in the early days, with the drugs and the shackles—in a strange, hateful sort of why, I understand why you did that to me. It was horrific, unforgivable—yes, of course it was. But back then, I was a stranger to you; you hated me, I hated you, and neither of us gave a fucking damn about what we did to each other..."

A lonely tear escaped, only for the wind to wipe it away.

"But then, after I had given you *everything*..." Hatred formed, swirling at the base of my belly, rising up to my throat as the words spat like venom. "To do what you did, to force me even when I *begged* you to stop..." A twisted laugh mocked my misery, echoing around our enclosed space. "No Mason, I'm not coming with you. Not today, not *ever!*"

Mason's jaw clenched. A violin swarmed with angered intensity.

"You asked for time," he said. "You asked for time I could not give."

"Oh, and how has that worked out for you? Funny, had you stopped yourself, I could have been ready by now. Maybe I would've wanted to try again.

But here you are, so desperately trying to convince me to come with you, after everything you've done."

Another bout of hateful laughter escaped my throat, carried by the breeze. "Tell me, Mason, why should I give myself back to *you*?"

"Because if you don't," Mason said, in barely more than a whisper. "If you don't come with me, right now, I will not be merciful. I will punish you in ways you cannot begin to comprehend." His eyes fell to my hands, still rubbing the small scars upon my wrists. "You've not seen what I can do to you, not by a long way. Yes, I've given you tasters, but you were pregnant when I formed those scars and that offered you a protection you simply don't have now. You're not pregnant, neither will you be when I eventually find you, when I have destroyed every last piece of this fucking Rebellion." He took a small, teasing step closer. "Would you like me to give you more scars?"

The pain of that morning: the fear, the terror, the desperation for it to be over. I felt the shackles biting into my skin, Mason's cruel, carnal satisfaction as he ripped the tube from my nose. Echoes of pain tingled my nasal cavity, which I hastily rubbed away.

"You don't know what you're doing," Mason said. "You're flooded by anger and resentment. I *understand* that. I understand why you hate me."

"You don't understand at all! How could you? You didn't feel your sons die within you. You can't possibly understand why I can't go through that again!"

"So, you'd rather align yourself with the people who *destroyed* them?" Mason scoffed to himself, running his hands through his hair. It remained sticking up at odd angles, continually fluttering as the truth of his words punched me in the gut. A truth I couldn't bear thinking about.

"Alira," he said, flooded with desperation he seldom showed. "Just once more. Become pregnant, carry to term, and I swear that I will *never* touch you again..."

The words were upon my tongue. They teased existence, so close to my lips. Emilia's words flew back to me, begging me to go back to him, to reconsider my current course of action. She crudely observed that I'd only have to endure the conception: a selection of minutes that would last hours. But still, survive through that, grit my teeth through the sensations, and I might yet continue. I'd have a baby at the end—the only thing I'd ever really wanted, the little bundles of happiness that had been so cruelly ripped away on two occasions. I missed my children, I mourned them still. Standing before Mason, my future seemed so clear, so tangible. All I had to do was go with him. Abandon Campbell, much like he had abandoned me.

Mason would destroy the Rebellion; I would have his child. He'd be something I'd be able to hold, to see grow up, to love with all the motherly adoration that still infested every surviving piece of me.

Lips trembling, I stared at the sand. Each grain nestled against each other, so unique, so old and stubborn. How long had this beach existed? How old were those individual grains of sand?

Mason's black boots came into my vision.

Of course. The beach was formed almost one-hundred-and-eighty-five years ago, when Ragnarök occurred. When Mason slaughtered almost two billion men, women, and children. If one listened closely, the ghost of their screams could still be heard upon the waves, crashing with thunderous intensity against the shore.

Another tear slipped down my cheek. Slowly, I took a step back. My decision had been made.

Mason saw this; he surely heard the determination of my music. It mixed with something else, almost inaudible, that spilled tears from my eyes.

"You stupid, senseless girl..." Then he listened harder, to the music inside his head. "You don't want to do this..."

Something changed in him then, as desperation filled the gaps in the anger. "You feel like you have to, because you think it's the right decision."

"Your Masonians are looking a little lonely," I said, the words sounding strangled and alien. "You best not keep them waiting."

"Alira, don't do this!"

"No," I said, staring at those diamond eyes and wincing at the sharp knot of coldness inside my brain. "I'm not coming with you; I'm not having your fucking child!"

"You are, Alira," he said with a bitter glare. "And when I find you, you're going to regret this moment."

A strangled laugh escaped my throat. *"Fuck you."*

Mason's eyes widened with a profound, deadly sense of hatred. It sucked me in, reigniting the same dread that consumed me the night of that dinner party, when I insulted him before his dinner guests. That fateful night sealed the marks upon my wrists forever.

Sand crunched behind me. "Time to go, girl," Campbell said, gripping my arm in a gentle vice.

"Alira, wait!"

I stopped, simply out of courtesy, with Campbell's hand still wrapped around my arm.

"Emilia," Mason said, unable to look at me. "Was she at peace, at the end?"

Those grey eyes, so doleful and shiny. The skin like paper, the personality that was just as stubborn and proud as it always had been...

"Yes," I called back. "Yes, she was."

A small, almost imperceptible nod. Then Mason returned his hands to his pockets and marched back to his Masonians.

The parley was over.

5

———

Joe Matheson collapsed to the floor.

He recovered quickly, spitting out dots of bright red that shimmered in the swaying light. The steady motion of the train rocked him gently from side to side as he knelt before the fury of all five commanders.

"Come on, Campbell..." Crimson teeth shined as he smiled. "I'm sure you can do better than that."

Campbell shook the pain from his fist, reformed it, and punched Joe again. It was harder this time, sending him sprawling across the floor. With a heavy groan, he rolled onto his chest and hoisted himself up, manoeuvring around hands tied together with mouldy, black rope.

"You piece of shit..." Campbell's bared his teeth in a snarl. "Give me one reason why I shouldn't kill you right now."

"Because Alira's right." Joe spat blood to the floor again, his nose oozing thick lines of red. One eye could barely open. "You need to know what I told Mason."

"What *could* you have told him?"

"Whatever I could to keep myself alive."

Campbell removed his jacket. The gaping holes in his black jumper compressed as he rolled up his sleeves and marched towards Joe and—

"No, wait!" I shouted, throwing myself before them.

"Girl, *move!*"

"'Tis no use breaking his jaw before he's told us anything."

Incensed, Campbell wiped a dirty hand across his mouth, perhaps trying to wipe away the stampede of curses that lay there. He remained pacing, his broad shoulders rising with each angered breath.

"You know he's the reason you're in this situation? He sold us out, he told the Masonians we'd be at Waterman's Quarry!"

"I know," I breathed in reply.

"Then why are you protecting him?"

"Because he's helped me. I know he's responsible for a lot of shit, but when I was a Slave, he gave me weapons to protect myself with, information to survive. Joe, as idiotic and treacherous as he is, *never* told Mason who I really was. He could have—it would have made him a prince in Mason's eyes. But he didn't and you *owe* him for that! We both do."

Campbell considered this very carefully. Those glacial-blue eyes flicked to me, then to Joe, then back to me.

"*Fine,*" he spat, marching into the shadows, steam still spurting from his ears.

Ashworth waved his revolver in Joe's face. "Go on, then. Tell us."

Joe stared at the gun, rusted, old and hardly alluding to the death it could inflict. He swallowed, blood trickling down his throat. "He knows you're on a train."

"No shit, seeing as his Masonians have chased this very train."

"I told him you're using the freight tracks."

That stopped Ashworth. The usual smugness dropped to his brown boots, replaced by a frown. "Very well. And what else?"

"No, no, no." Joe laughed, but his voice was strained and unsettled. "I'm not a bloody fool. As soon as I tell you everything, you'll just throw me off this train and leave me to the wolves. I need assurances."

"Oh, I'll give you fucking assurances." Ben Carter spun the crowbar in his hand and slammed it against the wall. Golden sparks danced around the air. "Tell us something worthwhile and I *assure* you that I won't pound your skull in like a fucking melon!"

"Carter, stop!" I shouted. "Just *stop!*"

"Get out of my way."

"No, you're not going to kill him—*no one's* going to kill him!"

Carter took a step closer, until he fumed stale cigarettes upon my forehead. "I said, get out of my fucking way. Or I'll kill you."

"Go right ahead," I said, my lips forming some depraved smile. "Death will be a welcome reprieve compared to when Mason eventually gets his hands on me. Why wait until that happens?"

Music swarmed inside my head: furious, resentful, utterly devastated. I could still see the disappointment in those diamond eyes, swirling with viciousness, merging into something truly horrific. Images of my future laid bare before me; no part of it was happy. I doubted I would get to see my child—my eyes would be gouged out, long before my child was born. There would be another Isobel Hutchinson to replace me, another woman who'd be called *Mama*.

Yes, Mason had known me long enough to know exactly where it hurt.

Ben Carter gripped the back of my hair, yanking my head to meet his sneer. "Mason isn't the only monster you have to worry about, *girl.*"

I spat in his face. Carter recoiled, wiping my spittle from that colourful eye, before he lunged towards me with the crowbar held high—

Campbell grabbed him in the air, ripping the crowbar from his hand. It clattered to the floor, kicked somewhere unseen. Ashworth jumped in and pushed the two men apart. Profanities spurted from Carter's gullet and he marched from the compartment, slamming the door shut so hard the metal groaned.

"Now, ladies and gentlemen, let's continue as adults," Theodore said calmly. He sat at the table, next to Isla, who had been massaging her temple for the last half-hour.

"Tell us all that you know, Joe," Ashworth said. "Or we'll give you to Carter and he can do with you what he likes. You lost him quite a bit of merchandise the day the Masonians captured you, so I'm sure he'll want some sort of recompense."

Joe spat red on the floor. "Fuck you!"

"You first, sweetheart," Ashworth growled. "Tell us what you told Mason."

With a heavy sigh, Joe finally conceded. "I told him you're looking for Sebastian Svellec, that you're hoping for Svenja's lost information."

Now it made sense, why no hint of Sebastian's whereabouts remained in Jury's Alpine.

"What else?"

"That you're running low on numbers, that it's only by Ben Carter's contribution that you can even class yourself as a Rebellion at all."

"What?" I breathed, then faced Campbell. "How many Free People are there?"

"Almost a thousand."

"Alira," Joe whispered, shadowed with blood and bruises. "Ask him how many of these one-thousand Rebels are fighters?"

"It's true," Theodore said from the outskirts. "Our numbers of fighting men and women are somewhat limited."

"How many?" I said, taking slow, angered steps towards him.

"The majority of our Rebels are refugees, freed Slaves—men, women, and children who are either too sick or too scared to hold a gun or a sword. Without Carter, our numbers fall around two-hundred."

"Two-hundred?" A horrible, doubtful laugh erupted from my lungs, where only scepticism now remained. "Are you telling me we're meant to fight Mason with *two-hundred* Rebels?"

"Almost seven-hundred, with Carter's help," Campbell added.

"And what if he leaves, hm? What if he decides that we're all just a waste of his time? How do you expect to fight with *two-hundred* Rebels when there are... I dunno, ten thousand Masonians—*at least?* And if *that* wasn't enough, how do you expect to kill Mason when the very ground cracks and rumbles beneath your feet?"

"Calm down—"

"Don't you *dare* tell me to calm down, Campbell!" My cheeks flushed red, a sharp finger pointing. "I've just told Mason, to his *face*, that I'm going to fight him with you. You don't have any comprehension of what he'll do to us if this fails!"

I threw my hands in my hair, parting the strands stuck together with grease and sea-salt. Panic burned my lungs, the urge to gasp that musty air too powerful to ignore.

I was an idiot. I was a fucking idiot.

"Listen to me, girl," Campbell said sternly. "We have more than enough people in the Rebellion to make a difference. All it takes is a single bullet, right through Mason's skull and we've won. Have faith."

Faith. A strange little word. Able to denote so much power, so much arrogance in even the most grounded of people.

"Fine, whatever." I washed my hands of the lot of them and wandered to the door.

"Put Matheson in a cell," Campbell grumbled to Ashworth. "If he stays here any longer, I'll kill him."

* * *

Away from the coast, the sun burnt away the cloud. Blue sky intermittent with white, fluffy clouds surrounded us. The train chugged through a low valley, surrounded on both sides by the towering grey rock, the mountains framing us with their majesty. Occasionally, a break in the view exposed flattened trees, their roots pulled up and needle-like leaves ripped from the branches. The snow remained, consuming everything. It was the fingerprint of an avalanche, rolling down the mountainside some weeks beforehand.

The tracks had already been cleared, most likely by the legitimate freight transports. We shared these train tracks after all, and occasionally we'd hear a lonely bellow in the distance. The Rebel train would slow, meandering through the mountains until the conductor was certain the legitimate freight train was far enough ahead.

Mason knew we were using the freight tracks. He would likely be studying them as I sat upon the edge of that compartment, my leg dangling from the train, my head leant against the open door as I considered my decisions.

Regret was not a word I liked to use. There was no point in considering the past, for what could be done about it? Decisions had already been made, the wheel of time had turned and there was nothing anyone could do to roll it back. The choices we had made, whatever we had done, we simply had to live with. No, I did not like the concept of regret.

Fear. That was a better word. The fear of what was to come. The anticipation, the terror of what fate had planned for me.

At this point, two options stretched far ahead. Both seemed equally out of reach.

The first was to carry on. I would fight with the Rebels, reach the ultimate goal of killing Mason. He deserved it after all. He was a slaughterer, a tyrant. How many people had he killed over his two-and-a-half-century existence? It was a stupid number. An abhorrent number. Yes, he deserved to die.

The second option was more likely, easier to touch with my shaking fingers and feel its cold truth sinking into my bones. Should this Rebellion fail, I would run. I'd been running most of my life, after all. Mason would not find me, for I had accepted past mistakes and I was a good learner. I would avoid retribution, of that I was certain.

I had to be certain, for if I doubted my ability to survive without pain or terror, then what was the point in sitting on that train, gazing towards my supposed freedom? Should I truly believe my future was hopeless, I would have taken Mason's hand beneath that grey sky, confused by the plethora of emotions crashing upon the shore with my surrender.

Relief seemed an odd emotion to feel if I'd so readily given myself back to him. It was a strange occurrence, so abnormal for me to even be hateful of its existence. Yet, I was certain it would be there, hiding within the grains of black sand.

The more I considered *why* relief would find me, why it would sink its claws—however unmercifully—into my chest and join the music's evil laughter in my soul, the more I understood. Imagine: no more running, no more fear. No more pain, other than what I had already endured, what was already described in the contract I would sign the moment my fingers touched Mason's. Indeed, if I'd surrendered to him that afternoon, then I'd be pregnant, if not at that hour, then very soon after. Another baby I would have to grow within me and pray for its survival. The thought was sobering.

But no. That's not what happened. I had delved into the back recesses of my stubborn brain and reminded myself of just what a monster he really was. Everything he did to me, everything I'd suffered through, could not be easily forgotten by a simple brush under the rug. There was no rug thick enough to cover everything. No, there would always be a part of me who was a victim, a sufferer, a prisoner.

It was a terrible cycle: that *R*-word, then pregnancy, then miscarriage. It went on and on, over and over inside my head. No way out, except sitting on that train, watching the world rock by, feeling freedom's icy breath as the mountains soared above.

No, I would not spread my legs and grit my teeth. I would not give him a child, only for the Free People to rip it from my womb.

I would fight him. I would stamp out the future that continued to torment me, end his cruel regime and stop the cycle for a hundred—a *thousand* —more innocent people, for I was not alone in this world. It was a sore truth that I had long accepted. The seven, formally eight rings upon my ear were unkind reminders: all the men and women who thought my life was worthless, defenceless, open for the taking.

How many *Jason Montgomerys* were out there? How many more *Tia Kingsleys*?

Yes, this was right. This was the right thing to do.

I regret nothing.

A grunt and a series of footsteps shook me from my reverie. I openly groaned when Ben Carter sat down directly opposite me. His long coat was flung behind him, the spurs on his boots catching against the metallic floor as he cast a leg out of the compartment door. It swayed with the motion of the train, encased in denim jeans covered in black grease.

"Seriously?" I said, utterly tiresome. "What, there are thirty carriages on this train and you choose to sit in this one?"

He smirked, a salacious glint in his eye. "I like the view."

He reached into the inside pocket of his coat and brought out a small leather satchel containing cigarettes, took one for himself, then offered one to me. "What the Hel," I grumbled, and plucked one out.

Scraggy and evidently homemade, it had thick fibres decorating the end. A subtle sniff. It certainly smelt like tobacco.

Perhaps sensing my trepidation, Ben Carter's lips smirked around the cigarette held between his lips.

"I can get you something more potent, if you prefer."

"No, that won't be necessary. I was just checking."

Carter finally found the lighter and hastily lit the cigarette, shielding the flame with his hand. His cheeks became gaunt with the inhale, emphasising that mammoth scar. The first hints of stubble shadowed his face, made obvious as he leant his head into the sunlight and threw me the lighter.

"Didn't take you as having a stick up your arse with nature's narcotics," he said.

I inhaled the warm smoke, the inner heat deliciously familiar. "I don't," I mumbled around the cigarette. "I'm just cautious. I like to know what I'm taking."

Carter caught the thrown lighter with one hand and returned it to his pocket. "I respect that," he said through puffs of pale smoke. "Mason's got his fair share of drugs and relaxants. I suppose it must have been difficult for you in the early days."

My eyes closed around the memories, forcing myself to relax into the smoke. "Why are you helping the Free People?" I asked.

"I would have thought it was obvious."

"But *why?* Forgive me, but I don't understand why you'd go to all of this trouble when you already have the Icelands under your control."

Carter met my questioning stare with sinister intensity. "I saw what Mason did to Erinton's Cavern. Place was obliterated, just like that. *Gone.*" Another inhale of smoke, the end of his cigarette smouldering with orange light. "It was only a matter of time before he'd destroy the entire Territory, and all of us with it."

"He'd never do that. He created the Territories, he loves them."

Carter just looked at me. "That bastard doesn't love anything. Not the Territories, not you, and especially not me."

Memories of my miscarriages surfaced, when Mason's violin sang with such grief. No, as wretched as he was, he had loved two things.

"Yeah…" I sighed out the smoke in my lungs.

Carter leant against the wall, his tongue scraping against yellowed teeth. "Must have been a generous deal he gave you today. I'm surprised you didn't take it."

My face twisted with disgust. "You go to him. Go on, off with you. Spread your legs wide and then see how you like the sound of his deal."

"Sounds a lot better than a whole lifetime of torture."

"It's not just that, it's…" I sighed out the smoke. "It's the whole package. It doesn't matter."

Carter inhaled one last time and stubbed the remainder of the cigarette on the metal floor. "From what I hear, you were once very excited about *the whole package.*"

"That was before you people ripped him out of me."

"Not me." Carter smiled and threw the cigarette's remains out of the carriage before retrieving a second. "I arrived after that lovely display."

"Oh, how fortunate for you. Yet I've no doubt you were glad of such things."

"Can you blame me? The thought of Mason's continued obscenities does not get the juices flowing."

I glared at him through the mist of cigarette smoke. "Bit hypocritical of you though, ain't it?"

Carter's face glowed orange again. "You sound bitter, girl," he said, returning the lighter to his pocket.

"How many people have you killed, Carter? How many women have *you* forced?"

"At least I have the decency to die. That's more than I can say for Mason, or at least, so it used to be."

Carter sighed out another lungful of smoke, staring at the mountains. "The world is changing out there, girl. Let's just hope you're on the right side when it does."

"What the Hel's that supposed to mean?" The taste of dirty cinnamon started to unsettle my stomach.

Carter's thin lips twisted. "You may have the others fooled, but not me. You and I both know that not all your fucks with Mason were forced. What happened, he suddenly get on your good side? You suddenly start liking the feel of him inside of you?"

Anxiety pressed my fingers against my rigid thighs. "You have no idea what I went through. We do a whole manner of things to survive; I'm sure you realise that."

"Oh, I do. But from the look of pure devastation on your face, or the way Mason looked like he was *begging* you to return to him, well... One can't help wondering if your relationship was more than superficial."

"You're disgusting," I said, grimacing. "How can you possibly think such a thing?"

"Tell me I'm wrong."

"You're wrong," I said, my hands squeezing tight. "You're *so* wrong."

A low chuckle rumbled Carter's abused chest, then he flicked the cigarette from the train and stood to his full height.

"You're a terrible liar, girl," he said.

6

In the cold, dark carriage that reeked of urine and damp, Joe Matheson sat upon the frosted metal floor. Legs crossed and head bowed, his bruised body swayed from side to side with the train's perpetual motion, his hands tied with rope secured to a metal loop on the floor.

Yet, despite everything, those seafoam eyes still shone as I entered, Anya in tow.

"Didn't expect to see you here." His voice sent slivers of familiarity through my muscles, his sharp jaw mottled with stubble and injuries. So strange, to see Joe Matheson this way. He was always so charming, so gleeful and cheeky. That boyish charm had been eroded by Masonians and Rebels alike, the smile chipped away one small piece at a time.

"We've brought you some food," I said, kneeling before him. Anya joined me with a brown sack containing a few pieces of bread and a leather water bag.

"Nothing glamorous," she muttered, handing Joe the bread. He took it greedily within bound hands, crumbs spilling from his mouth before he washed it down. A few coughs echoed around us, the art of eating suddenly so new to him.

"Campbell will hit the roof if he finds you both in here," Joe said, flicking his stare between us. "Helping someone like me ain't going to work in your favour."

"Yeah, well..." I sighed, crossing my legs beneath me. "The majority of the people on this train want me dead anyways. A conversation with you ain't going to change that."

Joe Matheson's stare turned pitying. "I'm sorry you're in this, girl. I'm sorry I left you with him, that I didn't try to get you out of there."

"You had to run, Joe. You were on his kill list as soon as he found out who I really was. I'm glad you ran."

Relief spilled from Joe's bloodied lips with the rest of the crumbs. "And what about you, Anya? Freedom after all those years must be quite overwhelming."

"Freedom?" Anya's lips twisted around the word, the taste disgusting her. "This isn't freedom, Joe. We're prisoners here, just like you."

"Just like me?" A quick pull on the rope, the fibres squeaking with the strain. "Don't see you tied up, left to fester with the rats."

"No," Anya admitted. "But, just like you, we're trying to anticipate Ashworth's next move. And Mason's, for that matter."

"Joe," I said, lowering my voice. "We need to know everything Mason knows. We need to know what you told him."

A spiteful, sneering laugh percolated the small, dank space. "So that's all I am to you, is it? Information?"

"Of course not," I said, shaking my head. Strands of hair gently tickled my cheeks. "Despite everything, despite the things you've done, I still consider you my friend."

His eyes lined with silver, those unshed tears full of memories: when we were both truly free, drinking mead and singing to a crowd of drunken revellers. Campbell was with us, laughing at our brazen hysteria.

"Joe," Anya said, leaning forwards. "Ashworth is dangling precariously close to failure, you know this. Should Carter decide he wants out, this Rebellion is doomed and Mason is free to walk all over it. We need to get out before that happens."

Joe's eyes slid to mine. "You can't run from him, girl. He'll find you, he'll punish you for—"

"He's going to punish me for a lot of things." A heavy sigh as *regret* still pressed at the base of neck; a stiffness I couldn't quite stretch out. "But that's why I need to anticipate actions, as best I can."

"Please Joe," Anya said. "Help us out here. Tell us what you know."

Joe's stare sank to the floor, scanning each little glimmer of frost, each trembling stone as they rocked against the metal. Eventually, perhaps anticipating his own future, his chest rose on a large, defeated sigh.

"I don't know much, and what I do know is fragmented. A series of whispers from Masonians, the odd sentence I managed to catch."

"I'll take anything I can, at this point."

Joe chewed against his cheek, racking his memories. "This Svenja Svellec... She's important, to both Mason and Rebels alike. She knows...*things*. It's imperative to Mason that the Free People do not find her."

"But Svenja Svellec is dead," Anya said, frowning. "Mason killed her, over a year ago now."

"Sebastian was dead too, once upon a time." Seafoam eyes switched to me. "I meant what I said to you in Blackberry's Clearing, about his obituary being read in Bolton Square. As far as everyone knew, Sebastian Svellec was dead and yet here he is, old and withered but still very much alive."

I chewed the scar on my lip, contemplating. "What do you know of Sebastian?"

Joe shrugged. "Very little, I'm afraid."

"Hm." I continued to chew my lip. Tallis told me that Sebastian wasn't human; that he was immortal, his wrinkled skin forever held in a state of perpetual age.

"What are you thinking, hon?" Anya asked, trying to catch my eye. I sighed, shaking away that curious conversation, one spring afternoon a long time ago. I was pregnant then. I still had my Flowerbook.

"Nothing," I said.

Anya remained doubtful. Those bright blue eyes continued to study me before they returned to Joe's colourful face. "Do you have any idea of Mason's next move?"

"If I did, I wouldn't be here. He squeezed every last piece of information out of me and then threw me to Ashworth, Campbell, and Ben Fucking Carter. A death-wish, under the guise of mercy." A bitter huff escaped his lungs. "*Bastard.*"

"What else does he know?"

"From what I told him? Nothing else, I don't think. He knows you're on a train, he knows you're using the freight tracks..." His eyes grew dull, the hope draining a little faster. "This place isn't safe anymore. You need to get out."

"You mean escape?" My lips twisted into a smile. "And go where, Joe? I don't have the contacts anymore. I'd be easily recognisable."

A lamb, waiting for the gates of the slaughterhouse to open wide, so she could wander right in.

"I can tell you where to get them: the coloured contacts, I mean," Joe said, his eyes wide and urgent. "A man sells them in a village called Leo's Landing, three miles south of the Snowland-Iceland boarder. Look for the house that has a bright green door."

I nodded, carving such key information into my memories.

"It's impossible anyway," Anya said, hugging her knees close. "Contacts or not, both of you seem to forget that Ashworth isn't going to let you go. At the very least, you're useful to him."

"Useful? How?"

"You're a bargaining chip, honey. You're the only assurance he has that Mason won't just bury us all under a mountain."

Frost inched its way up my spine, cooling my blood. I hadn't considered such an option, for this train to be crushed beneath layers of stone. Indeed, he could destroy us all with a blink of an eye or a flourish of a long finger. Should Ashworth lose me, Mason would just flick his wrist and the train would be flattened beneath a glacier—the last in a long line of icy marvels, born from rusted metal and blood.

"This Rebellion is doomed," Joe said, with a soft shake of his head. "Forget Ashworth, he's as good as dead. All the Free People are but you still have a chance to run, to escape. You need to get away from these people, girl!"

My head throbbed. A stabbing, icy cold pickaxe behind an eye that had already been whipped by a broken violin string.

"I-I don't know what to do," I admitted. "I feel so useless."

"Honey, don't say that." Anya flicked her attention to Joe. "Svenja Svellec. You said she's Ashworth's best hope, yes?"

"That *is* the word in the Barracks," Joe muttered dryly.

"Well then, she's our best hope too." Anya practically looked celebratory.

"We still don't know where she is, or if she's even alive. Mason said he killed her."

"He said he killed Campbell too, if you remember," Anya retorted, eyebrows raised. "When are you going to learn that Mason's a liar?"

I rolled my eyes.

"Look," she said, edging forwards. "The Rebels are convinced Svenja Svellec is alive and are going after her and Sebastian. They clearly believe she has important information that will give them the advantage, and that works in our favour too."

Joe Matheson scowled around the lingering breadcrumbs. "You're not seriously considering staying here?"

"It beats trying to escape, only for us to be killed or captured." A cloud of pearly mist escaped Anya's lips. "We're safer here than we are outside. At least here, the Rebels don't want Mason to find Alira any more than we do."

"Anya, don't be ridiculous!" Joe said, edging as far as his bound wrists would allow. "You're no safer here than you are anywhere else!"

Exhaustion plagued me. I lacked the energy to make my own decisions.

"Anya's right," I said, eventually.

"No, no! This is a bad idea! Think about it, girl," Joe said, his bloodshot eyes wide and pleading. "You don't know what Mason knows—"

"And what exactly does Mason know? C'mon Joe, if you know something we don't, you need to tell us!"

He sank back onto his ankles, his head falling. "I don't *know* anything. All I heard were whispers, rumours."

"That say what, exactly?"

Seafoam eyes portrayed genuine, unmitigated terror. "I lied to Ashworth. I never told Mason you were using the freight tracks. I mean, yes—I told him thinking it was good information, but they already knew!"

A shadow descended across that compartment, shrouded with fear and unease.

"What are you saying, Joe?"

"Girl, I'm saying someone on this train is a traitor."

7

———————

Pacing. Back and forth, back and forth. It's all I seemed to do those days —in a compartment stinking of mould, no less.

I debated whether to sleep, but the damp bedsheets just didn't appeal to me. Specks of frost glistened on the walls, catching my eye every time I passed, as did the bucket of water—once warm, but now one with the frigid air.

I had been pacing for what felt like hours, my muscles tight and rigid. The perpetual motion of the train rang against the music inside my head.

Mason was angry, of course he was. His music was loud and deafening, stabbing behind my eyelids. My piano had also reappeared, persecuting me in the back corners of my brain, mocking my own, stupid choice to escape my destiny.

You can't escape us, each note seemed to taunt.

I continued pacing.

The door to the compartment opened wide. Campbell's glacial-blue eyes scanned my appearance with a concerned frown.

"When was the last time you slept?" he asked.

"I-I can't sleep, Campbell." Energised blood flitted around my body. "I-I mean, h-how can I sleep at a time like this?"

"Oh, come here..." Campbell's large paws grasped my arms in a comforting hold and I sank into his warmth. My tremors lessened as he literally squeezed away the fear.

Campbell pulled back and held me at arm's length, picking away a stray strand of hair from my face. "Now," he said softly. "Talk to me. Tell me what's on your mind."

I didn't want to admit Joe's disclosure. I didn't want the Rebels to consider Joe a useless asset, to throw his lifeless body from the train like they had done with Emilia's.

"How well do you trust the people on this train?" I whispered.

Campbell frowned. "I don't follow."

"I mean, I know this alliance with the Mulch Gang is strained, and I-I know that things haven't been easy for anyone lately, but... How much can these people be *trusted?*"

A heavy sigh escaped Campbell's lips, bordered with thick black stubble. "Girl, you know I won't let anything happen to you."

"I know you won't," I said, and I believed it. As Campbell gently wiped away a tear with his thumb, I *knew* Campbell would never let them hurt me —not again. He was *my* Protector. "But what if... I mean, what if..." I licked my lips, the words struggling to arise. "Campbell, I'm afraid there's a mole on this train."

"A mole?" Campbell raised bushy eyebrows.

"A spy, or a traitor, or *someone!*" I shook his arms off and continued to pace around the room. "Campbell, what if a Masonian has infiltrated the Free People? Someone in disguise, pretending to be a Rebel and then feeding Mason information?"

Campbell heaved another sigh—in frustration, this time. "Who have you been talking to? Is it Carter? Has he been filling your head with nonsense?"

"No, it's just..." I collapsed onto the bed, the metal frame squeaking in retaliation. "Campbell, what if I'm not safe here anymore?"

"This is the safest place for you in the New World."

"Is it though? Really?" I ran my fingers through my long hair and cringed at the brittle, scraggy ends. It used to be so glossy and vibrant, styled to perfection.

Campbell eased down beside me and placed a warm hand upon my jerking knee. "You should sleep. It's been a rough couple of days. You must be exhausted."

He was right—of course he was. Sleep beckoned to me like an old friend, begging me to slip into her tranquil embrace. And I wanted to. I wanted to go to sleep. I wanted to rid myself of the terrible music inside my head and escape into my dreams. They were the only place I could feel safe, the only place where I could hold my sons in my arms. Yes, I liked my dreams.

The violin shrieked, angry and insistent and *furious*. I whimpered with the pain, curling forwards as my fingernails scratched my skull.

Campbell rushed to his feet. "I'll get Zackery."

"No!" I grabbed his hand and pulled him back down. Gradually, as the pain lessened, I lifted my head to meet his pity. "No, I-I'm okay..."

"Can you tell what he's doing?"

He obviously wondered if I knew what Mason was planning; to sense his thoughts, or to have an indication of his next move across the chessboard.

"No," I replied. "It's just his emotions."

Campbell's jaw clenched, his teeth grinding. "It'll get better, girl. Soon, you'll be free of him and the music, and you'll never have to live in fear again."

I didn't believe that. There was always something to live in fear of.

"Campbell, what if Mason knows where we are?" I asked, unable to look at him. "He already knows we're using the freight tracks, so what if he's just biding his time? Surely it's safer if I leave?"

Campbell recoiled from me as though bitten, his face twisting with barely suppressed outrage. "*Leave?* And go where? You're our only hope—if he finds you, then—"

"I know what will happen when he finds me, Campbell!" My internal cauldron started to simmer, then continued to heat.

"You're not going anywhere..." There was something else behind that stare: some unspoken warning, a desperate beg for obedience. "You need to trust me when I say that no one here will harm you, and there sure as hell isn't a traitor on this train."

Too tired to argue, I sank back into the bed, letting the thin mattress caress my curves. Metal bars pressed into the base of my spine, sending a chill its entire length.

Eventually, I nodded.

Campbell smiled. A small smile, but genuine. "I'm curious as to why you're so concerned. Who's been putting ideas into your head?"

I debated lying. I concocted many names: some real, most fictitious. Indeed, there were hundreds of names I could relay, and even more nameless faces. A whisper in a secluded corner, a note slipped into a pocket... There were so many explanations for my concerns, so many fantasies I could create...

"Joe," I conceded, and then quickly avoided Campbell's stern disapproval. "He said Mason knew things. Things he could only know if he had someone on this train."

Campbell listened with ever growing concern, his bushy black eyebrows set far down his brow.

"Joe's the traitor, girl." Sadness lingered, perhaps, as he remembered old times: of drunken laughs in a longhouse, or a shared tankard with an old friend. "He sold us out, he's the reason we're all in this shit. Why are you trusting him?"

I thought long and hard about that question. Indeed, why should I trust Joe Matheson? He had proven on several occasions that he couldn't be trusted. Joe Matheson was a selfish man, caring for no one but himself and dragging us all through the mud.

Why should I trust him?

"Because he's also dead if Mason gets his hands on him," I said. "He only cares about his own skin, and if he thinks it's in danger, he will do all he can to save it. That includes telling us the truth."

"Maybe he's playing us," Campbell said, shrugging broad shoulders. "Maybe he's working for Mason, maybe he's been offered mercy in exchange for all of us. Maybe he's trying to play you, to coerce you to escape simply so Mason can pluck you from the snow. Ever think of that?"

No, I hadn't.

Indeed, how far was Joe Matheson willing to go? What part of his soul was he prepared to sell in exchange for his life, his freedom, or even a dry roof over his head? What part of our last, lingering friendship would he be prepared to throw away?

Perhaps I best not know.

With a tight smile, Campbell tapped my knee. "C'mon, girl. Up."

He jumped to his feet and my face twisted. "Huh?"

"C'mon, I want to show you something."

Out of curiosity, I followed him through the bowels of the train.

Campbell led me into one of the compartments near the rear. Motor oil's heady stench suffocated the air, the lightbulb flourishing weak light across a selection of black vans.

"What's all this?" I asked, meandering around the neat line stored down the middle of the compartment, filling most of the space.

With a grand smile, Campbell slapped his hand on the bonnet. Metal grumbled in defiance. "These are our getaways. Mole or not, we can get these out within five minutes, and then I'll have us roaring along the tundra in no time at all."

Curious, I crouched down. No spiked tyres. "Won't get very far. Vans will just skid all over the place."

Campbell chucked to himself. "Reminiscing of your driving lessons?"

Pfft. Driving lessons, indeed. Nothing more than a stolen Masonian trunk and only half a tank of fuel to practice. Despite Campbell's tutelage, I'd never got the hang of skids, even with the spiked tyres.

He opened the door to the closest van and gestured me inside. I caressed the cold leather of the steering wheel, my feet resting upon the pedals as the gear stick loomed at my side. I reached down and startled at how neatly it fit in my palm.

"See, you'll drive us all to safety in no time." Campbell smiled, his entire face lifting to the sparkle in his eyes. I focused on that sparkle, a small smile teasing my own lips.

But those Masonian Barracks flashed across my vision: of a similar sparkle, created—this time—by tears.

Enslave her, Campbell's voice echoed.

"How did you escape?" I asked, then shocked myself by realising this was the first time I'd wondered such a thing. Had I really been so preoccupied that I hadn't asked him *that*, in all the weeks I'd been there?

Maybe I was just so relieved that he was alive, and not a rotting corpse in a ditch somewhere.

Campbell's smile faltered, his stare falling to the tyres. He kicked one, his shoe bouncing against its firm, rubber skin.

"I was imprisoned in the Barrack's holding cells. A young Masonian, no more than sixteen, guarded me. There was a distraction, he turned and..." Campbell trailed off. "I had an old shoelace in my pocket, so I strangled him with it."

A grimace twisted my features. I thought of Tallis, probably still nestled within a Maelstrom hospital bed, and prayed the Old Gods would take pity on him. Maybe Odin would keep Tallis' legs broken for a little while longer, so he might survive Campbell's shoelaces.

Campbell sighed. "I took his keys, let myself out, and ran from the Barracks under the cover of darkness."

A single tear trickled down his cheek, disappearing into his stubble. "I looked for you, girl. I found a ledger of all the prisoners, but your name wasn't there. I knew they'd already taken you to Maelstrom."

"That's why you went looking for Ashworth?" Compassion sparked inside my voice and my eyes burned. After what happened to Harrison Dagger, and all the rest, Campbell despised Rebellions. And yet, he joined the Free People for *me*, to get *me* out of the Fjordlands...

"Yes. I couldn't get into Maelstrom, let alone get you out. God, I wished they'd taken me there—I would have bashed down every Aristocratic door until I found you."

My heart, so bruised and battered, bloated inside my chest. I easily fell into Campbell's warm embrace.

I closed my eyes, inhaling his familiar scent of leather and gun oil. It was so easy to be with him, like this. I felt protected.

Campbell placed a small kiss upon my head. "Come on, it's getting late."

The protection disappeared. Cold seeped into my clothes, reminding me very much of his absence, and my predicament.

And the mole aboard that train.

I suddenly had to get away from him. As my looming choices grew ever more certain, the last thing I needed were reminders of Campbell's protecting warmth, or his sacrifices. I felt the ache of guilty tears and I hastily sniffed them back.

"I'm going to call it a night," I said.

"Yes, you need to sleep." Campbell patted me on the shoulder. "And try not to worry. You're perfectly safe here."

I forced a smile.

We returned to my room with a silence that was almost awkward.

"Night, girl," he said, a little curtly.

"Night," I replied.

* * *

As expected, the bedsheets were damp when I entered their embrace. They mocked the comfort I craved, only forcing my mind back to the Palace. Still ruined—nothing more than clumps of charred bricks and mortar. And yet, the memory of its soft, warm bedsheets sunk into every muscle, reminding me of their soft, clean adoration. I recalled the Reading Room, the cosy fire, and the windowsill where I'd just sit and read.

My thoughts returned to that cold compartment, and the knapsack of stolen books sitting patiently in the corner. I hadn't touched any of them yet. I simply lacked the energy.

I thought of Campbell's reluctance to listen to me. I thought of his sacrifice, his devotion to the Free People that completely clouded his judgement, his *senses*.

A cautious knock on the door revealed Anya. Ginger hair glinted in the light from the bulb, still swinging on the wire.

"Well?" she asked, hands in her pockets. "Did you speak to Campbell?"

"Yes."

"And? What did he say?"

A bitter huff left me, and I drew my knees up to my chest. "He doesn't believe me, Anya. He's not going to let me go."

Anya released her stalled breath, and her last tendrils of hope along with it. "Zackery didn't believe me either. He said I was crazy."

"*They're* crazy. They're living in a dreamworld, ignoring the warnings being spat in their faces. They think they're impenetrable." I winced as the violin screeched around my cranium. "Oh Mason, just go to sleep already..."

Anya perched on the end of the bed. "Are you sure you want to do this? There'll be no going back if we do. We *will* be prisoners if they find us."

"We don't have a choice," I said, wiping the tear squeezed out by the music. "If Mason truly does have a mole on this train, then Ashworth is leading Mason both to Svenja Svellec *and* me. Two birds with a stone that's being bashed down by Ashworth's fucking arrogance."

"You'll be betraying Campbell," she whispered. "Are you sure you want to do that?"

I sighed into my lap, concentrating on the growing ache inside my chest. Campbell's eyes screamed at me, so bright with hope and trust. Could I betray him? Could I leave him like he left me?

"I don't have a choice in this," I said, fighting the twisting in my gut. "I love Campbell, but if he chooses not to believe me, then I have to leave him."

The words tasted stale on my tongue. Even then, as my decision crystallised around my soul, I could see the tears well in Campbell's eyes—the fractures in our foundations widening, one betrayal at a time.

"Then it's settled." Anya jumped to her feet and removed her jacket and ripped jeans. Pale limbs scrambled into her own damp bed. "Are you sure you want to tell Orzo and Heidi?"

"Yes," I said, staring at the ceiling. White specks dotted across my vision, brought on by my migraine, and resembled stars on a dark sky. I wished I could see the stars. "We're getting off this train, Anya. The least we can do is offer."

* * *

THE NEXT MORNING, as the train chugged lethargically through the snow, Anya relayed our plan to the open ears of Orzo and Heidi.

I leant against the door, listening to her argument, the cold wind blowing away the cobwebs tickling my soul. I tasted freedom in that wind—a very different flavour to the motor oil and gun grease choking the life from that train.

Basking in the wind's tender touch, snow sprinkled my skin and I thought of the world itching at our fingertips: the mountainous peaks doused with fresh snow; the trees, shrinking as we travelled further north; the lakes with their flat, smooth skin easily recognisable against the drama of the land-scape. I relished those visions and the cold upon my skin. I wanted to crawl into that cold, to be blown away from that Rebel train with the rest of the snowflakes.

"A mole? Are you sure?" Orzo's voice was deep and steady, and did not agree with his boyish haircut.

"It's what Joe said," Anya said, thin arms crossed.

"He tells the truth?" Heidi asked. Out of all the Palace Slaves, Heidi had bounced into Rebel life extremely well. She remained optimistic towards the future, doing her chores with a newfound enthusiasm. Her Tribe traded with the Free People after all, so perhaps it was akin to coming home.

Maybe she just needed something to do.

But still, as the skin paled against her dirty blonde hair. I saw fear for the first time in young Heidi. Perhaps it was the fear of death, or the threat of punishment, or returning to her life bound by Slavery's shackles. Maybe, after everything, she was simply afraid of losing.

"Yes, honey," Anya said softly. "We think he's telling the truth."

"But how can you be sure?" Orzo piped up, pacing the entire length of the compartment. "How can you trust him after everything he's done?"

"Because why would he lie?" Eyes shot to me, and to my resolve and that veil of snow carried in freedom's fingers. "He's got no reason to lie anymore. Telling us about this mole puts him in more danger—from Rebels and traitors alike—so why would he tell us such a thing if it wasn't the truth?

"If this mole is so dangerous, why hasn't he told Ashworth?"

"They didn't believe us," Anya said, deflating with a sigh. "They've got no reason to think the Free People have been infiltrated. We already tried to tell them and they called us crazy, or assumed Joe's lying."

And if Mikael Ashworth thought Joe was lying, another body would be thrown from the train. Rolling down the bank, left to fester with the fungi in the trees.

"What are you going to do then?" Orzo said, the first licks of irritability scraping down his tongue. "You'll leave this train, and then what? Go walking about the wilds, out in the open for Masonians to find you? You'll be outnumbered, unprotected, un—"

"Orzo, I know how to manoeuvre the wilderness. I'm a Herder, remember?"

Orzo's stare grew nasty. "A Herder, really? Because the last time I checked, you were a fucking Aristocrat!"

A roll of my eyes returned me to the view. He was right of course. How many times had my dinner been served on the backs of Slaves?

I did not want to think about it. I basked in the sun's warm, cleansing rays.

"Orzo, that's uncalled for and you know it!"

"No, it's not, Anya! You're actually considering leaving the only safe place there is! Jeez, it's like you *want* him to find you!"

Rage spat through my glare. "Fuck you, Orzo. If this place was *safe*, we wouldn't be having this conversation and you *know* that!"

The air fogged up with tension.

"Come with us, or don't come with us," I eventually said, as their silence grew deafening. "But we're getting off this damn train, with or without you." Pushing myself away from the view, I left them to decide their fate.

* * *

A FEW HOURS LATER, as the last musical note fluttered in the air, I sighed at the silence inside my head. So rare it was, to hear *nothing*. So precious and fleeting.

Mason's slumber had finally removed the pain, and his violin with it. No more furious tones, no more painful punishment for his anger.

In its place, tranquillity reigned. Peace and quiet. *Finally.*

With trembling fingers, I replaced my hands in my lap. The piano stared at me, its golden skin shining in the sunlight streaming in through the open compartment.

A tentative knock lifted my head. Orzo's kind stare grew guilty as he gently closed the door behind him. "I'm sorry, am I disturbing you?"

I offered a tentative smile. "Not at all. I'm just enjoying the silence."

"He's asleep?"

"Yes, for the first time in days."

"Good, he should finally be giving you some peace."

Peace. A strange word. A short, abrupt word that sounded very much like the atmosphere it alluded to. Strange, how every word seemed to have its own sound.

Calm. Serenity.

Fury. Rage.

"Yeah, well..." I sighed again and closed the key lid, protecting each note within the golden case. "It won't be for long. He'll be awake in a few hours."

"But you still have a few hours' reprieve." Orzo revealed a hip-flask from his inside coat pocket, its silver skin mottled with black. "Care for a swig?"

"Of what?" I asked, smirking.

"I honestly couldn't tell you." He knocked some back and shuddered. "Though it packs a punch."

A tender smile stretched across my lips, encouraged by Orzo.

"Come on," he said, with a raised eyebrow. "What do you say? For old times' sake?"

There was something in his eyes; something I couldn't quite distinguish. But our last sour conversation lingered in my memories and I wanted to cloud it over, to cover it up until nothing but good echoes remained. Hugged by precious silence, why shouldn't I enjoy Orzo's company?

"Yeah," I said. "Why not."

We sat on the metal floor with one leg swinging outside the compartment. The cold tried to puncture our jeans, all but blown away by the alcohol that warmed our bellies. Blood filled with heat.

In that tranquillity, we just talked. About everything and nothing.

Two old friends, reminiscing over past lives.

"Do you miss Emilia?" I asked, passing the hip-flask. We'd already drank most of it, the liquid already swirling around our throats and burning away our rigidity, one little sip at a time.

Orzo gladly took the flask and indulged in one more swig. "Yeah, I miss her. She was an incredible woman. Kind, even for an Aristocrat."

"Yeah, she was certainly a rarity. *Kind* isn't usually a word associated with Aristocrats."

"I dunno..." Orzo smirked. "You were pretty up there."

"Really?" My doubting lip curled as Orzo passed the hip-flask. I took an extra-long swig to burn away the taste of Aristocratic bullshit.

I shivered as the alcohol reached my belly. The room spun. "I was a bitch, Orzo. I got sucked in by all the jewels and the nobility and became everything I despised."

"You weren't all bad. Besides, you were sucked in because Aristocracy provided an escape from your reality. Terrible things happened to you. The comfort of Aristocratic life would have been a draw for anyone in your position."

My fuzzy attention wandered to the mountains, and the warmth of Orzo's alcohol that rubbed away the perpetual anxiety. Yet relieved tears still threatened, burning behind my eyes. Did someone *finally* understand why I had succumbed to the life Mason groomed me for?

"May I ask you something?" he asked.

Inflated by alcohol's courage, I sniffed back my tears and smiled. "Of course."

Orzo licked his lips, dried from the cold weather. "Do you miss him?"

The ache reappeared inside my chest—strong, forceful and all too sudden. I drew in a deep breath as I considered his question, mist flowing through my open lips as I wondered what to say.

I didn't miss him. I didn't miss my tormenter.

But why was Orzo's question so painful?

"I miss the simplicity of it all," I said, shocked by my own admission. "I was going to have his baby, by my own volition as well. He was happy about that. He was nice to me."

"And now?"

Guilt and anxiety tried to rise, only to be whipped away by alcohol's shield. In that stillness, I considered Orzo's question with a deep frown and a heavy heart. "Now? Well, now it's not simple. I'm choosing to run from him, and he doesn't like that at all. Now, I'm living my life in constant uncertainty, and I'm constantly terrified because of it."

"Are you scared of what'll happen if he finds you?"

"I'm scared of everything. Of what will happen to me, and to you and Campbell, Anya and Heidi... Of Joe Matheson's life, of what Ashworth intends to do with him. Or the fear if—Gods forbid—I do become pregnant again and I lose another one..." A heavy sigh, my breath floating around us. "That's what terrifies me the most, Orzo... I'm scared of going through that again."

"You won't, Alira," Orzo said, edging closer, along with his scent: a potent mix of sweat and coal. Strangely masculine. "I won't let him find you, not again."

I smiled at his words, and the sun and the mountains and the warmness of alcohol's courage inside my blood. That precious silence entombed me, urging me to look up.

I stared at Orzo, at the kindness within those brown eyes, and remembered the look upon his face when he sacrificed himself to Erik Doncaster. There was horror behind his eyes that night—most certainly. But there was also desperation, dare I say a little...*pride?*

"Why do you care about me, Orzo?" He was ever so close to me, his hair rippling in the cool breeze. "Why, after everything I've put you through, do you still want to protect me?"

Orzo's hand lifted. Long fingers picked a wayward strand of hair from my face and curled it around my ringed ear.

Mason used to do that, frequently. His fingers were warmer than Orzo's.

"Isn't it obvious?" Orzo whispered.

Is it? *What* was obvious?

I startled as Orzo's clammy hand touched my cheek, his fingers like little icicles that still caressed warmth into my skin. Pure, loving *warmth*. Why did I relax into his palm? Because it felt good. It felt so good to be caressed, to be cared about...

His hand moved into my hair, holding me oh-so-gently as he tilted closer.

His eyes closed, then his lips parted.

Oh.

That was obvious?

Mason thought it was obvious, that night at dinner, when he threatened Orzo's future. I thought Mason was just being...well, *Mason.* Could he have been right all along?

Orzo's fingers tightened in my hair, urging me closer. Confused by such *strange* affection, I let him.

Somewhere in the background, my piano loudened.

That music could burn in Hel, so I closed my eyes and accepted Orzo's kiss.

The piano tried to scream, to yell her furious admonishment, but alcohol's fiery breath blew away her musical scolding, like leaves on the wind.

Alone, free from musical persecution, I concentrated on Orzo's kiss, and his lips, and the feel of his hands upon my skin. The feel of another's touch—a *kind, genuine* touch—for the first time in my life.

My heart pounded, *painfully*, as Orzo pulled me closer. He tried to deepen the kiss, licking his warm tongue across my lower lip, trying to entice my mouth to open, *to let him in.*

Panic ballooned.

I felt the prickle of his beard, the dryness of his lips... As I inhaled his sweaty aroma, or the lingering hint of gun grease and machine oil, I realised one, startling truth—the thing that terrified me most of all.

He was not Mason.

I abruptly pulled away. "Don't," I breathed, unable to look at him. "Just... don't."

It wasn't right. *This* wasn't right. Betrayal rose inside my aching heart—a betrayal I could scarcely believe existed, or one that I'd just helped perpetuate... Destiny's invisible chains still encircled my throat, and I was a fool to think they'd loosened.

Shame heated my cheeks and angry tears burned. I hated myself. I hated Mason. I tried not to hate Orzo.

Orzo's brow lowered. "Is it the music? Is it causing you pain?"

Yes, I was in pain. But it wasn't the music.

"Y-you better go," I said. Alcohol's fog disappeared, blown away with the rest of my courage. If only the pain in my chest would abate just as easily.

I needed to be alone. I craved the company of my past and a future that was just as empty as my present.

"Erm..." Orzo cleared his throat and stared at the metal floor. He tapped his thumb against the side of his leg, as though considering something.

He picked up the hip-flask. "I could get us some more liquor."

Confused, I just looked at him.

"It helped, right? I-I mean, we were able to kiss so..." He cleared his throat again. "I mean, the music let you kiss me for a bit, so if we have some more to drink then maybe we can carry on, and then—"

"And then *what?*" Anger bristled. All my fear, all my dread for the future —all my shame for the past—was obliterated beneath Orzo's proposition.

And his kiss and his emotions and all his fucking *desperation* for me to feel what he did…

The rage came hot and bubbling, and she was not merciful.

"What, Orzo? You think I'm going to *fuck* you? You think I'm suddenly going to forget that I'm *Mason's* and just so readily drop my pants for *you?*"

Stunned, Orzo remained stoic and silent, like the sheets of snow outside.

I laughed. A bitter, resentful sound that did not agree with the tears in my eyes. "I will never touch you again, Orzo! Not if I'm drunk or stoned or just goddamn desperate! I'm Mason's *mate!* I always have been, I always will be, and your hip-flask full of battery acid will never change *any* of that!"

"But I… I thought…" Tears itched Orzo's eyes, his lower lip quivering. I glimpsed at that lip, and the specks of dried skin, and my stomach lurched.

"You thought what? That I *love* you?" I laughed again, but the sound was mean and bitter. "No, Orzo. Of course I don't."

More silence. Wind whistled through the compartments, the air between us so thick and suffocating.

Orzo quickly wiped his face and stood to his feet. "Well, thanks for clearing that up."

As he marched to the door, the anger died. Instead, guilt ballooned, squishing away the hate and the rage induced by Orzo's first act of real tenderness. How long had it been since he'd kissed someone he wanted to? How long had it been since he'd consensually made love to another?

What the Hel have I done?

"Orzo, I'm so sorry, I—" I rushed to my feet, but the door had already slammed shut. I groaned, running my hands through my hair.

The piano teased in my peripheral vision. I stabbed my fingers against the keys, playing the song with newfound ferocity, suddenly wishing for something to fill that dreadful silence.

8

————————

I hadn't seen Orzo since my outburst. As the hours ticked on—as Anya, Heidi and I patiently waited with our bags packed and our resolution firm—I admitted that maybe his absence was for the best. There were just too many memories, too many echoes of hurt and failure. Yes, Orzo should stay behind. Maybe he'd find someone kind and genuine. Someone who liked the feel of his lips, the scent of his skin. Yes, he needed someone whose stomach fluttered in his presence, whose heart would sing at his every smile.

Orzo deserved to be loved. He deserved better than me.

"Well then," Anya said, looking at the aurora in the sky. "We better get going."

Blue and green hues danced across the black, hiding the stars that lay patiently beneath. It created that wintry glow against the snow, the same ethereal hue that filled me with such awe. My stomach flipped at the thought of walking beneath those dancing colours, away from the stench of war and Rebels.

I had played the piano frequently in the hours beforehand. My inner music, drunk off piano notes, slept off her musical hangover. When would she reappear?

According to Anya, who'd heard it from Zackery, pianos were now all the rage across the New World. Rumours of my musical prowess had spread fast, it seemed—clearly people had a sick fascination with the music that tortured me. Nevertheless, if such things were true, I hoped we'd find one of these pianos before my own music woke up.

Towns—they were our best hope. Not too far away, perhaps a seven-day trek through the valley, a town nestled between the peaks of the Brüster Mountains, right at the northern Snowlands, where only the hardiest of men would reside. There, in the midst of drunken revelry, we hoped a piano would be found. If not—if our instincts about such a large town were wrong...

Well, we'd face that problem if and when it came.

Either way, our minds were set. Like Hel were we going to stay on that train, waiting for the day Mason's mole ratted us out. How long did we have until Masonians ransacked us? Until Mason himself wandered upon that very train?

None of us wanted to find out. Even those little, annoying reservations at the back of my head silenced themselves.

But if we'd been mistaken—if the mole was nothing more than a misheard assumption, or a ploy to instil doubt and panic among the Rebels —then the train remained safe. Mason would believe I was still wandering its metal belly and he wouldn't dare destroy it unless he ensured otherwise. Such knowledge helped mend the pit in my stomach. I had to live with Campbell's shattered trust and disappointment, but at least I didn't have the entire train on my conscience.

The only obstacle now was Joe Matheson. Like Hel was I going to leave him there, to fester in his cell with the rest of the cockroaches. No, if we were getting out, then Joe Matheson was coming with us.

We just had to figure out how to do it.

"I could distract them," Anya said, pushing a thick strand of hair behind her ear. "The guards on the door, I mean. I could convince them to come with me, keep them occupied for an hour or two. That would give you more than enough time to get Joe out."

I listened to her plan with ever growing disgust. "Anya, *no*. You can't seriously be considering whoring yourself out?"

"It's nothing Mason didn't make me do," she muttered.

A wave of disgust rose with the guilt of having willingly shared a bed with that man.

"No, Anya, I'm not allowing you to do this! Not here, not after everything he made you do in the Palace..." I straightened my spine and crossed my arms. "No, we'll think of another way."

"Honey, this is my choice," Anya said, gently, trying to catch my eye. "This isn't like the Palace. This time, *I* have a say and I *want* to do this."

"We'll find another way, Anya, so just shut up and think."

Smooth hands cradled my face, forcing our eyes to lock. "It's okay, honey," she said. Her smile, warm and soothing, melted the ice upon my skin. "Just buy me a beer."

A shameless wink and she released me.

I looked at Heidi, silent and subdued, probably too young to fully understand what Anya was offering. Yet, perhaps wise beyond her years, she simply sighed out her innocence and nodded.

"We need to get off this train," she said.

Heidi was right. So was Anya. I was the only one disagreeing, the only one stubborn and stupid enough to search for an *easy* option.

"Okay, fine," I said, rubbing a hand across sore eyes. "As soon as the coast is clear, we'll get Joe out—"

Words shot down my throat as three men burst into the compartment; faces smutted with soot, clothes marred with engine oil and black stains. Eyes perused us like we were rotting meat: disgust, hatred, revulsion... Each emotion sang gloriously upon hard faces, the bulk of their anger settling firmly upon me.

"Come with us, Alira," one of them barked. Only then did I see the guns in their hands, gripped with white-knuckle force. "Ashworth wants a word with you."

* * *

MARSHALLED through the train at gunpoint, I stayed the stampede of curses at my throat and did my best to follow orders. I didn't like following orders, not anymore. *Obedience, cooperation*—I was done with them both. They were just words, blown away with the flurries of snow. But as gun barrels stabbed my spine, I bit my twitching tongue and once again did as I was told. Escaping that train would be easier without chains.

Anya, of course, was less enthused about cooperation and spat vicious insults. Grips on guns tightened, the sound of grinding jaws growing ever more noticeable.

Heidi remained behind. Forgotten, like the rest of the orphaned children who had nowhere to go.

Ashworth stood before the table with that weathered map and several more carved pawns. Behind him, Isla sat with her arms crossed, her lips pressed tightly together. Theodore and Ben Carter were on opposite sides of the room, both staring at me. Theodore's stare contained disappointment. Ben Carter's stare was an unsettling mix of hatred and utter hilarity. His, by far, was the most unnerving.

Armed men stationed themselves behind us, blocking our only exit. Campbell was nowhere to be seen.

I took a brave step forward. "Ashworth, what's this all about?"

"What indeed." There was no humour behind his smile, no kindness or sincerity. Just hatred. Raw, unyielding hatred.

A cold chill worked punched the soles of my boots, creeping up my legs once small inch at a time.

"You've got a bloody nerve!" Anya piped up, seething. "You march us in here—at *gunpoint*—without so much as an explanation!"

"Oh, we have an explanation, and our actions are more than justified." Ashworth leant both arms on the table, revealing the smatter of knives secured beneath his coat. He pulled his dirty blonde hair back from his brow and suddenly looked far older than his twenty-three years. In that moment, for the first time since I'd been on that train, he looked like the leader of the Free People's Rebellion.

He looked like the man who'd executed my unborn children.

"What's going on?" I asked, unable to hide the bitter shake in my voice. "Why have you brought us here?"

"We've received some new information," Theodore said, glaring. "Very unsettling information, at that."

"Oh really?" I sneered at them. "And what sort of information have you received, *Sir?*"

Theodore's head lowered until his eyes bathed in shadow. "Mr Carter, please would you fetch our guest?"

Ben Carter grinned. "My pleasure, Mr Addington."

In three long steps, he was beside me with a stench of tobacco and weed. He caught me staring at him, so he stopped to lean in close, puckering his lips as if to kiss me. I recoiled and he laughed quietly to himself.

Carter returned with another man, the meagre light highlighting the red threads in his patchy beard.

"*Orzo?*" I breathed.

We locked eyes. Betrayal screamed in the space between us. It mixed with something deep: once a light, vibrant emotion that had twisted and deformed into something dark and grotesque, like black tar.

Emotionally fraught, Emilia's voice sang inside my head.

"What the *hell* is going on?" Anya shouted behind me. "Orzo, what are you doing here? Why are we being held at gunpoint?"

"Because, Miss Whittaker," Theodore said, "some new information has come to light that makes us question Alira's loyalty to our cause. And yours, for that matter."

My heart solidified, sinking to my stomach like a cold pebble.

"Orzo..." I whispered. "What did you say to them?"

Ashworth plucked an item from his pocket: small, delicate, and glittering in the swaying lightbulb. My stomach imploded a little more with each twinkling teardrop link. The bracelet Mason had once gifted me sparkled vehemently, finally boasting its luxury after its long imprisonment.

Anya stiffened behind me.

"Where did you get this bracelet, Alira?" Ashworth said. There was menace behind his eyes; there was contempt.

When I didn't answer, he said, "Silence will not work in your favour. I suggest you answer us."

I opened my mouth to speak. Words remain elusive, so I cleared my throat. "It was a gift," I whispered.

"From whom?"

"Emilia."

"She's lying." Orzo lifted his head so each pitted scar shone. "Emilia didn't give her that."

Ashworth's stare hardened. "It's a bad idea to lie to us, girl. So, I'll ask you again: who gave you the bracelet?"

I licked the scar on my lip and felt the raised, hardened skin. I remembered how I got that scar. I remembered Verity Ulster with a knife to my mouth, about to cut out my tongue until Orzo descended those stairs. *Harm me instead*, his kind eyes once begged.

That was a long time ago now.

"Mason..." I eventually said, barely audible. "Mason gave me that bracelet."

Ashworth nodded, a triumphant smirk on his face. One spiteful look at the bracelet and he threw it away like the rubbish he thought it was. It clanked harshly against the metal floor and settled precariously over the grid beneath Ashworth's feet. I inched forwards, ever so slightly, my fingers twitching to save it.

"And why, dare I ask, did he give you that bracelet?"

A single tear threatened to fall, to drip from my chin with the rest of my deception. "Because I liked it. I saw it in a shop in Maelstrom. He caught me staring at it."

"He was trying to seduce her," Anya said quickly, her skin radiating anxious heat. "He did it under a guise for her good behaviour."

"And did this seduction work?"

A sad, sneering smile worked my lips. "Well, I'm here, aren't I? I'm trying to rid myself of him, to help you kill him. So, you tell me if it worked or not."

Hate and pity soured Isla's beautiful face. "If what you say is true, then why keep the bracelet? Why hide it?"

"I thought I could sell it or trade it for weapons or ammunition. I kept it hidden because I didn't know you people, and I didn't trust you'd believe my intentions." All true.

Ashworth and Isla exchanged glances. Ben Carter's attention remained fixed on me, a subtle smirk tickling his lip. Yes, a truly horrific man.

"Well," Ashworth said, producing a shameless, lying grin. "That all seems well and good, but Orzo here has another interesting story."

My attention shot to Orzo. Only then did I see the red lines around his eyes, and the hatred that seethed within them.

"Mr Atkinson," Theodore said, straightening his spine, looking down upon us all like the weaklings he thought we were. "Do tell us, in your personal opinion, if Alira was seduced by Mason."

"Yes," he whispered. "Yes, she was."

My heart jumped, wanting to claw its way into my mouth.

"Interesting..." Theodore purred. "And tell us, Mr Atkinson, do you believe that Alira was a prisoner in Mason's Palace?"

"A prisoner? Oh, no..." Orzo's throat bobbed with a large swallow. "She stopped being his prisoner a long time ago."

"Orzo, don't..." I breathed. "Please, don't..."

There was a small, spiteful curl of his lip before he puffed up his shoulders. "Her second pregnancy was consensual."

"*Orzo!*" Anya screeched, jumping to my side. "That's *not* how it was, that's—"

"Shut your face, Anya!" he spat. Anya startled back, shocked to hear such viciousness from Orzo—*kind, selfless, sweet* Orzo. I remained silent, trembling, disgusted by the truth he regaled so triumphantly... "Because that's *exactly* how it was and you know it! Have you forgotten the way you warned her? The way you begged her to come to her senses and remember what sort of *monster* he really was?"

Bloodshot eyes slid to mine. "Because you did forget, didn't you? You forgot about *everything*: the times he's hurt you, the atrocities he's committed... But I didn't forget. I didn't forget when you kissed him, or shared his bed, or grinned at the prospect of having his fucking child!" Hateful eyes lined with silver. "Yes, Alira, you *are* Mason's mate. You *always* will be."

I wanted to crawl away, to disappear beneath the metal wheels of the train and be cut up into little pieces.

Ben Carter barked out a laugh. "Just like I said to you, girl: a terrible liar."

"Do you have anything to say for yourself?" Theodore said, that pointed nose lifted in evident superiority.

His question roamed around my head. All those lies I could concoct, all those excuses I could create for my behaviour...

"I did it to survive," I whispered. Plump tears quickly formed, racing down my cheek. "You don't understand, I-I did it to—"

"Don't make me laugh!" Orzo spat. "You didn't do it to survive! You did it because you *liked* it and because *he won!*"

To think, I once believed he *understood* me... But no, he didn't understand. Not at all.

Anya charged forward, her face twisting with anger, her sharp finger pointing. "You don't have a clue what she went through, Orzo! You didn't see what he did to her, what he—"

"She's not the only one who's been assaulted and tortured!" Orzo's contempt spread around the compartment, like toxic smog. "We've *all* suffered under Mason's regime, Anya, and yet you don't see us running towards our tormentors with our legs wide open, do you?"

I cracked.

I lunged towards Orzo, fingernails twitching to claw down his pale, pitted face.

For a split moment, his anger disentangled. In it was the emotion he felt: the obsession, the longing, the *hope.*

And there, beneath it all, I saw his hope crumble.

Hard hands gripped my shoulders, right down to the bone, and dragged me from the room. Anya's screams matched my own. She yelled and clenched her fists, swinging them in a desperate rush. Rebel guards dragged us both through the train. People stared, orphans cried, eyes bore into us with such deathly certainty.

They knew we had betrayed them. They knew I was not nearly as innocent as I'd once claimed.

Joe Matheson scrambled as far back as he could, escaping the torrent of angry Rebels pouring into the prison carriage. They dragged me to the floor, silent and petrified, as they tied those mouldy ropes around my wrists. Anya berated them for their lack of sympathy, kicking everything that moved.

Her yells slammed against metal walls as the room emptied. Then it was just the three of us. Bound prisoners in a rat-infested cell.

Behind Anya's raving shouts, Joe Matheson scooted closer. "Girl, what happened? Did they realise you were going to escape?"

I stared at the strands of hay on the floor, at the cracked mud and the sheen of spilled grease. How could I explain? How could I admit something so disgusting?

The door burst open. In marched Campbell with his face flushed, his eyes sore and glassy. He fell to his knees and cradled my face within those two large paws.

"Tell me it's not true," he said, his lower lip trembling. "Please, tell me it's not true..."

I wanted to. Gods, did I want to.

"I'm s-sorry..." Emotion pooled out of me, all the hatred and anger rushing from my body in a series of sobs. Great, gut-heaving sobs. "I-I'm s-so sorry, I-I just didn't w-want him to h-hurt me a-again..."

Campbell's face softened, and from eyes that spoke such sorrow, a single tear escaped. It raced down his cheek, merging with his stubble. My cries loudened, my eyes squeezing shut to hide my own guilt, my own sordid shame.

Campbell crushed me into him. Large arms wrapped tightly around my trembling frame and rocked me back and forth. "Shh... It's okay... Shh, don't worry, girl. It's okay..."

He slowly eased me away, meeting the tears that blurred my vision and raced down my cold cheek. He wiped each away with the pad of his thumb, like he had when I was small and scared. "Listen to me," he whispered, his voice hoarse. "I'm going to speak to Ashworth, I'm going to make sure he sees reason."

"H-he hates me, Campbell. They all w-want me d-dead..."

I didn't blame them. Not now, not after everything they knew, every last little confession squeezed out of my eroded, Aristocratic skin.

Campbell pressed a hard, chaste kiss on my forehead. "I'm going to make them see sense. Don't worry, I'll get you out of these ropes in no time."

"Campbell, I-I'm—"

Campbell forced a small smile. "Trust me, girl."

Trust. Did I have any left?

He fled the compartment, leaving us to the stench of rats and urine.

In Campbell's absence, the silence returned. Was Mason asleep? No, he was simply listening, trying to gauge the trauma I faced on that train.

Joe Matheson scooted closer, his worn shoes scuffing against the frosted metal floor.

"You gave into him," he realised. "You wanted a baby too, didn't you?"

Painful memories resurfaced. The tears came harder.

"Shut up, Joe…" Anya breathed.

9

———

Trapped in that stinking, frozen cell, we waited with the squeaking rats. None of us had the energy to speak—to make forced, dull conversation that no one cared about. Our plans had been ruined.

I'd switched from a Rebel to a Rebel prisoner. No doubt Ashworth was rethinking his strategy, wondering how long they could keep me, in what ways they could use me before I lost my worth. How long until they threw *my* lifeless body from the train? Perhaps I would roll into Emilia's grave, be reunited with her at the end.

Mason was probably laughing at my stupidity.

Regret.

I tried not to think of it, yet there it was. It popped up when least expected, berating me no matter how hard I tried to fight it.

I tried to fight Mason too. Look how that ended up.

But no, it wasn't all hopeless. Campbell was still my friend, he was out there, fighting for my life, my cause. He would not abandon me, not again. He was my Protector, regardless of what I had done.

I remembered how eager I was to leave the train—to leave *Campbell*—and my stomach crunched. More tears swam down my cheeks, the urge to hug him—to apologise for *everything*—just so damn potent.

Perhaps Campbell understood. Perhaps he realised the reasons for my actions, the catalysts for all my betrayals—past, present, and future.

Because yes, I'd already betrayed him. I'd already sliced that knife through his pride, his *trust*, and cut him deep. I'd made love to his enemy, the enemy of us all.

Perhaps I deserved their hatred.

Orzo deserved mine. The *bastard*. If—no, *when*—Campbell untied my wrists, I'd be sure to pay him a visit. I imagined his eyes—each speck of emerald green within the brown—and wished to see them in ever ominous detail. I imagined the feel of his curly hair around my fingers, holding him still as I glared into those eyes. Would *regret* surround his soul as he shattered beneath my stare?

Commotion outside the carriage. Shouts coalesced with panicked, frantic footsteps.

Another yell, followed by a faint rustle and hum. It intensified, growing into a low, ominous drone.

"What is that?" Anya asked, as the noise grew louder.

Brakes fired. Compartments creaked and squeaked into a single, deafening clatter. We lurched forwards as the train clamoured to stop.

"W-what the hell?" Joe shrieked, hoisting himself up.

"Shh!" I pressed. There was noise outside, movement.

Gunshots.

They peppered the air in all directions...

Surrounded.

"Oh my God," Anya breathed, her colour draining. "Quick, we need to get out of here!"

She pulled against the rope with newfound ferocity, her beautiful face scrunching beneath the pressure. Joe kicked the wall, trying to prize his tethered hands away, groaning and grunting through the strain.

I remained silent, utterly terrified, as I listened to the violin inside my head. *Excitement, hatred.* Strings plucked in time to each echoing gunshot...

He's here...

The door barged open. Anya shrieked, scrambling back. Then her anger exploded, *"You!"*

Orzo did not flinch beneath her writhing hatred as he dropped to his knees and untied my hands.

"I-I'm sorry, Alira." He stumbled around the words, his tongue unable to follow. "I-I was angry but that gave me no reason to—"

His words were meaningless. A sharp shove against his shoulder and I scrambled to Anya's aid. Orzo remained still, like a lost child.

No sooner had I loosened Anya's restraints, than she leap towards Orzo and slapped him hard across his cheek. *"You bastard!* How *could* you? How could you betray her like that, after everything that's happened?"

Orzo remained silent, his eyes large and glossy, his lower lip trembling through his beard. A single hand caressed his cheek, glowing red with Anya's handprint, but he kept guilty eyes fixed to the floor.

"Thanks," Joe whispered as I quickly freed him and helped him up. Despite his bent posture and unsteady legs, he managed a swift limp to the door.

"Talk to us, mate," he said. "What's happening out there?"

"I-I don't know..." Orzo remained staring at the floor, unable to lift his head. "Th-there was an avalanche and they came out of nowhere."

"Masonians?"

"Yes."

The violin loudened, its tempo accelerating. I closed my eyes, absorbing the power of his music, allowing it to fill my blood with heated adrenaline. "Mason's here."

"Ah, *shit!*" Anya shouted. She dug her fingers through her hair, as though hope lay buried within the greasy copper strands. "How'd he find us?"

"I told you there was a fucking mole," Joe grumbled. He opened the door, a creak rattling as a singular line of light cut his face in two. "Looks like your sudden imprisonment forced Mason's hand. He was probably afraid they'd execute you."

Understanding hit Orzo. It winded him, knocking air out of small, tense lungs. He glimpsed up, only briefly. He met my eye, only for a second, and within their seething spill of diamond, Orzo saw exactly what I thought of him.

He dropped his gaze, afraid of witnessing any more.

"We need to go," Anya said. "We need to find Heidi."

"I'll get her," I said, the music igniting whatever determination I had left. Orzo's actions had buried deep, igniting my muscles with adrenaline. I would not allow his vengeful idiocy to be the end of me. I would not give him, nor Mason, such a pleasure.

"I'll come with you—"

"No, Anya. Help Joe, head for the trees. I'll find Heidi and join you there."

She reluctantly nodded, then slapped Joe's shoulder. "Can you run?"

"To get off this train? You bet your damn life."

"I-I'm going to stay here." Orzo's voice was so small in that compartment. It was lifeless, lacklustre, as though the light that once burned bright inside Orzo's heart had been doused in the same black tar, the same stinking grease that smeared its way across our friendship. It created a stain difficult to scrub clean.

"Orzo," I sighed, my defeat audible. "Masonians are everywhere, you can't possibly stay." But then I remembered the feel of his lips and hatred boiled inside my belly. I pushed it down, far away. There would be plenty of time to hate Orzo later.

"No, I'm staying," Orzo said, louder this time. "My actions brought Mason here. The least I can do is try and clean up my mess."

Anya marched past Orzo and took a firm grip of my arm. "We don't have much time," she said.

I looked at Orzo, debating whether to hit or hug him. Beneath the inherent apology in his eyes, resentment still lingered, so perhaps he wondered the same thing of me.

"Go," he said.

I did not say goodbye.

* * *

PEOPLE SCREAMED. Rebels and children rushed and scattered between compartments buried in mounds of snow.

Bodies marred the scenery. Men, women... I ignored the sight of children, their small limbs peeking from the snow. Masonians were there too, their blue coats popping against the white. Gunshots percolated the air. Shouts, shrieks—falling bodies merged with the clanks of metal against metal. Explosions spurted fire and shrapnel. Golden, angry heat encapsulated the frosty air.

I peeked outside the compartment. Blue coats stroked the snow, just before a wall of Rebels. Another explosion somewhere ahead, the train trembling in its wake.

My heart thumped in my throat as I faced Anya and Joe. "You need to get off this train—run to the trees, as fast you can, and I'll join you with Heidi."

Joe gripped Anya's upper arm and pulled her towards the open door. She remained reluctant, unable to leave me.

"Go!" I pressed. "I'll be fine, just get out of here!"

Tears saturated her lower lashes, her eyes sparkling like sapphires. "Be careful," she whispered.

I watched them sprint through the air of violence and merge into the trees.

Heidi.

I ran through the train, wading through the flood of Rebels, grabbing tufts of blonde hair and exploring the faces of terrified strangers.

"Heidi!" I yelled through the bedlam. People pulsed to the ground, ducking below speeding bullets. I pushed past them all, parting the frenzied crowd.

Through the bash of shoulders, I found Zackery. He knelt over a woman cradling a bloody hole in her abdomen. I pushed my way to his side.

Panic prickled his features. "The hell are *you* doing here?"

"Where's Heidi? Have you seen her?" The tide of people threatened to carry me away. I brutally fought my way back to him.

"You don't understand, he's here, he's—"

"I'm not leaving without her so tell me where she is!"

Zackery pushed a dirtied towel into the woman's bleeding belly. She groaned through the pain, life deserting her. "Four compartments down," he said. "I saw her hiding behind the flour bags."

Limbs ignited with newfound urgency. "Thank you," I said, and fought my way through.

The crowd of people lessened further up the train, leaving only the slow trickle of Rebels running for their lives. The tide of gunshots grew quieter, the bulk of Masonians moving to the other end of the train.

I bashed down doors, skipped over the fallen bodies doused in both brown and blue coats. Heart thumping, I reached the fourth carriage. Fires raged on either side, blistering the tree trunk piercing the ceiling. It had buckled the carriage when it fell, knocking over the supply boxes. Cans of food had spilled across the floor.

"Heidi!" I shouted. "Heidi, you in here?"

I heard a squeak. Nothing more than a small vocalisation. I held my breath, forcing myself to ignore Mason's exhilarated violin and focus on the sounds that enveloped me: the crackling fire, the distant echo of shouts and gunshots, the explosions somewhere outside...

Another squeak, a familiar tone of voice.

"Heidi!" I pulled back the sacks of grain and potatoes. I saw a leg first, covered in spilled flour. Next, a torso, an arm. Heidi's blonde hair, completely saturated in the white flour, peeked from the fallen sacks. "Gods, are you okay?"

She nodded, puffing white clouds.

Footsteps sounded, and more than one. We were too far from the door; the tree was blocking our way—

"Quick!" I pulled Heidi to the far side of the compartment. We nestled behind boxes of canned food, directly beneath the flickering flames. It was too hot, but we endured quietly. Positioned between a gap in the boxes, I had a good view of the cans littering the ground, between the spent bullet cases and pools of spilled flour.

From the front of the train—from the few compartments the Masonians had already vandalised—arrived a screaming woman gripped by two Masonians. Ebony hair flowed down her back like sheets of slick oil.

"Isla!" Heidi breathed.

She inched forwards and knocked into one of the boxes. A can of beans rolled from the top of the crates and clattered to the floor.

I slammed my hand over Heidi's mouth, holding her flush against me as the can rolled lethargically across the metal floor. It hit the side of a black boot. The Masonian stilled, listening.

Please don't let them find us...

Metal crunched. Sparks rained upon us as the tree lifted from the train. I grimaced at each hot prickle on my scalp, protecting Heidi as best as I could.

The tree dropped with loud thump and the door opened, showering us with specks of snow racing in from outside.

A new pair of feet banged against the metal. My heart stuttered. I recognised those pounding footsteps...

"Ah, we meet again, my dear..."

The rich, velvety sound of Mason's voice sank into my bones. Fear rose up, trembling my muscles. I closed my eyes, inhaling deep. *Control your music, girl...*

Heidi stilled, her skin cooling despite the fire's heat. I held her closer, my palm still fixed against her lips.

Mason's boots appeared through the gap in the boxes. I saw the sway of his blue coat, the occasional glint from his bloodied silver sword.

"Well, things do often have a way of going in circles," he said, approaching Isla with another Masonian at his side. "I remember a similar scenario with your mother. She was on a train too, if I recall."

Isla tried to edge away but was lurched back just as quickly. Mason inched closer. "Time is in short supply, so why don't we make this easy for each other, hey? Tell me where she is, and I might just let you live."

"Go to hell!"

A spitting sound and Mason recoiled, laughing to himself. "Oh, how disappointing," he said, lifting his arm.

A hard whack and Isla was flung far over, only to be hoisted back up.

"Now, let's try this again," Mason said, skulking ever closer. "Tell me where she is, Isla, or—just like your father—I'll make your final hours very uncomfortable indeed."

"Do what you want with me. I don't care—I'll *die* before I tell you anything!"

But her bravado was failing. Terror spewed from each forced word, each courageous syllable. Her voice, though loud and filled with emotion, was trembling.

Mason sensed her fear. He was a predator, after all.

"Oh, you are sorely mistaken," he said calmly. "You see, I won't allow you to die. I will ensure you remain conscious, perfectly receptive, as I mar that flawless skin of yours."

Mason removed a knife from behind his back, hidden beneath his coat. A large, shiny thing: completely free of blood and bone, yet the curved blade glimmered with murderous precision. Expressly designed to cause pain.

I watched, heart to my throat, as Mason lifted the knife to Isla.

"Now, the way I see it, this little conversation could go one of two ways. Either you tell me where Alira is being kept, or I start slicing. Shall we start with a finger? How about an eye? Come now, my dear, stay still for me..."

Isla's scream curdled the air. Heidi shook violently in my arms and I held her tighter through the wailing until—

"*Stop!*" Isla's piercing howl reverberated through the entire carriage. *"I'll tell you everything, just please stop!"*

Mason lowered the knife. Glossy drips of crimson fell to the floor, peppering the puddles of spilt flour.

"Where is she?"

"T-the prison carriage..." Isla gasped, her voice hoarse. She could barely hold herself upright. "S-sixth carriage down... We...we tied her up, n-next to Matheson."

Mason's violin rejoiced with a thousand jovial notes. *Relief* sang its hearty way around the tune. "Thank you, Isla," he said. He wiped the curved, bloody blade on his sleeve.

"Let me go..." Isla's voice was weak, exhausted... Plagued with failure.

"Later, my dear. You're a Rebel Commander, after all. You don't expect my Masonians to waste such an opportunity, do you?"

Sickness rose. It was a feeling Isla and I shared.

Mason marched to the end of the compartment, his polished black boots catching the firelight. "Keep her entertained," he said.

In his absence, the Masonian dogs grew excited. Wolf-whistles and lewd remarks now filled the space. Isla's cries grew louder as they forced her to the floor, her limbs spread and held down by two Masonians. The third stood over her, unfastening his weapons belt. It eagerly clattered to the floor.

Very carefully, I removed my hand from Heidi's mouth. She stared at me, her eyes large and glassy, her skin devoid of colour. I placed a single finger to my lips. She nodded, cowering with her knees tucked beneath her chin.

Isla's guttural wails grew louder as the Masonian kneeled between her spread legs.

I crawled to the side of the compartment. The sharp, metallic edge of a can glinted in the meagre light. Yes, that would do nicely.

A hessian sack winked at me, its floury contents all but emptied across the floor. I placed the can of beans inside, twisting the sack tightly closed, strangling it like a Masonian throat.

Fresh panic thickened the air. Isla's desperate screams loudened...

I rounded the crates and struck the sack down upon the Masonian's head. Blood spurted from the dent and he fell upon a writhing Isla. I heaved the sack and collided it with a Masonian's jaw. He collapsed against the stack of crates, helpless as they fell and crushed him with an almighty crash.

Strong arms encircled me, heaving me away, ripping my floury weapon from my fingers. My feet left the floor entirely. I kicked the wall, propelling us back into the fire.

Blue fibres ignited. Flames ensnared him, turning him into a burning ember and licked his flesh clean off. Fiery arms flailing, he raced from the compartment, sprinting through the snow until he collapsed in a convulsing heap. His movements lessened, then stilled, and he remained a burning beacon of orange light against the black.

The sound of squelching percolated, followed by crunching. I quickly turned to see Isla, blood pouring down her cheek, pummelling a Masonian skull with a food can. Bits of his head spurted in all directions, like some perverted fountain.

"Isla!" I yanked her away by her shoulders. "He's dead, Isla! He's dead..."

The bloodied can slipped from her fingers, rolling a few miserable feet away.

Tenderly, I took her face and turned it towards me. Mason's torture pooled blood into her eye, thankfully still intact, and drenched her cheek. I swallowed hard at the remains of her right eyebrow, hanging from the upper rim of her eye socket.

I quickly removed my green chequered scarf and held it against her brow. She winced and whimpered with the pain, recoiling.

"You need to stop the bleeding," I whispered. Gently, I manoeuvred her trembling hand to the scarf and made her press down firmly, spurring another cry.

"Fucking dogs..." Isla eventually managed. She stared at the Masonians, her good eye now growing red. "Sick bastards..."

"Isla, you need to get off this train. Campbell, Ashworth—where are they?"

"I-I don't know. The avalanche came so quickly, we didn't even have a chance to arm ourselves. I was thrown from the train with the impact, that's how they found me. I don't know where the others are, or if they're still alive."

No, no! They have to be alive!

I licked my lips, suddenly so dry. "Y-you need to find them, Isla. Or if not, get to safety."

"What about you?" A green eye, so glassy and transparent, locked onto mine. "We imprisoned you, Alira. I told him where you were..."

Yes, she had. No doubt Mason's relief would deform rather quickly when he discovered I was not where I should have been.

"I would have done the same," I admitted, in barely a breath. "Few people would have done differently, Isla."

She nodded, more to herself than to me, and gestured to the food cans littering the floor, now stained with bits of Masonian tissue. "Take as much as you need, but you need to go quickly."

She was right: Mason was far too close for comfort and time was not on our side. I grabbed a hessian sack and threw some cans inside. I heaved its immense weight upon my shoulder, quickly ushering Heidi out from behind the crates.

"Where will you be?" I asked, holding Heidi's hand. "In case we need to find you, I mean."

"We have contacts in every town from here to the Lightlands," she replied wearily, her voice still hoarse. "If you need us, you'll find us."

"Thank you, Isla," I said, and rushed from the compartment.

Snow crunched beneath my boots, hot flames whispering at my back. Heidi ran at my side, leaving nothing but snowy footprints and poofs of flour.

Gunshots ahead. From the line of trees, torches shone bright and ominous against the black.

Panicking, I looked back to the train. Masonians were still on there, *Mason was still there...*

Blue coats emerged from the forest, polished swords gleaming in the moonlight.

"No, come on—this way!" I shrieked and dragged Heidi back to the train. The compartments were emptying, people scurrying like rats from a burning furnace. Gunshots peppered the air as they ran, bodies falling, red streaking the snow.

Fire swarmed, the air hot, heavy and saturated with sweat and gunpowder. I cast my view outside, trying to find a gap through the carnage.

A flood of terrified, shrieking people slammed into us. Heidi and I were caught in the flow and my hand slipped from hers.

"Heidi!"

Buried beneath mounds of people, we stumbled from the train. I collapsed in the snow, protecting myself from the stampeding feet.

I searched for Heidi as the crowd dispersed.

"Heidi!" Panic tears threatened. I couldn't see her!

Ahead, a group of Rebels cowered in deep ditches. I scrambled through the snow, my hands numbing.

Something grabbed my hair. I shrieked, grasping at the fingers and the hand they belonged to. My stomach tumbled as I was lurched onto my back.

"Hello, sweetheart." General Alden's scarred face twisted into a mocking smile. "Mason's going to be happy to see you again."

Trees whispered to me, begging me to run to them, to free myself!

"Oh, shush now," he crooned. "Such whimpering does not become you."

Alden knocked the air from my lungs with a swift kick. Groaning, I spat the snow from my mouth and turned to snarl a vicious insult when—

A sickening squelch rippled the air.

Alden's face twisted, his eyes wide and...*dead*?

He fell to his knees, his black trench coat spilling like tar across the snow. Blood leaked from his ears and nose.

Sweat froze upon my back as the *Rebel*, whose crowbar lay buried in Alden's skull, snarled at me with flawless white teeth.

"You fucking bitch!"

He ripped the crowbar out with a squelching sound that sent cool nausea bubbling in my gut.

Words—screams, shock—ripped back down my throat. I'd expected to see a Masonian, or even Mason himself. But as I stared at this *Rebel*—at the great bushy beard that dominated his sharp features, or the matted chocolate-brown hair that tickled his shoulders—the bright lustre of those heartless, emerald eyes left little doubt of *who* Mason's mole was.

Ivan Ulster glared with sinister longing.

"I'm going to make you pay for what you did to her!" Blood dripped from the crowbar, held tight by white knuckles. I scrambled back, fighting his homicidal march.

"I should have let her gut you back in that basement. Oh, but no, she spared you—and for what? You were her *end!*"

I coughed up my fear, my vocal cords spluttering, "Ivan, w-wait!"

"She was my sister..." I saw the despair within his features, the *grief...* It swiftly malformed into something wicked, reeking of vengeance. "I'll make you scream before I give you back to him!"

The crowbar lifted high...

A gunshot ricocheted around the space. The crowbar slid from limp fingers. Ivan Ulster's lifeless body collapsed, blood pooling from his open cranium.

Behind him, crouched in the snow, Heidi trembled. She held a gun with white fingers, a thin line of smoke still rising from the barrel.

"Heidi..." Relief pooled in my gut as I scrambled over and gently removed the gun from her cold fingers. Her tremors matched my own, those honeyed eyes still gazing mindlessly ahead. "C'mon Heidi, look at me..."

With a gentle vice, I moved her face to meet mine. Those eyes flicked up, meeting my own. They seemed so young, so innocent.

"Come on," I said. "We need to go."

With a slow nod, she grabbed our sack of food.

Ivan's corpse still leaked red across the snow.

"Joe was right," I whispered. Only the Old Gods would have heard me, but I needed that truth to escape. *Joe was fucking right.*

Through the screams and the stench of death, I searched his fake Rebel coat and pulled out a few random papers, scrunching them in my pocket.

"What are they for?" Heidi asked with a croak.

"Insurance," I replied.

The forest beckoned us like a lost lover.

Carnage surrounded us: Masonian trucks charged through the snow, spilling blue coats and bullets. Men and women screamed, buried behind thick snowbanks or crouched behind charred vehicles.

More trucks rolled up but we just needed to break the barricade, to slip beneath the long shotgun barrels and disappear into the trees beyond.

A nearby truck exploded. A shockwave of light and heat slammed into us, knocking the air from my lungs. Flown back, I landed with a loud grunt.

Ears ringing, head pounding, nausea churning. Stars glittered across my vision, the sky spinning in tight, woozy circles...

"Alira!" Campbell's rough hands plucked me from the snow. "Look at me, are you alright?"

Swallowing vomit, I wiped away the warm wetness trickling down my throbbing brow. "I-I've been worse... Wh-where's Heidi?"

"Here!" she called, stumbling forwards.

Relief shook my knees. "Oh, thank the Gods."

"Girl, I'm so sorry..." Campbell said. "You were right... We've been played and for God knows how long."

Joe was right.

"Ivan Ulster," I said, slamming the stolen Rebel documents into Campbell's open palm. "He was Mason's fucking mole! I last saw him almost two years ago but he's been away *on business.*"

"*Shit!*" Campbell yelled with bared teeth. He scrunched the papers in his pocket and sent a longing look towards the train. Masonians still clung within, infecting its metal walls with their murderous stench. "Girl, I've got to help get this train running again."

"What? Campbell, no—there's no time!"

"Not for you." He presented his old, worn revolver. "Take this and head for the trees. The avalanche buried the forward compartments, including the ones with the getaway vans, so you'll have to make it on foot."

Realisation hit me with another shockwave from an exploding train carriage. Screams merged with the sound of cracking metal and wood. "No, Campbell—you need to come with us, please!'

"I need to stay; you don't!" A panicked look over his shoulder at the Masonian reinforcements. Our window of opportunity was rapidly closing shut... "Head to Eagle's Overlook and speak to Harald, the Innkeeper—he's an ally, he'll know where to find us."

He thrust his revolver in my hands and placed a desperate, final kiss upon my forehead.

"I'll see you soon, girl, I promise. Now, *go!*"

Heart hammering, I grabbed Heidi's wrist and *ran*. The trees grew closer, the snow deeper, and as the sounds of gunshots merged into the distance and the cold slithered up our legs, the forest embraced us like a mother welcoming her lost children.

Moonlight fought through the branches, aiding our passage with thick streams of silver. Heidi's breaths were loud and audible, fearful cries close to bursting.

I loosened a few Herdinese words of encouragement, for us both.

"Hey!" a familiar voice rang around the trunks. "Hey, over here!"

I quickened my steps just as Anya came into vision.

"Oh, thank the Gods…" I breathed through bruised lungs. I threw my arms around her, teary relief spilling down my cheeks. "Is Joe with you?"

Joe materialised some distance away, his gaunt face flushed. "Oi, this is no time to relax!"

A sharp wave of his arm had us following him through the trees. We rushed through dense undergrowth, away from the echoing gunshots.

"We'd almost given up hope," Anya said.

"It was eventful," I muttered. "We saved Isla and—"

Music.

It slammed its defeated, *enraged* form through the trees until it found me.

Anger, rage, fury—the emotions split my skull in two, throwing me to the ground. *Disappointment, misery, panic* soon followed, shrieking those violin notes inside my head with unbridled, unrelenting power!

Somewhere behind us, dogs barked.

"Shit…" Joe breathed. "We need to move, *now!*"

Strong hands grasped my arms. "C'mon, you have to run!"

But I couldn't run. All strength had left me, whipped away by the strings of a raging violin. Masonians were behind us, tracking us, for Mason knew I was no longer on that train…

Blood dribbled from my nose and dripped red pearls onto the snow. My skull audibly cracked and I screamed.

"Give her to me, now!" I was passed to Joe, who lifted me upon his back.

And then, we ran.

10

SPRING

Sunlight shone through coniferous needles. It fought through each tree, reaching the remnants of slush and snow. Birds chirped high above, their black shadows crossing a cloudless sky. Splotches of snow slumped to the ground, dripping from thawing trees.

We trudged through the undergrowth, stepping over fallen trees, traversing ditches, avoiding boulders.

Joe's strength quickly faltered, for I was still sprawled upon his back and he barely had the strength to stay upright. His legs trembled with the strain, small grunts escaping his throat.

Slowly, with great effort, I lifted my sore head. Dried blood tightened my lips and stained my tongue with iron. Even beneath the trees, the light was too bright, too dazzling.

Anya's foot caught beneath a branch. She fell with a small shriek, her limbs like lead.

"Oh-okay," Joe breathed. "We'll... We'll stop here for a while..."

He slowly sank to his knees. I rolled off him, falling to the wet ground. The world was sickeningly bright...

With one great, heaving retch, I vomited up the last of the musical pain. Nothing but bile, it dissolved the snow into a sickly mess. A yellow hole steamed in an otherwise untouched landscape.

Heidi's cold fingers pressed against my forehead.

"How is she?" Anya asked, trying to stand. Her face twisted with pain, her legs shaking.

I washed my mouth out with snow. "I'm fine."

"Don't bloody look it," Joe said. Each breath seemed to pain him, his entire body sprawled against a fallen log.

I cradled my throbbing head. "The music is fading. It's not as bad as it was."

As the agony rose and fell with each throbbing beat, maybe Mason was falling asleep? Perhaps he was otherwise engaged, torturing Rebels for information. Maybe he was training more dogs after the last pack had lost our scents.

I squeezed my eyes shut, determined to halt the growing trepidation.

Slowly, as we listened to the quiet of the forest, our breath returned, our strength recovered, the shakes in our limbs subsided. In this perpetual quiet, only our thoughts remained, more frantic than ever.

"What do we do now?" Heidi's voice, small and feeble, permeated the frosty air, as if the Masonian attack had filled her lungs with tar. Dreams of freedom had been warped, replaced with nothing but ominous foreboding. It seemed to age young Heidi, the experience carving deep lines into her forehead.

Indeed, as the weight of Heidi's question sank into the icy ground, we remained silent. The weight of indecision was just as great as the alternatives, yet no one had the courage to speak.

"Eagle's Overlook," I whispered, when the silence became unbearable. "Campbell said the Innkeeper will be able to help us."

Joe snarled. "You shittin' me? Eagle's Overlook is the largest town in the Snowlands. It'll be crawling with Masonians."

"Then what's the alternative?"

"Oh, I dunno..." Joe deflated into the ground, wiping a grubby hand across his eyes. "Did Campbell say anything else?"

"No... But they were trying to get the train back up and running. It must have been their only escape route."

"Of course it was," Anya added, her hair shining like a mound of pure fire. "The train had all their weapons and food, not to mention all their medical supplies."

"Speaking of which..." Joe said, stumbling upright. He hobbled a few paces and leant against a tree, scrutinising the area. "Anyone got any food or water?"

I glanced at Heidi.

"I dropped the sack," she whispered under her breath.

My heart sank. All that canned food—enough for two weeks—was now lost, buried beneath the snow.

"It's okay, honey," Anya said, but her cheeks noticeably paled.

"I have this," I added, holding up Campbell's rusted, black revolver.

"Oh great." Joe sardonically chuckled. "Have you heard the bang on that thing? We'll catch the attention of everything within a mile's radius."

He threw his hands in his hair and expelled a long stream of groans. Cogs were clearly turning inside his head.

"We need a town," I said. "Look at us, we're in no fit state to go Roaming."

No food, no water. No weapons and no supplies. We'd be dead within the week, and that was being generous.

Joe stared at his own ripped rags. He knew I was right. We needed supplies, and the bustling market towns were our only hope.

His attention turned upwards, eyes squinting in the sun. "Heidi, you know how to climb trees?"

As it happened, Heidi did know. She was up and down that tree within fifteen minutes, directions to a nearby town safely stored inside her head.

"Great, how far?" Joe asked.

"Maybe two days?" Her face scrunched as she took a pondering look at the state of us. "Maybe three."

Joe's heart audibly sank. "We'll never make it. We'll freeze to death well before that."

Heidi's eyes filled with tears, her lower lip wobbling.

Anya whacked Joe so hard he flinched. "Don't listen to him. We know how to build fires to keep warm, and we can melt snow to drink. I'm sure we can set some traps to catch something... I mean, c'mon—we've come this far!"

My lips quirked upwards. It was refreshing to hear such unadulterated hope.

"Anya's right," I said, because I needed something to cling onto. "We'll be fine."

Joe, evidently doubtful, had little choice but to agree. "Well, let's at least use the daylight while we can."

He limped over and pulled me to my feet. The world convulsed with sickening motion, blood rushing to my head. I swayed a little, but soon steadied.

"Can you walk?"

"Yeah, I think so…"

"Good."

Joe exhaled a sharp burst of air, kicking through the undergrowth until he found a long, narrow tree branch to use as a walking aid. "Well, come on, then."

Without objection, we followed.

* * *

MY HEADACHE LESSENED as the sun climbed higher. Soon, the musical agony was nothing more than an ache, easily blown away by the breeze. Fresh, cold air cleansed my lungs and icy crunches soothed my blistered feet. Before long, hope surfaced—perhaps a foolish notion, yet I eagerly accepted its warmth. It had been a long time since freedom felt so tangible.

Beneath the towering trees and a sky streaked with birds, I thought of my childhood. Of similar treks with Campbell, traversing between towns and longhouses full of laughter and mead.

Campbell's revolver weighed heavy in my hand; its rusted skin gleaming beneath each ray of light. I whispered a silent prayer for Campbell, for him to be alive and on that train, escaping through the mountains.

Yes, I'd see him again. I was sure of it.

We'd escaped, and had Campbell's blessing to do so. A small mercy, given what happened, but it still helped stitch the fabric of our trust back together. I smiled warmly at the thought.

Trudging through the snowy undergrowth, I thought back to the Masonian attack. I thought of Isla, blood pouring down her cheek, and remembered her parting words. Perhaps this town, whichever one it was, would have some Rebel contacts. Maybe I could pass on a message, to let Campbell know that we were alive and well.

I voiced my idea to the group. It was either met with silence, or Joe's doubtful laughter.

"Don't trust the fucking Rebels. Their idiocy is the reason we're out here, remember?"

My brow scrunched. "That's unfair, Joe. They didn't ask to be attacked."

"You told them about the Masonian mole and they did nothing. I'd say they were asking for it."

Ivan Ulster's face flashed across my retina. There had been such raw hatred behind those blazing green eyes, such...*grief.* It had never occurred to me that Verity Ulster would be missed, that she would be mourned, avenged by those who loved her...

I shook away the thoughts, disgusted by them.

Beside me, Heidi's hair glimmered gold in the passing rays of light. I recalled the look on her face as Ivan fell dead, his brain spilling out for the dawn birds to feast upon.

I whispered a Herdinese words of thanks. Heidi smiled in return, though it was a perhaps a little too forced. Ivan Ulster was her first kill, evidently. I remembered the shape of Verity's soul, the way it cracked beneath the power of my stare. Mason was right: the first times were always the worst.

I put my arm around Heidi's shoulders, holding her close. She leant into my touch, her tight shoulders drooping.

The sun grew heavy in the sky, drenching our path in dirty yellow. Night would be falling soon, along with the temperature. Pearly mist eagerly escaped my lips, my fingers and toes already numb. We reached the edge of the forest just as the red sun bled across the horizon.

"Well, look at that," Joe muttered, leaning against his staff.

A frozen lake loomed ahead. Surrounded by forest, its smooth skin spread to the base of enormous cliffs. In the middle of the frozen lake, perched atop a rocky island, a lonely shack beckoned.

"Do you think anyone lives there?" Anya asked. The wind rippled her hair until it resembled red flames in the dying sunlight.

"Doesn't look like it," Joe said, narrowing his eyes at the small chimney. No column of smoke emerged. "Place looks abandoned."

"Well," I said, taking a step forward. "Let's find out."

Covered in a delicate layer of snow, thick ice glowed red beneath the setting sun. Ominous creaks echoed beneath us as we edged forwards, one delicate step at a time. The sun had long died by the time we arrived at the shack, replaced by an aurora that shined blue and green against the grassy roof. The wooden walls, softening with damp, supported a structure that was thankfully still stable, but the door peeled straight from the hinges as Joe forced it open.

"Ah shit," he mumbled, kicking it to the ground.

As expected, the shack was empty. It had been for some time.

"Evidently left it in a hurry," Anya mumbled, fingering the charred remnants inside the cooking pot. I stared at that metal thing and saw the worn engravings on the side: *Jones and Sons, Ltd. Birmingham. Est. 1878.*

I frowned at such odd script—*remnants of the Old World, perhaps?* —and threw my gaze elsewhere.

Sacks and straw boxes littered the wooden floor, all empty. They had left little behind, which had since rotted completely.

Yet, some blankets remained. Albeit damp and sporting unsightly patches of mould, they'd do for a night or two.

A few bits of wooden furniture had also survived, including a stool and a cot. Plagued with rot, they were easily broken into small pieces and set below the chimney. The damp wood was stubborn to set alight, but as smoke eventually formed and glowing embers settled between the wooden fibres, the first hints of warmth dragged a sigh from my lips.

"This should keep us going for a while," Joe said. He secured one of the blankets above the open doorway, protecting us from some of the outside chill.

In the safe confines of that abandoned cabin, the exhaustion returned. Sharp and heavy, incredibly stubborn.

"Where do you think we are?" Anya asked, also fighting sleep.

"Snowlands," I replied. The frozen lake left little doubt.

"Eagle's Overlook is in the Snowlands," she whispered.

Joe immediately bristled. "We're not going to Eagle's Overlook! I'm not risking a meaningless chat with Campbell, only to end up on a Masonian whipping block." He sighed heavily, his muscles stiff and rigid. "Jeez, they'll kill me next time."

"Lucky you," I muttered.

Annoyance flicked across Anya's delicate features. "Then what would you do, Joe?"

Her question stunned him. Those seafoam eyes disappeared into the flames, the bruises on his face growing darker by the minute. "I don't know…" he whispered.

I shook my head, hoping to dislodge the unease that trickled into my lungs. "We can discuss this another time. For now, our plan is to go to the town, gather supplies, and *then* we can figure out what to do. No use stressing about it now."

"Since when did you become so mature?" Joe's cheeky smile reappeared, reminding me of a longhouse, a tankard of mead, and the humble suggestion to go to Waterman's Quarry.

"Slavery has a tendency to do that, Joe," I replied, glaring.

The smile dropped to the floor, as did his gaze. "Don't throw that back at me. Please, not now. Not after everything we've been through."

Guilt bloomed again. "You're right. I'm sorry."

Everything suddenly seemed so complicated. I just needed to sleep…

I gathered a blanket and settled down in the far corner of the room, the warm firelight caressing my back. I traced each blemish on the wall and listened to the occasional pop of wood, or the crackle of fiery heat. The violin was quiet too, finally.

I closed my aching eyes and listened to the calm.

* * *

I STOOD in the foyer of the Theatre. Plush, red carpet cushioned my boots, the polished marble walls gleaming. A chandelier dripped with diamonds, refracting prismatic light in all directions.

How did I get here?

Music resounded ahead. Such beautiful music…

A man stood before two ornate doors, waiting for me. Aged skin hung from his bones, yet youthful eyes gleamed with as much golden lustre as his teeth.

"They're waiting for you," Sebastian Svellec said.

"Who?" I asked.

"The Family. They've saved a seat for you."

"Oh..." I chanced a look over my shoulder, at the thick layer of snow that now smothered that plush carpet. *How did* that *get there?*

I turned back to Sebastian. "Are you joining me?"

"Oh no." He grinned widely, *menacingly.* "I'm waiting for my sister."

Sebastian Svellec opened the door wide. "But *they've* been waiting a long time for *you.* Best not keep them any longer."

Agreeing—though not quite understanding why—I stepped through the door.

A stage loomed ahead. Instruments stood proudly, waiting before empty chairs.

I took my seat in the audience, the red velvet cushions so plump and round. I was the only one present: a single viewer in an auditorium built for hundreds.

People walked upon the stage. Beautiful, enrapturing people... Elegant dresses, vibrant and stunning, matched the sparkling jewels that dripped from ears, necks, wrists... Black tuxedos were pressed to perfection, each bowtie so pleasingly symmetrical...

They stood behind their instrument, handling it with love, respect, *adoration.*

Twenty-six pairs of diamond eyes sparkled vehemently in the chandelier's light.

Another man walked in. A white suit, this time. It matched his hair, the colour of alabaster. His face was indistinguishable, but I knew his diamond eyes shone most powerfully of all.

The others *bowed* to him.

He took residence at the podium, his back to me. Power brimmed from beneath his neatly stitched suit, pulsating through the air like waves of shimmering heat.

The orchestra sat, cradling their instruments, holding them high and ready in their hands.

The man lifted his arms, a conductor's baton held delicately between his fingertips...

Music erupted. A wave of tunes and notes swarmed upwards, vibrating in the air. Each instrument fit with complete harmony—the most sublime musical jigsaw that rippled my very soul. Each chord stroked my skin and pulled the hairs on the back of my neck, willing me closer, wanting me to fall into the captivating tune.

The song I knew all too well exploded from an orchestra of diamond eyes and sublime dresses.

The Conductor's arms pulsed and swayed, guiding them as *his* music sang. He traced shapes in the air, thrusting his arms, moving his entire torso with the beat, the tempo. I wanted to step closer to that powerful music, to fall headfirst into it.

The orchestra birthed the frightening melody with the might of *generations* worth of power and passion, torment and rage. Arms swayed, lungs expanded, fingers twitched...

Near the front of the orchestra, Mason played his violin with fervour, pure and unadulterated. His eyes sparkled with alluring intensity; his soft lips parted to release focussed breaths as his bow swept against the strings...

"Beautiful, isn't it?" said Sebastian, suddenly sitting beside me. *How did he get here?*

I turned back to the orchestra. "Yes," I whispered.

"They're one instrument short."

I stared at Sebastian, my brow furrowed.

"Look harder." He grinned again, gold teeth gleaming.

My eyes instinctively found Mason, and then scanned the rest. The beautiful women, their faces hiding so much conflict... The handsome men, reeking of power, of domination and contempt...

A piano.

It lay near the back of the orchestra, its cushioned seat beckoning. It called to me, *begged* me to play it, for me to stroke my fingers across its smooth, ivory keys...

The Conductor raised his hands and with a jolting movement, the music stopped. Only its echo was left, quivering in the air—and in my lungs, my heart, *my soul.*

Twenty-six pairs of diamond eyes bored into me. Judging, *waiting...*

Mason's stare was the brightest of all.

The Conductor's head twitched, ever so slightly.

"Come," he said. His voice was so succulent, so powerful...

Just like the music.

"Join your Family," *it* said.

Panic festered. My limbs trembled.

This isn't right, something isn't right!

"No..." I whispered. I didn't want to. *I don't want to!*

I jumped from the cushioned seat and raced up the aisle. Instruments screeched in agony as a violin sobbed inside my head.

I burst through the doors, expecting to see the foyer with the red carpet and snow, but I was on the Rebel train. It swayed gently upon the tracks— back and forth, back and forth.

The train was empty, devoid of everything. No ammunition racks hugged the walls, neither did food cans roll from one side to the other. Moonlight flooded the compartments with silver, the large doors open and boasting the mountains around us. Snow covered them, glowing beneath an aurora's light. It danced above a sheet of stars, carrying the whisper of a song upon the breeze.

I walked aimlessly ahead.

A closed door stood before me. Without restraint, I opened it.

Aqua eyes glared above a face stitched together with thick black lines.

"Hello, Maya!"

Jayson Montgomery hit me. I fell onto the carriage floor as panic seized my lungs.

"Don't worry, Maya," he said, leaning over me with that manic white smile. "Who knows, you might even enjoy it."

I tried to scream but no sound came. I was suffocating, restrained by an impossibility.

Jayson Montgomery was dead. *You're dead!*

His cold hand pressed against my mouth. I tried to scream, to *breathe*, but it was no use—he was too strong!

I can't breathe!

Jayson's face morphed before me. The skin aged, forming jowls that hung from a jaw that grew thinner, longer. Platinum-blonde hair sucked back inside his skull, whitening into steely grey. Aqua eyes changed to the same golden lustre that now coated his teeth.

And there, as the metal walls of my dream disintegrated into the warm nightmare of that shack, I felt the very real hand upon my mouth. It matched the cold blade of the knife against my throat, and the hating, infuriated glare of Sebastian Svellec crouched over me.

Life shocked into muscles. I struggled, trying to scream through his hand.

Sebastian pressed the knife against my throat.

"Quiet or I'll kill them," he whispered. The same raspy voice, the stench of cigars and whiskey...

From the corner of my eye, I saw Heidi sleeping soundly. Beside her was Anya, her breaths slow and steady. Joe snored somewhere behind them.

Tears prickled my eyes, my stare growing pleading.

"Now," he said, leaning close until his foul breath fluttered across my eyelashes. "You're going to come quietly with me back to Mason, and then you'll give him a son. Or I'll slit the throats of everyone you care about, starting with the little one. Do you understand?"

A few careful nods, my vision blurred with tears.

Sebastian grinned, his teeth catching the dying firelight. They gleamed with menacing lustre.

Slowly, he removed his hand from my mouth to reach for his gold walking stick. His knife was still pressed to my throat as we carefully stood upright. We took steady steps towards the doorway, the blanket still swaying in the breeze.

One of the floorboards creaked.

Heidi's eyes opened. We locked stares, only for a second.

Heidi screamed.

Sebastian kicked the pile of burning logs. Sparks exploded, raining down upon the shack as flames licked the air. Heidi scrambled into Anya, who startled awake with a shriek.

Spidery hands buried in my hair and dragged me towards the door. With an angered yell, he threw me from the shack. I landed with a painful thud as rocks punched my spine.

The roof of the shack choked with smoke, orange heat blaring through the decaying walls. It blazed behind Sebastian, silhouetting him with orange light as he marched closer.

"Do you know what you've done to him?" Sebastian screamed. *"The position you've put him in?"*

I scrambled back and reached the lake. My heeled boots skidded across the ice—I couldn't find a foothold!

I finally clambered upright with lungs threatening to burst.

Sebastian's stick whipped across my shins. I shrieked, pain radiating up my body, unable to support my weight. A spidery hand found my hair and dragged me behind him, moving at startling speed across the ice.

"Just wait until he gets his hands on you, you troublesome *bitch!*"

From the belly of the burning shack, Joe erupted with Heidi under one arm, Anya in the other.

I screamed until my throat bled.

Anya ran to me, a burning log in her hand. She held it high like a weapon, her teeth bared and ready to strike.

Sebastian rounded on her and slammed his walking stick between her feet. An ominous echo skimmed across the lake. Ice cracked. Anya descended up to her chest in the freezing water. She gasped, her fingernails scraping against the ice as she desperately tried to claw her way out.

"Anya!" I fought harder against Sebastian, my boots flailing helplessly across the ice.

Joe raced towards us and grabbed my foot. With a maddening howl, Sebastian whacked his stick across Joe's jaw. Blood spurted and Joe fell to the ice in a groaning heap.

With Sebastian's attention elsewhere, I got a tight hold of his finger and yanked it back. The satisfying pop of bone as Sebastian's grip faltered.

I freed myself, jumping to my feet, crouching low like a wolf waiting to pounce.

I sang my Name around my skull: *Wolf-Charmer, Wolf-Charmer...*

Sebastian stared at his crooked finger. Tucking his cane beneath his arm, he gripped his finger without so much as a cringe. A sudden jolt, a sickening crunch, and gold teeth shone through his smile. He continued to circle me, the tip of his black coat mere inches from the ice, the gentle pat of his cane resonating with each controlled step.

"How long do you think you can run from him, hm? How long can you defy your destiny?"

"*Fuck* my destiny." I matched each of Sebastian's steps, keeping the distance between us.

From the corner of my eye, I saw Heidi at Anya's side, trying to pull her from the freezing water.

"Arabella thought the same. She evaded William for *years*, formed countless Rebellions, killed thousands of his men. And do you know what happened to her, my dear?"

Heidi finally freed Anya from the ice, shivering wildly, yet very much alive.

"She was betrayed by one of her oldest friends." Sebastian smiled, savagely. "The simple promise of diamonds, that's all it was. A bag of jewels in exchange for Arabella's whereabouts. Mason was born less than a year later, just as destiny prescribed."

From behind Sebastian's back, Joe stumbled to his feet. Blood dribbled from his mouth; his steps uneven.

"So, tell me, Alira," Sebastian scowled. "What makes you believe your fate will be any different?"

The aurora shone brightly above, flowing into my smile. "You tell me, you old prick."

Joe leapt onto his back, ripping the golden stick from his grasp.

Sebastian grasped the knife from within his belt, flailing it madly behind him. Joe grabbed his wrist, holding back the blade with audible effort.

Anger clenching my jaw, I leapt towards Sebastian and buried both thumbs in his golden eyes. Liquid, metallic gold oozed from his eye sockets and pooled around my thumbs. I pressed deeper.

His scream was monstrous, inhuman. The knife slashed into my forearm. I shrieked, ripping myself away from him, cradling the gaping cut as his knife clattered against the ice.

With a great howl, Sebastian heaved Joe from his shoulders. He slammed him down with a loud grunt.

Sebastian was soon upon him, clawing his blind body up Joe's torso until spidery hands wrapped around his neck. "Mason should have killed you when he had the chance, you wretched *boy*, you fucking *whore-son*, you—"

The knife danced into my fingertips. I leapt upon Sebastian's back and sliced the blade deep across his throat. A fountain of liquid gold rained down upon Joe, gagging and squealing as he pushed off Sebastian's shaking body.

But Sebastian's shakes did not lessen. They grew bolder and more forceful until his entire body spasmed, jolting viciously across the ice. Spurting gold blood covered a face that seemed to mould and change shape. Those spidery fingers grew shorter as they clenched silver hair that lengthened in a matter of seconds. His voice, shrieking and gargling, changed pitch entirely.

And then, as Sebastian grew still, Joe and I watched in horror as he rolled upon his belly and pushed himself upright.

Shrieking and panicking, I lunged forwards with the knife held high—

"No, *wait!*"

I skidded to a halt, frowning at the two dainty hands held up to me, then at the woman whom they belonged to. My scarred lips parted as I gasped and gawked at the shoulder-length hair, the sharp nose, the large golden eyes set in a face heavily lined with wisdom. Through the thick layer of bloody gold, rosy lips surrounded a mouth full of golden teeth.

Against all the odds, I lowered the knife.

"Alira, I presume," she said with a breathless smile. "Good to finally meet you, girl. My name is Svenja Svellec."

11

———

Flames engulfed the shack, roaring higher and brighter with every second. The grass roof collapsed, throwing billions of sparks upwards to join the stars. Delicious heat spewed in all directions: a bonfire we were eager to sit around.

We thrust the few surviving blankets around our shoulders, staying the worst of the bitter night's chill. Anya, shivering profusely, utilised most of these blankets with her lips tinged blue. Yet, her mind was as shrewd as ever. She remained staring at the woman with the golden teeth, unable to accept she had been Sebastian Svellec less than an hour ago.

"So, let me get his straight," Joe croaked, eyebrows raised high. The cold, damp cloth he held against his swollen jaw made speaking difficult, as did the black finger-marks on his neck, yet he was determined. "You and Sebastian are completely different people? Different personalities, different memories, the works?"

"Yes, that's right," Svenja said. She wiped a wet blanket down her neck, removing the last of Sebastian's golden blood. Or was it *her* blood? I was still unsure.

"As soon as one of you is killed, you just turn into the other?"

"Well, it's not as simple as that..." She bobbed two silver eyebrows, contemplating. "But yes, I suppose that's the easiest way to look at it."

"Can he hear us?" I asked. My limbs were still full of adrenaline, rigid from fear. I expected Sebastian to come clawing back at me any minute, wanting *my* eyes as recompense for his own. "I mean, is he in there, observing us through you?"

"Not at all," she replied with a tender smile. "Yes, he is in me, somewhere... But he is unaware of anything I do or say. He's unconscious for as long as I am alive, and this time I intend for it to stay that way."

Another wall collapsed into the flames. Sparks raced to the stars and disappeared into the aurora's dancing light.

"So, whose side are you on, then?" I asked, scrutinising this strange woman. Echoes of Sebastian still lingered in her features, and I did not trust them to stay quiet. "Sebastian would have thrown himself on swords for Mason, so why should you be any different?"

Svenja smiled. A strange smile, somewhere between amusement and sympathy.

"I understand your trepidation, but you have nothing to fear from me. While Sebastian's purpose is to help Mason, mine is to hinder him, by any means possible."

"Why?" I asked with a wary frown. "Why are you and Sebastian so different?"

"Why are you and Mason?" she retorted with a smirk.

My brows lowered as I considered such a thing—at just how *different* we really were. Echoes of Verity's soul came back to haunt me, as my inhuman stare forced it to crack. How many of Mason's victims had met a similar end?

Svenja threw the blanket down beside her. "At any rate, you can ask Heidi for reassurances of my agenda. I've helped the Free People, and her Tribe, numerous times. Isn't that right, sweetie?"

Heidi lifted her head. Between the greasy locks of blonde, those honeyed eyes twinkled.

"My Tribe is *dead!*" She jumped to her feet and stormed away, arms tightly folded.

Heart bloating, I glanced at Anya. "Should I go after her?"

With a heavy breath, Anya gently shook her head.

"That was my fault," Svenja said. "I sometimes forget she's still only a child. Her experiences could test even the strongest of us."

Heidi stood at the periphery of the rocky island, kicking the edge of the lake's smooth, frozen skin. Lost within her own thoughts.

"We need to find Ashworth," Svenja said, some moments later. "Do you know where he is?"

Joe groaned beneath his breath.

"No," I said. "But Campbell suggested we go to Eagle's Overlook. Apparently, the Innkeeper—"

"Harald, yes. Good idea, he'll know where they are."

Joe scoffed to me, "Why go through all that effort trying to escape the train if you're just going to run back to them?"

"Because I'm here now," Svenja said, before I could answer. "And I—and by extension, *we*—need to find Ashworth."

"Why?" Anya asked.

"I have important information that will greatly benefit the Free People—and all of you. It's imperative Ashworth has it."

Seafoam eyes narrowed. "What is this information?"

"I'll tell you when we find Ashworth."

Pfft, power-hungry wench, indeed. But...Svenja *knew* things no other person should—that had always been a certainty. That's why Mason wanted her dead, I was sure of it. Given that, I'd absolutely no doubt that Svenja's information *could* change the course of Ashworth's Rebellion—but for better, or for worse? I didn't know, and a little chime in the back of my head told me to *run*—to forget about her and Campbell, and race through the trees.

I didn't trust those thoughts, not with those musical claws buried in my soul, ones that so readily danced with the strings of my fate. But that musical trepidation made me consider the cards Svenja held—both the ones in her hand, and those hidden up her sleeve. I needed to be there when she put those cards on the table.

"We'll help you find the Rebels," I said, and quickly ignored the pummelling stares. "But only if you tell us that information, too."

"When we find Ashworth." Svenja's grin gleamed. "Deal."

* * *

THE SHACK HAD REDUCED to nothing but glowing embers. A pillar of black smoke rose high into the sky, tinged lilac from the dawn light and streaked with clouds the colour of ripe peaches. Indeed, the sun would be arriving soon.

In the rising light, the smoke quickly became a loud and threatening signal, calling to all Masonians within a fifteen-mile radius. *We're here, come and get us*, the smoke continually sang.

That same smoke was heavy on our backs as we traversed the frozen lake. It was a frosty morning, despite the spring sun. I blew a pillar of mist into the air.

Leading our little troop, Svenja Svellec marched ahead on a clear mission with that golden cane aiding her unequal steps. Her limp was on the opposite side to Sebastian's, I noticed. Still, the long black coat and silver hair filled my heart with unsettling dread. Visions of Sebastian, his eyes gushing liquid gold, hung heavy in the dense, chilly air.

I concentrated on Mason's violin. Angry, as always, but no different than usual. Clearly unaware of Sebastian's fate.

A shaky sigh escaped my lips, my boots striking hard against the lake's smooth, frozen skin.

For the most part, our plan remained the same: head to the nearby town, gather supplies, then make the long and perilous journey to Eagle's Overlook. Joe emphatically refused, and yet he didn't have much choice but to join us. His only alternative, it seemed, was to traverse the New World alone. Even he decided that was a bad idea.

So, we continued on.

I inhaled that fresh, still air. So different to that Rebel train stinking of damp and mould. Did Campbell succeed in restarting that train? Had he and his fellow commanders escaped through those freight tracks?

Anya came to my side, the blankets still tightly wrapped around her shoulders. Her cheeks had regained an inkling of colour, yet her eyes remained numb and utterly exhausted.

"I think you should talk to her," she whispered, as though the very air was eavesdropping.

"Who?"

"Svenja Svellec."

I shook the thought away. I didn't want to speak to her. I didn't want to see Sebastian's teeth as she smiled. "No, I don't think so."

"She has information," Anya said delicately. "She's not going to tell us everything until she finds Ashworth... But you might get *other* information out of her, like about Mason's Line, or his Family."

There it was again: the heritage—the destiny—that kept following me, yapping at my heels like some insistent puppy.

As my hair blew across my shoulders, I found myself surrendering to the thought. Knowledge beckoned, limping ahead with that golden walking aid.

Ultimately, and with a heavy sigh, I agreed.

Svenja Svellec was surprisingly fast, given her delicate frame. Her body, old and withered, contained so much raw, resounding power that, appearances aside, she certainly could not be described as *old*. I had no doubt she could kill us all without breaking a sweat.

"Hi," I said nervously.

Svenja smiled as I joined her side. "Come for a chat?"

"I suppose."

"I'm not surprised. This must be a difficult time for you: running from your destiny and all that."

An uncomfortable silence followed. Upon the lake's smooth skin, I felt exposed, like a gaping wound. I looked longingly towards the line of trees ahead, wanting to disappear into their comforting embrace.

"I'm glad we have a chance to talk," Svenja said. "I've been waiting many years to meet you."

I met her sincerity with wide, startled eyes. "You have?"

"Of course." She sent me a knowing sidelong glance, the corner of her lip quirking up. "Mason wasn't the only one looking for you, girl."

"Campbell was good at hiding me."

"Evidently." She chuckled quietly to herself. "I even persuaded a woman to fill your shoes and keep Mason occupied, in the hopes I'd reach you first."

The Pretender's long blonde hair floated across my vision, framing those colourful, opalescent eyes.

"You told her things about me, didn't you?"

"I told her just enough for Mason to believe she was Alira." Another sly look, that smirk persisting. "I needed to keep him off your trail for a while, to give me the chance to find you first. Yet despite all that planning, all that effort, he still beat me to it."

I looked over my shoulder, at Joe's seafoam eyes surrounded with purple bruises. After everything, could he say he'd redeemed himself?

"Why did you want to find me?" I asked. Other questions roared inside my head, each fighting to reach the surface: what I was, what *she* was. I forcibly pushed them back, determined to keep them subdued and obedient. Svenja Svellec, as powerful as she was, was as skittish as a hare. Like the good little hunter, I had to bide my time. I did not want to spook her.

"Why? To protect you, of course! I'm here to help you, girl."

"I thought you were here to destroy Mason."

That earned me a hearty laugh from lungs riddled with mucus. "It's one and the same."

Another uncomfortable silence. Questions rose again, begging me to throw them at Svenja's lined face.

"Can Mason be killed?" I asked, carefully.

"Yes, if the circumstances are right." A quick look up and down my frame, at the leather coat smattered with mud and liquid gold. My own blood still caked upon my skin: an ugly reminder of musical pain. "You're evidently Connected to him, so that's a start."

"And my soul is broken," I whispered. The pain arose, bloating my heavy heart as my hands balled. Svenja observed my mannerisms, her face hard and unyielding.

"Then yes," she said, her pointed nose held high. "So long as circumstances do not change, he can be killed."

The pain inside my chest changed, diverging from mournful grief into something else entirely. A sudden inhale and I pushed it away, unwilling to be anywhere near it.

"So, what was it then?" Svenja asked. "Was it by accident, or design?"

"What?"

"Your soul. Did you break it yourself?"

Hatred swarmed. Nails punctured my palms as I squeezed my fists into ever-tightening balls.

"No," I said, my tone bitter and resentful. "It was the Free People, both times."

I recalled Ashworth's face and bit back the anger. No, this was not the time to fuel the anguished hatred. The past—theirs, mine—it didn't make any difference. For better or worse, we were working together now. I had to throw past grievances aside.

Or bury them in a little box, hiding at the back of my subconscious, secured with rusted chains.

"Ah, I see..." Svenja tone changed, turning pitying. "I didn't realise it happened twice."

"Yeah, well." Angry words grew bitter on my tongue. I swallowed them with a shiver. "Now you know."

The line of trees was almost upon us, no more than an arm's throw away.

"It must have been difficult for you," Svenja said gently. "I'm sorry I didn't find you sooner, that I didn't get the chance to explain."

My steps halted, my eyes squinting in the early morning light. "What is there to explain? Knowing the reason *why* wouldn't have made it any better."

"Perhaps." Svenja sighed, expelling a long steam of cloudy air. Dark shadows formed in the crow's feet at both corners of her eyes. "Arabella was rather reluctant too, in the beginning."

"What changed her mind? Why did she suddenly turn her back on her destiny and try so hard to kill Mason?" There was an air of disgust that I desperately tried to hide. No doubt Svenja was questioning my loyalty, as I hers.

"She spent too much time with me," she replied, almost proudly. "I had a way with words with her, and she knew what was at stake."

"Didn't work though, did it? Mason was born regardless."

"Yes, he was." Svenja took a strained look at her surroundings, silently absorbing the snow, the lightening sky, the jagged teeth on the horizon... "Mason did a good job with this World. William would be proud."

Seemingly lost in her own thoughts—her own *failure?*—she hobbled to the trees.

"What was he like?" I asked, jumping to her side. "William, I mean."

"Oh, very similar to Mason. Ruthless, sadistic, incredibly cruel..." Svenja's pace slowed, a lined, blotchy hand massaging her cane's polished bone handle. "But he was honest, all things considered. If he was going to kill you, he'd scream it to the sky. None of these broken promises or false senses of security that Mason so readily enjoys. No, that has Arabella stamped all over it. Mason learnt from her well, it seems."

"I thought he hated her."

"Oh, he does. But you can't help the traits you've inherited. He's still half *her,* after all."

"Hm."

I thought to my babies, wondering—for what seemed to be the thousandth time—what they would have been like. Would they have been cruel, like Mason? Would they lie and taunt, just like him? What aspects of *my* personality would have shined through?

Perhaps they would have been gentle. Maybe they would have been artistic, like me, and drawn their own sketches or created grand masterpieces from the mountainous views.

What instruments would they have played?

"What instruments were they? William and Arabella, I mean."

"William plays the oboe, and Arabella the cello."

Clearly Mason's obsession with string instruments was also inherited from his mother. I thought back to my dream—to the Family Orchestra—and wondered if my subconscious had placed Arabella in her rightful position.

"I had a dream last night," I said, staring vacantly ahead. "I was in a Theatre, watching an orchestra play the music in my head."

"Ah yes. The *Family.*" She practically spat the word out.

"There was a man—the Conductor." I tried to keep my tone neutral, only occasionally stealing a look from her.

"That would be Grayson."

Grayson. I recognised that name.

Memories flashed: Anya and I, exploring the names on Sebastian's withered document. "He's the Head of the Family?"

"You could say that." Her tone was decidedly clipped.

But I was determined... "Who is he?"

Silence remained. *Did she hear me?*

"I wouldn't delve too deep into Mason's Family, if I were you," she said.

"Why not?" I avoided her gaze and stared to the snowy bank. The ice was brittle here: pebbles from the lakebed easily punched through.

"Mason will be dead soon," Svenja said. "So, quite simply, what's the point?"

12

———————

By the time we reached civilisation, two days later, the sun had long since disappeared.

People lined streets covered with dirty slush. The sky was a mess of stars, dulled by the light spewing from the braziers littered about. With those damp blankets pulled low across our brows, we scurried through the town, all the while searching for Masonians.

All except Svenja, that is, who marched ahead with that walking stick clanking against the cobblestones.

"Oh, well that's a great way to look inconspicuous, innit?" Joe hissed in my ear.

Nestled close to the Glasslands' borders, Gowan's Crossing contained a handful of wooden houses and a central square, still choked with stalls despite the blackness of the sky. Thick billows of smoke obliterated the mountainous wilderness, until only the thunderous creaks of hidden glaciers remained.

Directly ahead, a large building's structured roof and carved border made it easily recognisable as the town's longhouse. People decorated the entryway, laughing to each other with glazed, drunken eyes. I squeezed Heidi's hand as we passed them, for they ogled her innocent structure like hungry owls would a baby rabbit.

Inside, sticky heat tingled my chapped cheeks. Dried herbs hung from the rafters: strings of garlic, thyme, and branches full of dark green dill. The heady aromas infiltrated the stuffy space, merging with the stench of sweat and smoke surrounding a chandelier of elk antlers.

Tables littered a floor covered with sheepskin rugs. Servers in their stained aprons perused the scene, gladly delivering large tankards of mead and platters stuffed with roasted lamb, root vegetables and roasted potatoes. One of these platters passed by us, the scents tingling my nasal hairs. I inhaled their aromas, hiding the insistent grumbling in my stomach.

We invaded an empty table, hidden in the far corner of the longhouse. Wooden stools creaked ominously as we rested our tired legs, the table wobbling beneath our elbows.

"Oh." I startled at the tankards of mead being delivered, then whispered to Joe, "We have money?"

Svenja smirked, a plump cigar hanging from her lips, and boasted the collection of gold coins in her palm.

"A little present from Sebastian," she said. "Found it in his pocket."

I could've kissed Svenja as a platter of lamb was placed before us. Rich, meaty juices coated my tongue, and I practically groaned at the taste. Gods, when was the last time I had a proper meal?

Anya probably served it to you, my snide little voice chimed.

As the hours wore on, and as the remains of the lamb lay scattered and gnawed upon the platter, I sipped my tankard of mead in the emptying longhouse. No use travelling until morning. Until then, we needed to lay low, stay hidden, and be quiet. It was only a blessing that Gowan's Crossing was free of Masonians. Perhaps our luck was growing?

Svenja Svellec counted the rest of her stolen coins upon the table. As the last one tipped from her fingers, she dropped her shoulders with a large sigh.

"Not enough?" Anya asked.

"For a room at the inn, yes. For blankets and ammunition, no. We have enough for a couple cans of food and some warm clothes. Anything else is wishful thinking."

I groaned into my hands. We could never reach Eagle's Overlook with that.

"Wh-what about this?" Anya said. With a pained expression, she reached into her pocket and plucked out something long and silver, sparkling dimly in the light.

My heart stopped. "Where did you get that?" I whispered, gazing at the bracelet's teardrop links.

"I found it, back on the train. I spotted it just before we escaped." She appeared sheepish, her bright blue eyes darting between me and the table. "I-I'm sorry, I just thought—"

"It's okay, Anya." A hard swallow as I avoided her pitying gaze. "We should be able to sell that for some quality goods."

"Absolutely!" Svenja was practically euphoric. "I'll get to work, scout some potential Merchants."

I swallowed the rising ball of hate and watched, helpless, as Svenja gathered the bracelet, marring whatever lustre it had left with lamb grease. Gusts of chilly air and snowflakes entered as Svenja left the longhouse.

"I don't trust her," Joe said, once the door slammed shut. "She used to be Sebastian Svellec, for Odin's sake! I've still got his bloody fingerprints on my neck."

I sighed, fiddling with a frayed seam in my coat. "Mason hates her—Hel, he *killed* her—and that's good enough for me."

"Earning a spot on Mason's hit-list ain't exactly a comfort."

"If Svenja wasn't on our side, then you'd all be dead and she'd have delivered me to Mason by now." Another sigh, the weight of the lamb sitting heavily in my stomach. "Besides, what other choice do we have?"

"Alira's right," Anya said. "She seems genuine enough."

"Yes, well. Be it on your heads, then." Joe took a strained gulp of mead.

Frigid air pulled the hair on my arms as two men walked in. Long leather coats, woollen hats, cracked teeth, and a modest selection of guns strapped around their hips, they were clearly in someone's pocket.

My gaze slipped to the bartender. Her skin grew ashen, her chest pulsing up and down with each breath. Without a word, she poured them a large tumbler of clear spirit, then scuttled down into the cellar to hibernate through their visit.

Clearly these men had a reputation. I tugged the blanket low across my brow.

"Two guys over there," I said, in barely more than a whisper.

Joe glanced over his shoulder. "Ben Carter's lackeys."

Anya eyes widened. "Gang members?"

"Maybe they know where the Rebels are?"

Joe's faced scrunched. "I know you care for Campbell, girl, but running back to him and Ashworth is a piss-poor idea."

My expression remained stony. "Why the Hel would you think I'm running back to Ashworth?"

Joe's scowl slackened into shock—an expression the others shared. I smiled as sweetly as I could. "I'm not setting one foot back on that train, Joe."

For the first time—perhaps in his entire life—Joe seemed lost for words.

Anya chewed her lip until clarity brightened her features. "This isn't about seeing Campbell, or the Rebellion. You're just after the information Svenja's going to give Ashworth."

I nodded. "If that information is as imperative as she claims, we'd be fools to run away from it." I sipped my mead, the honeyed sweetness tingling my tongue. "Svenja says she'll only spill her secrets in front of Ashworth, and I'm not optimistic or stupid enough to think she'll do it sooner."

"So, we find Ashworth, stay long enough to hear the information, and then...what? Relay our gratitude and just wander into the sunset?" Joe sneered to the musty air. "Do you really think he'll let you go?"

I stumbled around my words until Anya chimed in, "I doubt we're going to run into Ashworth anytime soon, so we've still got time to figure that out."

I offered her a small smile of thanks. She gladly reciprocated.

"Besides, I'm pretty sure Svenja will be a useful asset if we run into any Masonians, given how Sebastian held his own in a fight." I nodded to the reddish-purple bruises on Joe's neck.

Those two gang members had finished their drinks and were about to leave. Joe sighed—either in defeat or reluctantly agreeing to my plan—and called over his shoulder, "Oi, where's your boss? We need to speak to him."

The two men met us with stunned, suspicious eyes. "Oh yeah, and what's it to you, prick?"

Anya stood to her feet, pushing a long band of copper over her shoulder. A quick flutter of her eyelashes, those blue eyes ever so pleading.

"We were on the Rebel train," she said. "We were separated from the others when we were attacked, and we're ever so lost. You wouldn't know where to find Ben Carter or the rest of the Rebel commanders, would you?"

It took less than two seconds, and a salacious wiggle of Anya's hips, for the two men to concede.

"Sure, sweetheart," one of them said, boasting teeth that were chipped and discoloured. He downed the remainder of his drink in a single breath, then burped so loud the room shook. "But we need your guns first."

His stare rested on the table, and Campbell's black revolver lying upon it.

"Why?" I asked, with narrowing eyes.

The stranger just grinned, exposing his hideously cracked teeth. "Don't worry, you'll get it back as soon as the Boss says so."

Even on a good day, it was a bad idea to be defenceless in the New World. But this wasn't a good day. Far from it.

Yet, these men were our only chance to find the Rebels—and Ashworth. Besides, we were all on the same side, right?

With some tender words of encouragement from Joe and Anya, I reluctantly surrendered the gun.

"Wonderful." He grinned, tucking it in his belt. "Now, follow us."

* * *

SNOW FELL IN THICK, steady waves. Each white flake peppered my brow, cooled the inside of my nose and dug against my lungs. It was freeing, to be in that cold. It was purifying, *sacred.*

"Word of warning, sweetheart," the man said, strolling next to Anya. "Mike the Mulch has got a nasty temper at the best of times. I'd stick close to me if you can."

Anya simpered and tittered, playfully slapping his shoulder. Someone called him over and, in his absence, her face easily dropped.

What would Anya do once all of this was over? Would she return to waiting tables in some sketchy inn? Perhaps she would settle down, start a family of her own, kiss someone she loved, and who loved her in return. A small smile as I imagined her happy, surrounded by her loving horde.

Gang members materialised from the veil of snow as we neared an enormous wooden building. A barn, or so it looked. Gaping double doors were lodged open, despite the weather, and revealed the crowd of armed men inside.

Joe skulked to my side. He kept his head down, his eyes glued to the footprints in the snow.

"Girl, I'll meet up with you later," he whispered.

"What? Why, where're you going?"

"I don't have the best history with Carter. He's still after my balls, remember?"

Shit. Joe was right. Carter was ready to kill Joe back on the train, and he didn't strike me as a man who'd forget even a mild grudge. With a gentle nod, I whispered a Herdinese word of good luck.

A gentle squeeze of my shoulder and Joe's paced slowed. He began to separate himself from the group, his head still bowed.

"Oi! Where're you going?" A brutal shove returned him to my side. "You're not going anywhere, mate."

More men stepped closer, like hunters stalking their prey. Our colleagues gradually turned into our captors.

"Joe..."

"Stay close to me..." His cold hand grasped my own, slicked with sweat.

The barn rose high above up, melding into the opaque sky. Thick black cables streaked the area, attached to electric spotlights. Powered by generators that rumbled against the howling wind, white artificial light bled across the area.

Inside the barn, the sea of angry, armed men parted to reveal a table smattered with weapons. Revolvers, rifles, even an axe. They were being catalogued under the watchful eye of Ben Carter.

His attention flicked to us as we approached, his cerulean eye surrounded by a thick layer of dried blood, originating from a cut on his brow. That same layer of mottled red reached the corner of his mouth, which curved upwards in an unsettling smile.

"Ah, yes," he crooned. "I wondered when you'd all turn up."

Floorboards creaked as he took controlled paces around us all, the spurs on his boots echoing.

"Awfully glad to see you, girl." Smiling, he yanked the blanket from my head. "I was beginning to think you'd betrayed us. Y'know, running back to your lover, spreading your legs wide for him."

"You really are a pig, Carter." I glanced at the boxes of ammunition nestled between fat sacks of canned food. "You look like you're planning an attack."

"In a matter of speaking, yes." He prowled to Anya, took a gentle handful of her copper hair, and sniffed. Anya recoiled from his touch, her shoulders hunched. Smirking, Carter continued to circle us, like a starving polar bear.

"Do you know where the Rebels are?" I asked.

"Why d'you want to know?"

"We've found Svenja Svellec," Joe chimed in. It was a courageous attempt to appear cooperative, perhaps a little threatening, but Joe's puffed shoulders deflated at Carter's scowl.

"Have you really?" he snarled. "Looks like you lost her though. You really do have a knack of losing valuable shit, don't you, Matheson?"

"Look, Ben..." Joe displayed apologetic palms. "There's plenty of time to kill me, later, but right now, we need to stop Mason. C'mon, where're the Rebels?"

"I have absolutely no idea, mate." Carter grinned, exposing yellowed teeth. "Last I saw, they scrambled onto that bloody train and steamed off with their tails between their legs."

"Shit..." I sighed, rubbing my sore head. The violin had returned, insistent and nagging. "Then do you know where we can find them?"

Carter just shrugged. "Y'know, girl, I don't much care anymore."

One hand in the pocket of his long, scruffy coat, Ben Carter fingered each of the guns on the table. A grubby, scabbed hand moved down each polished barrel, caressed each trigger...

"I'm beginning to lose faith in Ashworth's Rebellion. It all seemed like a good idea at the time, but as more of my men die from Ashworth's stupidity and his ridiculous attempts at bravado, I'm getting a little pissed off."

Carter turned to us, leaning against the table. Nestled within his grubby hands, a large revolver loomed.

"Ben," Joe began, carefully, "you know Ashworth is the best chance we have at killing Mason, at—"

"And how many more men am I going to lose? Another hundred? More?"

He laughed bitterly into the stagnant air. "Do you know what Ashworth promised me, once all this shit is over? He said I'd have the Icelands, free at my disposal, to be my own little kingdom. And I want the Icelands, I really do."

Carter could detect my fear, like blood on the wind. He smiled.

"Y'know, it really was a generous deal Mason offered me on that beach. I'm thinking to reconsider."

My heart sank, then thumped around my chest. "Don't... Carter, please don't..."

"If I remember correctly, all that's needed is a little exchange." He tilted forwards with a maddening grin. "Do you remember what the exchange was, sweetheart?"

I took a step back and felt the cold barrel of a shotgun against my spine.

"He won't do it! He'll never give up the Icelands!"

"Yes, well..." Carter gestured towards the room filled with death's instruments. "Why do you think I have all of this? If he doesn't play fair, I'll blow your brains clean out. Y'see, I'm not giving him much of a choice here."

He pushed himself from the table and took two terrible steps towards us. The blood on his face glistened with sinister lustre.

"Boys," he said, "dispose of the spare parts."

Hands grasped us, squeezing the flesh, heaving us apart.

"Oh, apart from the redhead." Carter smirked. "I'll keep her for a while."

Anya and I were dragged to one side of the barn, Heidi and Joe to another. I threw my fist against a jaw. A sickening crunch made the man double back, cowering. Something hard hit my stomach and I fell to my knees, unable to catch my breath, holding back vomit as pain echoed around my torso.

Through my hazy vision, Heidi screamed as they pressed a gun hard into her temple. Joe was just ahead of her, grunting with each punch. He fell, spitting blood, cowering through the stampede of kicks.

I tried to reach them, *protect* them!

A hand buried in my hair and dragged me towards Ben Carter, who stood cleaning his gun with utmost care.

Think, girl! C'mon, you have to—

Something metallic rattled inside the barn. Screams stopped; punches paused. Even Carter lifted his head to see the object leisurely rolling towards him. It came to rest in the middle of the building, directly beneath the table of weapons.

In a moment of startling clarity, Ben Carter realised what he was looking at.

"Move!"

The grenade exploded. The table flew up in a flurry of fire and shrapnel. Guns spattered in all directions; blades soared with deadly intent and demanded a series of groans.

Those nearest the blast were killed, their bodies mangled, their faces mottled with cuts and abrasions. The rest of us were left reeling, our heads spinning, our ears buzzing with deafening intensity.

As fire licked the ceiling and screams flooded my senses, I turned to Anya, sprawled on the floor with a large cut decorating her cheek.

"Anya!" I shouted, cradling her face. *"Anya!"*

She startled awake, her eyes darting. I dragged her to her feet and crossed the labyrinth of bodies. We heaved Joe from beneath a fallen rafter and charged towards the door.

Heidi was already there. *"Come on!"*

The barn sang with angry heat. Sparks fell to the ground, siring more fires and igniting men.

Anya and I supported Joe's weak frame as we rushed into the snow. I passed the man from the longhouse and quickly plucked Campbell's revolver from his unconscious body, holding it firm against my chest, taking comfort in its weight. Sweat peppered my brow, instantly chilled by the frigid air.

The trees. If only we could make it to the trees!

A man jumped before us. I stared down the long barrel of his gun, frozen and waiting until—

A loud thud. The man collapsed in a heap.

Behind him, grinning stupidly, Svenja Svellec held a shotgun high and proud, the butt glimmering with blood. "Well, c'mon then," she pressed.

The forest beckoned, the roar of the burning barn at our backs.

Bullets peppered the air, bits of bark exploded from nearby trees. Svenja Svellec leading the way, we followed her rushed limp.

A bazooka's projectile swooshed past and exploded in the mess of trees ahead. It threw us back with nature's shrapnel—a violent shower of sharp wooden stakes and splinters. I landed on something soft: Joe, who grunted beneath my weight.

Svenja Svellec jumped to her feet. "On your feet!"

Anya stumbled upright, grabbed Heidi's hand and pulled her into the safe darkness of the forest. "Alira!" she yelled after me.

I scrambled upright and tugged at Joe's hand.

He didn't move.

I noticed his leg—and the large splinter embedded in his inner thigh. Blood gushed from the puncture, saturating his jeans.

"It-it's okay," I stammered, inspecting the wound. "I-I can s-stop it, I-I just need—"

But the Mulch Gang were regrouping themselves, fanning out from their burning base like ants from a nest.

Joe cradled my face, forcing our eyes to meet. I stared into those eyes glazed with moisture, scratching the surface of the soul within. It was a good soul. A *kind* soul.

A single tear trickled down his cheek. "Go."

"No, I-I'm not leaving you!" I slapped away his hands and examined the wound again. Calls of angered men lingering behind us, racing closer and closer...

Joe grasped my face again, wiping the tears from my cheeks with the rough pads of his thumbs.

"You need to go, girl," he said, his lower lip trembling. *"Please..."*

No, I couldn't leave him—*I can't leave you!*

Joe's face paled. Blood gushed from his leg, marring the white snow beneath.

A single, gasping sob erupted—from me, him, both?—as I threw my arms around him. He embraced me in return, burying his face in my hair.

"I'm so sorry," he breathed. "I'm sorry for everything—"

"I forgive you," I said through the tears. "I forgive you!"

Joe kissed me desperately upon my forehead.

"Run," he whispered, barely able to focus. His blood darkened the snow.

Trembling, I clambered upright as Joe removed his belt and wrapped it around his upper thigh. He groaned through the pain, using the last of his strength to pull it taut.

Campbell's revolver became heavy—*too* heavy. Joe looked so hurt and helpless, and I couldn't just leave him bleeding and shivering in the snow.

"Take this," I said, and threw the revolver in his lap.

Shock twisted his paling features. "No, absolutely not, I can't—"

"You want me to run?" I shouted, tears blurring my vision. "Fine, I will—but *only* if you take it! Or I'm staying!"

It was a foolish, selfish admission, but it was the only way he'd agree.

"I'll hold them back as long as I can," he said. I saw his pride, his triumph, as he gripped Campbell's revolver with white-knuckle force. *"Now run!"*

Stifling a sob, I raced to the trees just as they appeared. Joe Matheson pulled the trigger, the murderous *bangs* pushing me further and faster to the forest. A few seconds of laboured gunshots, then deafening silence reigned.

* * *

RUNNING THROUGH THE TREES, the burning barn became nothing but a distant crackle in the night. Angered shouts still cut through the shadows. They were close; I had to hurry.

The others couldn't have been far ahead. I zipped between the trees, hoping to spot the burst of Anya's copper hair or Svenja's flash of gold.

Speckled by falling snow, the forest bathed in an eerie orange light. I stared harder into the shadows ahead, fighting the growing panic in my chest.

The Gang was close now.

I heard something. A name, spoken by another.

It was my name, shouted through the trees.

Anya.

My lungs swelled; the cold air suddenly able to penetrate. An exhausted smile tinged my lips as I took the first relieved step.

Something slammed across my mouth. I startled, inhaling with the shock. A sickening stench of chemicals flew down my throat.

I tried to scream but my words were muffled by the cloth, and the bloody hand that pressed it against my lips and nose.

"Shh..." Ben Carter crooned down my ear. "Just relax, sweetheart."

Arms filled with concrete. I tried and failed to drag his hand away. The world darkened. My eyes fluttered closed as chemicals swarmed inside my lungs.

A dangerous lightness filled my head. Strength left me. I couldn't move.

Ben Carter lowered me to the ground as the blackness swallowed me whole.

13

I saw Mason.

He played a violin on an empty stage.

Music surrounded him. So beautiful. I wanted to fall into that music, for my bones to be pulled and tugged by each chord, each melody...

The bow danced against the strings; Mason's body pulsed with the beat. Slowly, I moved closer. I wanted to touch him, to trace my fingers against the smooth material of his dinner jacket.

"Come closer, my dear."

A bump. I jolted awake. Stuffy air reeked of sweat and stale barley. Did I have an empty grain sack over my head? Through my pounding skull, I opened my eyes. Blackness greeted me in return.

A sudden inhale forced stale air down my dry, sore throat. Something pressed against my mouth—*in* my mouth—inhibiting my speech. I tried to cough against the pressure, resisting the urge to gag.

Confusion inched across my dizzy mind. *Where am I? What happened?*

Another bump and my body jolted hard against the cold floor.

I tried to move, to claw away the blackness. My hands were tied. I groaned, pulling at the bindings around my wrists, then around my feet, ankles, legs... Loops of rope dug deep into my flesh.

Panic grew, like fierce waves rising towards the shore. Memories surged beneath the sack: Joe's sacrifice, Ben Carter's sneering spit, the cloth saturated in chloroform...

I screamed as loud as I could.

Some scuffling ahead of me, then something pinched my nose through the sack over my head.

I couldn't breathe, for my mouth was full of that bitter-tasting cloth. I kicked aching legs in every possible direction.

"Are you done yet?"

Rage boiled. I tried to free myself, jerking and writhing. I thrust tied ankles ahead of me, always fruitlessly. Lungs burned as they gasped for air. Dizziness grew. White dots speckled my vision until I had no choice but to still.

He released my nose and I desperately inhaled that stuffy, stagnant air. I curled my limbs and cowered in a small ball.

Questions raced. Where were they taking me? What atrocities would I face when we eventually arrived?

Another bump, followed by the numerous sounds of jingling ammunition. How many people were with me, guarding me? I guessed four, perhaps five. Was Carter one of those people?

I was his property, after all. It would do him well to ensure I was unharmed when he sold me.

Tears prickled my eyes. I squeezed them tightly shut, doing my damned hardest to remain composed.

Mason's cruel smile remained etched in my memories. Scars ached, stronger than ever, as my foul future reared its head again.

I thought of Campbell and Ashworth... Would they know where I was? That I was taken, not by Rebel moles or Masonians, but by their greatest ally?

A cruel twist of fate indeed. I could almost hear Mason's snide, *I told you so.*

I prayed sincerely—*desperately*—for Joe Matheson. That infuriating, misunderstood man. Please, dear Odin, may he still be alive. Somewhere, *somehow*, he could still be alive...

Life passed by in a series of flashes: *Maya Doe, Mason's Mate, Mother, Traitor...*

Was it too immature to hope I was dreaming?

How wonderful that would be, to wake up on a snowy mountain, next to my Papa. Would he be proud of me? Would he be glad that I had run away from Mason, denied my destiny?

Regardless of my decisions, he would smile through a greying beard and place a loving hand upon my shoulder. He would say everything would be fine, because to him, it would be. *Things always have a way of working out*, he would say.

No use considering the past because the wheels of time had already turned.

Regret nothing, he would say.

We rumbled to a stop before a wall of frigid air blasted into the van, hard and unforgiving. Cold buried deep into my bones, deforming my breaths into short bursts, sharp in nature and all too desperate.

The Ice Territory, I abruptly realised.

Hard hands yanked me outside. My boots collided with the ground, crunching through the uppermost layer of frozen snow. Biting wind clawed through my coat, prickling my skin, licking it with raw perversion as I failed to contain my shivers—from fear, or the cold?

I was held steady as the ropes around my legs were cut. Blood rushed to my numb feet, tingling ferociously. Strong arms dragged me into an abrupt blast of warm air, but my shivers didn't lessen. *So, it's fear, then.*

Wooden floorboards squeaked beneath my feet, the air heavy with the stench of cigars and weed, so thick it was almost unbreathable. Bursts of drunken laughter mixed with screams—a terrifying paradox, foretelling a place riddled with both debauchery and malice.

I lost all sense of direction: a series of corridors here, an opened door there. Buried somewhere deep inside that labyrinth, I was thrust into a wooden chair and my bound wrists secured to the floor. I tested the restraints as the men released me, but it was no use. The binding rope was taut and would not give.

Ben Carter took a seat opposite me just as the sack was yanked off. My eyes squinted against the meagre bulbs, hanging haphazardly from the ceiling. The room was completely bare, save for a wooden table between us, and an ashtray containing nothing a few piles of ash and several cigarette butts—as if I needed *another* reminder of Ben Carter's presence.

Another cigarette sagged against his lip—*of course it did*—as he plucked his lighter from his coat. It fell to the table in a dull clank once he'd enjoyed that first, sumptuous drag. I expected him to say something—*do* something—but Carter just stared at me, motionless except for the corner of his lip. It inclined upwards in a state of perpetual amusement and I wanted to claw his entire face off.

"Well," he said eventually. "Welcome to my home, girl."

Still gagged, I just glared at him.

"So, what d'you think? Hardly compares to the luxury of Mason's Palace, of course, but..." That cerulean eye winked at me. "I trust you'll find your stay here more than comfortable."

I forced a noise around the cloth in my mouth.

"Oh, I'm sorry, I didn't catch that."

He leant forward and removed the gag: a hideous piece of grey cloth that lengthened upon removal. I gagged as Carter threw it to the floor, my throat sore and scratchy. Eyes watering with the strain, I licked my dry lips with an equally dry tongue and forced an uncomfortable swallow.

"I said, *fuck you*," I croaked.

Carter forced an overly hurt expression. "I don't know why you're getting your knickers in a twist. You're going to see Mason again, and we both know how much you miss him."

Something twisted inside my stomach: a foul concoction of fear and dread. "You're not going to win, Carter..."

"I don't intend to *win*, sweetheart, I intend to form a deal. No harm done; all sides win."

"Ashworth would disagree."

Carter's expression twisted with contempt. "That *fucking* boy," he snarled, pinching the cigarette from between his teeth. "He's as good as dead, and you know it. Don't try to pretend that you actually believed in that fucking Rebellion?"

"I have to believe in it because what other fucking choice do I have?"

"We all have a choice, girl," Carter scowled. He stabbed the cigarette on the table, despite the ashtray, and hastily plucked another from his pocket.

I tried to keep my fear in check, but one of my tears was stubborn and escaped my grasp. Carter saw it for a brief second and lit his cigarette. He truly didn't care.

"I don't have a choice though, do I?" I said, my fearless mask slipping down my cheeks. "*Please*, Carter, I'm *begging* you—don't send me back to him!"

"Or what?" he said, leaning back in his chair, his arms crossed with that smoking cigarette between his fingers. "What are you willing to offer me instead? Not much, by the looks of it. Always your body, of course, but even then, I don't particularly want a musical axe stabbing at my brain. So, tell me: within those limiting set of parameters, what can you possibly offer me that I don't already have?"

Nothing, was the answer to that. I had *nothing*.

Carter knew this, and his smirk reappeared. "At any rate, none of that would fix the problem, would it? I want the Ice Territory and the only way I can have it is by giving you to Mason. I'm afraid my hands are tied."

"Carter, you can't seriously expect him to just...*give* you the Icelands! He created them, for Odin's sake!"

"He can create another." A lazy shrug of his shoulder, the glowing cigarette siring a wispy line of white. "I'll admit, I don't know what awaits you with Mason, but, frankly, I don't care. The Icelands are *mine*, girl, and I don't care how I get them."

Heartless. That was an ample adjective. Ben—*Mike the Mulch*—Carter was a selfish, *heartless* bastard.

How could he ever think Mason would agree to such a plan? Perhaps the decades of power and chemical intoxication had muddled his perception of reality. Or maybe he was just too arrogant to think clearly.

Two men marched in carrying a wooden box surrounded by cables.

"Ah, finally," Carter mumbled over the fag.

The box opened to reveal a black telephone inside, clumsily assembled with colourful wires sticking in all directions. Yet the dial tone rang clearly as Ben Carter rotated the number wheel with a single finger. It clicked and clanked with the movement, Carter continuously puffing away.

A knob turned, the dial tone loudened, and Ben Carter sat back in his chair with an arrogant wink.

"*Yes, how can I help you?*" Her voice crackled as the signal clawed at the Icelands, yet her shrill, Aristocratic tone was evident.

"Put me through to Lord Mason, sweetheart," Carter said, tapping a mound of ash to the floor. "Tell him Benjamin Michael Carter wants a word."

"*Of course, one minute please...*"

Carter and I exchanged glances; his was amused and pitying in equal measure.

The dial tone stopped.

"*Carter...*" Mason's loud, rich voice echoed across the room, his violin pulsing with each syllable. Gooseflesh raced up my arms, tingling with chilled fear. "*What an unpleasant surprise. Are you going to offer me surrender?*"

"Nothing of the sorts, my good man," Carter replied, mocking his accent. "However, I've had a change of heart in recent days and am more than willing to discuss your deal."

"*Deal? What deal?*"

Carter smiled at me. A hideous smile, full of wickedness and yellowed teeth. "I've someone with me who wants to say *hi*."

My jaw clenched tightly shut, my hands balling through the tremors.

Carter's smile dropped. "Oh, she's a little shy. Hang on, mate..."

He wandered behind me, pinching that cigarette between stained fingertips. He pushed my head down, exposing the back of my neck and my limbs yanked helplessly at the restraints when—

A sharp, stinging pain as Carter pressed the smouldering cigarette butt into my skin. It burned my flesh, sizzling. I bit my tongue, trying to keep it in, but it hurt so much and—

An agonised shriek burst from my throat just as Mason's violin screeched. "*Carter!*"

Carter removed his cigarette and tossed it to the floor, returning to his seat with a quick slap of my head. Breathless, I silently groaned through the lingering pain, my flesh raw and burning.

"*You have my attention,*" Mason said slowly. "*What do you want?*"

"You know perfectly well what I want. In fact, you made me such an offer at Giant's Respite."

"*That deal was refused.*"

"Then let's remake it." Carter grinned again, picking at the bits of grit beneath his fingernail. "I have something you want; you have something I want. All that's needed is a simple exchange of goods."

Goods—that's all I was to him. Not a living creature, not a person who had already been through Hel. Just *goods*.

"So, I'll have the Ice Territory, and you'll have that big, happy family you've always wanted. How does that grab you?"

Mason paused, deliberating.

"She remains unharmed," he said, his tone low and steady. *"Do you hear me, Carter?"*

"Alira's fate really depends on you, my good Sir. If you're not at Draco's Pass in—oh, I'm feeling generous—let's say two weeks from now, then it's really out of my control. How many more years are you willing to wait until another *Alira* Comes of Age, hm? Twenty years? Fifty? That's an awfully long time, wouldn't you say?"

"If you so much as touch her—"

"You'll do what?" Carter snarled. "Destroy the Territory, with Alira in it? Ha! And then you'll really be up shit's creek, won't you?"

The violin screamed inside my head; so out of tune, so terribly conflicted...

"Alright, Carter." Mason's anger crawled through the handset. *"You have a deal."*

"Wonderful! See you in two weeks, mate."

The telephone cut off.

14

I hit the cell's stone floor with a grunt, coughing around bits of hay and dust.

"Enjoy your stay, wench."

Rage reignited and I scrambled to my feet, shrieking, and charged towards the door.

It slammed shut just before I could reach it, but the anger didn't retreat, the rage did not lessen. I pounded on that wooden door, helpless to stop the thugs' raucous laughter outside. The wood trembled, hinges rattling against the frame, but the door refused to budge.

Dejected, I slid down the wood and collapsed into a heap at the base. There, the reality of my position sank with brutal understanding. Panic festered, bloating my already full heart with dread and the precise, unmistakable fear of my future.

Laughter faded, the thugs finally leaving me to my isolation.

In the deep quiet, I took a strained look around my cell. A bare room: wooden walls, a bucket, and a stone floor speckled with frost and hay. The only window was the one in the door, covered with a black metal grid that glimmered with frost.

I pressed my knees to my chin, hugging them close.

Fear was a difficult emotion to shift. I counted the seconds inside my head, a terrible countdown to the reunion with my torturer...

Memories flooded my head, of when our Connection was young and fervent, when Mason took pleasure in seeing me hurt.

I stared at the scars on my wrists and felt the pain of that morning: the despair of each assault, the way Mason's diamond eyes sparkled with so much hate, so much malice and contempt. I rubbed the scars hard, feeling the shackles bite into the skin, remembering the agony in my nose as he ripped the tube out.

But even after, when the physical pain was over, the emotional turmoil Mason inflicted was no less damaging, no less difficult. The isolation I felt, the witless wanderings through those empty, desolate halls. I remembered the knife in Luna's hand, the sickening dread of feeling Mason's wrath simply because I had spared another's life.

Because I had tried to *protect* her.

I bit my tongue, hard, tasting the iron tang of blood and painting the memory of what such a thing felt like. My eyes squeezed shut, wanting to save them at all costs.

I rubbed my belly, empty of everything, and saw flashes of Isobel Hutchinson. Would another woman paint my baby's room? Would another woman be my son's *Mama*?

The word *regret* threatened to emerge. It scratched the back corner of my mind, dancing around my brain, skipping over the box of emotions that still lay buried. It was jovial, singing its way back into my heart and suffocating my lungs. I was drowning in the word, for its bitter taste was everywhere.

I tried to force it back, to push away the rising tide of emotion. *The wheels of time had turned*. There was no point ruminating over past events or painful decisions. What good would it do to mock past choices?

But there, in the decaying filth of Carter's cell, that word became harder to ignore.

It clawed into me, biting at my flesh until I had no choice but to accept its presence, to ponder the choice I had made that day.

Visions of that black beach, where the waves crashed with thunderous intensity, where the frigid wind caressed my cheek, flit across my eyes. I saw

Mason, his diamond eyes glowing beneath the dirty sky, and remembered the promise of an upturned hand.

And there, as regret pressed into my spine, I imagined myself taking it. I imagined a life where I'd wake up without fear, without hurt, without the knowledge of the pain I would inevitably face. No more torture, no more spilled blood.

Joe might still be alive, had my choices been different that day.

I thought to the son, yet to be created, and wondered if I might have the eyes to see his first breath...

Regret.

Finally, in the cold darkness of that cell, I allowed that word to fill me. It rose through my stomach, rising higher and higher up my throat until it burst out in a series of sobs. I curled myself tighter, cursing myself and all my *stupid* decisions. The truth could no longer be ignored or pushed aside.

I wished I had taken Mason's hand that day. I wished I had a future to be excited for, a son I could hold and nurture.

But no, that future had been wiped away. It had been carried off by the same calamitous waves that donned that black beach. That future had been thrown to the Endless Sea the moment I turned my back to Mason, the instant I chose Ashworth's future instead of my own.

Emotion built inside my lungs and I screamed my pain to that empty cell, releasing all that I had denied myself, all the lost hopes that had fed my gullible heart.

Pouring my heart upon the walls, I remained alone.

15

A rat skulked ahead. Black fur, short and shiny, reflected the light from the bulb above. Occasionally it stopped, its front paw raised, its pink nose twitching in the damp, stuffy air.

For a moment, I watched it. Still and silent. Fixated upon its every movement.

Scuttling a little more, the rat met the scattered remains of food dropped through the grate in the door. Leftover pieces of bread had grown mouldy, green spores already mottling the surface.

The rat worried not and took a large crumb between its paws.

Its eyes were black and shiny, like two beads. It stared at me as it ate, perched upon its hind legs, its tail stretched far behind it.

I tilted my head as I watched. Fascinating creatures.

The rat finished its morsel, then took a hesitant step towards my boot. Its nose twitched. Perhaps it had seen something, stuck in the rubber gutters in my sole.

I willed that rat to come closer, urging it to come clawing at my clothes, to scratch away the perpetual numbness.

Pounding footsteps startled us both. The rat scuttled back to its nest, disappearing through a hole in the wall.

A key scratched in the lock. The door opened wide. Two thugs picked my weak frame off the frozen floor and dragged me down the corridor.

Smoke—tobacco and weed—infested my lungs. I coughed loudly, for the scent was cloying. It burned my eyes.

Up a flight of stairs, I was shoved into in a small room. Once again, the only thing of any importance was a small table with an ashtray. And Ben Carter, of course. He stood before the open window, the gentle breeze ruffling his dirty brown hair. His face, hard and unyielding, scowled at the view.

"Do you know what that is, girl?" he asked.

Cautiously, I followed his attention. The Icelands stared back.

Such a barren landscape: a harsh, frozen environment. Few trees dotted the scenery, but those that did were short and stumpy, like they had been denied growth. One half of all visible trees were smattered with green needles, shining like dull emeralds against the snow. The other half was barren, the leaves shredded or ripped away by immense winds that carried shards of icy glass.

Numerous boulders scattered the landscape, covered with lichens and snow. No roads, for the snow was too thick and unyielding. Ahead, the northern edge of the Brüster Mountains cut the horizon, their jagged, snowy peaks ablaze with the crimson light of a setting sun. The two tallest peaks met like the edges of two serrated knives, fitting perfectly in place and forming a winding, narrow path through the mountain range.

"That there is Draco's Pass," Carter said. "Don't suppose you know its legend?"

I shook my head.

"Thought so." Eyes narrowed in the red light, the sky quickly darkening. "Well, the story goes that two dragons sought a golden egg, borne from the sun. They each wanted to own the egg, to own the power inside of it. When they eventually found it, they fought until they were both beaten, bloody, and close to death.

"Then, the golden egg hatched, casting its golden light upon them both. They stared into that egg, consumed by the promise of power, yet nothing happened. So, they waited. Centuries passed, and their skin turned to stone, their wings to snow. They were immortalised in the rock, still fighting over the egg that promised power but delivered nothing in return."

Abused lungs inflated with a large sigh, the tips of his stained fingers tapping nervously upon the table.

"Of course, the story is bullshit. There were no dragons, no golden egg. Those mountains were formed during Ragnarök, no more than two centuries ago. Your mate formed those mountains, not the dragons."

A few more taps against the table, the setting sun bleeding red light across his features. "And yet, I feel like one of those dragons. I feel like I stared into the golden egg, waiting for power and got nothing more than fucking disappointment."

As the urge got the better of him, he thrust his hand into his pocket and pulled out a cigarette. The scar down his face glowed orange with the first, delectable inhale. Shoulders softening beneath the hit, Carter held the cigarette between his fingers and still tip-tapped against the table.

The sun dipped lower, flooding the sky with tendrils of orange, crimson, gold… It highlighted the snow with a bloodthirsty glow, shredding through the arms of those last remaining trees.

"I'm not surprised you haven't heard that legend, girl. It's synonymous with those born in the Icelands but rarely falls on outside ears. Up here, we learn that legend the moment we learn to breathe, passed from one generation to another."

His tone grew bitter, the dying light casting shadows across his face. "I bet Mason hasn't heard that tale. I'd wager he doesn't know about the dragons fighting over the golden egg, immortalised by the power they craved. No, he's barely stepped foot in these lands, and yet he claims ownership of them? I was *born* here, I'll *die* here! I am more of their rightful owner than he ever will be!"

Anger fluoresced behind that cloudy eye. Another strained inhale of smoke, his face glowing with amber light.

"Two weeks ago, I made a deal with the Destroyer of the Old World. Given the circumstances, I thought he'd make every effort to be here on time. And yet, my scouts inform me that Draco's Pass remains empty. It seems our dear Lord Mason is a little distracted by other affairs."

Ben Carter's glower slipped from Draco's Pass. "I don't like it when people are late, girl. It makes me *tetchy*."

"He'll be here," I said, my defeat audible. "He wants me back; he wants a son."

"Oh, I don't doubt that at all." Another drag between those dried lips; another satisfied exhale. "But I'm a businessman at heart, and I find his tardiness a tad insulting."

"It's not the new day yet," I said, but Carter returned my reassurance with a contemptuous laugh.

"I've kept my side of the bargain: I've left you unharmed. You've been my guest, all things considered. Yet, he still dares to insult me?"

With a grotesque chuckle, he threw the cigarette out of the window. "Come with me," he said.

Like Hel. I didn't move.

Carter plucked a revolver from behind his back and held it low at his side. "Don't test me," he growled. "Now, after you."

* * *

CARTER'S DEN WAS A LABYRINTH, a honeycomb of rooms and corridors that led further into dank, smoky bowels. Eventually the corridor opened into a large room where layers of wooden benches clung to the periphery of a wide, open space. It looked like an auditorium—complete with a central pit, which Carter nudged me towards.

"I'm not known for my patience." He spat a large, yellow blob into the deep pit, surrounded by wooden poles. Sand smothered the base, stained with dirty red blotches and streaks.

Blood.

"Do you know what this is?"

I didn't reply. A crowd gathered around us, taking their seats with smouldering spliffs.

Carter spat in the pit again. "Well, it's a place for people who annoy me. I planned to put Joe Matheson in here, one day."

A smile crawled across his face, lifting his expression with sick amusement. "Your mate has annoyed me, girl. Yet, he's not here for me to throw in the pit."

I took a step back, my heart racing. "Carter, I—"

"You are though, and I reckon Mason will be able to hear everything you experience through that sweet little Connection of yours. Isn't that right?"

"Wait, don't—"

Carter grasped my arm and pushed. I fell ten or eleven feet and landed in the bloody sand with a *thump.*

With starling alarm, I scrambled upright. "Carter, what the *Hel* are you doing?"

Cater crouched at the pit's edge, rubbing his hands with that sick smile on his face. "Oh, I'm going to make Mason realise that he can't keep people like me waiting. This is *my* Territory, after all, and we play by *my* rules."

From the corner of my eye, I noticed a dusty chalkboard being wheeled in. On it, scraped down its marred surface, was my name—*Alira*—next to an uneven table full of betting odds. Terror gripped my bones as the seated men —the *spectators*—exchanged money, cigarettes, and little bags of white powder.

I swallowed hard, squeezing my fists to stop them trembling. "Carter, what is this?"

Carter's grin widened. "Let's see if Mason will pick up the pace, hey?"

Ben Carter lit another cigarette as he wandered through the cheers and wolf-whistles to the top of the auditorium. Of course, he had the best seat in the house.

I ran to the smooth wooden poles that were impossible to climb. Chalk scratched against the blackboard high above...

"Okay lads, open her up!"

An ominous creaking filled the pit. Slowly, I looked over my shoulder. A section of the wall detached from the rest, raised high by the ropes looping from the ceiling. Behind it, a dark tunnel belched the acrid stench of faeces and rotten meat. I suppressed a gag—*fear, disgust*—and took a laboured step back.

Footsteps sounded: loud and muffled, completely inhuman. Low grunts echoed from the shadows, the stench of sweat and mud growing with terrible intensity...

I saw her shadow first, moving through the tunnel. But as she drew closer, light illuminated her black muzzle, those dark brown eyes, her grubby white fur. Ribs pressed against her torso, beneath the layers of fur and skin. Teeth bared in a ravenous snarl.

Standing—no, *cowering*—I could do nothing but watch, breathless and terrified, as the polar bear stood on her hind legs and *roared*. Black claws grew, their long, curving points catching the light.

Cheers and shouts rattled into the pit. The chalk had stopped scratching.

A pure, wretched terror infested me. My muscles ached to freeze, every movement like a creaking gate. I carefully manoeuvred around her. For a moment, she watched. Observing me from her immense height, inhaling my scent, looking down upon my meagre morsels with hunger in her eyes...

Claws descended. I rolled across the bloody sand. She charged at me, huge jaws snapping. I scrambled between her flailing limbs, thrusting away my fright as my blood filled with power, speed, agility and—

The bear whacked the air. Four long claws slashed through my leather coat and sliced the top layer of flesh. I shrieked, hot fingers of pain spreading down my back.

The crowd cheered and hollered. Ben Carter's laugh was the loudest of all.

Pushing away the pain, I shrugged the coat off, twisting the slashed fabric. Our eyes locked—diamond with obsidian—as we circled one another. Blood dribbled down my back, dropping like small jewels in the sand below. The bear raised her nose, sniffing.

She roared and bounded towards me. I slapped the twisted coat at her face. She startled, trying to kill the coat. I ducked behind her view, hiding behind her.

A group of thugs rushed into the auditorium and whispered to Carter. His face fell with a frustrated huff. "Alright, show's over—*get her out of there!*"

The bear took the shredded coat in her jaws, ripping the seams apart, licking the drops blood until she realised with a roar that my meat was not in it. She bounded around the pit with a ferocity that made me whimper. Above me, creaks and clinks as the rope slowly lowered.

I kicked the bloodied sand towards her. With an almighty roar, the bear startled back, distracted by the new flurry of scents.

I gazed up at the rope, slowly descending. It was so close, *so close!*

The bear quickly recovered, stamping its huge feet. It lunged.

I threw myself out of its way in a cloud of dust that covered my face, my hair, the wet blood upon my back. I doubled around her, her jaws clamping just above my head. I grabbed a handful of sand and threw it in her eye. She startled back, groaning, pawing at her face.

"Grab the rope!"

Not needing to be told twice, I jumped and caught it with both hands. Men shouted and the rope rolled up, carrying me out of the pit.

The bear saw her dinner exiting and took one final leap. I kicked at her, evading her snapping maw as I was finally pulled free.

Limbs shaking, blood pouring from my back, I collapsed onto those wooden floorboards. Thugs surrounded me, suffocating me with their stench and their sick amusement, paying up their losses or collecting their winnings.

My heart hammered inside my chest, the lingering drips of adrenaline leaving me at last. In its place was a full, unrelenting exhaustion—and *pain*. Lots and lots of pain.

A hoarse laugh preceded Ben Carter's presence, pushing himself to the front of the crowd with a horrific grin. "What a show! No bad feelings, of course. I'd no doubt you'd get out of there alive."

Profanities and *Curses of the Old Gods* lay at the tip of my tongue, aching to be spat over Carter's scarred, smirking face. But all my energy had gone, pulled back inside that pit with a starving polar bear. I could still hear her roaring, groaning for my flesh...

"As it so happens, the show had to be cut short," Carter said, crouching down. "My scouts have spotted a Masonian convoy approaching Draco's Pass. I daresay your mate has finally arrived."

Slowly, I forced myself to hear the violin. Its relief sang back; a response to hearing my own melodies of safety. What did it sound like when I dodged snapping jaws? I'd been too preoccupied to listen.

Carter perused my bloody body, his cracked lips twisting. "Oh, look at you. We can't possibly deliver you to Mason like that: you're filthy. Can't have rumours spreading about my hospitality, can we? There's a ridiculous tale that I feed my guests to a polar bear, after all."

16

—————

W arm water ran across me. How freeing it was, to be buried beneath that water. To let it flow across my pale, damaged skin and carry away all the filth.

Kneeling inside the tub, I scooped another cupful of steaming water and sloshed it down my back. I audibly groaned with the pain, watching the blood pool around my knees. It ran in red streams around me, diffusing to all corners of the tub.

Carter had stationed a guard outside the door while I bathed. Not that I trusted him. I had scoured the small room, searching for any cracks in the wood, any holes some would-be pervert could exploit. Alas, the room was secured. I could wash in peace.

Tenderly, I felt the cuts upon my back. Five of them, running from shoulder to sacrum. I grimaced with the pressure from my fingers, my entire back throbbing. Tears itched the corners of my eyes and I succumbed to the stings.

I thought to my Jörmungandr tattoo and wondered, quite sadly, if the great snake still held his tail in its mouth. Did he still represent a sense of calm, of order in this wretched world? Or had that tail been ripped out by the claws of a starving polar bear?

I took another cup of water from the steaming bucket and doused myself in its warmth. I didn't have long left, a matter of minutes.

With great effort, I pushed myself upright. Large drops of blood seeped from the wounds, dribbling down my buttocks. I had to ignore them, for time was short.

I hobbled to a crate of clothes. All women's: trousers, jumpers, blouses, even a dress. How the Hel had Carter amassed such a collection?

I recalled the way he sniffed Anya's hair. *I'll keep her for a while*, he'd said.

A shiver ran the entire length of my burning spine, following each oozing cut. Carter was clearly a sadistic bastard, but...*this?*

"Oh Gods..." I whispered, but I was beginning to think they'd stopped listening.

With my other clothes ripped and bloodied, I'd no other option. My blood would now mar some other woman's clothes. Perhaps my friend's. With a thick swallow, I began to dress.

Each scrape of material against my skin felt like an electric shock. I shouldn't have been in those clothes—they deserved to hug another's body, to be warmed by another's skin. Wearing those clothes was so perverse, so utterly *wrong...*

Breathe in... One... Two... Three...

A glint of sparkle caught my attention: a pair of earrings. Cheaply made, for their diamonds were nothing but chipped glass, I tested the pliable metal and stretched the metal loop into a long point. A weapon, perhaps? I placed it inside my pocket, just in case. Given the fate their last owner endured, they'd probably insist I take it.

I knocked three times on the door. It opened with a creak and I was escorted to Ben Carter. His gaze slipped from Draco's pass and trailed me up and down.

"Ah, lovely," he crooned. I strenuously ignored him, pulling the coat around my middle. The jeans were too small, the black jumper too large, the coat the colour of claret... That colour, in particular, was an unwelcome reminder of all the times I'd served wine in Mason's Palace. Still, at least the boots fit: brown leather and bulky, they were the only things suited to the outside weather...and I liked them—even if admitting it felt like a sin.

"Now, if you don't mind," Carter said, picking a thin length of rope from his pocket. Surrounded by thugs and devoid of strength, when Carter slowly tied my bruised wrists together, I simply glared.

"Oh, when you look at me like that, it makes me wonder what's going through that beautiful head of yours." He had the audacity to wink.

"Go to Hel, Carter."

He grinned. "I'm already there, sweetheart."

* * *

THE TRUNK LUMBERED on as I pulled my tied wrists up from the loop on the floor. They did not budge, my hands moving less than one measly inch.

At least, this time, there was no sack. I could plainly see the thugs puffing away on homemade fags and spliffs. I couldn't decide which scenario was better—at least with the sank over my head, I was left in ignorance.

Gods, it fucking *stank.* Like the very air choked on their foul concoctions.

No windows. Only the rough metal of the truck's walls stared back, teasing me with the unknowable. How close were we to Draco's Pass? How far away had my freedom—my *future*—been thrown?

I pulled against the binding ropes once more, alarm swelling in my gut. Moisture prickled the corner of my eyes as the minutes ticked ominously on.

Keep it together, girl! Ben Carter was approaching with that sick, satisfied grin and I refused to give him any more pleasure.

"Well, our time together is almost over. Although, I must say, it has been *delightful.*"

I spat on the floor.

He mocked a hurt response, his cracked lips pouting, and produced a long, grey cloth from his pocket. I fought against the restraints as his fingers buried into my hair.

"If it's any consolation," he said, forcing the gag into my mouth, "this is not personal. You were simply a means to an end. A bargaining chip I could use to my advantage, to gain what I already own."

He pushed the cloth far down my throat, muffling my moans of defiance, and tied a second muzzle around my head.

With a heavy sigh, Carter sat back and studied me. "I like you, girl, all things considered. You've got spunk."

We shuddered to a stop. Thugs stood to their feet with ammunition jingling in their pockets. A blast of icy air came gushing in, along with small beads of snow whipped up from the ground.

Carter looked at me, a smirk tickling his lips, and pulled me out. Beautiful mountains mocked my dire situation, the blanket of overhead stars laughing at my predicament. It wasn't too late—I could still get out of there. But the rocky walls were too steep, too treacherous. The only way out was behind Carter's black trucks, crowding the pass. I struggled against Carter's hold, clinging to the last bits of desperate hope. His stained fingers buried deep into my flesh, until they felt bone.

Light smothered the rock, headlights beaming like the eyes of some snarling beast. Mason's convoy stopped a little further down the pass, spilling a gaggle of blue coats and long, glinting swords.

I struggled again, shoving at his shoulder. Carter dug a thumb into my back, pressing it into the raw, swollen cuts. Pain swelled, rising to my throat in a long, anguished groan. He removed the pressure and I sagged against him, gasping frigid air through my nose.

Masonians' sharp eyes scrutinised the scene, their eager hands caressing the guns as Mason approached us. The sword upon his hip was mottled with dried blood, hiding its usual gleam. He'd purposefully left it dirtied, as a reminder of the lives he'd taken. To most, Mason's approach would be a sinister sight—the prowl of a monster, a predator, with powers and strength incomprehensible to a thug like Carter. But I knew Mason, perhaps better than any of them. Oh, he'd tried to hide it, but I saw the fragility that clung to him, the exhaustion beneath eyes that still shone wildly, dangerously in the dim light.

With a sharp tug of my arm, Carter approached.

"Mason," he said, smiling. "Pleasure to see you this far north. Not often you grace the Icelands with your presence."

"Extenuating circumstances," Mason spat in response. His eyes briefly flicked to me. "I asked for her *unharmed*."

"Oh, so you *could* feel that, huh? How interesting..." He shrugged. "Well, she's still alive. At any rate, a little adrenaline never hurt anyone, least of all her. She's a wild thing!"

"Yes, I am aware." The violin grew agitated inside my head. "Time is in short supply, Carter. I am a busy man."

"Of course, I'm sure you two have much to discuss. Have you decided on any names yet?"

Mason glowered, a shadow falling across eyes that penetrated the space between us.

"Give her to me." His voice was low, dangerous.

I struggled, panic tightening my chest as Mason came closer and closer... Tears burned my eyes, my entire body rigid, petrified.

Masonians gripped their swords. Carter's thugs loaded their shotguns with exhilarated, wild grins.

"So, looks like I have the Icelands," Carter said. "Agreed?"

"Yes. They are yours."

"Wonderful."

Carter threw me to him. I collided with Mason's chest, radiating angry heat, and quickly doubled back. Mason grabbed my arm, so hard he bruised the bone.

"Enjoy your time with the Icelands, Carter," Mason spat. "Mortal lives are ever so *finite*."

Carter smirked over his shoulder. "You'd know all about that right now, wouldn't you, mate?"

I grimaced around the violin, singing with sickening intensity. Rusty engines roared as Carter's trucks moved away, celebratory shouts and hysteria puncturing those rough metal walls.

Mason dragged me to his own convoy and threw me in the back of a black van.

This is it, I thought. I squeezed my eyes shut, terrified to see Mason's sadism, his hate and his vengeance come punching my pale cheek...

But it was a Masonian who came. He secured my tied hands to a loop in the floor and left me alone.

And then, as disturbing questions sang around my skull, the van doors slammed shut, catapulting me into blackness.

* * *

How long had we been driving? An hour, perhaps a little more.

The truck rumbled and groaned as it fought its way up the steep incline, atop a bumpy, ill-maintained road. Tyres fought hard to cling to the icy mountainside, their sharp spikes sinking deep into its frosty skin.

We lurched to a stop. Footsteps crunched the snow as the slam of metal resonated around my little motorised cell.

The van's door opened, the rush of biting cold prickling my features. A Masonian untied my restraints and, with a tight grip of my arm, pulled me out of the van.

No trees up at this altitude. Only grey rock, smattered with patches of snow.

No sign of Mason.

The Masonian led me a little way up the path. Just before the rim, he stopped. He turned to me and unsheathed his sword. I startled back, gasping, but he tugged me closer and—

Cut me free?

The rope fell from my wrists. With a grating cough, I removed the gag from my mouth and met my freeing Masonian with questioning eyes.

He slid his eyes to the top of the path, where the summit was just out of sight.

Rubbing sore, discoloured wrists, I debated running. I imagined leaping down that mountainous slope, using the snow to carry my body all the way to the base.

Perhaps reading my face, the Masonian plucked out his gun and held it low at his side. *Make a move,* his hard eyes seemed to say, *I dare you.*

My wrists were sore, my back throbbing—and I didn't want to feel any more pain. Was that so wrong of me?

So, I climbed the path.

It led to a rocky ledge that overlooked the entirety of the Icelands. The Territory stretched far ahead, disappearing into the horizon. To the right, a series of short mountains, their tips eroded by the harsh winds, their flanks carved with a patchwork of erosion scars. To the left, the snow-covered land fell into the Slushy Sea: a calamitous ocean, with waves the size of small buildings, smattered with icebergs that glowed silver against the black.

And yet, as the wind howled and the distant thunder of waves found my ears, it was beautiful. A dynamic landscape, untouched by corruption. It was the ultimate frontier, owned solely by the elements.

Standing at the edge of the platform, Mason watched his world with awe. Arms low by his side, he remained stoic as the bitter wind caressed his features.

Cautiously, I approached.

"Beautiful, isn't it?" he said, staring at the view. "The grand, untouched majesty of the last true wilderness of this world. Erinton's Cavern was the last town that littered this landscape, though that too was wiped clean away, like dust upon a table."

Mason turned to me. Eyes sparked a whirlwind of colours in the silver moonlight. "Would you like to see where it was?"

No, I didn't. I didn't want to see the remains of a glorious, bustling town that now contained nothing but bone and ash.

And yet, as hostility quivered those violin strings, I knew better than to test his patience.

His arm slinked around my waist, holding me close. I shivered, despite his warmth.

He pointed to some lonely mountain, placed in the belly of two curving glaciers.

"There, see?" he said, leaning into me. I felt the heat of his cheek, the vibration of his throat with each velvety syllable... "That used to be home to almost six hundred people. A marvellous town, carved directly into ice."

He pressed his mouth to my ear shell, inhaling my scent like a man starved for air.

"Did Campbell take you to that town, Alira?" he asked, his lips stroking each of those seven golden rings. "Did he show you the tunnels of Erinton's Cavern?"

"Yes," I breathed, barely audible.

He smiled, the flat enamel of his teeth brushing against my skin. "Then you saw how beautiful it was, how those six hundred people filled its icy walls with such colour, such vibrancy." A deep sigh, a cloud of pearly mist rising to the stars above. "But then it was infected. Consumed by Ashworth's Rebels, by Ben Carter's thugs. That vibrant town became poisoned by their greed, their guise for *righteousness*. It was a shame, what happened to Erinton's Cavern. It was a travesty it had to end that way, corrupted by filth."

Mason removed his hand from my waist, taking a laboured step forward.

"Ben Carter has corrupted the Ice Territory. He has smeared it with his revulsion, bastardised its beauty. These once pure, exquisite lands are swarming with filth, and he dares to think he can claim ownership?"

A harsh, sneering laugh escaped him.

"I built this Territory! I carved it from my conscious mind, sculpted it with my very hands! Ben Carter is nothing but a parasite on *my* creation!"

The wind stopped. It was sudden, as though someone had flicked a button somewhere.

"Tell me, Alira, do you know how many people live within this Territory? How many brave, innocent souls reside within its boundaries?"

"No," I whispered.

"Three-thousand, eight hundred and two." The world became still, devoid of sound. Even the waves grew silent upon the shore, as though nature itself had bowed beneath Mason's rich voice. "Almost four thousand people—through no fault of their own—have come to reside under Ben Carter's *rule*. The thought is quite nauseating."

Mason glimpsed over his shoulder, smiling. "Well, my dear, I hope you like what fate you and Ben Carter have sealed for these lands."

"Mason, I—"

"Perhaps you should send a prayer to your *Old Gods*. Maybe you should scream to the Icelands and pray they hear your apology."

I outstretched my hand towards him. "Please, Mason," I gasped through the ache inside my chest. "You know I didn't have a choice in this, that I didn't—"

Mason laughed loudly, spitefully, towards the view. "Oh, my dear Alira. If you really believed that, your music wouldn't be screaming with such guilt, remorse... You know what you've done, the part you've played."

My hand dropped to my side. Heavy, much like the truth Mason fed into my muscles, the guilt he now smeared inside my stomach.

"It doesn't matter now," he said, gazing ahead. "Fate comes for us all, one way or another."

In the stillness of that mountaintop, Mason raised his hands.

It was slow at first: the low rumble beneath our feet, the distant howl of wolves, the flurry of birds as they rippled from the few remaining trees...

Mountains trembled. Rocks tumbled down the steep slopes and cascaded to the quaking ground below.

And then the very ground cracked.

Mountains collapsed beneath their weight, the ocean raced along the shore in a seething, thunderous wave. Trees fell into great, bottomless pits, the ground convulsing beneath the power of Mason's lifting hands... His fingers twitched, ever so gently, and glaciers exploded. Millions of icy shards ripped into the landscape.

Pillars of dust reached high into the sky, clouding the destruction with a thick layer of dirt and dust. But yet, beneath that impenetrable veil, the first itch of fire sang. It rose from the ground, glowing embers of liquid rock that oozed into the snow. Steam hissed across the Territory.

The quakes grew. Air roared with the Iceland's last breath...

The land buckled. Rocks collapsed, the earth twisting and turning, destroying everything. It was a pit of destruction, an entire landscape of convulsing ruin...

The encroaching sea flooded giant, angular boulders. Those boulders were the only things left of the Ice Territory.

As the echo of screams licked the cold, dusty air, Mason lowered his hands.

I fell to my knees, unable to support myself. No tears for the Icelands, no words of despair or prayers to the Old Gods.

There was just shock. Pure, numbing shock.

As the waves crashed and tumbled against the rocks, Mason turned to me. The violin sang with disappointment—with anguish and regret—but there was no anger inside his music. Just sorrow. Mournful melodies for a land that lay ruined beneath his fingertips.

Unable to move, unable to feel, I was still as Mason crouched before me. His sword scraped against the frozen ground, his eyes taking a final longing gaze to the destruction.

"This is *my* World, Alira," he said. "It was born from my imagination, laboured by my hands."

As he'd so often done, Mason pushed a single piece of hair behind my ringed ear. Using all my effort, I moved my sore eyes to meet his. They were heavy and bloodshot. Incredibly despondent.

"You were born from the World I created. Your very soul was a result of Ragnarök, all those years ago and without me, my dear, you would not exist. You are not meant to fight me."

Mason's stare grew sinister, his eyes overshadowed with the anger I knew so well.

"But yet, here we are. So much remorse for your actions, so much turmoil. Did Ben Carter share that same turmoil, that same guilt, as his *reward* buckled and cracked beneath his feet? Did he and his fellow Gang regret their actions as their *prize* came tumbling around them?"

He stared at the Icelands' remains. Screams dispersed as the calamitous waves licked away the survivors.

"It doesn't matter now, does it? The Icelands are no more. Ben Carter is with them, entombed for eternity within their remains."

A gentle breeze rippled his back hair, his tired eyes squinting in the cold.

"But not us. We linger on. We survive the slaughter and the turmoil. Why? Because it is what we are made for, my dear. You, as well as I. We both have a purpose in this World, a part to play. We are nothing but two instruments in an Orchestra built for a hundred, and yet our place is so important, so necessary for the music to sing in all of its glory…"

Mason turned to me again, with contempt.

"You're not the only one to have run, Alira. There have been many, many more before you, and yet destiny always prevails. More mountains are moved, more people die. Don't you see? One man's actions—Carter, Ashworth, Anders—have no bearing upon our future because what are they but ants upon a mountainside? So easily squished as that same mountain crumbles beneath their feet."

A gentle pinch of my chin, the heat of his breath as he moved closer.

"And mountains *will* crumble, Alira. My Family's Line has endured for over three-thousand years. I'll be damned if it ends with me."

17

———

The van rumbled against uneven ground. Sitting in its metal belly, I awaited my fate with numb understanding. Opposite me, the Masonian's eyes were sharp and alert, ensuring I did not cause trouble.

The shackles, sharp and biting against my wrists, stung as I moved. Slowly, I tested the holding chain that connected me to the floor. It was taut. For fear I'd wear my wrists down to the bone, I'd given up trying to fight it.

After Mason led me down from that mountain, he threw me into the van and slammed the door with a ferocity that nearly burst my eardrums.

A few short minutes later, the doors sprung open again. I expected to see Mason. I thought that was it, that my torture would begin. I imagined the Masonians guarding a van that rocked back and forth...

But no, that's not what happened. I was left unharmed, with the only tell of Mason's sadism etching into my bruised wrists. Now, only that watchful Masonian kept me company. An older man, years of experience and a nose left crooked from a firm right hook. But he remained inside his own bubble, with only the occasional flick of a brown eye.

And so, I waited.

Visions of the Icelands kept coming back to haunt me. Flashes of their destruction kept speeding across my vision. I forcibly shook them away. No, I couldn't think about them. I couldn't imagine all those innocent lives lost to my fucking stupidity.

Choices have consequences. That much was obvious. Never did I believe an entire Territory had to pay for my decision on the beach that day.

No, it's not your fault, girl. I was tired of blaming myself for the actions of others.

Yet, as a solitary tear trickled down my cheek, I closed my eyes and allowed the irrational guilt to fill me, to trickle down my limbs until its toxic taste consumed everything. I knew it was ridiculous to blame myself for Mason's depravity, yet those thoughts still buried deep inside my bones, merging with the marrow until they were impossible to claw out.

After a while, I simply accepted it.

The van shuddered to a stop. It was sudden, evidently unprecedented. My watchful Masonian hopped out of the van, demanding to know the problem.

"Avalanche," a voice replied. "Completely covered the road."

I struggled forwards to see Mason march through the snow, a rolled piece of paper in his hand. Most likely a map. I tried to keep them in my line of vision but the van doors slammed shut.

I held my breath, listening to the commotion outside: muffled words, the occasional shout of frustration. Yes, they were preoccupied.

I quickly spat the hidden earring—taken from Ben Carter's horrific chest of clothes— into my hand, having slipped it beneath my tongue just before Mason grabbed my arm on that mountainside. Now, as my captors were otherwise engaged, I bent the hook. The keyhole in the shackles glinted at me, begging to be taken. I grimaced through the stings in my wrists as I picked the lock.

The earring jammed. I fought harder against the shackles, squeezing tears from my eyes.

Come on, you fucking bitch...

The shackles clinked open.

No time for relief. I removed the shackles and lowered the chain to the floor, without a single sound.

I positioned myself; calmed my raging heart. I only had one shot at this...

The Masonians' plan was simple: turn the convoy around, take the long route. A good plan, all things considered.

Snow crunched. Doors unlocked.

I kicked sharply against the doors, throwing the Masonian into the snow, and jumped from the van. Ten—no *fifteen*—Masonians looked at me, shock percolating their features. Mason's expression was the most noticeable of all.

I turned to the veil of trees and ran.

"Leave her," I heard Mason grunt. "She's mine."

I clambered my way through the unyielding blanket of snow, my shoes slipping against the branches buried within. Moonlight poured over the forest, bathing my route with silver as the aurora danced blue and green at my impending victory.

Mason's heavy footsteps grew louder, closer. I quickened my pace, terrified to glimpse back and see each swirl of *rage* within those gorgeous eyes...

But my cuts were oozing. Pain throbbed down my spine. My pace slowed and I tried to keep up the speed, begging my treacherous body to ignore my injuries and keep running, but the ferocious pain grew hindering.

My toe caught beneath a hidden branch. I tumbled forwards.

Mason was upon me. He grabbed the back of my coat—the colour of claret—and pulled me back. I slipped my arms out of the fabric, desperate to maintain the distance, desperate to *run!*

Cold fingers gripped my baggy jumper. I pulled against him, stretching the fabric. Something hard dug into my back, directly in the middle of a deep, oozing cut.

I gasped, my back arching with the pain. It radiated down my spine, throbbing with each heartbeat.

"No, s-stop!" I shrieked, as he dug his thumb in harder.

I tried to double round, to rip his hands away. Arms encircled me.

We fell.

I tried to crawl away, to find a foothold and propel myself up and—

Mason grabbed my ankle and pulled. He rolled me on my back and crawled over me, pinning me down. I tried to fight him, to buck him off. I rolled from side to side, but his weight easily held me down. My bruised, bloody wrists were held tight above my head as his knees spread my legs.

His mouth twisted into a sneer. "This all looks very familiar..."

I tried to buck him off again, to propel him to one side or the other. It was no use. The pain, the fear—it overwhelmed me.

I sank into the snow. No more fighting, no more struggling. I consigned myself to my fate with a pounding pulse and eyes thick with unshed tears.

Mason just watched me, his face devoid of colour, his cheeks gaunt and shallow. A shadow of the man I knew, a mere echo of the man with whom I once shared such passion.

"What are you doing?" he hissed; his voice, though laced with anger, was so small and fragile. "I want you to *run*, Alira. I want to feel you fight beneath me. I want to hear you *scream.*"

Specks of snow prickled my cheeks. Beneath those icy waves and a sky dancing with blue and green light, exhaustion clung to each of those sore, *tired* muscles. As my fragile body sank deeper into the snow, I abruptly realised the irrational release in just...lying there.

"What's the point?" I whispered. "You'll always win."

Mason huffed out bitter amusement, then grimaced, as if he felt pain —*my* pain—inside his head.

"What do I sound like, Mason? Angry, relieved, terrified?"

Mason stared at me, his eyes swirling with colour. I gazed into those eyes, skimming the outer edges of his angular, jagged soul. Our Connection reignited, spreading numb fingers through my skull.

"I want you to hear my music," I whispered. "I want you to listen to it, to feel it scratch and shriek inside your head."

The despair rose: a nagging, bloating ball inside my heart. It mixed with the ache, suddenly so forceful, that rose high into my chest.

"No, Mason," I said, my voice breaking. "I won't fight you. I won't try to stop you. It's inevitable, what you will do to me, so what's the point of running anymore? What's the point of delaying what I know will happen? So no, I won't scream. I won't make a single sound because I want you to hear— to *feel—everything.*"

Something changed in Mason's eyes. Only for a second: a swirl of some unknown emotion. As soon as it was there, it was gone. The anger swiftly returned, making a mess of Mason's hidden emotions.

Without a word, he heaved us to our feet.

✱ ✱ ✱

WE TRUDGED THROUGH THE SNOW, towards the vans.

His violin continuously sang: so quiet, so consigned to the inevitability of his future actions. No doubt my piano rung equal inside his head. Did it sing dread or regret? I delved into my own emotions and realised that I couldn't tell the difference anymore.

Occasionally, Mason's eyes would flick to me. Only a brief glance. They scanned my complexion and quickly returned to the forest ahead.

We continued in silence.

The trees dispersed, revealing the convoy between the frosted trunks.

Mason's pace slowed. He tugged on my arm, halting my advance, and gazed ahead with narrowing eyes.

Gunshots peppered the air, echoing throughout the trees. Heart to my throat, Mason and I watched his Masonians fall to the ground. One after the other, their crimson life seeping across the road.

Brown coats moved up ahead and the frantic shouts of armed strangers cut through us.

"Let's go," Mason hissed.

A sharp tug back into the trees, his grip tightening.

The first stranger stepped into the forest, studying our footprints.

"Run," Mason said. "Run, *now!*"

Even as Mason's hand slid from my arm, I remained running by his side, desperate to escape the claws of ravenous, dangerous men at our heels.

I tripped, collapsing to my knees. Mason heaved me up, back to his side. Gunshots roared on either side of us, the panic—the *terror*—growing in my lungs with each pounding step.

Mason fired shots at our pursuers. The bangs percolated the space, ricocheting around the trees. We ducked as more gunshots whipped passed our ears and hit nearby trees. Splinters of wood spat from each collision.

Throwing me aside, Mason took his aim with cheeks flushed with anger and eyes spitting malicious light. Bullets whizzed past his ears, but he was too incensed to care.

One attacker fell to the ground, followed by another, then another. Out of bullets, Mason unsheathed his sword with an incensed howl and held it high above an injured, scrambling man. A fast swoosh, a sickening squelch, and the forest returned to silence.

With great, relieved breaths, Mason closed his eyes. The aurora's light caressed his features as his violin breathed gentle melodies.

Trudging towards me, Mason sheathed his bloodied sword.

"We need to move," he said. "I doubt they're the last and—"

He stopped, delicate lines marring his brow.

I returned his stare, vacantly, as the numbness spread from my belly. Slowly, with great effort, I looked at the blood seeping through my jumper, dripping to the pristine snow below. That same blood coated my trembling fingers.

I looked at Mason.

"No..." he breathed.

My legs collapsed beneath me. For a short moment, as I lay in the deep snow, I gazed at the aurora above. I thought of my Pa, smiling, welcoming me with open arms.

It's time to come home, my little Wolf-Cub.

Mason skidded to his knees and cradled my face, his quickly losing colour.

"Stay with me," he whispered desperately.

He lifted the hem of my jumper to inspect the bullet wound. *"Fuck..."* he hissed beneath his breath. Large clouds of mist erupted from his mouth as he frantically searched our surroundings.

The aurora was so pretty, dancing across that star-studded sky. I wanted to touch it, to wave my fingers through its pastel hue...

Blackness encroached along the sides of my vision. Mason's out-of-tune, erratic violin slowly faded from my mind.

"Fuck!" he yelled. He cradled my face, forcing our diamond eyes to lock. "No, you're not leaving me, not now—not when I'm this close!"

A large groan escaped my throat as Mason plucked my numb body from the snow. I absorbed his heat as he carried me; such a beautiful contrast to my icy blood.

Everything became disjointed. A whirlwind of visions that were erratic, without context.

First, a forest smattered with tall trees, caressed by those dancing lights that shimmered strange and colourful prisms upon the snow.

Next, a town, its braziers alit for the whole Territory to see. A haze of orange bled across the sky, all but smothering the lustre of the light above.

Screams punctured my ears. Through the forced slits in my eyes, I saw people running, escaping Mason and the trembling ground beneath their feet. Pots were knocked over, deep cracks formed in the ground, dogs barked and whined, livestock shrieked and squealed as they all ran from the town's impending doom.

Mason kicked a door open. He grunted, then moved to the next one. Another door was kicked down. A family cowered inside: a mother held her two children close, covering their eyes as the Destroyer of the Old World stood in their doorway.

Mason cursed beneath his breath and moved to the next building: the town's inn. People cowered beneath the tables, escaping the torrent of dust and rubble pouring in great waves from the rafters. The room was ablaze with the fiery, orange light reflected in Mason's frenzied eyes.

"Get out!" he yelled.

A stampede of feet as the world continued to quake.

Mason hurried further into the inn. Strange, I'd never heard him so breathless.

I felt myself being placed upon a stool. Mason supported my weak body and cradled my fingers upon rough, cold keys.

A piano.

But no teasing tingles raced up my arms.

He pressed my finger down. A singular, beautiful note erupted.

The music found me, digging its claws deep, deep, *deeper* inside my soul. My fingers danced and I cringed at each of those harsh, out-of-tune keys and yet I was unable to stop, unable to think, feel, *breathe*. The music devoured me with each chord, each note, each piece of musical bliss that caressed my injured flesh.

Those five long lesions healed, the skin stitching itself together with musical thread. My wrists, so bruised and raw, returned to their usual colour. Sensation returned to my numb body, warmth exploding as a bloodied bullet clinked between my feet.

And then, through the bursts of musical ecstasy, exhaustion came. My eyes closed, my muscles grew heavy. No sooner had the last musical note echoed, than my awareness slip away, falling into Mason's open arms.

18

Fire crackled.

I heard it first, prickling at the first hints of my consciousness.

Next, that warm glow. It caressed my face, my features.

Sensation spread.

I flexed my muscles. No pain, no aches of injury. Only the delicate release of tension, as if from a long, satisfying stretch.

I twitched my hands. They remained resting upon my belly, bound together with rope.

Slowly, my eyes creaked open.

Fire burned. A modest size for a campfire, for its flames were tall and healthy. It spread its golden glow upon the rocky walls of the cave, highlighting each little crevasse, each minuscule crack, every winding vein of black, white, olive, red...

The firelight gleamed against a bloodied sword, carefully placed against the wall. It lay next to a silver revolver, emblazoned with an emblem of a stag.

My eyes scanned further, to the hessian sack that spilled a few lonesome potatoes. Next, across the smooth skins of six spent bullets, still scattered across the floor.

Mason leant against the rocky wall, both legs bent before him. He was still except for his hands, pulling apart the remains of a charred potato and periodically placing a steaming piece inside his mouth.

Those dangerous, *beautiful* eyes fixed on me. Bloodshot and bordered with dark circles, those diamond irises clung to the glow of the fire and sparkled like two orange garnets. Yet, their fragility shone. It intensified the gauntness of those cheeks, the ashen hue to his skin...

He looked exhausted.

Slowly, under those two watchful eyes, I pulled myself up. The entrance to the cave was large and wide, boasting the view. We looked to be on the side of a small cliff, level with the tips of those snow-covered trees. Mountains punctured the distance, stretching to an aurora shining brighter than ever.

"Where are we?" I asked. Cold punctured my healed back as I leant against the wall, directly opposite Mason.

"Does it matter?" Steam rushed from the potato in his fingers as he placed a cooked morsel in his mouth.

I studied the sword to his side, followed by the piles of spent bullet littering the cave. "Who attacked us?"

A heavy sigh inflated Mason's chest. "Difficult to say. They could have been stragglers from the Mulch Gang, or Ashworth's Rebels."

"No..." I said, shaking my head. "Must've been Carter's thugs. Ashworth doesn't want me killed."

"They weren't aiming for you," Mason spat.

I sank beneath the intensity of his glare, falling further against the wall as his violin turned spiteful.

I tested the rope around my wrists: immobile. The tips of my fingers tingled and I saw the fresh bruise covering those scars. A hard swallow as I scanned my clothes, shifting on the stone, trying to decipher—to *feel*—any evidence of assault.

Frowning, I met Mason's tired glare. "You haven't... I-I mean, did you—"

"You almost *died!* I barely got you to that piano in time, so forgive me if that doesn't get one *in the mood.*"

The silence was so tense, I couldn't even feel relief. I swallowed around the knot in my throat, unsure with how to proceed.

"Thank you for saving me," I whispered, after far too many heartbeats.

Mason huffed and threw the potato's remains into the flames. Sparks erupted to the rocky ceiling. "Don't flatter yourself. I'm just not prepared to wait another few decades for a child."

Another difficult swallow, this time across the sudden ache in my chest.

"How long was I out?" I asked.

"A few days."

I looked to those bloodshot eyes and the fatigue clinging to his skin. "When was the last time you slept?"

He did not reply.

Only the fire could puncture the thickness of the air between us.

I chewed the scar on my lip. "So...what happens now? What are you going to do?"

Mason's glare could cut ice. "I bet you'd love me to answer that, wouldn't you? So you can run all the way back to Campbell and spill all my plans." Another huff, directed to the fire. "You can't wait to go running back to him."

"Is that why you lied to me?" I snapped, my inner temperature rising. "Is that why you told me he was dead, to stop me from running back to him?"

"Perhaps. Maybe I just wanted to save you from an uncomfortable truth."

"Oh really?" I scoffed. "And what truth might that be?"

"That he left you to me, my dear," Mason said, with a cruel smile. "He knew the fate that would await you the moment he put Slavery's shackles around your wrists."

"He did that to save me, he didn't have a choice but to—"

"Campbell *abandoned* you, Alira. He left you to Slavery's shackles—he left you in Maelstrom, within easy reach of me—and now you're so ready to sacrifice yourself for *him?*" Mason laughed darkly to the flickering flames. "Where is his devotion to you, hm? What possible reason do you have to throw away your entire life, your *destiny*, for a man who gives you nothing in return?"

His echo lingered in my skull. "How *dare* you! Campbell didn't *abandon* me; he isn't just *using* me for his own gains!"

"Isn't he?" Mason raised two dark eyebrows, a callous smirk on his lips. "Did Campbell ever tell you how he escaped?"

"Yes, actually," I said, scowling. "One of your Masonian stooges forgot to confiscate his shoelace, so he strangled him with it and escaped the Barracks."

Mason's mouth formed a wide, unsettling grin. "Is *that* what he told you?"

A soft chuckle broke the barrier of Mason's chest, racing over the fire as my skin cooled. "No, my dear, he wasn't in the Barracks—not this time, at least. He was in Maelstrom, about to be hanged in Bolton Square, but Ashworth got wind of his immediate execution and ransacked the place. In the struggle, they freed Campbell and escaped Maelstrom without even a backwards glimpse."

Campbell's words rushed back to me with the breath of outside wind: *I couldn't get into Maelstrom, let alone you out... God, I wished they'd taken me there —I'd would have bashed down every Aristocratic door until I found you...*

Mason saw my heart sink, heard my piano quiver, and his smile grew.

"So, what stopped Campbell from saving you? With all that firepower, with my Masonians lying dead, why didn't he save you from Emilia's clutches? He knew where you were of course, I was sure to spit it in his face mere hours beforehand. So then, why didn't he save you?"

I remained quiet. Excuses swirled around my head, swimming in and out of those angry violin strings. I swallowed each of them, unwilling to have Mason wipe away my last bit of faith.

There must have been a reason why he left me: not enough firepower, too many Masonians... Maybe he was injured, relying on Ashworth to get him out and save his own skin.

Maybe Mason was just lying to me. Again.

Whatever the truth, I couldn't hide my inner turmoil. Mason revelled in it. "You see, my dear, Campbell doesn't care about you. As soon Ashworth cut his ropes, the Free People's Rebellion was his only priority. You were simply collateral, plucked from my grasp as soon as they realised you could be useful to them. And you are useful, aren't you?"

"I'm helping them, I—"

"For what?" he yelled, eyes blazing. "*Why* are you helping them, what possible motive could you have?"

"You dare ask me *why*? I want to be rid of you, Mason! I want to live without pain and fear!"

"But you're not going to live at all if Ashworth wins! You'll die with me, for God's sake!"

Emotion halted. My mind empty of all except Mason's words. Mason observed my startled reaction, and his nasty smile grew.

"They haven't told you, have they?" A guffaw of laughter to the rocks above. "Oh, this really is priceless! All this time, you've been berating *my* dishonesty and yet failing to see the absolute *flurry* of lies your precious Campbell's been spitting in your face."

"I don't believe you…" Campbell wouldn't lie to me about something like that. He just wouldn't.

Mason laughed again, shaking his head. "We're Connected, Alira. If your body dies, your soul lives on in a new body. But if *I* die, that's it. My body and soul are gone forever, and our Connection will ensure that your soul is destroyed along with mine. Not that Ashworth or Campbell care about that, of course. To them, it's just two birds with one stone, in a matter of speaking."

"Campbell *cares* about me, he wouldn't want me dead!"

"Campbell wants *me* dead, and if that means losing you in the process, then so be it." Mason leant against the wall with a bitter huff. "Whether you like it or not, I am your only hope at a future."

"What future?" I scoffed, a lone tear trickling. "Do you think I'm *excited* for my future with you? You think I'm *excited* to have my eyes gouged out or to have my children taken away from me?"

Mason stared vacantly ahead. "You made your choice at Giant's Respite."

"Because what other choice did I have!" My voice echoed around the stillness of the cave, dragging down Mason's unapologetic eyes. "Why would I come with you after what you did?"

"You didn't give me a choice."

"No, you *chose* to hurt me, after I'd given you everything!'

"*I needed my immortality!*" His voice echoed around the cave as wolves howled in the distance, sharing my pain as birds rippled from nearby trees. "I wish I could have given you time—I really do—but I needed to crush the Rebellion!"

A horrible, dejected smile tickled my lips. "I would have given you a child, Mason. You know I would have."

"After how long? A month, a year? How many more men would I lose before you willingly conceived? How many more bombs would it take before they finally finished us off, hm?"

The ache in my chest grew. It bloated inside my heart, my lungs, until I could barely breathe. "That's all I am to you, isn't it? I'm just a machine, a simple tool for you to gain your immortality."

Mason scoffed beneath his breath, rolling his eyes to the ceiling.

"You're my *mate*, Alira," he said. "What part of that fucking title don't you understand?"

More silence threatened. I stared at the fire and wiped my wet cheeks with bound hands. There, spurting our demons on the walls of that cave, I thought of my past, my life with Mason. I thought of my sons, existing for the shortest of times.

"I miss them, Mason," I whispered, my voice as broken as my soul. "I miss them *so* much..."

A short pause, my words dispersing through the empty air.

"I know," he replied, gently.

Another pause echoed, only cut by the crackling fire.

"Ashworth killed them, Alira. You're helping the man who *killed* our children..."

His violin sang loudly inside my head, filled with such grief, such resentment. I bowed my head, unable to look at him. That truth swirled nastily around my belly, washing away my retort.

Mason huffed bitterly beneath his breath. "It doesn't matter anymore, does it? You made your choice."

"And you made yours," I angrily shot back. "Don't you dare believe that you're blameless in this, Mason."

"Oh, I know I'm not. Unlike you, I can admit my mistakes."

"You think I can't?"

"Of course, you can't. You're so fixated on vengeance, so obsessed with making me pay for what I've done, that you're blind to your own self-destruction. You're at the precipice of some great cliff, about to walk straight off the edge and yet unable to see it."

"I know the mistakes I've made. I know I made the wrong choice at Giant's Respite."

Mason's bloodless lips tilted into a bitter sneer. "What changed your mind, hm? Was it when you knew I'd find you, when you heard the Ice Territory's last breath? Don't insult me by pretending your *regret* was anything more than your own self-pity."

"Then what do you regret, huh? You regret the deed itself or the fact that you lost me?"

"You're here, aren't you? I didn't *lose* you—"

"You lost me the moment you *forced* me, the moment you threw it all away—our only chance to be a proper family!"

"*Family?*" Mason laughed darkly. "You know *nothing* about Family!"

"I was a *mother*, Mason! But what were you, huh? A *monster*, not caring for me or the life I was creating, but for your own selfish gain! You don't care about me; you don't care about your child!"

"And what do you care about, hm? Killing me? You'd rather throw away your only chance—your *only* chance to live a blissful existence—to try and spite me? *Why, Alira?* Why are you doing this? *Why* are you throwing out your *entire* future for Ashworth and his *fucking* Rebellion?"

"*Because I loved you!*"

Silence.

It encompassed the space between us, ripping away Mason's retorts. In that silence, he just looked at me. Eyes wide, his jaw clamped firmly shut. Shell-shocked. Utterly stupefied by my disclosure.

Over the lingering silence inside my head, I took a deep, shaky breath.

"Why did I join Ashworth? Because, even after everything you've done, everything you've done to *me*... I loved you, Mason..."

Tears roared down my face. "I was so happy..." I whispered through shaking, despairing breaths. "I looked forward to the future, I wanted so much to believe that my life would get better—to be free of all the pain and the suffering... And it was—those eleven weeks were the happiest of my entire life..."

Disgust ballooned inside my belly at such a disclosure. Not at the words themselves, but the *sincerity* of them. And there, from within that ball of shame, anger rose and spat from my grimace.

"That's what the music—my destiny, this *life*—has done to me, Mason. That the only form of happiness I've ever had was with the likes of *you*..."

Fists clenched around the rope. "And I *hate* you for that..."

And there, as I listened to the stillness, I swallowed past the pain in my chest. The guilt, the shame of my own emotions—my own *weakness*

—remained as a tightly wound ball, hidden someplace deep. I wanted to throw that ball away. I wanted to rip it apart, to destroy it much like Mason had destroyed me.

And yet, despite everything, I couldn't. It remained elusive, forever hiding somewhere inside of me.

So, I just listened to the stillness of that cave, hating myself.

* * *

A while had passed.

The aurora had changed colour, morphing from a veil of blues and greens into more pinkish hues. It sat gloriously atop an indigo sky. Occasionally an owl would swoop by, its long feathers rippling in the breeze.

Mason gazed into the fire. He was stoic, unmoving. His violin had returned inside my head: quiet, subdued, trembling with disbelief.

I stared at Mason, and the exhaustion that clung to his every seam. His eyes, though open, were forever fighting the weights dragging them down, forcing them to look ahead despite the urge to roll back inside his skull.

I looked to my bound hands. My future dangled by a fraying thread; my entire existence determined by a man such as Mason.

Did my abhorrent disclosure change the course of that future? Perhaps. Perhaps not.

The Icelands' screams trembled in my ears. How many people did he say? Almost four-thousand?

My heart sank at each lost life. Those poor people, those *children*, that now lay buried beneath mounds of lifeless rock.

Mason had already caused one Ragnarök. What was to say he wouldn't cause another?

Regret was already looming, burning a hole at the back of my head. But then, what was the alternative? To bow beneath Mason for the rest of eternity, to stand back while thousands more perished beneath his fist?

He did not deserve my loyalty. He did not deserve my cooperation.

I stared at the man who was my captor and remembered how happy I was. I remembered the smiles we shared, each loving caress. The way he gazed at me, enraptured by my smile. I remembered the warmth from his hand, pressed against the small bump that pushed beneath my clothes. Through the disgust, the *abhorrence* of such memories, I missed that life. I missed waking up without fearing my future.

Tears licked my eyelashes. I lifted my head to the ceiling, determined to keep them subdued.

When my head lowered, Mason stared at me. Motionless, yet he housed so much indecision.

"Alira," he eventually said. His voice was so weary, so...*fragile.* "I want you to have a future. I don't want you to be so...*consumed* with vengeance that you destroy us both."

He licked his lips, his tired eyes glowing orange in the firelight. "Forget Ashworth, forget Campbell. Let us forget the errors of the past and move forward with our lives."

"How can we?" I whispered, meeting that diamond stare for the first time in what felt like centuries. "Mason, you've killed so many people, hurt so many more... Even me, even after..."

More tears escaped as the words just kept coming. "You just don't get it. I stopped being afraid of my future and do you know how hard that was? To look past my early imprisonment and fully *enjoy* the prospect of spending my life with *you?*"

A violin sang loudly, mournfully inside my head. So much regret lay inside those vibrating strings, each one singing a tune that spoke of such penitence.

Everything was so heavy, the very air weighing me down. "That future's gone," I said, utterly exhausted. "You wiped that future clean away, so forgive me if I'm not running back to you with my arms wide open."

A deep sigh inflated Mason's lung. He was so fraught, so...*apprehensive?*

"But we can make another future," he said, quietly, as though the walls would crack. "I'm not asking you to forgive me for what I've done, I'm simply asking...*begging* you to reconsider your current course of action before we do something we *both* regret."

The pause weighed heavily upon the firelit air.

"And you *will* regret it, Alira," he whispered, dangerously. "But I don't want it to come to that, I never have. So now, this is a chance for both of our past decisions to be wiped away. A new start, one not of happiness but of *contentment*. We'll both get what we want, without any more pain."

Regret. I could already feel it, climbing up my gullet. What part of that cave would I regret the most when Mason eventually dragged me out of it?

I stared into those hard diamond irises and saw the pleads, the hope that sparkled with glorious intensity.

"Forget Giant's Respite," he said, with a tired shake of his head. "Forget my threats, my anger... I'm asking you to give yourself—to give *us*—a future. And it won't be one filled with bubbles and rainbows—of course it won't be —but it will be a future nonetheless."

A light, warm and comforting, shone upon the notion of having a future at all.

"I need a child to regain my immortality," he said bluntly, eyebrows raised. "But *you* need a child because you are a Protector, and God knows you will be a spectacular one."

I imagined my belly being round and bulbous, pulsing delicately with the movements from within. For a fleeting moment, a rush of excitement rose inside my chest. It was quickly replaced with longing—a hard and desperate longing— and although I knew it was my own sordid destiny pulling the strings of my heart, I was helpless but to imagine a future where I could hold my baby in my arms.

"I'm scared, Mason. I don't want you to take my son away..."

"I won't," he replied, softly. "You have my word, Alira."

His *word*. What use was Mason's *word*, his false promises, his disclosures of fucking mercy only to cut me where it most hurt.

Yes, his word meant very little.

But as I saw the pleading behind those eyes, as I heard the desperation within each of those quivering strings, perhaps there was some truth to Mason after all?

Maybe, despite all of this, there was some hope for a future I could smile at?

A leap of faith was all it took. I traversed the cave and fell to my knees before him. For a moment, he simply stared. Drinking me in, like he was parched for me.

The music was mellow, soothing, as his lips touched mine. I tested their familiarity with delicate movements, and as the hate and disgust swirled nastily around my belly, I just pushed it away, far away. I locked it in a broken box, only held together with chains and unequal slabs of wood, so I might consider my actions later.

But at that moment, as our tongues danced with the aurora, I could only focus on my future: the glorious promise of a life without fear, without running—a life where I could *finally* hold my son, to beam at the sparkle within his own eyes...

Mason's hands climbed my arms, holding me so gently. Slowly, he lowered me to the ground.

Control. I needed *control!*

I quickly rolled him over, straddling him. Here, feeling the warmth of his body, I forced aside the rush of memories and focussed only on that cave: the cool breeze fluttering my hair, the gentle flicker of the firelight that slowly burnt away the last of my morality.

I deepened the kiss. Excitement ballooned inside my torso, willed on by musical desperation, and I *needed* to touch him, to move my hands across his body.

Mason could see this, could sense my hands aching. He reached around his back and brought out that curved knife. Excitement deformed, whipped away by the shape of the blade, the sinister lustre of the polished bone handle...

As Mason swiftly cut the rope from my bruised wrists, I stared at that knife, frozen and horrified. How many people had that knife cut? How many lives had it claimed?

As Isla's agony echoed around my memories, my looming choices suddenly felt so heavy...

Mason followed my fearful gaze and threw the knife to the opposite wall. It clattered loudly against the stone floor, ringing my head.

"No, don't look at that." He cradled my face, forcing our eyes to lock. "*Look at me.*"

So, I did.

I stared hard inside those diamond eyes, relished the cold numbness inside my skull. It was so freeing, so liberating that I could think of nothing else...

As our lips collided, as I moved my hands beneath his shirt and unbuckled his belt, all I could think of was how *right* this was. Even as our moans echoed around that small cave, as our pleasure spiked in one agonising release, I did not think of the consequences of my actions. All I could think of was *him*, and the future he dangled before my eyes.

I craved that future, with every fibre of my being.

19

The jumper scratched my skin as I dressed. I rubbed my hands up and down my arms, trying to dispel the lingering sense of...*unease* that squirmed just below. The wool was stiff, for it was still caked in my blood. I admired the circular scar on my abdomen; a good shot, all things considered.

"There's a Masonian camp around ten miles from here." Mason quickly buckled his belt and set to work on his weapons, securing them around his hips. "With luck, we should be there by nightfall."

I nodded, silently, and hastily buttoned my jeans. I felt dirty, like I had taken a bath in thick, black grease.

Dawn approached. A line of pale blue inched across the horizon, tickling the tops of those snow-covered trees. The aurora faded with every passing minute. Now, without its ethereal glow, darkness loomed. Shadows engulfed the trees, hiding their grandeur within inky blackness. The forest looked frightening.

Mason touched my arm. I quickly recoiled, as though burned by him.

"You should take this."

I followed his gaze to the curved knife he held; the blade hidden by a leather holster that neatly contained the screams. Visions of Isla's tortured expression loomed around me, teasing the slick skin of her mutilated eyebrow. I swallowed the images with difficulty, and took Mason's knife.

"Why are you giving this to me?" I met his eyes, for the first time in what seemed like hours, and saw their inherent sparkle, their sheer will to dominate everything. They scared me.

"The men who attacked us are likely still out there. We may need to defend ourselves."

"But aren't you immortal now?"

Something squirmed deep inside my gut. Some horrible concoction that sent cool nausea rushing.

Mason sighed. "There are no guarantees. We should know in a week in or two."

His hand twitched, as if to touch me. He ultimately decided against it and wandered to the other end of the cave, searching through that hessian sack until he picked out a small box of ammunition. Bullets clinked as he reloaded his revolver.

With a heavy sigh, I strapped the dagger around my hips and tucked it beneath my jumper.

"Regardless of my immortality, you can still die," Mason said, sending me a wary glimpse.

Dread sank into my heart, already heavy with the weight of my choices.

"Yeah, thanks for reminding me," I muttered dryly.

Mason smiled to me. A tender smile, so full of pride. It lifted his entire face, wiping away the fatigue. "Try not to worry, my dear. Once we reach Black Ice Cavern, starving mountain lions won't be able to sniff you out."

I managed a small smile yet was unable to meet his eye.

"Let's go," Mason said, kicking the smouldering remains of campfire. "The sun will be up shortly."

* * *

OUTSIDE THE CAVE, a merciless cold fluttered through the strands of my hair. I closed my eyes, listening to the tenderness of Mason's music as the wind carried my breath.

Deep snow crunched loudly beneath my boots as the world continued to lighten. Colour inched across the horizon, hugging the layer of trees. Before long, it would turn red, then gold, then bright blue. A new day beckoned, aching to cast its light upon the New World.

Despite everything, this world was my home. Whether by Mason's hand or Ashworth's, I didn't want to see my home destroyed. I wanted to *protect* it. Was that why I'd screamed my pleasure around that firelit cave? Perhaps that was one reason. One of many.

Ahead of me, Mason trudged through the thick snow. I stared at the back of his blue coat and remembered the bullet holes I'd once seen plague the fabric. They evidenced something entirely taken for granted, tokens of an impossible truth that just kept screaming.

But now, such evidence was gone. Stitched away, with whatever was left of Mason's invincibility.

A tender hand fell to my belly, imagining the possibilities within.

It snapped away just as quickly, scalded by the burning truth of what such a thing would mean. I blinked back guilty tears.

Mason's head twitched, ever so slightly. He must have heard the sudden change to my music, the way my inner *humanity* scolded my decisions. Hands balled at his sides, then relaxed just as quickly.

Carefully, I listened to his violin. It remained calm, singly softly within my skull.

We continued on.

I remembered the first time Campbell told me about Mason. How he said, with no ambiguous tone, that Mason wanted to kill me, to erase my diamond eyes from his reality before they had time to destroy us all. Everything was so simple back then: run from Mason, whatever the cost.

As it turned out, the truth of destiny was far from *simple.*

Campbell's lie still stung. It was a lie fed over so many years. So many falsehoods he had spoken, so many lies fed over our campfires. Would he lie to me now? Was he *still* lying to me?

Trust seemed awfully hard to find. There was always a reason to lie. Very few could call themselves free of fabrication.

That was something Mason was so incredibly guilty of. He enjoyed the way his lies tasted upon his tongue.

Was Mason lying to me now? Was the future he dangled before me nothing more than bait, concealing the sharp end of a torturer's hook?

But then, what was the alternative? To continue running from him? Yes, I could survive the wilderness on my own—I was a Herder, after all. Aside from everything else, I was born in the harsh cold of Mason's World and grew up surviving its wintry embrace.

But it would be a lonely life. Incredibly lonely.

The sun peeked above those trees, dousing the world in young light. Beneath her gaze, I thought to the wider members of the Rebellion. All those innocent people who also deserved to live in Mason's world.

What would he do to Anya and Heidi and all the other people under Ashworth's dirty fingernail?

"Mason," I said, rushing to his side. "I need you to promise me something."

"Go on," he said.

"I need your word that you'll be merciful."

His pace instantly slowed, his eyes returning to their usual glare as they slowly slid to me. "If you even breathe Campbell's name—"

"No, it's not him," I said—a hard truth, but I knew his fate had been sealed with Mason long ago. "It's Anya and Heidi."

Mason thought for a moment, his tongue tightly pressed into his cheek.

Through the growing annoyance of Mason's violin, I quickly said, "They were taken, too—from the Palace, I mean. They didn't willingly join the Rebels and they were only following my lead."

"Are they with Ashworth?"

"No... I-I mean, maybe... I don't know. I don't think so."

Mason just looked at me.

"We were separated," I conceded with a sigh. "I was looking for them when Carter kidnapped me, so as far as I know they're still with Svenja Svellec."

"*She's alive?*" His violin exploded. I cowered beneath the pain in my head, suddenly so vicious. Mason grabbed both my arms and held me tight. "Listen to me, Alira." Through the anger, his panic sang. "You need to stay away from her, do you hear me?"

"But why?"

"That woman is dangerous—*do you hear me, Alira?*"

"Yes, yes—I hear you." I wriggled free and wandered to the edge of the cliff, where the fresh air could blow away the musical pain. Gradually, as his violin dulled, I chanced a look at him. "Who is she, Mason?"

Mason lifted his head to the sky and inhaled cold air. Eyes closed, he did it again: breathed in, then out. It was a form of meditation, a way to scrape away the incessant rage. It was reminiscent of what Emilia taught me so long ago.

Breathe in... One... Two... Three...

As his music subsided, he met my questioning gaze. "She turned my mother into a monster. She violated her soul: twisted her instincts, her very personality."

"I'm not Arabella, you know that."

"Yes, I do." He captured my face, his cold hands freezing me in position. "You are the exact opposite of Arabella, and Svenja won't like that at all. She'll take more drastic measures if she has to."

Anxiety shrivelled my stomach. "What do you mean?"

Mason licked his lips and briefly scanned the trees. "She wants to keep our souls broken, by any means necessary."

Before I could react, his hand moved down to my belly and...*caressed* it. It was such a simple gesture, so sudden, but his eyes sparkled with emotion and my traitorous heart skipped a beat.

"Please, Alira..." he said desperately. "Join me or join Campbell—but stay far away from Svenja Svellec."

* * *

MASON'S WARNING echoed inside my skull.

Stay away from Svenja Svellec.

It was not a threat, but a plea—a rarity for Mason, indeed.

As the sky clouded over and delicate flakes of snow fluttered in the air, I followed Mason and did my best to understand the woman with the gold teeth. She'd already said that she had a way with words with Arabella, for she was *reluctant* in the beginning. She was a Protector, after all.

Did that mean Arabella once craved a child, like me?

No, that was preposterous. I could never do what Arabella did, or what she tried to do, at least. Mason trudged further ahead—clearly her efforts didn't pay off. If she had succeeded, then I wouldn't exist. Neither would the New World, and the souls of those two billion people who once lived in the Old World would have been left to live, to grow old, to die as their original destinies prescribed.

Funny how the mind wanders.

Mason threw out his hand, pausing our advance.

"What is it?" I asked, coming to his side. He remained still, taking long, cautious stares through the trees. I followed his gaze but saw nothing beyond the thick veil of snow. "Mason?"

A bullet fired through the air, hitting the tree beside my head in a flurry of splinters.

Mason grabbed my arm and ran, blindly firing his revolver. I could barely breathe as Mason pulled me to a halt and gripped my shoulders. Adrenaline wiped away his fatigue as those dangerous eyes shone brighter than ever.

"Black Ice Cavern is another three miles East of here. Go, I'll distract them."

"But—"

"*Go!*"

He threw me away like some stuffed toy. A sword in one hand and his firing revolver in another, he was quickly veiled by the falling snow.

Bullets cut through the dirty grey light. It was late in the day, the sun hanging low and almost completely covered by thick clouds. I concentrated on its subtle warmth on my back as I ran East.

Gunshots gradually died. Limbs trembling, lungs burning, I supported myself against a tree trunk, willing up the energy to continue.

Black Ice Cavern. A bloody Masonian camp. Only I was fool enough to walk *towards* that pit of murdering animals.

Yet there I was, stumbling ahead. Blindly following Mason's instructions if it meant I stayed on his good side. Jeez, if he even had one.

No, that was unfair. Of course, he had a good side—that's why I was doing my fucking best to stay on it.

Regret nothing, girl.

I sighed, curling my arms around my chest as I did as I was told.

Movement ahead. I stopped, narrowing my eyes. Mason, maybe? Or a Masonian? Perhaps I had already made it to the camp. Perhaps my decision had already been made for me—and such a thought lifted the moral weight off my chest.

But there were no flashes of blue or glimmers of bloodied swords. Only faded leather, and belts of ammunition strapped across torsos.

Not Mason. Not a Masonian.

Shit!

I stumbled back, panic growing. The scar on my belly already ached, anticipating the next bullet.

But I don't want to die! Not now, not when I finally had a chance!

Panic burned my lungs. I turned, ready to run, and collided with a chest.

Rough hands squeezed my wrists. I screamed, struggling against their strong grip, fighting with all my might to escape and run back to—

"Girl, it's me!"

I opened my eyes to the faded black leather on my attacker's arms.

"Campbell?" I breathed. Glacial-blue eyes overlooked a wide, relieved smile that was almost completely smothered in stubble. *"Campbell!"*

I threw my arms around him. Desperation surfaced, not with escaping, but with holding him close. I reverted back to the orphaned girl, so scared and alone and just so exhausted with the world.

"Thank God..." Campbell sighed into my neck, his protective arms squeezing tight. "We thought we lost you."

With a gentle push, he stood tall and studied my features, rubbing the rough pad of his thumb against my tear.

"We heard Mason found you." Disappointment shone; not at me, but at himself.

"Carter sold me, Campbell," I whispered above my falling heart. "He fucking *sold* me."

Campbell's expression was nothing less than pained. "Traitorous *bastard*."

Straightening his spine, he puffed out his chest and placed a gentle hand between my shoulder blades. "Come on. We've set up camp in a small village not far from here. Even got a piano, would you believe."

That Masonian camp screamed inside my head. A faceless, unknown place that held such promise...

Campbell's eyes narrowed. "C'mon, what the hell are you waiting for?"

My mouth opened, but no sound came. I couldn't tell him. I couldn't breathe a word about what transpired in that cave, or the deal Mason and I had just made. To do so would put a great red cross above my head: a target, a prisoner, a *traitor*. I couldn't deal with those labels—not now, not when I already struggled with my choices…

Campbell's loyalty was to the Free People, not to Mason's regime, and though I wished to all Gods that I could just break down and explain myself, I was scared of telling him the truth.

My realisation hit me as a sudden, frosty inhale.

I was *scared* of Campbell.

"I-I…" I forced my mouth closed.

With a large sigh, Campbell cradled my cheeks. Warmth flooded into my skin. "Mason is still close by. We need to hurry if we're to get you away from him, before he hurts you again."

Before he hurts you again.

It was a simple truth.

Too simple.

Dazed and petrified, I ignored the nauseating pressure that swarmed my stomach as I allowed Campbell to lead me to Ashworth's camp.

I'd been right, when I first glimpsed the Rebels through the trees: the choice had already been made for me. But it didn't lift the weight off my soul. Quite the opposite, in fact.

* * *

WHEN WE ARRIVED at the small village with the piano, now overrun with Rebels, cracks still streaked the muddy ground. Large, unsightly things: deep, black chasms in the earth, scarring what would have been a rather charming little village.

Modest huts and a single inn surrounded a huge brazier, still knocked over from the quake a few days ago. Its charred remains still marred the snow.

The village itself seemed to persevere rather well. No huts had collapsed beneath Mason's power, neither had any fallen into the cracks that scarred the landscape. The grass roofs had remained intact, and all residents were accounted for. Those residents now watched Rebel intruders with intrigue and agitation, and both in equal measure. It was public knowledge that Mason was close by, and a village reeking of Rebels would most certainly grasp his angry attention.

That anger was something I was entirely focused on as Campbell led me to the inn: a beautiful building with an intricately carved doorway and a grand chandelier of elk antlers. It housed a selection of flickering candles that highlighted the dirt in Ashworth's scruffy blonde hair.

"Ah, she returns!" He threw a sarcastic arm on either side. "We were beginning to think you'd forsaken us!"

I rolled my eyes at him, then noticed the piano sitting in the corner. My fingers twitched with the memories, echoes of those healing notes still swirling around my skull.

Ashworth followed my gaze and that cocky smile grew.

"We heard Mason forced a dying girl to play the piano," he said, meeting my eye with an amused sneer. "What happened? A bit too rough with you, was he?"

With a frustrated huff, I lifted my jumper to reveal the small, circular scar.

"One of your men got a bit too trigger-happy, Ashworth," I growled and threw my jumper down. "I barely made it."

"Well, of course I'm happy you're still alive, otherwise we'd have Mason's immortality to contend with." Ashworth smiled tightly and cast his attention to a large table in the middle of the room. On it was a map, complete with those little tokens. A pang of sadness as I noticed the entire Icelands crossed off with unsightly red marker.

"What's the situation, Ashworth? How many fighters do you have left seeing as the entire Mulch Gang is buried beneath layers of rock?"

"Oh, all in good time, girl." Ashworth studied the map, drawing his finger across its stained surface. "In the meantime, we need to ask you a few questions."

"Oh great," I mumbled, rolling my eyes again.

Campbell was quick to grumble something inaudible, then stood by Ashworth's side. Both expelled threatening auras.

Zackery arrived looking a little worse for wear, for his face was a mess of black bruises and his glasses were only held together by tape. I was about to ask him if he was alright, but he barely looked at me as he handed over a small glass jar.

I scowled at Campbell. "The Hel is this?"

"We need a sample."

"Of what?"

"Urine." Ashworth puffed up his narrow chest. "We want to know if you're harbouring more than you look."

Pregnant. They thought I was pregnant.

"This is ridiculous..." I snapped. I dropped the jar on the ground and angrily kicked it away, surprised that it didn't shatter. It collided with Campbell's foot—a man who was stiff with indifference. "You're so full of shit, Ashworth."

"Oh, so Mason didn't take advantage of you, then?" Ashworth raised fair eyebrows to Campbell. "Did you hear that? Clearly Mason isn't the sick bastard he'd have us all believe."

I winced at his words, and the sarcasm behind them.

"Girl," Campbell said, gently. "You've got nothing to be ashamed of. We know it wasn't your fault."

That same unease squirmed inside my belly, tightening those stiff knots. I stared blindly at the jar by Campbell's foot, unable to meet his eye.

"But," Campbell continued, "regardless of what happened, we just have to make sure."

"There's no need! I-I'm—"

"Stop lying," Campbell said—a little harsher than he must have meant to. Fighting back frustrated tears, I listened to the violin. Quiet, tentative notes sang back. Was he already at his Masonian camp? Was he still waiting for me?

Campbell picked up that abused jar and threw it at me. I barely caught it.

"C'mon, don't be a child," he snapped, finally losing patience.

"No, this is ridiculous! I'm not doing—"

"Just piss in the damn pot," Ashworth glared. His holstered gun glinted in the candlelight.

Perhaps cooperation worked in my best interests. Yes, the Rebels didn't want me dead, but that had less to do with my welfare and more their impending victory. How lenient they were prepared to be—how tolerant of my defiance—was entirely dependent on my behaviour. They did not need another reason to hate me.

So, with trembling limbs, I slowly took the jar to an adjoining room.

When I returned, Zackery had a strip of paper in his hand.

"Put it there," Ashworth snapped, pointing to the edge of the table. Silently, I did as instructed. Nausea bubbled ripe in my stomach.

Zackery placed the strip of paper into my urine. He held it there for a couple of minutes and then studied it carefully, his brow slightly creased.

"Negative," he said.

An audible sigh of relief spilled across the room.

"Oh, thank God," Campbell breathed to the chandelier above.

A heavy ball of tears burned behind my eyes. I blinked it away before anyone could notice.

"Don't get too excited," Zackery said. "Could be too early for a conclusive result."

Ashworth's face fell. "What're you saying, Doc?"

"I'm saying, how long has Alira been with Mason? Two weeks?"

They clearly had no idea *when* Carter sold me. I wondered what they'd do if I told them I'd only been with Mason for a few days, or that we'd had sex mere hours ago?

They'd probably kill me where I stood.

As shame swelled my chest, I'd probably let them.

No, you have a new start waiting for you, girl.

I scoffed around my own thoughts. Pfft, a *new start*. It wasn't a *new start* at all. Gold chains were still made of metal.

Zackery stared at the strip of paper. "This is very promising start, but we're not completely out of the woods yet."

A small, victorious smile worked its way across Ashworth's thin lips. "Get Theodore," he said.

Zackery nodded and left the room, taking my sample with him.

I didn't care where he was going, or why. I was just glad he took that fucking test-strip with him.

Ashworth cleared his throat. "Alira, you're going to tell us all you know about Mason's whereabouts."

I scoffed. "He doesn't exactly trust me, y'know. He wasn't particularly forthcoming with his plans."

"Granted, but you must know where he was taking you?"

"We're just looking for a rough area," Campbell said, trying to catch any lingering bits of trust. "You're a great tracker, girl. You must have a vague idea?"

I stared at the mud stuck on my boots, at the way it caked and cracked beneath the hearth's light.

"C'mon..." He took my bony shoulders within large paws and tried to catch my eye. "You know I'll do all I can to keep you safe."

Mason's voice rang inside my head: Campbell had escaped Maelstrom and left me stuck beneath Mason's boot. Doubt tried to claw into my skin. I rubbed it away before it could materialise.

Mason was a liar. I knew that. He'd proven that several times.

"Your silence makes us question your loyalty, Alira." Ashworth's glare was just as dangerous, just as threatening as the hands upon my shoulders. Strange, how Campbell's hands didn't feel as comforting as I remembered.

"Alira," Campbell whispered, tears in his eyes. "Where was he taking you?"

"East." The word just...*slipped out*. Dropped without my control into the air between us. I shocked myself upright, blinking away my surprise as Ashworth scoured the map. "I-I mean, maybe, he never—"

"Only place close is Black Ice Cavern," Ashworth said. "That ring any bells?"

Campbell must have seen the spark of familiarity upon my face. "Thanks," he said.

With a final pat on the shoulder, he returned to Ashworth's side. I curled my arms around myself, biting the skin around my nails, wondering how in Hel's name I'd explain myself to Mason, Campbell—*all of them*.

A blast of chilly air entered the inn, followed by Zackery. Theodore was just behind him, his bald head concealed in that woollen hat. And there, hobbling along—with a wooden stick, this time—was Svenja Svellec.

She grinned wildly when she saw me, boasting her gold teeth. "Ah, Alira! Wonderful to see you here, girl."

Stay far away from Svenja Svellec…

I immediately avoided her gaze.

"You alright?" she asked, coming closer. "You look like you've seen a ghost."

"I'm fine."

Svenja sighed. "Ah, Mason's been bad-mouthing me, hasn't he?"

I remained silent, unable to meet her golden eye.

"Well, I'm afraid I'm not nearly as *savage* as he makes me out to be." She clicked her tongue and gripped her cane with white-knuckle force. "Shame on him. He should let you make your own decisions. You're entirely capable of thinking for yourself, aren't you?"

Was that sarcasm?

"At any rate," she continued. "Time is ticking on. We need to hurry."

She hobbled towards Ashworth and suddenly remembered the *information* she claimed she had. I bet she'd already told Ashworth—and as grating as the thought was, the Rebel glares made my own questions fall back. I'd get that information out of her—damn right I would—but perhaps now wasn't the best time for those sorts of conversations. I doubted they trusted me enough to tell me, anyway. I didn't have the right—or the audacity—to be bitter about that.

I joined Svenja at the table and noticed the obvious omission: "Where's Isla?"

"On the train," Svenja said. "With your friends Anya and Heidi too, as a matter of fact."

My entire body lifted, erupting from that stuffy inn. "They're okay?"

"Oh yes, they're fine."

"They and the rest of the Free People are waiting to depart our stronghold in the Woodlands," Campbell explained, with a tender smile. "Just have a few more stragglers to pick up and then we'll meet them about fifty miles from here, not far from Eagle's Overlook."

I grinned stupidly, excitement brewing at seeing Anya's glorious copper hair, or Heidi's blushing smile. To hear they were alive, unharmed, filled my blackening heart with such lightness that I barely remembered who I was with.

That, of course, all came crashing down when Svenja removed a small bottle from her pocket. She placed it on the table, directly before me.

It was bottle of pills. The ones Anya gave me, all those months ago. The ones I so willingly swallowed, with hate and vengeance in my heart, to inhibit Mason's growing immortality. That felt so long ago now. How times had changed.

"Where did you get these?" I asked weakly. The bottle was cold in my fingers, each excited pill jingling within.

"I took them from Anya," Svenja said. "She let slip that's how you got rid of Mason's more...recent attempts."

I grimaced, unable to hide my spite. I could explain my slip-up with the camp to Mason, but *this?* "You expect me to take one?"

"But of course."

"No." I threw the bottle on the table, as though burned by it. "I'm not taking one! There's no point—you've already tested me!"

"You know that was inconclusive," Campbell said, his annoyance festering like a putrid wound.

"I don't care! Y-you can't make me—I refuse!"

My soul shuddered, cracks widening as those musical claws hunkered down.

I pushed myself back from the table and headed for the door. Two Rebels blocked my path, their revolvers held in twitching hands.

"There are ways we can make you, Alira," Svenja said. We locked eyes— diamond to gold. Beneath that inherent fragility, danger shone. It glinted off each golden tooth as she sneered. "These are desperate times, girl. We need to ensure Mason remains mortal."

I rounded on her, glaring. "Why, Svenja? Ashworth, Campbell—I understand their motivation. But what's in it for you, huh?"

She grinned at me: wide, unsettling, and entirely reminiscent of Sebastian. Indeed, the likeness was startling.

"For over three-thousand years, I have watched this Family do nothing but *destroy*. Don't you think it's time for that to end?"

Echoes of the Icelands surfaced, the screams of all those poor people still hanging upon the air. Their deaths were pointless, barbaric.

Yet, there I was, so willing to run back to the man—the *monster*—who caused it all. And he'd do it again, if he so wished. We were nothing but ants beneath his boot, scurrying up a mountain doomed to crumble.

Tears licked my eyeballs, not just for me but for all those I had betrayed the moment I unbuckled Mason's belt.

Campbell placed heavy hands upon my shoulders again, pushing me down beneath the stares—the *wants*—of the Free People.

Every part of me roared in defiance. Knees trembled beneath me and I wanted to collapse, to curl myself in a little ball. Whose side was I on? Mason's, or Ashworth's? My gut and my soul seemed to have very different ideas.

But what did I *want to do?*

I didn't know. I just didn't know anymore.

Guns cocked. I felt their aims at the back of my head.

"Killing me is a bit redundant," I said, with none of the snark I intended.

Ashworth smiled tightly. "You're swallowing that pill, girl. Whether you want to, or not."

I stared at Campbell, my eyes burning. "You agree with him?"

He couldn't meet my eye. "We need to be sure," he said, softly.

I closed my eyes, trying to imagine a scenario where I did not have to do this. The beach at Giant's Respite came to mind, with those thundering waves upon the shore.

I could already feel Ashworth's dirty fingers in my mouth, prying open my jaws as Svenja stuck those pills far down my throat. I should just save them both the bother and get this over with—at least then I'd retain my freedom.

Or what little I had left of it, at least.

I angrily shook off Campbell's arms and marched to the table. The pill was so small, so frivolous. It fit perfectly in the grooves of my palm, its powdery skin totally unable to catch the light. Such a small, pointless thing and yet it carried so much weight.

I couldn't think about it. So, I just threw it into my mouth and swallowed quickly. It was dry against my throat, sticking as it slid to my stomach.

"There," I said. Campbell grabbed my arm before I could turn away.

"We need to be sure," he repeated.

Only after Svenja had inspected my mouth, searching for any hidden pill, were the Free People satisfied.

"You've made the right decision. Just you wait, Mason will soon—"

"Shut up, Campbell," I breathed, and stormed on shaking limbs from the inn.

20

———

The world had gone murky. Though the snowfall had finally ceased, cloud smothered both the setting sun and the aurora above. In their place lay a sheen of grey—thick and unyielding—dousing the landscape in dullness. As the sun finally dipped below the horizon, the residual light of the world did nothing but emphasise the shadows. It wasn't even twilight. It was just dirty. Like pond water.

Yet, the village still bustled with life. Lit with full force, braziers cast their warmth across the pack of Rebels darting in and out of each hut, each house. Scurrying about, almost aimlessly, cradling guns soaked in Ashworth's ambition.

Sitting on a fallen log a little way up the hill, I watched them all. I spotted Campbell, idly talking to a few of his compatriots. He'd have hushed conversations and then move onto the next. Occasionally, Ashworth was with him, monitoring everything.

No sign of Svenja Svellec. She remained inside the inn, hidden from view.

Cold wind stroked my cheeks. I enjoyed the bitter feel of its fingers, the way it parted my hair. It was freeing, to feel the wind. So natural, so right.

I spotted Theodore strolling up the hill. His hands were encased in his gaping sleeves and his bald head only protected by that woollen hat. Frayed strands formed a slight halo and the wind fluttered her fingers through those wayward fibres, mocking the baldness that lay beneath.

"Remarkable view," Theodore muttered. "Isn't it?"

Yes, it was. The village hugged the southernmost base of the Brüster Mountains, rising high into the cloud above a dense forest. The dirty grey light made for an effortless atmosphere: brooding and sombre. Indeed, the entire landscape appeared to be meditating.

"It's beautiful," I said, sincerely.

Theodore perched upon the log beside me, his hands still concealed within the arms of his robes.

"I never liked the wilderness," he said, gazing ahead. "For many years, I despised everything outside Maelstrom. I always thought it so dirty, so uncivilised."

A bitter laugh beneath my breath. "Maelstrom is uncivilised. All those Aristocrats cheering, leering as poor, innocent people are stripped and sold, or celebrating when an innocent neck snaps. Maelstrom is barbaric."

"Yes, I see that now." Small eyes narrowed, licked by the incessant cold. "But when you are raised in such an environment, it becomes habitual. There is an awful sense of normality that sticks to our bones until forcibly pushed out. Only by looking in, as an outsider, can you see the true form of Maelstrom's rotting heart."

"Is that why you're here?" I scowled to the snow beneath my feet, bitterness itching on my tongue. "Is that why you're suddenly so social, to remind me how monstrous my destiny is?"

"No, my dear, I'm simply here for mutual comfort. I know how difficult it is to throw away the life we crave."

"And yet, here we are." I looked at those small eyes, like little grey pebbles set in the rosy roundness of his face.

"Yes, I'm here. An Aristocrat, trying his damned hardest to fit in."

My eyes spotted Campbell again, strolling ahead with that antique sword swinging from his hips.

"Campbell's an Aristocrat too," I stated.

"Campbell always despised his heritage. His family did unspeakable things to rise so high in the social hierarchy, insofar that they were frequent visitors at Mason's dinner parties. Such things did not sit well with Campbell and he couldn't wait to leave Maelstrom. Indeed, Campbell has not been an Aristocrat in a very long time."

"So, then what about you? Are *you* an Aristocrat?"

"Of course, I am." Theodore's cold eyes slid to me. "I readily enjoyed the frivolities of Maelstrom. Forsaking everything I knew, everything I had worked so hard for, was not an easy decision."

The swallowed pill sat heavily in my stomach. I could feel it, like some swollen ball of decision that refused to dissolve.

"Then why did you? Why leave the comfortable life you loved so much?"

Theodore's wide chest expanded on a large, laboured sigh. His eyes fell to the moody scenery, lines carved deep into his forehead.

"Mason took something from me. Something I loved very much." Theodore met my eye, a bitter smirk on his lips. "And no, my dear, I do not mean my testicles."

"Then what?"

Theodore stared into the line of low cloud. It caressed the trees, gradually rolling down the mountainside. As the light continued to die, the mountains ahead and the distant forest bathed in opaque grey.

Just when I thought our conversation had ended, Theodore replied, "I was a member of Mason's Social Circle, once. My heritage was important in Maelstrom, for my mother's family owned the largest retail store."

Harrisons. I knew it well. Mason had bought my diamond bracelet from there.

"And," he continued, "like many of Maelstrom's Aristocrats, I owned Slaves. I owned a lot of Slaves, in fact. Mostly female, of course."

Theodore glanced at me, a sparkle in his eye. "I wasn't always like this, you understand. Before my unfortunate...omission, I was quite a looker. I even had hair, would you believe."

I wondered what colour his hair was.

"But I did something unspeakable. A cardinal sin, in the eyes of Maelstrom." Behind Theodore's eyes lay some deep pain, bored into his very soul. Just like the music bored into mine. "I fell in love with one of my Slaves," he said.

After witnessing Theodore's sour demeanour, the notion that he could *love* anything was entirely unfeasible.

"As I said, I wasn't always this way," he said, raising a thin eyebrow. "But nevertheless, I did love her. She was gorgeous, both inside and out. The kindest, most beautiful soul I've ever had the privilege of knowing."

Something resembling sympathy, perhaps even pity, rose in my chest as Theodore wiped a tear from the corner of his eye. "What happened?" I asked gently.

"I invited our dear Lord Mason to dinner one night. For no special reason, it was simply to boost my ego." A bitter huff, shaking his head from side to side. "Oh, he noticed her instantly."

A familiar scenario rose to my mind, concerning a Slave called Maya Doe. "He wanted her, didn't he?"

"Oh, he certainly did. He was with Verity Ulster at the time, but that didn't stop his eyes from wandering, wanting. Such a selfish, greedy man. When he visited my house the next morning, I naively assumed it was to congratulate me on a successful night. Never did I anticipate that he wanted to buy her from me."

I recalled a similar conversation between Mason and Emilia. He offered her crates full of gold for the apprehension of my *services*.

"And did you?" I asked. "Sell her to him, I mean."

"No. In fact, I emphatically refused." A large sigh decorated the air with white mist. "So, he said he would just take her, without payment, whether I wanted it or not. He gave her two hours to pack her belongings and then left me reeling from our conversation.

"But...I couldn't let her go. I truly loved her, and I knew the reason Mason wanted her in his Palace. It was sickening, to think of him owning her like that. I refused to let him have her.

"So, I decided we would run away. We would travel to the furthest corners of the New World, where Mason would never find us.

"But he did find us, of course." Theodore sighed again, his gaze resembling the oncoming wall of fog: cold, impenetrable. "They found us in the Forest Territory. Mason transferred her to his Palace, but me? Oh, he stayed with me for a little while. He ensured that I would never continue my family's noble Bloodline."

"I'm sorry, Theodore," I said. "Truly, I am."

"It's of no matter. My fate is shared by many across the New World, but that is not the reason I joined the Rebellion. It was revenge, certainly. But not for me."

Theodore's eyes glossed over. They were thick and shiny, concealing so much emotion.

"What happened to her?" I asked.

"She died. She was killed in the same Palace that had already destroyed her, several times. If she was with me, if Mason hadn't forced her from me, then she would still be alive. I would still be with her. We would still be happy."

How refreshing it was, to hear such hope. Perhaps Theodore's own hatred, his own stewing thirst for vengeance, had clouded the very real fact that he was still a Slave Owner. Did she love him back? Impossible to say, but refusal would not have worked well in her favour. Perhaps, had fate worked differently, Theodore would have turned into the very sort of monster he now despised.

With a heaving huff, Theodore stood to his feet.

"Ashworth wants you in the inn by dusk," he said, shuffling through the snow. "I would avoid pushing him to send a search party."

I groaned beneath my breath. I wanted to bask in the freedom on that hill, to inhale that dense atmosphere. The thought of returning to that stuffy inn, among the eyes of hating Rebels, just did not sit right.

But I just didn't have the energy to deal with Ashworth's attitude, or his groping men. With a heavy sigh, I followed Theodore down the hill. I thought of his story, of his descent into the Free People. I thought of the Slave whom he had loved, who lost her life in the bowels of Mason's Palace.

"Theodore, if I may, the Slave Mason took from you. What was her name?"

Theodore's pace slowed, his eyes falling to the floor. They contemplated for a moment or two, lost in their own memories. "I believe you knew her," he said. "Her name was Tia Kingsley."

* * *

DARKNESS DESCENDED QUICKLY THAT NIGHT. The clouds smothered everything, emphasising the shadows of the surrounding forest. Torches were hastily lit and placed around the periphery of the village. I stared at those torches and wondered what the violin tried to sing to me.

Mason's music was ever so quiet, as though contemplative. Worry entangled each note as anxiety sang loudly between the strings.

No anger. Not yet, at least. Perhaps he still had hope.

Campbell's sword glinted in the torch's light as he came marching over. "You doing alright there, girl?"

"Fine."

I wasn't.

Campbell sighed. "It'll get better. Soon, all of this will be behind you."

I recalled that cave, and Mason's pitying laugh. "Campbell, c-can I ask you something?"

Campbell looked at me, a frown cut deep into his brow. "Of course."

I led him to the edge of the trees, away from prying ears. "W-when I was with Mason, he...he said..." I licked the scar upon my lip, unsure with how to proceed. My tummy wound up like a coil of cold, rusted metal. "I won't...*die*, will I? If you kill Mason, I mean. Regardless of our Connection, my soul can still survive without his...right?"

Campbell flashed a compassionate smile, a heavy hand resting upon my shoulder. "Of course, it can," he said tenderly. "You're going to survive this."

"You promise?"

"Yes, of course. Mason will say anything to convince you to join him. He's a terrific liar, don't believe anything he says."

I knew it.

I swallowed the growing ball of lead lodged at the back of my throat and formed a shaky nod. That seemed to be enough for Campbell, who led me back into the village's belly, infected by Rebels. I eyed them all, looking at each face, at each speck of dirt or stain of black grease.

I saw a face pitted with acne scars. Above it was a mop of curly hair, and a jaw covered with a patchy beard...

Orzo?

He was gone as soon as he appeared, enveloped within the mounds of Rebels. Blinking away the fleeting image, I blindly followed Campbell towards the inn.

Shouts behind us. Campbell stopped, turning on his heels. A loud *swoosh* as he unsheathed his sword, holding it with whitening knuckles.

"Girl, get inside."

But I did not move, transfixed by the curious shadows in the trees...

Bullets burst. Screams followed, Rebels and innocents darting like scared rabbits.

I threw myself into the snow. Campbell was with me, low upon his elbows.

"Alira, run!" he said.

"But Campbell—"

"No *buts*—if you die, we *all* die!"

With a great heave, Campbell pushed me to my feet. I ducked as bullets sped past my ears and ran into the forest, the warmth of those braziers chipped away one frantic step at a time.

As the sound of gunfire dispersed, I was left alone. My pace slowed; my burning lungs gasped for air. Both hands upon my knees, I bent low to the ground and regained my stamina.

In that moment of rare quiet, I grew annoyed. I was rather tired of people throwing me away, casting me out into the wilderness as soon as danger came knocking. I deserved better than that.

Grumbling, I pulled myself upright and stomped through the forest. Away from the braziers, natural light shone a dull silver. Moonlight punctured a gap in the clouds and snow reflected this silver light, illuminating everything. Ominous and beautiful.

Beside me, the world dropped sharply into large lakes that resembled flat pearls. To my other side, the mountain stood as vertical cliffs. Water roared somewhere in the distance.

The forest opened up and a waterfall shone silver against the cliff. A great pool lingered at its base, supporting angular boulders. The water continued to snake its way across the ground, carving deep gutters in the snow, before rolling off the cliff's edge into another waterfall, taller than the last. Far below, water hit the ground with thunderous intensity, shedding large clouds of rising mist. In the stillness of the night, the noise was deafening.

I edged towards the stream. The water was fast, tumultuous—a seething cauldron that would easily carry me over the cliff.

No, there must be another way across. I turned my back to the roaring water.

A sound grasped my attention. I stopped and peered over my shoulder.

I saw his coat first. It was that glorious shade of blue, beneath it a bloodied sword that still gleamed a mottled silver.

Across that roaring water, Mason repeated my name.

"Come," he said.

Through the slow, monotonous pounding of my heart, I found his outstretched hand. It stretched over the stream, beckoning me.

I took a step closer, then stopped. All those screams echoed in my brain, each telling of a lost life.

I had so many scars. All of them hurt...

Mason could see my hesitation, hear my fear.

Licking his lips, he stepped closer to the edge. Some of the snowy bank dropped away, flung over the cliff with the rest of the water.

"Alira, I gave you my word."

I wanted to believe him. I wanted a future...

I remembered the pill I'd swallowed, the location I betrayed. How would I explain myself? What would he do to me?

Maybe he'd understand. Maybe he'd realise that I only did what I had to do to survive, to cling to the Rebel's lingering trust—*my* last scraps of freedom. Maybe I'd remind him how much easier it was to take his hand without Ashworth's chains weighing me down.

Perhaps there was still time to make amends.

I stepped forwards with the urge to be free of fear, free of the lies and chains and the Rebel noose tickling my neck. Mason's eyes sparkled brilliantly, vehemently, and my body was not my own as my traitorous fingers twitched ever closer...

"Alira!" Ashworth's voice penetrated the space. "Where the *hell* have you been!"

The water roared, louder than ever, as my hand snapped back to my side. Mason's did the same, those bright eyes suddenly overshadowed with something dark, sinister, as Ashworth prowled into our—*our*—space.

Ashworth's pace slowed. His gun lifted, aimed directly at Mason's startled, stunned eyes and he pulled the trigger—

A dull click. The clip had already been emptied.

Mason stumbled back as his violin screamed with relief. That same relief echoed inside my heart, slamming against a piano's keys as Mason's eyes briefly found mine. A few deep breaths, from us both, as Ashworth lowered his gun with a frustrated glare.

"You lucky bastard," he muttered.

"Ashworth..." Mason managed a sinister smile. "You appear to be out of bullets."

"The same applies to you, I reckon. Otherwise, I'd be dead already."

Mason's smile fell. "I don't need bullets to kill you, *boy.*"

"Then what are you waiting for?"

Mason's eyes flicked to me. A fleeting movement, barely noticeable, yet Ashworth saw it clearly. "Oh, of course! You can't risk moving any mountains here, can you? I'm too close to your precious mate."

Ashworth gripped my arm, startling a shriek out of me.

Mason edged forwards, fingers twitching. But no, should the ground move beneath Ashworth's feet, it would move beneath mine as well. Mason could not risk me falling to my doom, for Ashworth had the leash pulled tight.

"Ashworth, the deal I offered is still on the table. Give me Alira, and you and the Free People will be spared."

I tried to shake off Ashworth's hand—*to take Mason's*—but his fingers merely gripped tighter.

Ashworth laughed to the sky. "Oh, I bet you'd love that, wouldn't you? To regain your immortality and then destroy us all? Just like Carter and the Icelands?"

He tugged me harder to his side, spurring another shriek.

"You foolish boy..." Desperation shone beneath Mason's glower. "You know this will not end well for *any* of you unless you give her to me!"

I struggled to free myself from Ashworth's fingers. Mason saw my fruitless efforts and his violin sang with such failure. Tears licked my eyeballs, numbing in the bitter cold.

Ashworth observed Mason, then me. Studying us both, carefully. His grip around my arm tightened.

Then he smiled.

"Y'know, Mason, I don't think you understand just how much help Alira has been to us of late."

I shot my eyes to Ashworth. He met my silent begging and that nasty smile widened.

"Where was his camp again, girl? *Black Ice Cavern?*"

Mason's brow marred with lines. Then he looked to me with a wounded expression, as though Ashworth had stabbed him with a rusty knife, twisting the blade.

"Oh, she has been a whirlwind of cooperation, I must say!" He laughed loudly against the roaring waterfall. "She's been ever so kind in halting your immortality too, haven't you, sweetheart?"

Something hard twisted inside my belly. Some horrible, deep sense of dread and guilt that sang gloriously inside Mason's head.

"Ashworth, don't…" I whispered.

Ashworth glanced at me, and his smile grew. It was a wicked smile, designed to lap up every last bit of hope that Mason—that *I*—had clung onto.

From within the depths of his pocket, Ashworth picked out a bottle. As each pill clinked and clanged inside, I felt the intensity of Mason's confusion. He was sceptical, hesitant to understand the words Ashworth spat with such enjoyment…

"Deeply sorry, mate. But it looks like your most recent efforts won't come to fruition either."

He threw the bottle across the stream. Mason caught it with a single hand and slowly—reluctantly—inspected the small, clinical words on the bottle. Those diamond eyes found me again and I saw the betrayal—the *devastation* —behind each sparkling speck.

"I'm sorry…" I whispered, sobs aching my throat. "I'm so sorry…"

I listened to the ferocity in Mason's music, the depths of betrayal that spurt from those devastated eyes. I saw the revulsion, the utter abhorrence… Oh yes, he hated me in that moment. He *despised* me.

My scarred heart bloated, and as that persistent ache reappeared, more suffocating than ever, I gasped back my tears and tried, with all my might, to express how *sorry* I was. I needed him to understand that I didn't have a choice back in that village, that Ashworth might as well have pushed that pill down my throat, one painful inch at a time.

Did Mason see that? Perhaps—but I knew then that it wouldn't have made a difference.

With a weak movement, Mason threw the bottle of pills into the river. I watched it for as long as I was able, until it spilled over the cliff and tumbled into oblivion.

An exhausted laugh escaped him as he turned his back. His violin, battered and broken, kept singing as he disappeared between the trees.

When he was out of sight, Ashworth's grip loosened. I threw myself away from him, angry tears spilling.

I screamed at him, "*Why did you do that? Why did you tell him?*"

Ashworth rounded on me, his teeth bared into a disgusted snarl. "Because I think you've forgotten whose side you're on! I'm not a fool, and don't you dare expect me to believe that you'd so readily fight for *us* when he was dangling your hope on a fucking breadstick!"

"You had no right, you had—"

"My *right* is to kill Mason! That's the only thing I care about, the *only* reason you're still alive!" Ashworth's hot breath beat down on my forehead. "And mark my words, you dare consider running back to him again and I'll cut your fucking legs off!"

Ashworth gripped my arm and dragged me back to the village.

21

Cramped inside a truck rolling across a bumpy and uneven road, we slowly traversed the Snowlands.

Rebels grew cocky, especially Ashworth, for the Masonian attack had been swiftly debunked as a decoy. Two men—three at the most—caused a bombardment of bullets that left only a small handful of Rebel losses. Nothing more than a distraction, a ploy to coerce the Rebels to scatter and to entice me to run through the trees, where Mason was waiting for me. He was trying to save me, to carry me back to his camp so we might both survive this Rebellion.

Of course, that's not what happened. Mason's will to save me had deformed beneath Ashworth's disclosure. Stamped out beneath his boot, until nothing but mulch remained.

He would never forgive me. Not for this.

As the Snowlands rumbled by, I wiped silent tears from my cheeks and listened to the despair, the *anger* in Mason's music. It was a painful melody inside my head, each note shrieking pain that radiated behind both eyes.

Yet, I managed its painful insistence and remained listening. I needed to hear what Mason was feeling, to understand if there was—if there ever could be—some hope for my future. So far, only dread sang back.

My heart ached, so fucking much, not for Mason but for a future that was now just as horrific, just as uncertain as it had always been. A deep breath escaped my lips, trying to dispel my lingering torment.

I was not alone in the truck. Ashworth and Campbell studied a map, speaking at length about some tunnel between here and Eagle's Outlook. They argued beneath their breaths, both insistent in their differing courses of action. Theodore listened intently to their argument yet had little energy to intervene.

Svenja Svellec was there too, just silently watching me, her nose ever so slightly lifted. Her, I ignored most easily of all.

A shooting pain stabbed through my...*belly?*

I knew that pain. I knew what it meant.

Oh no...

I groaned through the sudden, stabbing agony, my legs rising to my chest. Some deep breaths and the pain finally subsided. I relaxed back into the chair, fighting the urge to throw up.

"Hey, you alright, girl?" Campbell asked.

I didn't answer and turned away from them, fighting back tears.

"The pills are starting to work, by the looks of things," Svenja chimed in. She cocked her head to one side, almost in admiration.

Another stab of pain. I keeled over, hugging myself with gasping breaths.

"Should they be doing that?" Theodore asked, mildly concerned.

This was normal. I had felt this before, back in the Palace. It had startled me back then, yet my anger towards Mason was still so raw that I'd lapped up my pain, wanting him to hear it all. Yet I was still perplexed when, a few hours later, I saw the blood in my underwear. Despite Anya's warnings, it still came as a shock.

Watching me, Svenja smiled. "Alira's body is trying to resist the chemicals, at all costs."

I begged her, "Please, shut up..."

The violin screeched inside my head. He knew what was happening. It only made him angrier.

I closed my eyes and tried to erode the last twelve hours. I should have been in Black Ice Cavern, discussing my uncertain future with the monster I once loved.

Not now. That future had been wiped cleaned away, not by my own hand, but by Ashworth's. I glared at Ashworth's cocky brazenness, and the arrogance behind those young, immature eyes. Mason was right: he was just a *boy*.

If it wasn't for him, my children would exist. I would still have a future.

The anger rose, like water on the precipice of boiling. The hatred, the pure, seething *rage* that tingled inside my veins forced my heart to beat faster and faster until—

A blast of pain hit me, like a bolt of lightning inside my womb.

The pain wiped away the anger, leaving exhaustion in its wake. I closed my eyes, so utterly done with *everything*, and willed my life to just...carry on. I didn't want to feel anymore. I didn't want to fear or to love or to hurt, hate...

I just wanted to exist. To remain numb to everything. It was so much easier when I didn't feel anything...

I leant against the cool metal and concentrated on each bounce, each low rumble, and tried to figure out where it all went so wrong.

* * *

THE CONVOY STOPPED. Ashworth's ears perked up, like a mountain lion detecting danger. Or food.

They burst from the truck like pus from a wound: Ashworth first, then Campbell. Svenja sent me an unsettling smile and followed. Theodore, the gentleman that he was, allowed me to go first.

Frigid air caressed me. I breathed it into my lungs, desperate to forget the van's stuffy air. The aurora danced above; so mellow, so beautiful. I stared at it for a little while, lost in its prismatic colour.

Campbell called my name. I blindly followed—I always did. He stopped at the edge of some great cliff, overlooking a field of snowy, jagged mountains. Train tracks curled around the base of the closest mountain and disappeared down a tunnel's gaping maw.

"Where are we?" I asked, curling spilled tendrils of hair behind my ear.

"About twenty miles from Eagle's Overlook," Campbell replied, a map in his hand.

"What are we doing here?"

"We're going to put a real downer on Mason's day."

Ashworth marched over with a portable radio. "Alright, Isla, where are you?"

Isla's static returned through the handset, *"Just approaching the final leg of the tunnel now. About to lose signal."*

"Noted, see you on the other side, girl."

"Allfather Guide You, mate."

Static roared through the radio until it finally clicked off. Ashworth replaced it in his pocket, sniffed, and just admired the view with a squint.

I turned to Campbell. "What's happening?"

Campbell smiled and unrolled the map. Each Snowland settlement and mountain gleamed in crisp, exquisite detail. Eagle's Overlook, in the mid-east of the Territory, was encircled with bright red marker, as was the exit to the tunnel just down the cliff from us.

"See this tunnel," Campbell said, skipping his finger across a dashed line through the mountains. "This is the only direct route in or out of Eagle's Overlook. The mountains are just too dense and too treacherous for traversing by foot or vehicle."

"What's your point?"

"Well, should this tunnel just...*disappear*, then Mason's gonna have a rather hard time crossing the Snowlands."

"But he can just move mountains," I countered.

"Ai, he can, but such things take great physical effort on his part. You saw how weak he is, how exhausted." Campbell sighed into the view, expelling his misty breath. "These are a lot of mountains to move, girl."

I recalled the days after the Lightlands' creation, where Mason slept for those twenty-seven hours. As exhaustion pooled beneath his eyes, it was obvious just how drained, how *fragile* he had become.

Campbell continued, "Should that tunnel go, Mason will need to decide what's more important to him: completely utilise his energy and power on a wild goose-chase to reach us, or to save his energy, stay alert, but waste weeks on a detour."

Campbell's lip quirked upwards in a blatant display of triumph. "Whatever the bastard ultimately decides, it will greatly benefit us."

"Yeah, but what about the tunnel," I said, nodding towards the gaping black hole.

"You let us worry about that," Campbell said with a wink. A final smile and he moved away, speaking to Ashworth just out of earshot.

Another stab of pain made me grimace. The attacks were becoming more frequent, more vicious. To ignore the pain—the *consequences*—I just gazed at the aurora above. I examined each line of colour, each flicker of light. The way it danced, undulating across a sky dotted with billions of stars, illuminating the snow with its unique, wintry glow...

"How you doing?" Svenja asked, coming to my side. She observed me with a conceited little smile, so full of condescension. Sebastian screamed from her features.

"Fine," I replied.

Svenja grinned, boasting an array of gold teeth. "By the way, how's Mason? I never asked."

My suspicious eyes slid over to her. "Why d'you want to know?"

Svenja shrugged. "I've known him since he was a boy. His welfare is important to me."

"*Pfft.* Only because you want him dead."

Svenja's smile faltered. "Don't you?"

Her question, though simple enough, filled my blood with such numbing conflict. The answer remained somewhere buried. Hidden, completely out of view, even from me.

"Hm," Svenja purred. "How interesting."

I stared at her—at the wisps of grey hair blowing in the wind, at the muddle of age spots upon papery skin—and felt the power seeping from her. It flowed like pure heat, creating a shimmering veil that hovered a few inches from her skin.

"What are you?" I asked.

"I am just a simple woman, trying to save billions of innocent people."

"And Sebastian?"

"Sebastian is a just simple man, trying to ensure the Family's Line continues."

A shaky breath as I stared at the view, tears tickling my eyelashes. "Why am I the End of Everything?"

Svenja looked at me, her eyes swirling like pools of molten gold. The corner of her mouth tilted upwards, ever so slightly.

Campbell suddenly snapped at Ashworth, who seemed visibly disturbed. "No, this is ridiculous—you can't do this!"

Ashworth stared at the radio like his very soul was trapped inside its shell. His jaw clenched, but occasionally his lips would part for a long, slow exhale.

"Campbell," Svenja said, hobbling to his side. "What's the problem?"

Campbell threw his hands into his hair, panting, unable to stand still.

"It seems," Theodore began, observing with taut superiority, "that a Masonian garrison has followed the train into the tunnel."

"And?"

Ashworth's eyes finally flicked up. "There are almost three-hundred Masonians in that tunnel."

"And over four-hundred innocent people on that train!" Campbell's cheeks flushed, emphasising patches of raw skin flaked by the cold. "You can't seriously be considering this..."

My eyes wandered to the small box tucked into Ashworth's belt. Upon it, protected by a glass casing, was an ominous red button. Down below, Rebels flooded from the tunnel's black entrance and scattered towards the trees.

"How many explosives are in that tunnel?" I asked.

"Enough to flatten the whole mountain!" Campbell shouted. "The train needs to be clear before you blow it, Ashworth!"

"And how many of my men will that cost?" he snapped back. "Here, we have a golden opportunity—*three-hundred* Masonians, Campbell! When else will we have the chance to wipe out those sorts of numbers?"

"At what cost!" Incensed, Campbell prowled to Ashworth like a mountain lion going in for the kill. "For God's sake Ashworth, Isla's on that train!"

So was Anya, so was Heidi...

"Ashworth..." I took careful steps forwards, my numb fingers outstretched, my boots crunching the snow. "Please don't, think of all the people on that train!"

Ashworth lunged to me with a sharp finger outstretched. "Don't you dare lecture me about saving innocent lives!"

I remained immovable to Ashworth's steady assault as he beat hot, stale air upon my forehead. "I don't need to be lectured by *you*, the End of Fucking Everything, about saving lives!"

He spat in the snow. "You don't get a say in what I do, the things I'll sacrifice to win this war!"

"Ashworth," I tried again, my voice trembling. "There are *children* on that train…"

Ashworth paused for a moment, glaring with utter incredulity. "You fucking hypocrite," he growled.

Something curled around my gut. Some deep, horrible sense of unease that tried to peek at the world, to make its truthful presence known in my conscious thought. I pushed it down, far away. *Don't think about it.*

"Listen to me," Campbell said, forcing a gentler tone. "Just let the train get clear, *then* blow the tunnel."

He gestured towards the gaping black hole and the thick layer of snow just aching to tumble down the mountainside…

But Ashworth didn't stare at those things. He cast his gaze up, towards the aurora. Its soft, gentle light caressed his features and stroked his greasy hair. His eyes closed as he absorbed those colours, and the chill of the wind and the fresh air.

I expected him to be renewed. Recharged by nature. For him to open his eyes with newfound vigour and clarity.

But when those eyes opened, they portrayed anything but. Instead, they contained corruption. They contained greed, desperation.

They contained contempt for the New World, and everything in it.

Ashworth lifted the radio. "Prepare for detonation."

"*Are you crazy?*" Campbell rushed for the detonator but Rebels ripped him away, kicking and screaming.

"Ashworth, don't—*please!*" I gripped his dirty coat, trying to capture any last bits of mercy in his young, immature eyes. All I saw was his arrogance, his selfishness. "Don't do this, don't—"

Ashworth threw me away with a hard whack. I collapsed against a boulder, whimpering around the sudden and intense ache in my core.

Anya's face flashed before me. So did Heidi's.

Get up, Alira!

Through the aches and the spasms, I found a foothold and leapt up. I could see the button in his hand, the protective cover up and the red button plump waiting and—

A low drone resonated. The train chugged out of the tunnel, puffing black smoke into the air. A wide smile stretched across my lips as carriages exited: five, then six, then—

Brakes screeched, the echo bouncing down the valley. Mountains trembled; rock quaked beneath us. A great cloud of smoke burst from tunnel, embracing the train with its dangerous, fiery arms.

Rocks poured down the slope. Cracks formed in the sheets of snow upon the mountain.

Helpless, we watched those layers of snow slump, then collapse in a roaring cloud of white. It was an animal, ripping away everything in its path, uprooting boulders and trees and tumbling down the slope.

The avalanche grew hungrier. It consumed the train, ripping it entirely from the tracks.

With the back half of the train still buried, *smouldering,* inside the tunnel, the front half ripped clean away. I watched, shaking, as that half rolled down, pushed and shoved by the avalanche.

The cloud of white settled. The train remained smattered across the snow. Destroyed.

And there, standing upon that mountain, we just watched.

Ashworth removed his thumb from the detonator.

22

The snow was deep here. Boots sank into its powdery embrace.

I trudged through that snow with burning lungs and a foul, abhorrent fear.

Screams howled in the air. Fires burned as small outcrops of angry heat, surrounded by broken bits of metal, branches, and the mangled, distorted train. Carriages were strewn across the snow, those frosty metal walls still convulsed in a perpetual state of shock. The front of the locomotive had erupted entirely into flames, those coal stores still feeding the furnace. It remained a fiery haze of red at the end of the wreck.

People stumbled around me; their faces covered in blood. They walked around the bodies of men, women, children...

I found Bentley buried in the snow. His hair was still slicked back—with blood, this time. Those sharp, obedient eyes remained open, gazing out eternally.

Breath caught in my throat. I stumbled on.

The screams dispersed further up the wreck. Ashworth's remaining Rebels attempted to save those still buried in the tunnel, to drag them from those few surviving carriages before they collapsed beneath the weight of a whole mountain.

But such efforts were fruitless. Where would terrified people go if three hundred Masonians were at the tail of that train?

To the front, of course.

I left Ashworth and Campbell to pull the remains of their Rebellion from the wreckage.

Bodies grew into piles. Some were buried in snow, limbs sticking out at odd angles. Others were crushed by boulders or slabs of metal, or the ripped appendages of trees.

Heidi was under one of those trees. A trunk, frosted and rutted, crushed her torso. Kneeling besides her, I caressed the soft swell of her cheek, closed those lifeless honeyed eyes, stroked a strand of gold behind her delicate ear...

No prayers to the Old Gods. Not this time.

A pained whimper escaped my throat. Again, I stumbled on.

More faces peeked from the snow. Ghostly, empty expressions. Half were peaceful, half anguished.

A glint of gold peeked from inside a train carriage, the black and white keys of Sebastian's piano teasing me from within the wreckage.

I saw long copper waves fanning out upon the snow. They shimmered beneath the light of the burning coal stores, roaring just ahead.

I breathed her name, the sound barely audible. I ran to her, dragging my feet through the snow, and fell to my knees at her side.

A metal spike erupted from her torso, embedded just below her right rib. It impaled her to the snow. Cries inched up my throat, the wails growing just beneath. I swallowed them all away and placed a trembling hand against Anya Whittaker's pale, frozen cheek.

Blue eyes creaked open. They were so dull, so shiny, yet their glorious colour jumped as bloodless lips formed a desolate smile.

"Alira..." she whispered. Her hand moved up and grasped my own. I startled at the fragility of her frozen fingers, like icicles about to snap in the breeze.

"Hey," I said, leaning close, so she could feel my warmth. "What are you doing here?" I forced a smile, running my thumb up and down her cheekbone. "You're the one who keeps *me* out of trouble, remember?"

Anya's lips quirked up. "Can't let you have all the fun..."

Blood oozed from beneath her torso.

I swallowed hard. "Look, you need to hang on, okay? I-I need you to promise me that."

Anya grimaced with a sudden intake of breath. "Heidi... She... She was just beside me..."

"Don't worry, I'll find her," I said confidently—because I already had. Those honeyed eyes were already burned into my retina. A lonely tear escaped, sinking into Anya's t-shirt until only a dark stain remained. "But I'm going to stay with you for a bit, okay?"

Anya nodded, but the very action was strained, exhausted, as her body slumped. Even her eyes sank deeper into her skull. Filled with moisture, they sparkled in the firelight like balls of blue glass.

"It's so cold..." Another inhale, her face twisting. "Am I... Am I going to be alright?"

Emotion balled at my throat. I stared into those glass-like eyes, skipping across the tender warmth of her soul, glimpsing at the floods of compassion —of *virtue*—that spilled from within. And as she struggled with each strained breath, the aurora reappeared on a sky studded with stars. I saw its reflection in Anya's eyes.

"Yes, Anya..." For the very first time, the lies came easily, without hinderance or doubt. "You're going to be just fine."

To hear those words from a woman who had always been incapable of lying... Hope sparked in Anya, drawing a beaming grin upon her face. She held my hand tighter as her gaze fell to the aurora, utterly enraptured.

Life seeped from her, relaxing that smile, dulling the intensity of those eyes. Finally, I closed them, protecting that precious blue stare.

Silence returned, and, in that stillness, I allowed the emotion to rise. I expected the wails to punch my throat, for that growing ball of anguish to explode as a series of sobs.

But it never burst free. It remained trapped inside of me and spread like a cancer, slow at first, then faster and faster until it trickled down every limb, to the tips of my toes and my flaked fingernails. The familiar pot of anger simmered over the same fire that illuminated that glorious copper hair.

Tears of acid stoked my cheeks. Tremors took a strangling hold.

I imagined a knife at Ashworth's skinny neck and I felt *excited*. I saw the bullet digging into his eye, wiping away his arrogance and his selfishness and his immorality.

In that one, terrible moment, I didn't want Ashworth dead. I wanted him *destroyed*.

My limbs were not my own as they stumbled upright. Through the nausea, through the *pain*, I was a visitor in my own body, idly following its instruction. Somewhere, as the violin's confused, anxious tones settled in my mind, I willed my piano to yell and scream inside Mason's head. I needed him to feel my anger, my vengeance, my desperation to stare hard inside Ashworth's shattering soul...

The door to that wrecked train carriage was easily pushed aside. Anger made me strong. It made me powerful.

I stumbled inside that ruined compartment, and as the final stab of pain echoed inside my belly, I stared at the remains of Sebastian's piano and willed Mason's immortality to grow unbridled.

The keys were misshapen, the strings stretched and warped, but as my hands fell upon them and music exploded around that compartment, I coerced it to sing strong and deep inside my body.

The song was powerful—angry and elated and just so goddamned desired. As each note screamed and shrieked around the metallic compartment, I called out to that music and prayed for it to sing louder, fiercer, to erupt inside that train wreckage with the full force of those twenty-eight musical instruments. I wished for every member of my fucking Family to sing with me, *in* me, to rejoice and scream and yell with lungs made of brass and wood and string!

Silence. It returned so quickly, so suddenly.

I stared at my trembling fingers as they hovered above the keys.

23

Rebels swarmed ahead. They were like ants, or rats. An infestation of some mundane description.

Campbell found me. We locked eyes, only for a second.

He said my name. He asked if I was alright.

I ignored him.

Ahead, Ashworth knelt in the snow beside Isla. A metal slab crushed her pelvis and both legs, but she was alive and held tight onto Ashworth's hand.

"Just do it..." I heard her say.

Ashworth rarely showed grief. He considered it a weakness, an unfortunate addition to human emotions.

Yet, that tear shone bright and proud as it trickled down his cheek. He wiped it away quickly, just as soon as he'd pushed his knife into Isla's temple.

Mikael Ashworth looked to the carnage, sniffing back all essence of supposed *weakness*.

"Take what you can carry!" he yelled to the masses, and trudged to his infestation of Rebels.

Campbell took a gentle hold of my arm. "Did you find them?"

His touch was painful, utterly unwelcome. I pushed it off and wandered to the trees.

* * *

THE FOREST GREW SILENT.

Such a glorious sound. Nothing but the rustle of the wind, the gentle scent of moss and wood...

Where was the violin? Perhaps he was asleep. Perhaps he was listening, gauging the intensity of my music, my turmoil.

Light flickered above me, caressing the snowy undergrowth. The trees were thick and yet the aurora did its best to punch through, speckling the ground with pristine blue light.

That same soft glow fell upon my hands; upon the blood that stained my fingertips.

For a long while, I just stared at it, unable to comprehend its meaning. It was such a small amount of red, seemingly so insignificant.

Yet, the consequence of that blood shone brighter than any aurora, screamed louder than any music.

It signalled that I was alone.

That I had lost *everything*.

As the emotionless itch of ice crawled up my legs, I refastened my jeans and wandered aimlessly through the forest.

* * *

SHOUTS SOUNDED BEHIND ME.

They were familiar shouts: urgent and sonorous.

"Girl, the hell are you doing?"

Campbell Anders took a sharp grip of my arm. I brutally snatched it back. He tried again, gentler this time, and leapt before me with his defensive palms open.

He opened his mouth to speak, to berate my sudden antisocial behaviour in these so *desperate* times. Words ripped back down his throat. I imagined what greeted him as he stared at me: the bloodless lips, the pale cheeks, the dullness of diamond eyes dragged down by red lines and blue bags.

"Jeez, girl..." he whispered.

I didn't need his pity, so I walked around him. Another grip.

"Come on." He tried to pull me back. "Let Zackery have a look at you, let's—"

I ripped my arm away. "How does it feel, Campbell? How does it feel to take orders from a mass murderer?"

Campbell licked his dry, chapped lips. "You know I didn't agree with that..."

An insane smile stretched my mouth. It pulled against the scar, formed by a knife wielded by a sad and jealous woman. That was such a long time ago.

"You didn't agree with a lot of things. You didn't agree with Elliot Trevelyan either, did you?"

Campbell's face fell. He took a cautious step forward.

"Everything I've done," he said with a nasty, despairing scowl, "has been for the good of the New World."

I laughed a maddening cackle. It echoed up into the trees, merging with the dancing light in the sky. "Is *that* how you justify Gainstorn?"

Campbell froze; his eyes wide, his lips slightly parted as guilt and horror spread like a stain upon his face. Even from that distance, I stared into those glacial-blue eyes and saw the turmoil, the self-condemnation.

Good.

"Tell me Campbell, when you shot an innocent little baby, right there in her cot, did you consider that act of pure, wicked barbarity to be *aligned* with the views of your fucking Rebellion?"

Stunned, he took a few moments to regather his thoughts. "You don't understand: Mason was there, he'd found her, he'd—"

"Mason found me too, eventually." I smiled. A great big sneering grin. "Was I your atonement, Campbell? Or was I just a means to an end?"

Campbell hurt was evident as tears streaked his cheeks. "Do you think Gainstorn was *easy* for me? Do you think I drank mead and celebrated after it was done?"

"Why wouldn't you? Mason was weakened, I was being born to another family..." My poor parents... If only they'd known how their precious baby would be their downfall. "I bet Harrison Dagger was laughing about Gainstorn. Until Mason cut away his smile, that is."

"Don't you dare..." Campbell's voice was low and all too dangerous.

"He was just another Rebellion leader, Campbell. Just another mass murderer you blindly followed."

Campbell shocked back, his hands trembling. "Harrison Dagger was the greatest man I've ever known."

I shot a nasty grimace. "Didn't stop him from letting you do his dirty-work though, did it?"

Tears disappeared into his stubble, his mouth twisting into a snarl. "I shouldn't have to justify my decisions—right or wrong as they were—to you. I *saved* you, I *care* about you."

"Yes, of course!" I laughed my contempt to the entire forest. "Did you *care* the day Ashworth plucked you from Maelstrom's gallows? Did you *care* when the Free People called your name and you left me *rotting* in an Aristocrat's basement?"

Campbell saw my anger. He was scared by it. "Alira, I'm so sorry I couldn't keep my promises."

Promises. All Campbell gave me was broken promises.

I smiled and a single tear squeezed out. "You've promised me a lot of things over the years. You've lied to me, too. You, Mason—you both just constantly *lie* to me..."

Wind blew its cold, silky fingers through my hair, pulling me back into the bowels of the forest.

"Y'know," I said, "it makes so much sense when I think about it. Of course you left me to Mason—what would be the point in saving me? You needed me pregnant with his child, so our souls could be broken, so he'd be mortal..." I leant forwards, ever so slightly as the word *collateral* sang around my skull. "Is that about right, Campbell?"

His throat convulsed on a large swallow, yet he did not reply. Fists clenched at his side, his knuckles camouflaging into the snow.

My bottom lip split as I grinned, and I *relished* the sting. "Y'see, I think, when Ashworth plucked you from those gallows, the Free People were the only thing you cared about—"

Campbell choked on his own breath. "That is *not* true!"

"But it is, isn't it?" I was done with the lies, the deceit. Mason was a monster, but now I saw Campbell for what he really was: a Rebel. And, like all Rebels, he wanted Mason dead, by any means necessary.

"I see it so clearly now," I said, eyes still burning. "You saved me when I was little to keep me hidden, to stop Mason from getting his hands on me. But then Ashworth gave you a chance to destroy Mason for good. How could you refuse such an offer? Once a Rebel, always a Rebel—hey, Campbell?"

No words erupted from Campbell's throat, but his face twisted. With despair, or with the gravity of the truth? Probably both.

With a bitter chuckle, I turned my back to him and walked through the trees. Snow crunched beneath my boots. "Thanks for making my life collateral, Campbell."

"Wait!" he shouted, his voice already broken. "You deserve a proper explanation, but not here, not now. Come with me and I'll explain everything."

There was a time I craved Campbell's warmth, his comfort, his protection. The memories were still there—*somewhere*—and yet they remained buried. They were hidden beneath mounds of snow, crushed by the same avalanche that ate Anya and Heidi.

Wind gently howled through the trees, rustling the snow-encrusted branches above. I closed my wet eyes as flakes of ice stroked my cheeks, meeting the single, betrayed tear that trickled down.

"No, Campbell," I said, and met his hurt with my own. With a choked breath, I wandered to the trees. "You're no different than Mason."

I heard Campbell's reaction: anguish, shock, betrayal... They coalesced into a single, ominous swish of an unsheathing sword. "Don't make me force you to come with me."

Such dangerous words...

Anger sparked through numb muscles. I rounded on him with a snarl. "Or what? Are you going to kill *me,* just like my predecessor? It's the same soul, y'know. A different body, of course, but when you looked into the diamond eyes of that baby, *I* was the one staring back at you!"

Campbell knew that. His guilt screamed it.

Slowly, my lips stretched into a smile. "Kill me again if you want. I'm defenceless, but that didn't stop you last time, did it?"

My smile grew wretched. "But I suppose it's all rather counterproductive, isn't it? You kill me and *poof,* Mason becomes immortal. Then how can you justify your *sacrifices,* hm?"

Campbell remained silent. The only tell of his pain was a laboured swallow, and the tears that disappeared into his stubble.

I smiled again as shadows encroached around me. "Mason was telling the truth, wasn't he? I'm going to die with him."

Campbell did not reply, but his stare dropped with my stomach, and that spoke a thousand words.

A bitter, despairing laugh echoed around the trees, embracing me within the same darkness that grew unbridled inside my veins. "Well, darling, I promise to give you a good finale. The curtain's about to fall, after all."

* * *

ONCE AGAIN, silence reigned.

No owls soared between the pines, no foxes scurried in the undergrowth, no deer pranced.

Only slivers of silver moonlight fought through the trees. It created a path through the muddle of trunks, an endless labyrinth of dark and light as I trudged through the snow.

My only company was the light in the sky.

And Svenja Svellec, who suddenly appeared through the mass of pines. She leant against a tree, both her arms and legs crossed, with her wooden stick tucked beneath her arm. Golden eyes narrowed atop a sneering grin.

"Evenin', Alira," she said.

My glare cut through the moonlight.

Svenja followed in my footsteps, snow crunching beneath her unequal steps.

"I always suspected Mason got his claws in you, along with the music," she said, behind me. "The Protector's soul can get a little *muddled* after the Connection. All the Destroyer's hate, all his anger pouring into her with the music can be a little...*corrupting*."

My teeth ground together, until I could feel the specks of white powder against my lip.

Svenja exhaled a subtle burst of mucus laughter. "Yet, with you, I genuinely believed there was hope. Campbell always said that no matter how much the anger consumed you, how deep the music buried inside your soul, there was still good in you. He always stipulated that, despite all the experiences your soul has endured over these one-hundred-and-eighty-six years, it still resembled just enough of its original shape to be amiable to my cause, to be truly *good*." Another laugh, bitter and resentful. "Looks like we were wrong."

Anger swelled and crawled up my gullet. "You want to talk to *me* about goodness, Svenja? Just talk to Ashworth—berate *him* about his fucking righteousness after what he did!"

Svenja lifted her pointed nose. "Ashworth fights for a larger cause," she said calmly. "He is risking his life, and the lives of others, for the prospect of freeing thousands, of saving billions."

"*Billions?*" I laughed wildly, manically to the speckle of stars above the trees. "What *billions*, Svenja? This isn't the Old World!"

"No, and I blame myself for that," Svenja said, with a bowed head. "I had too much confidence in Arabella. I grew cocky and that arrogance formed the foundation of Mason's New World."

That gold grin reappeared, brighter than ever. "But I've learnt from past mistakes, and as luck would have it, Ashworth now understands that countless innocent lives are at stake if Mason wins this war. He understands that four-hundred beings are a necessary sacrifice to ensure Mason's weakened hold. You know that Anya and Heidi would also understand—"

"*Don't you dare speak their names!*" I screamed, marching towards her with murderous intent.

Svenja matched my impending march by keeping the distance between us.

"No Rebellion is worth this!" I shouted hoarsely.

Satisfaction spread like treacle across Svenja's face. "Spoken by someone who is loyal to Mason's regime."

I shocked back, disgust trickling down my limbs. "I'm not loyal to him," I said, but the music kept singing, its aching claws clinging tight. I remembered that firelit cave, my eagerness to run to his camp, the desperate *longing* to create his child... I did those things because I craved a future—because I was selfish and scared—but that didn't mean I was loyal to him.

Did it?

Svenja formed a golden grin. "You hate this Rebellion. Regardless of its failures, its triumphs..."

I remembered all those lost lives, all those cries of pain and wails of grief, and I wanted to scream.

Svenja took a slow, arrogant step towards me. "This Rebellion simply tries to weaken Mason's hold, and your soul—being so...*consumed* by the music's hold—doesn't like that at all. As though you are preconditioned to hate all attempts to kill your precious mate, or to escape the destiny the music *desperately* wants you to complete. Does that sound about right?"

A bitter, disgusted laugh rattled around my lungs. "Fuck you, Svenja..."

She formed a spectacular grin. Moonlight gleamed against her teeth. "Just something to consider."

A fog of hate and grief invaded my brain, turning everything else into frozen, numb slush. It pushed the entire forest into the background of my conscious thought, throwing it away until I had the energy to notice it. Perhaps, if Svenja hadn't stolen all my attention, if she had not thickened the fog of obliviousness inside my head, I would have heard the crunch of boots behind me. Perhaps then I would have been alert enough to dodge the large branch that slammed against my skull.

But then again, perhaps not.

24

———————

Water splashed against my face. Cold, like little specks of snow prickling my cheeks.

I stirred, grimacing around their unwelcome chill.

More water splashed. It dribbled down into my mouth and I detected the echo of blood against my lip. I licked away its metallic taste and startled at the sting of pain. Had I bitten myself?

Slowly, my eyes creaked open. Only a blur stared back.

Flickering candlelight caressed the grey, frosted walls. The floor I was lying upon, smattered with bits of hay and mud, only supported a wooden chair, currently being utilised by a broad-shouldered man wearing a black jacket.

"Campbell?" I croaked.

With great effort, I pushed myself upright.

Pain spread, hot and thick, inside my skull. I groaned audibly and inspected the injury on the back of my head. Blood caked my hair, sinking its brown, clotted form between the strands. It was sticky against my fingertips.

Gradually, as the room began to settle, Campbell's form sharpened. I saw the bucket of water by his side, the knife strapped against his thigh. I saw look inside those glacial-blue eyes, suddenly so cold and smothered with guilt, pain and betrayal. They looked down upon me, disappointment splashing with the cold drops of water flung from his dirty fingertips.

"Hey, girl," he said, but the words were forced, almost alien.

Leaning against the wall, I held my throbbing head and observed the four stone walls. No windows, other than a small hole near the ceiling, covered by a metal grate. The door, concealed behind Campbell's ominous frame, was secured tightly shut but even then, I could see the flicker of torches behind the grid, as well as the guard stationed outside my cell.

My *cell*.

A horrible, sneering laugh stung my lips. "So, am I your prisoner now?"

Campbell's throat convulsed on a large, laboured swallow. "I didn't want it to come to this, but your loyalty has come into question."

A laugh, small and feeble, echoed delicately around my lungs. "Ashworth always wanted me as the enemy."

"No," Campbell growled, his cracked lips twisting into a scornful grimace. "You've done that all on your own. Quite spectacularly, too."

I forced my eyes to his boots. Such large things, with thick laces and brown spots of mud marring the black leather. What did they look like when Campbell originally found me, all those years ago?

"Jeez, girl," he said, through audible pain. "I gave you every chance in hell. I wanted so much to believe that your cause for this Rebellion was true, that it wasn't just some twisted way to punish Mason but to be rid of him for good!"

Hot tears prickled my eyes, my lower lip trembling through the sting. "I do want to be rid of him."

Campbell sniffed back his tears. "I don't believe you. Not now, not after the train and those *things* you said to me in the forest."

Memories swirled around the bloody hole in my head. The darkness that had trickled up my limbs, bloating my tongue with the vile words I was sure to spit, unmercifully, in Campbell's face.

"Tell me the truth, Campbell..." My teary face met his, so fraught with failure. "Why didn't you come back for me?"

"I wanted to. I wanted to go back for you in Maelstrom but there wasn't enough time, and we didn't have the numbers..."

But then his resolve grew, puffing up those broad shoulders with staunch resilience. "And then we heard that Maya Doe had become Alira, that Mason had found you, and before we had time to get you out of that shit-hole, you were pregnant." A quick wipe of his nose, another hearty sniff. "And I didn't want to put you through any more pain but what was the alternative? To let Mason's child live, to condemn you to an *eternity* of torture?"

"Don't do that, Campbell," I snapped over the ache in my throat. "Don't use *me—my* fate—as justification for what Ashworth's done! Ignore Ashworth's Rebellion and tell me what *you* want."

"I want him dead," Campbell said, exhausted. "I want him to rot in the foulest, deepest cauldron of hell for everything he's done."

Campbell scooted forwards. "And for the things he *will* do. Have you considered all the future pain, the continued suffering if Mason wins? And not just to us—this isn't about *us* anymore! This about the billions and *billions* of innocent lives that will be destroyed if Mason's Line continues!"

Defeated, Campbell slumped in the chair, deflating into its wooden structure until a small creak cried out from between the fibres. "I didn't understand the enormity of your destiny before. But now I do—I see the whole, unambiguous picture and it *scares* me."

Yes. Svenja had told them everything.

More tears begged behind my eyeballs. The End of Everything crawled into every cell I possessed, sinking into my bones through the pores in my skin.

"Why?" I whispered, faintly. Terrified. "What am I, Campbell? What did Svenja tell you?"

Campbell shook his head, ignoring my question. "Fate is screaming down Ashworth's neck too, and *that's* why he did what he did, why he sacrificed the train for the good of this Rebellion."

Tears broke the barrier of my resolve. Sobs ached to burst, wanting to feel the warmth of Anya's arms, craving the glint of glorious copper hair or Heidi's round cheeks bulging with peanut butter.

But I'd lost them. They had been stolen from me.

"I'm sorry about your friends. What Ashworth did was barbaric—I will *never* deny that—but at least his actions, as heartless as they are, stem because he sees the bigger picture."

"And what picture am I in, Campbell? The one where I've lost *everything* —all I ever cared about—because of some stupid Rebellion that won't win?"

"Oh, we'll win." Confidence exuded from the seams of his jacket, yet his words were whispered, almost as if their very presence could somehow turn the tide of fate.

That same tide forced another bitter laugh from my lungs. After everything Campbell had said and done, I realised with brutal understanding which of his lies hurt the most.

"And then what? I'm dead too, aren't I? Campbell, you're not just burying Mason... Y-you're burying *me*..."

Campbell grimaced as tried to halt the flood of emotion. He stared at frosted cobwebs in the ceiling, decorating the grey stone with little silver streaks. "I wish it didn't have to be this way. I wish we could go back to a long-house, clanking together great big tankards of mead and Roaming to our hearts' content... But Mason found you and that changed everything."

Campbell's heavy sigh filled the sudden claustrophobia in that cell. "I'm sorry I lied. I was trying to protect you, like I always have."

Mason lied to protect me too, or so he'd claimed. I curled my arms around my legs, fighting through the grief, the fear, and letting the chilly air numb my skin. A sad, longing stare to each of the walls of my cell, watching the specks of frost glitter in the swathes of silver moonlight, cutting between those metal grates.

"I am your prisoner," I stated. Campbell didn't correct me. "Are you going to keep me locked up in here, until I—*we*—die?"

A small, wretched smile tickled Campbell's bloodless lip. "We can't trust you. Despite everything Mason's done to you, all the torture you endured at *his* hands, you *want* to run back to him. Hell, you almost did!" He ran two hairy hands down his face, perhaps trying to pull away the truth that plagued him. "If we allow you to do that, it means death and not just for us, but—"

"For billions," I cut in, with a bitter huff. "Yes, that's been mentioned once or twice."

Air sat thick and viscous between us, clouding our once bright and caring relationship with the bitterness of betrayal, on both sides.

Through that viscosity, Campbell pulled his gaze down to me. I felt his eyes upon my skin, my hair, my eyes... Perhaps he was reminiscing back to the little girl, who once had her hand nestled inside his pocket, fondling those fourteen gold coins with grubby, stubby fingers.

"My father was a very cruel man," he said, eventually. I met his stare, listening to his tale with intrigue. He'd never spoken to me about his childhood. "He enjoyed his Aristocratic heritage and he certainly profited from it. God knows how many innocent people he sold into Slavery—somewhere in the thousands, most certainly.

"When I was old enough to truly know his business, I remember thinking, *how can he do that?* How could he so willingly sell all those people to a lifetime of pain?

"So, one night, I asked him exactly that. I went into the bedroom he shared with my mother. They were reading in their bed—a huge, obscene thing. Red cushions, four great wooden bedposts that were doused in red and gold velvet, a mattress that would cradle your very bones..."

He paused for a moment, perhaps wishing he was nestled within that comfy bed, far away from reality. I did too.

"My parents were most definitely irked by my question. I understood their irritation: the clothes on my back, the food on my plate, and the roof over my head were all down to my father's business. Without it, we'd all be starving on the streets."

Campbell's eyes glazed with moisture. "Yet, I wanted to know. I asked my father how he had no regrets about what he did, why no thought was spared for all the people he'd condemned to Slavery. I asked him how he could calmly sleep in that big fucking bed, without a single care..."

Campbell's eyes met mine, for the first time in what felt like centuries. "So, he put down his book and looked me dead in the eye. '*Because I don't care where* they *sleep*', he said to me."

Disgust pooled in the grooves at both corners of his eyes. "That's when I realised how fucked up my family was. It wasn't just what my father was doing or the lives he was trading, but the...*ignorance* of it all. He just brushed away the truth, just like that. Gone." He made a lazy movement with his arm, cutting through the thick air. His hand sank to his side and nearly dragged his body from the seat.

"And that's why I can't save you, girl, despite how much I want to. Because

—God above—I do want to, and it *kills* me to know that for Mason to die, you'll..." He couldn't finish. But beneath the pain and compassion in his eyes, stony determination shone. "I could've forgone the promise I once made to Harrison Dagger—to kill Mason, just like he killed my friends. Because when *you* saved *me*—when my life's purpose switched from *my* vengeance to *your* protection—I was content with that. If we'd never gone to Waterman's Quarry, I still would be."

I remembered Campbell's reluctance to find the Free People, in the beginning. Because yes, he despised Rebellions. He knew they always ended with pain.

This one was no different.

Campbell wiped his nose on his sleeve. "But I can't do that anymore. I can't just run away from this now that I know the truth of your destiny and..." Campbell stumbled over his words. A deep breath later, he licked his lips and said, "I'm not my father. Unlike him, I can't allow myself to just sit back and ignore the truth, to forget about the *countless* people who have and who will —at some point in the future— succumb to Mason's Family... I wouldn't be able to live with myself, and I'm so, *so* sorry..."

I chewed the scar on my lip, relishing the dull pain. As dread sank heavily in my stomach, shrivelling it into something hard and dry, I forced a shaky nod.

"I understand," I whispered sincerely.

Campbell exhaled a stream of air. In it was the relief; the certain, undeniable truth that—despite everything—a sliver of humanity had survived within my soul. Perhaps there was still some essence of the little girl he met all those years ago.

Campbell stood to his feet. He was so tall, his entire presence completely dominating the small, cramped space. "For what little consolation it must be, you'll be safe in here. No one will hurt or punish you. I've ensured it."

Wordlessly, I nodded, and while I knew I should feel some relief, I remained impartial to Campbell's final act of protection.

What did it matter? I'd be dead soon.

Campbell wandered to the door. Just before he reached it, he stopped. Indecision weighed heavy on his heart and dragged down his face. It aged him tremendously, emphasising his silver strands of hair, illuminated by the surviving threads of moonlight.

"About Gainstorn..." he said. "For what it's worth, you were my atonement."

Tears pooled inside eyes that spoke a thousand words.

"I know," I said, my voice breaking.

With a small nod, Campbell knocked twice on the door. It opened to reveal a smattering of guards, all armed with shotguns.

"Goodbye, girl," he said, before he was enveloped by the Rebels.

"Bye, Campbell," I whispered to an empty cell, as the metal door clinked shut.

25

Staring at the walls, pitted with cracks that glittered white with frost, I realised that no cell was the same.

I thought of my bedroom at Mason's Palace, and the view across the gardens, stretching to those mountains smothered with snow. Then there was my other bedroom, the one with the rust-coloured walls fitted with grand, painted scenes to create the illusion of freedom.

Then, there was the train compartment. Damp and dank. Even the binding ropes were riddled with mould.

Carter's cell smelt better than the train. No damp, you see. It was too damned cold for damp.

Could that firelit cave be considered a cell? I blinked back the tears such a thought pushed out.

And now, there I was. Sitting in a frosty, stone mausoleum. It was the last cell I would ever enter: the one that would become my tomb.

I wished for another life.

A while passed. Movements erupted outside the cell. Simply from reflex, my spine straightened. Totally still, like a startled doe.

Maya Doe.

So many prison cells: one for each life. I'd had so many lives.

So many lives had now been lost.

I wiped my face upon my sleeve, hiding from the Rebels who bounded into my cell.

Two Rebels rushed to me, as though I might vaporise before their dirty, dusty hands. The third held a loaded shotgun, pushing it hard into the crook of his shoulder with his hateful gaze never faltering.

"Be careful not to pull the trigger, mate." I smiled, madly, as I was dragged past him. "Otherwise, it would have all been for nothing."

They dragged me down the corridor. Fires blared down both sides and yet the chill of the stone walls and slate floor still cut through the air. I shivered, despite the desolate, depraved anger boiling my blood. Little bumps prickled my skin, soon squished away by those tight, merciless hands.

A part of me wanted to fight, to scream the name *Wild One* in their greasy faces. I remembered the way I once was, so willing to escape my predicament, so achingly eager to run, no matter what. Then, when that had failed, I had submitted. I became obedient and for a while I was happy, content with my entire existence. But it had all come crashing down, one huge avalanche at a time, rolling and convulsing as my fate—my future—grew more and more wretched. Through the bitterness of my current reality, I remembered the sweet taste of hope upon my tongue.

They made me: Campbell, Mason, Ashworth... All of them, one way or another, had pumped their hatred, their vengeance and their goddamn desperation into my veins, corrupting my blood, moulding my once spherical, shapeless soul into an irregular monstrosity.

And as those Rebels dragged through that corridor—for some maddening, insane reason—I smiled.

* * *

Svenja Svellec boasted gold teeth as I was dragged to my destination: a room, modest in size, fluttering with the orange rays of a heathy fire. Two Rebel lackeys stayed with me, both with fixed frowns upon oily faces. As for the commanders, Ashworth glared as I entered, a sick smile upon his face. Theodore, on the other hand, remained completely, utterly emotionless.

Yet, it was the wide, spectacular grin of Svenja Svellec that sent shivers down my spine. It was glorious, ecstatic—as though she had been waiting three-thousand years for this moment.

As dread formed hard and low inside my stomach, I glanced around the room, and the frosted window that shut out the world. Some blankets were folded and stored by the fire, supporting a large coil of rope. Beside this lay the curved knife Mason had given me, confiscated upon my imprisonment. In the centre of the room, a long wooden table had been cleared and cleaned for my arrival.

I inhaled the clinical stench of bleach and took a laboured step back, unsure of the scene I had been dragged into.

Svenja, perhaps sensing my rising panic, forced her scary grin aside and took an unsteady step forward.

"No reason to be afraid here," she said, though lies screamed beneath that sweet voice.

"Course not." I shook off my guarding Rebels, for their touch made me nauseous.

Slowly, my sight slid to Ashworth, then to Theodore.

"Where's Campbell?" I asked. Despite our fractured relationship, Campbell's absence twisted my stomach, merging with the anxiety into something quite sickening.

Ashworth's smile was wide and proud, all too celebratory. "Oh, he's leading the Free People to victory, my dear Lady. Mason's days are numbered, as are yours."

The violin thrashed severed strings inside my skull.

"Mason's not going to die easily," I said.

"Oh, I don't doubt that at all. But it doesn't change the fact that we're going to kill him."

"Then why are *you* here? Surely you'd want to see Mason's demise more than anyone?"

Ashworth's proud smile widened into a full, toothy grin.

"I know this is hard for you to understand," Svenja said, hobbling over to me. "A corrupted soul is difficult to reshape and sometimes we have to take matters into our own hands."

"Get to the point, Svenja," I snapped.

That golden grin reformed anew, although something about it had changed. It turned sad, disappointed. "You're the End of Everything. You will inadvertently kill billions of innocent people and we can't—"

I pushed past her, storming to the far side of the room. Those two Rebels scooted forwards, but Ashworth held out his arm, pausing their advance.

"Theodore," he said over his shoulder. With a silent nod, Theodore shuffled his way through the labyrinth of people and disappeared into that cold corridor. I wondered where he was going, but the door quickly shut with a defiant slam that wrenched my mind back to Svenja.

"Don't bullshit me," I snapped. "Mason doesn't want this world to end! He created the Territories and I felt his sadness—his *regret*—as the Icelands screamed and I'm telling you that he'd never willingly want to destroy—"

"It's too late for this World, Alira. I'm trying to save the next one."

Words whipped away, smothered by the same shadow that descended over her wrinkly features.

"What?" I breathed. Somewhere, deep inside, the familiarity of her words began to settle, peeling away the last scraggly bits of a label that had followed me my entire life, that had defined every action, every decision I had made over my twenty-two long, painful years.

No, not twenty-two. I'd been in existence for *one-hundred-and-eighty-six* years. My soul was a result of Ragnarök, after all.

How many times had I been killed because of that label? Mason once said that not even he could remember. I suddenly felt so tired.

Svenja's thin lips formed a brief, depraved smile. "A long time ago, I met a girl. A beautiful girl with diamond eyes. Her name was Arabella."

Her words washed over me, sinking into my pores and adding just a little more dread to a heavy, roiling stomach...

"I was with her for over a decade. I told her about her destiny, I told her why *she* would be the End of Everything. I told her that, if she was truly a Protector, she would *protect* the billions of people that would succumb at the hands of her destiny.

"By the time she Came of Age, her soul was so hard and stubborn that not even the music's claws could sink in, though it constantly berated her for it. And yet, she was absolute in defying her existence and was all too willing to sacrifice herself to end the Family's Line.

"Yet, despite all that planning, all that determination, William still found her. He Connected with her, tortured her... And despite everything she did to try and *save* the people of your Old World, Mason was born regardless. Another Destroyer, just waiting to carry out his own destiny.

"You see, Arabella's was complete the moment Mason left the hot, tropical islands of William's World and arrived in this one. Oh yes, the music cheered when your Old World crumbled. I heard it as I was thrown into its tattered ruin, forced to watch those two billion people die helplessly, needlessly, as Mason created his *New World*.

"And here, I have remained, flicking back and forth from Sebastian every time one of us steps on the wrong toes." A *pfft* of bitter laughter arose between her teeth. "Here I am, once again trying to convince another Protector to *protect* the innocent lives her son—the Firstborn, another Destroyer—will smother beneath the convulsing ruins of *his* New World."

I remembered Mason saying that he *arrived* in the Old World, that his parents were alive but *elsewhere*. I was confused by his choice of words and convinced myself that's all they were: *words*. Chosen to deny me the information I craved, chosen specifically to create that confusion.

But now I realised that Mason was—perhaps for the first time—entirely accurate in his description. He did *arrive* in the Old World. He simply appeared, jumping into this World from another—his *father's* World, where he and Arabella still lived.

Answers to impossible questions cut through me, as did Svenja's golden glare, and I became too halves. One was numb, without feeling. The other was filled with staunch defiance.

"No..." I whispered, as though the words were scandalous. But then my voice-box kicked back with roaring intensity. *"No*, I-I don't believe you!"

Through my shaking limbs, and the *abhorrence* of the words spewing from Svenja's throat, I remained shell-shocked and alone.

"It is inevitable, my dear," she said quietly, sadly. "You are the End of Everything because you are the mother of a World's Armageddon."

A single tear trickled down my skin. It clung to the delicate layer of fuzz upon my cheek and dripped to the stone floor. For a while, I simply watched the minuscule puddle it had produced, noticing how the firelight caught each essence of that liquid, squeezed out of a diamond eye.

Those eyes were the same as Arabella's. And the Protector before her. And the one before her.

So many women. So many *lives*...

I leant, trembling, against the wall, and I wanted to scream. I wanted my eardrums to burst with the pressure of sound, for it to drown out the truth that kept rising around me like hot bile...

It's not true, it's not true... But I no longer trusted my own thoughts. There, as I considered the words stabbing my stomach, I realised in one sudden, brutal understanding that I believed every single word of it.

In a room filled with Rebels and flickering firelight, I knew why I was the End of Everything.

Somewhere deep inside, I think I'd known for a while.

Truth hit me, powerfully, ripping away my strength one hard whack at a time. I collapsed onto that cold stone floor, shaking ferociously, cradling the music inside my head.

Svenja's walking stick trembled the floorboards. She crouched down, so we were level: gold with diamond.

"You understand now, don't you? You understand why we can't—why we never could—allow you to give birth to your son."

Tears streaked my cheeks, my breaths fast and shallow. Guilt rose, not for what I would do, but for what I would create. What sort of monsters would my lost sons have become?

But as Svenja's eyes gleamed with such *pity*, another little thought came worming, niggling into my brain, burying itself so deep that it couldn't be pushed out. Perhaps it was my defiance, the remnants of my own piano which—although silent—was buried so deep inside my soul that not even Svenja could dig it up.

"But..." I breathed with burning lungs, as though I had raced up a steep mountain, where the air was thin and dusted with frosted diamonds. "But you didn't even give them a chance..."

Svenja's eyes narrowed; her jaw slightly slack, her brow delicately lowered. "What?" she growled.

Resolve shone as bright as that fire, burning with sure, unbreakable heat. "You changed Arabella's personality..."

Illuminated by the golden light, I let the entire world dissolve. All that remained was Svenja and I, racing down opposite sides of that steep mountain. "She tried to kill Mason. You made her reject her destiny, *you* corrupted her soul to such an extent that she stopped being a Protector to her Firstborn..."

My eyes grew wide, desperate. "If a Protector doesn't have to protect, a *Destroyer* doesn't have to destroy."

My sons didn't have to destroy...

Svenja's entire posture shifted. Pity twisted her wrinkly features, spinning the entirety of her emotional spectrum before settling, rather firmly, upon hate.

"The Firstborn's fate cannot be changed."

"But you don't know that!" Hatred grew inside my belly, as searing and as fierce as that fire... "You condemned their fates before they were even conceived, doomed them to die before—"

"I saw the Old World crumble, *girl*." Her shimmering aura grew hot, dangerous, and I could do nothing but listen, both terrified and enraptured, as she hissed the words through gritted teeth...

"I witnessed the needless slaughter of two billion people. I heard their screams as the sea boiled, as their buildings collapsed and the big bells inside their towers tumbled around them. I saw children burning beneath ash, drowning in glowing rivers of melted rock and metal. I can still smell their charred flesh—do you have any idea what that smells like? The stench of millions of burning children?"

A tear trickled from her eye. In it, suspended within the clear liquid, was the minuscule shimmer of gold powder.

"I was forced to watch that. That was my punishment for failing—the consequence of Arabella's Firstborn. So don't you *dare* lecture me about what *could* happen if you create a Destroyer." She slapped the tear away, unwilling to show its apparent weakness. "I know what will happen. I've *seen* what happens, what *always* happens when a Destroyer lives!"

"I'm sorry, Svenja," I said, my voice cracking—torn between misery and hate, defiance and defeat. "But y-you don't know that! I'm not Arabella and so my son can't be Mason!"

With an angered groan, Svenja pushed herself upright. She looked down upon me with a disappointed glare and those teeth still grinding.

"You're right about one thing…" For the first time, I realised how much she *despised* me. "You are certainly not Arabella…"

Hands grabbed me, hurled me to my feet. My boots scraped against the scuffed floorboards, fingers digging with merciless brutality into the soft flesh beneath my arms.

"What're you doing?" I shouted, as Rebels dragged me towards the wooden table that stank of bleach… Panic grew, coiling around gut, wiping away my fear of Mason and my destiny, replacing it with the very real, very sudden dread of my fate inside that room.

With a great heave, they slammed my body on the table. A low grunt escaped my lips, the back of my injured head hitting the wood and sending rough shocks of pain throbbing around my skull. Stars dotted my vision, the dusty, webbed ceiling convulsing with sheets of light.

Those two Rebels—one at each end—held down my limbs as Ashworth approached with a thick coil of rope. "I'm sorry about this," he said, yet his smile disagreed with such an apology. "I gave Campbell my word that no harm would come to you, but there are biggest forces at play here."

Theodore returned with Zackery, carrying a leather satchel. Its contents rattled as he placed it beside my head.

Terror soured my insides. "W-what is this? W-what's happening?"

Bones bruised as those Rebels held my limbs harder, tighter, and my scars discoloured with red, angry swelling.

Svenja Svellec arrived in my vision, her teeth bared in a snarl.

"I made a mistake with Arabella," she said, staring at me as though I was soaked in my own excrement. "I naively, arrogantly, assumed that we'd done enough to prevent Mason's birth. I will not make the same mistake again."

Sharp breath burst from my lungs, my entire body trembling.

"W-w-what are you talking about?" I tried to move my limbs but was held down harder.

Metallic clinks arose from the satchel next to me. From within its black bowels, Zackery removed a knife: surgical, serrated.

He placed it upon the table. Next to that, a scalpel: perfectly cleaned, its blade reflecting the firelight. Only then did I have a terrible, horrific inkling for why I was held down upon that bleached table.

That *surgical* table…

Tears flooded my hairline. "I-I'm not pregnant, I—"

"We know you're not, my dear." Svenja circled me, her walking stick clanking. "But that doesn't mean you won't be, at some point in the future. Whether or not you willingly run back to Mason, it's only a matter of time before you bring a Firstborn into this world. I will not allow that, not this time."

For the first time in a long while, the tones of a petrified piano sang.

"We are going to remove your ability to have children. Permanently."

For a moment, I remained still. Completely motionless, unable to absorb her words. But as the brutal, sickening meaning sank into my freezing body, I screamed.

I yelled with the power of a soul that wanted, that *needed*, to remain intact. Such a bodily omission would certainly take a piece of my soul with it.

My soul would remain broken. Permanently.

"*Please, don't do this!* There's must be another way, there must be a—"

Svenja and Ashworth locked eyes and shared a fleeting, unspoken agreement to begin.

"Remove her clothes."

Rebel hands pulled off my boots. Cold, grimy fingers fiddled with the zip on my jeans. My legs were wild, flailing, but they continued.

"*Please don't!*" I begged between my sobs.

Theodore, who had been growing paler with every passing second, shuffled slowly to the door.

"I..." He seemed fraught, visibly distressed. "I can't watch this, I-I'm sorry."

He scuttled from the room, like a drowning rat.

My jeans were pulled down, clean away from my kicking, wild limbs. I screamed louder.

As Ashworth began to loop the rope around my torso, securing my shaking body to the table, I took a terrified, desperate look to Zackery's pale face.

"P-please, don't d-do this to me." I unashamedly begged him. "Zackery, *please!*"

Scalpel poised and ready, Zackery's large brown eyes gazed at mine. I could see the goodness in those eyes, the insatiable drive to *help* people.

Watching me restrained to that table, crying and pleading, did not agree with any part of Zackery's nature.

"I-I can't do this..." he said, his lower lip wobbling.

Ashworth tightened the rope until it dug into my torso. I wondered, rather horrifically, if I'd be able to scream properly when they started slicing.

Svenja marched to Zackery and slapped him hard across the face. "Pull yourself together, man! This isn't an innocent *girl*—it's the End of Everything! It's a machine built to kill billions so don't you *dare* make the same mistake Campbell did and start feeling *sorry* for it!"

Campbell. I remembered the warmth of his arms, his protective hugs. *No one will hurt you*, he said to me, *I've ensured it.*

I wailed even louder.

"Gods, someone shut her up!" Ashworth snapped. Svenja clanked around the table with a cloth smeared with black stains. I clamped my jaw shut but she easily prized my mouth open and stuffed me full of the cloth soaked in gun grease. I gagged around the taste, its potent smell clinging to the back of my throat.

With slow, lethargic movements, Zackery walked to the other end of the table. He appeared to be dazed, stuck between nightmare and reality, dragged between his morals and his orders. On either side of him, Ashworth grabbed one of my flailing legs, a Rebel grabbed the other.

Muffled screams burst through the cloth, my voice creaking and crackling, like I was stuck on a broken phone line.

Just as Ashworth yelled at a reluctant Zackery to begin, my piano loudened. Its panicked, hysterical notes were so brittle, so out of tune, completely dominating the screeching violin. My inner music, usually only singing to entice or to torture, now returned with a frenzied, excruciating yell:

GET THE FUCK OUT OF THERE!

Anger returned, willed on by the music, and flowed like liquid heat through my veins. I remembered the punchbag in Mason's Palace, the sheer power brimming inside my muscles, and heard Mason's sonorous voice inside my head.

"Give in to the anger," he'd shouted. *"Let it consume you!"*

I concentrated on that anger, relishing its feel, its heat. I turned the knob high on that boiling pot and willed each raging bubble to pop inside my muscles, to thread them with hatred, with driving *power*.

As Zackery prepared for his first cut, I willed that same anger into my legs and kicked and *kicked* with the full force of my soul—not broken but *surviving*. My experiences, as harrowing and as horrific as they were, threw strength down my limbs and made them *burn!*

The Rebel's hold loosened. I jolted my leg back, clean out of his sweaty hands and I kicked my big toe into the warm wetness of his eyeball. He screamed, loud and anguished, startling Zackery into lowering the scalpel. One leg free, I kicked Zackery's jaw and he fell back into the wall, allowing me enough time to throw my foot into Ashworth's bony cheek. He stumbled back and his hands slipped from my other leg.

The second Rebel held both my wrists with one hand and used his other in a panicked effort to grasp my free, flailing limbs. A single hand wasn't enough to restrain my heated rage and I ripped myself free. This Rebel, no more than twenty years of age, stared at me with wide, shocked eyes and I stabbed my thumbs into both of them. Warm blood squirted upon my face. I pushed my thumbs deeper and, in a seamless motion, ripped them out.

His scream was monstrous, inhuman. He stumbled around the table, clutching his blind, bleeding face and collided into Svenja. They tumbled to the floor, rolling around each other in a flurry of gold and blood.

I loosened the rope around my torso and scurried out. I slammed hard onto the wooden floorboards and quickly pulled the foul piece of cloth from my mouth, vomiting up the lingering taste of gun grease.

From the corner of my eye, Zackery regained his focus. His eyes darted over the floor, meeting the scalpel directly between us. Angry heat raged as I grasped it between my bloody fingers and sank its pristine blade straight through Zackery's palm, impaling him to the wall. He shrieked, cradling his oozing hand, tears pooling behind his glasses.

The remaining Rebel, the one my toe had stabbed, restructured his attack. The last surgical knife still sat patiently upon the table and for a brief, tense moment, we both stared longingly at it. He made the first move, charging towards it, his hands twitching.

But anger made me quick and dextrous. I reached it first, took its handle and sliced the serrated blade clean through his neck. Through the gargling blood, he spent his final few minutes twitching on the floor.

Something hard hit my legs. I shrieked and fell to the ground. Svenja was suddenly upon me, her hands around my throat, her teeth flickering in the firelight. "You selfish bitch! You know lives you're risking, the innocent people you're condemning to death!"

Svenja's spidery fingers compressed around my neck.

Kill her, the piano screeched. *Kill her, Alira!*

I buried my fingers in her wiry white hair and stared into those golden eyes, focussing on each speck, each metallic gleam.

A shape appeared: malleable, convulsing, like a ball of molten gold held in a perpetual state of fluidity. I stared hard, deeper, wanting to dive into that liquid ball but it changed shape and pushed me out.

I tried again, staring harder, trying to peel that golden ball apart and witness the flood of memories from within. Svenja's soul morphed around my stare, throwing me out every time I tried to gain entry.

Even my soul felt the strain. Numbness grew, dousing the fire inside my blood. My hold on Svenja weakened.

She prized away my grip, throwing me off. My eyes, though heavy and sitting like two cold marbles, focussed upon her frantic, flailing frame as her features began to morph. Like that ball of molten gold, Svenja herself resembled a liquid structure, fighting the rush of Sebastian trying to gain entry.

I'd weakened her soul, chipped away the power that held back Sebastian's control. Now, as they battled for dominance, Svenja's features quickly morphed into Sebastian's, then back to Svenja's. Only the teeth remained the same: gold and rigid, the jaw opened in a perpetual, silent scream of utter agony as she—*they*—writhed upon the floor.

"*What have you done?*" Ashworth's grating howl bounced off my thick, heated skin.

"I'm not apologising to you, *boy*," I said through the acidic tang. "You claim to fight for freedom, for *justice*, but nothing you do—nothing you've *ever* done—has been worth the *noble* cause you claim to fight for!"

Ashworth's narrow jaw widened into a detesting grin. "I'm going to enjoy gutting you."

We circled one another, like animals. Our steps careful, our teeth bared, we each craved the sweet taste of the jugular. That bloody, serrated knife peeked at me from the floor, begging for the warmth of my fingers.

Or Ashworth's.

I lunged for the knife. Ashworth pulled me back. I kicked the table, propelling us to the far wall. Ashworth hit it with a loud grunt, the tip of his long coat tickling the fire roaring just below. Flames rose, scratching at Ashworth's skin and he howled, loud and infuriated, as he threw me into that neatly stacked pile of towels.

As Ashworth ripped off his flaming coat, I stumbled upright. Mason's sheathed knife had been knocked upon the floor.

Behind me, Ashworth's incensed cry echoed around the room, readying for his attack.

In act of blatant desperation, I ripped Mason's curved knife from its leather holster...

I meant to threaten Ashworth, to halt his enraged advanced. I planned to scream at him, to berate his choices and all his *fucking* Free People and demand they let me go!

I turned with that knife grasped and ready to threaten...

Unbeknownst to me, Ashworth was already charging. He impaled himself upon Mason's unsheathed, sharpened knife.

For a moment, stillness reigned. Ashworth and I remained locked, separated only by Mason's knife and my sweating palm. Ashworth's brown eyes widened, his lips swiftly losing colour, as he took a laboured, shocked stare down to his abdomen. His warm blood seeped onto my fingers, sinking within each gap, each groove.

Our eyes met. Ripe fear swirled within his.

I'm sorry, I wanted to say, but no words came. As I pulled the knife from his torso and Ashworth tumbled at my feet, I realised that he didn't deserve my apology. He may have, once.

I looked at Mikael Ashworth's vacant, lifeless expression. A pool of blood grew beneath him, glossy and sleek, shimmering in the warm firelight. I stepped over it, leaving Ashworth's body to cool beneath the fire's dying embers.

Svenja remained cycling between Sebastian and her own soul. Writhing upon the floor, she pulled at hair that lengthened for exactly two seconds, then shortened just as quickly. I stared at those cycles for a little while, Mason's bloody knife still wrapped within my fingers. How would it feel if I'd cut her throat? Would it be satisfying? Perhaps it would, for a single second, before Sebastian's vengeful thumbs came clawing at my eyeballs.

Leaving her convulsing body, I returned to that surgical table and unwrapped myself from Mason's knife. Ashworth's blood still stained my fingers and marred my jeans as I hastily dressed. Dirty, bloody feet slipped back into my boots just as Zackery's pained shrieked jolted my attention.

"I-I'm s-so sorry. I-I swear, t-they weren't giving me a choice!" I scanned the thick tear tracks staining his cheeks, and the blood leaking from his impaled hand.

I threw a towel into Zackery's lap. "To stop the bleeding," I said.

I barely felt my legs as I crouched before him, holding the bloody tip of Mason's knife to the marble in his throat. "Where are we?" I asked.

"Erm, f-fifteen miles southeast of Eagle's Overlook."

I forced a shallow smile and ripped the scalpel from his palm, throwing it far out of reach. Zackery shrieked, holding his bleeding hand close, crying as he wrapped it in within the towel's warm, comforting embrace.

From the window, we looked to be nestled on a sweeping plateau, surrounded by a sea of jagged mountains. Moonlight blared bright and forceful upon the landscape, bathed with snow and silver. It beckoned me closer, willing me back into its wintry, wild heart.

"Don't come after me," I said, as Ashworth's blood coagulated on my hand. "I'll kill any Free People who dare come after me, do you understand?"

"Yes," Zackery breathed, fighting unconsciousness. "I'm so sorry..."

Without another look, I returned to the New World's cold embrace.

26

———

How long had I been walking?

The Rebel hideout had long since disappeared, covered by layer upon layer of fresh mountain.

Night gradually morphed into a pale pink sunrise, hanging below snowy peaks. Yet, a few stars remained, clinging to their sparkles before their daytime nap.

I continued on. Completely numb, be it from trauma, exhaustion, or cold. I couldn't tell anymore and yet, I welcomed the iciness. I craved its monotony, willed my tired body to just continue feeling *nothing*. I didn't want to remember that firelit cave, or the train wreckage, or the table donned with knives. I was so tired of remembering, of feeling. I was tired of being blamed —of being *mutilated*—for the actions of others.

So, so tired...

Eventually, a wooden shack appeared. Precariously placed on the overhanging ledge, the shack's position screamed *refuge*. Who built it? Impossible to say, but its inhabitants were clearly no longer welcome. The shack had been slowly eaten by the chilly air, the wooden walls warped and cracking with thick layers of frost, but as I stumbled inside its protective walls, the remaining blankets and metal stove gave some minuscule comforts.

No fire. I couldn't afford to draw attention to the lonely shack on the cliff-side. Besides, I was scared of warming up. I was terrified a fire would thaw my bones and muscles, and allow raw, serrated feeling to cut into me, just like that scalpel...

I curled upon that mouldy floor, wrapped in damp blankets, and listened to the howling wind. Hours passed and streaks of yellow sunlight cut through the gaps in the wooden walls. I forced my leg beneath one of those rays and relished its fleeting warmth.

Curled up inside that shack, my thoughts tumbled to Svenja. Was she still cycling? Probably. Only a bullet would stop her and Sebastian's struggle.

I rubbed my temple, concentrating on the dull ache that lingered there. Evidence of Svenja's soul still clinging to my own. Icy pain concentrated behind my eyeballs, telling of a very failed Connection. Her soul was so odd, so *inhuman*. Echoes of it still lingered inside my mind and if I concentrated hard enough, I felt her haunting presence. Like a layer of liquid gold had been smeared inside my skull, calling back to Svenja.

If I concentrated even harder, her soul even called back to me. Only briefly, like the echo of distant thunder.

I thought about when Heidi and I were enslaved in the bowels of Mason's Palace. She'd said she knew where Svenja Svellec was; a powerful *hunch* that she was in the Icelands.

Did Heidi, at some point and for whatever reason, stare into Svenja's soul? Had she unknowingly dipped her fingers into that ball of convulsing gold?

Poor Heidi. Tears leaked from my eyes, dripping into the damp, mouldy blanket. I hadn't mourned her and Anya. Not yet, not the way I wanted to. The events since their deaths had been so consuming, so horrendous that I simply lacked the time or energy to cry for them.

But I missed them, so fucking much. In a way, perhaps my lack of crying stemmed from denial. They weren't dead, they were just away. They were hiding from Mason in a lonely part of the New World, curled up around a healthy fire with a meaty rabbit sizzling upon the grill. I imagined them smiling, relaxed in the knowledge that they were *safe*, that no Masonians or Rebels could ever find or hurt them ever again.

I relaxed further into that image, comforted by it. Closing my eyes, I pretended that I would join them.

Put the kettle on, girls. I'll be there soon.

* * *

I STARTLED AWAKE.

No sunlight punched the wooden walls, no white glare foretold the sheets of snow. Daylight had long gone. Now, the shadowy depths of night were only cut by the aurora's cool, green glow. Remnants of its ethereal colour fell gently upon my face, pulsing through the gaps in the ceiling.

Slowly, I sat up. Nausea rushed.

With a great heave, I vomited the foul contents of an empty stomach. Acidity burned my tongue as the pool of bile steamed in the cold air. Sickness still lingered, yet I pushed it away, trying to forget about it.

Wrapped in those damp blankets, I walked through the mountains bathed in snow and coveted by the aurora's green glow. I basked in such freedom. Everything was so beautiful as I traversed those mountains.

But such calm was fleeting. Exhaustion ached my limbs and my stomach growled for food. I admitted that civilisation—though entirely unwelcome— was my only hope at survival. With little choice, I edged towards the lonely mountain of Eagle's Eye as soon as I saw the wide, smooth caldera it perched in. The whole geological feature reminded me of a basin in the kitchen of mountains.

It was foolish of me to visit such a large town, and one infiltrated by Rebels. No doubt word of my escape was already filtering through the Free People, along with Ashworth's demise.

But as my empty belly ached and my body shivered, I didn't have much of a choice.

Gods, I'm so hungry...

The fires of Eagle's Overlook burned brightly, grasping my eager attention from miles away. From a distance, I simply assumed the town crawled with Traders and Roamers alike—just like normal. Those fires belonged to heathy braziers, showering light and warmth across a whole manner of visitors.

Little did I know, Eagle's Overlook had a very different flavour that evening.

As I wandered into the town, the blanket pulled low across my brow, I gaped at the once vibrant, exuberant town, now transformed. Pulled by Rebels and thugs into a decaying pit of ruin and blood.

People weaved in an out of burning fires—not braziers, but *bonfires*—born from burning books and furniture, thrown into the mud from the Town Hall's grand interior. They burned as angry beacons of heat and colour that flickered upon graffitied walls.

Mud squelched beneath my boots as I walked, quite numbly, onwards. People danced around those bonfires, throwing bits of Aristocracy into the hungry flames, feeding the haze of salty, bitter smoke that suffocated the air. They were wild, like animals; half screamed with exuberance, the other with utter agony. Children weaved in and out of those flames—those *people*—crying and laughing in equal measure.

Huts smouldered, the grassed roofs so dry and blackened. Barrels of mead rolled from the inn and people huddled around them, pouring the contents into their palms as they drank with a speed verging on desperate. Were they trying to rejoice, or forget?

But the clear star of the town, suspended high and proud for the entire Territory to see, was the Governor of Eagle's Overlook. Held above a pile of charred books and furniture, his body was tied to a wooden bracket. Closer still, and I noticed that he had been scalped. Blood trickled onto a face that was far from its original colour, the white gleam of his skull enticing crows that squawked and circled. His white robes, completely drenched in blood and dirt, had been ripped open to reveal his bulbous belly, disembowelled, with the spill of his bloody, slippery ropes hanging down to his ankles.

Hot nausea rushed up my gullet, but I remained staring, unable to pull my eyes away. Gripped by morbid fascination.

At the base of this horrific, sickening display, a woman and three children lay sobbing.

Cautiously, I approached. Their clothes, once so clean and freshly pressed, were smothered with dirt and mud, caked with layers of humiliation and despair. *Aristocrats*, I sadly realised. Probably the Governor's wife and their three children.

I looked to the Governor's corpse, already discolouring. Each limb appeared stiff and cold, and thick lines of green and black streaked his drying skin. Yes, he'd been dead for a while.

Fire burst from the inn as a group of rejoicing men hurled flaming bottles of liquid. Harald, the innkeeper, rushed out, his beloved tabby cat wrapped within his arms, and berated the raucous attackers with his dissimilar eyes seething. Strange, I thought Harald worked for Ashworth, so why would the Rebels destroy his beloved inn?

Rebels. These people didn't deserve such a title anymore. They were thugs. Plain and simple. Their dream wasn't freedom. It was anarchy.

Flames roared higher, shocking life back into the Governor's widow. With a final sob, she forced herself upright and stumbled away, gripping her children's tatty clothing.

Something had dropped from beneath her cloak and squelched sickly beneath my boot. I saved the necklace from the mud, wiping my thumb across it. Two enormous diamonds sparkled, protecting an even larger gem. Amethyst, diamond, sapphire? I wasn't entirely sure, but its rich, purple hue reminded me of the dress I wore the first night I consensually gave myself to Mason. His violin had played so beautifully as he unzipped that dress, one torturous inch at a time.

"Hey..." I tried to call, but my voice was so broken and croaky, as though my throat was made of sandpaper and wore away the sound. "Hey!"

The woman abruptly turned to meet my demands. Absolute terror warped her neat features: the straight button nose, the gaunt cheeks, the deep blueness of eyes that had not slept in many, many days. She dragged her three children behind her, protecting them from me. From *me*.

Then again, given my destiny, she had every right to.

"Here," I said, and offered her the necklace. Its silver chain dripped between my fingers, still stained with blood and mud.

I was afraid she'd take one look at my violent hands and then scramble back, unwilling to be anywhere near them. But her fearful stare never made it to my hands. Nor did she notice my diamond eyes, just peeking from the lower rim of the blanket. In fact, she never looked towards my face.

Pure, unmitigated fear warped her features. She rushed back, desperately gaining distance between me and the children cowering behind her. My expensive hand dropped heavily to my side. I watched her run into the carnage of bonfires and yelling people, their lush cloaks fluttering.

Sighing, I stared down at the necklace. It didn't belong in my palm, soaked in mud. It deserved to be around her skinny neck. Still, perhaps I could sell it. Or trade it. I didn't care how much it was worth, so long as it tipped food into my mouth and a gun into my palm.

I chanced a concerned look at the crazed men and women, joyously ripping through the heart of this once proud town. Almost for comfort, my fingers stroked Mason's bloody knife, hidden at the small of my back.

I'd come here for supplies and food—something to settle my shivering bones and aching belly. Instead, I'd stepped into a cauldron of bitterness and boiling blood. A pit of utter carnage—not unlike the one filled with that starving polar bear. Just like that horrific auditorium, the cheers of crazed men and women smothered everything. Rebel thugs with violence in their hearts and hatred in their bellies, gorging themselves on chaos, wanting this proud town to just *burn*.

Was *this* how Ashworth envisioned his free world? *This* was what Anya and Heidi died for?

Commotion from behind us. A group of men rushed into the town's burning, smouldering square.

"Masonians!"

Like they'd been summoned from the pit of Hel, black trucks blocked our only exit and vomited up a gaggle of angry, seething Masonians. They charged towards us with their guns high and their swords unsheathed. Thick clouds of white erupted from their mouths as they yelled for our submission, our surrender.

I rushed back with the rest of the terrified, panicking people. Scrambling from the tide of bloodthirsty animals.

Some of the rioters decided to fight, throwing themselves with their flaming bottles and shards of glass. Others had guns and knives, shooting and slicing.

And yes—for a moment, I thought they might do it. I thought these violent thugs would destroy the Masonian ambush before it had even started. That they'd finally do something good with their lives and save the innocent people trapped in their filthy rebellion.

Masonian bullets cut them down before they even got close. Bodies littered the ground, smearing the mud with glossy red.

Masonians outnumbered the Rebels three to one. The Rebels were a single faction, already drunk off violence, alcohol—and Hel knows what else. But the Masonians were soldiers—an elite garrison of trained killers patrolling the Snowlands and cutting down every Rebel, Gang member and miscreant they stumbled across. Perhaps this was Mason's revenge for the tunnel explosion: it would take him a long time to traverse the Snowlands and he was damned sure to obliterate any whiff of Rebellion as soon as he smelt it.

And one could detect the burning smoke of Eagle's Overlook from miles away.

Trapped in the flood of terrified, whimpering people, I pulled the blanket low across my brow as we were marshalled down into the flat, snow-smothered base of the caldera.

Moonlight intensified each glare and gleaming sword. Terror sang loudly inside my stomach, obliterating the hunger. I gulped back the fearful vomit, too terrified and too exhausted to try and run from the crowd of people.

Stay low, was my plan. *Be inconspicuous.*

Masonians marshalled us into a little pool of crying, petrified people. As the aurora bathed us in glorious green light, I gazed at Eagle's Eye: the lonely mountain that held Eagle's Overlook halfway up its steep grey flanks. It proudly stood in the middle of the caldera, surrounded by flat plains of snow that rose into glaciers, creaking and slumping down tall mountains.

Screams rippled somewhere behind me. Masonians dove into the crowd and plucked out children, ripping them from the pool of hysterical people. They marched their trembling bodies back into the main town, eventually out of sight. As their cries grew quiet, I imagined them surrounding those blazing bonfires.

Perhaps it was just to keep them warm, but such lies grew bitter. They had a plan for those children, most certainly. I swallowed my trepidation, remaining still and subdued in the middle of that sobbing crowd.

Perhaps, should I remain completely silent, they wouldn't notice me...

I felt Mason's presence before I saw him: the air became still, the gentle breath of wind paused. My strength had gone, ripped away by Ashworth and

Svenja, so when Mason marched before us, glaring and snarling in equal measure, I couldn't scream, move, cower—*anything*. Frozen by the intensity of those diamond eyes, I forced myself to peek from beneath the hood and my stomach lurched up, high with the children in Eagle's Overlook.

Gaunt cheeks sat unhealthily upon his ashen, pallid complexion. Dark bags hung low and heavy beneath eyes that fluoresced powerfully—*dangerously*—in the silver moonlight. Perhaps Mason had been weakened. Perhaps his lingering mortality had chipped away his power, one minute fraction at a time.

But no, that was a fool's thought. Standing before us with his teeth bared and his silver revolver gripped in white knuckles, I understood that Mason, flooded with anger and desperation—consumed by the *fear* of his finite future—was more dangerous, more powerful than ever.

Ashworth didn't weaken the monster, I abruptly realised, *he simply made him angry.*

"Well, this really is a sight!" he snarled to us, perusing the scene like a ravenous lion waiting for the prey to run, so he could sink his teeth right in. "The *glorious* residents of Eagle's Overlook, reduced to whimpering beneath the light of your burning homes!"

Specks of snow whipped up from the icy ground, bowing in submission to Mason's pacing boots.

"Tell me, how does it feel to live in Ashworth's world? To have your homes, your livelihoods smouldering in the bowels of your once *spectacular* town?"

He laughed loudly, madly, to the dancing lights above.

"Eagle's Overlook is *mine* and you dare defile it? You *dare* desecrate its noble history with such barbarity, such lack of civility?"

Another crazed chuckle to the stars above, shimmering through the pastel green hue.

"You are *nothing!* You are ants upon a mountain, an *infestation* upon my World that deserves nothing but complete eradication!"

Standing there, illuminated by the heavenly tones of the sky above, I watched the man who once filled my scarred heart with such life. A solitary tear raced down my cheek, dribbling to my jaw.

I loved you, I had said to him. Perhaps I did, once. But there, as he shrieked his insanity—his *cruelty*—to the innocent, crying people of Eagle's Overlook, the *survivors* of his barbaric World, I finally remembered the hatred.

Not the hatred for what he did to *me*, not the hatred that had consumed his Palace's last surviving weeks. But the early hatred, before the music sang inside my head, before it had dug its musical claws into my soul and chipped away my morality, one deafening chord at a time.

I remembered the horrific stories Campbell told me about Mason, I remembered the bodies of the countless Herders—*my people*—butchered by his regime. Tia's face flashed across my memories, when Mason forced her compliance in return for protection from a sick man, whose only punishment was a temporary *demotion*.

That's all Mason did to Jayson Montgomery, for what he did to Tia. As she struggled to survive through her entire existence, Jayson was simply *demoted*.

And yet, I *had* loved Mason. I once craved his touch, we had mutually gushed over the little life I was creating, craving the blissful future that once seemed so tangible.

Perhaps that all it was. Maybe I'd never loved Mason. Maybe I just loved the idea of a *future*, without running, without fear. A future that teased happiness, for the first time in my life. Maybe that's all it was.

I hoped that's all it was.

"So," Mason continued, as his bloodless lips twisted into a wide, sinister grin. "I hope, dear residents of Eagle's Overlook, that you enjoy this little demonstration."

With exaggerated, sweeping arms, he gestured to the lonely mountain, and the burning remnants of a once grand town. "Here, as your children lay in the depths of the eagle's belly, I want you to witness what happens to those who *dare* defy me!"

Fresh fear rippled across the pool of people. I was one of them, wondering with deathly clarity if I had understood Mason correctly...

Mason turned to the mountain full of bonfires and crying children. His arms lifted; his fingers curled. Ground rumbled beneath our feet as rocks and boulders tumbled down the mountainside.

People scrambled forward; panic filled the cold air. Someone pulled a gun from beneath their clothes and fired at Mason. He startled and ducked as bullets poured around him. The Masonian to his left dropped dead to the snow; the one to his right was flung back by the bullet in his shoulder.

The attacker's clip emptied. He frantically fumbled with the gun, spilling bullets as he brought a fresh handful from his pocket. Masonians forced their way through the crowd and stabbed the Rebel attacker just as his reloaded gun clicked shut. We all rushed from his bleeding body, like coloured oil dropped into water.

Before us, Mason cackled. "You think you can kill *me*? *I will destroy all of you!*"

He turned to the mountain—those *children*—as the violin screeched inside my skull.

A woman screamed, rushing towards the mountain. It was the mourning Aristocrat: the Governor's wife. Mason took one bored look at her and curled his fist. A seamless spike of ice erupted from the snow and impaled her, slicing through her neck directly above her collarbones.

Blood poured down the ice with delicate wisps of steam. I gazed at her dying body and felt the weight of the necklace still nestled inside my pocket. Her throat deserved to be held down by that necklace, not *mutilated* like that...

All because she wanted to save her children. One more parent they'd have to mourn. Three more orphans in a world that just didn't give a damn about any of them...

A flurry of emotion—of anguish and anger—erupted inside of me.

Mason stopped, listening carefully to the music inside his head. His bloodless lips parted to release the first of three, long breaths.

I tried to stop it, to flush my emotions back down before their meaning could be understood. But I couldn't. Those feelings remained inside of me: a wave of thunderous, unrelenting emotion that screamed triumphantly inside Mason's head.

Heartless diamond eyes surveyed us all. Then he smiled.

"Alira," he crooned to the crowd. "How wonderful of you to join us here."

My heart sank at his widening grin. He took delicate steps closer. "Tell me, when Svenja Svellec tried to gut you and your music *screamed* at me, did you *regret* your decisions?"

Fear choked me. Even my breaths were too terrified to escape.

Mason's powerful eyes perused the scene. *"Find her!"*

Masonians rushed into the crowd. They grasped the back of innocent necks and stared into strangers' eyes.

Mason grew impatient. With a strangling grip upon his revolver, he shot an innocent woman. Her body tumbled in a bloody pile. People shrieked and screamed. His aim found the next woman.

"Stop!"

The word was out before I could stop it, hurling towards Mason's receptive ears. The crowd scrambled back, as though my voice was fire.

We locked eyes. Diamonds shined beneath ethereal green light.

"Ah." He smiled. "There you are."

Masonians encircled me, their swords unsheathed.

"I'm curious, my dear," he said, taking slow, menacing paces before me. "Which part of your life do you regret the most, hm? Was it when the poisoned wine passed your lips, or maybe your visit to Maelstrom? Then again, maybe it was the beach at Giant's Respite, or perhaps the pill that slipped down your throat."

He grinned menacingly, spectacularly...

"Well, my dear Alira, I will ensure you regret every single one of them."

Hate ballooned inside my belly—powerful, consuming—wiping away whatever *love* I had left. I returned his sinister glare with a clenched jaw.

"Such *fire...*" Mason crooned, that evil smile persisting. "Do you remember the night we first met, on the stage of that empty Theatre?"

Of course, I did. That night had been carved into my skull, along with the music. I Came of Age that night. I listened to the strange music inside my head and wondered how I was destined to end the world.

"From that moment, I wanted to keep your fire burning—to nurture it, to see it grow and watch it burn brightly, *fervently...*"

Mason's smile was a cold as the specks of ice that fell gently upon his cheek. "But not anymore. Now, I want to extinguish your fire. I want to *destroy* you."

A lonely tear trickled down my cheek. "You already have, Mason," I whispered, with all the energy I could muster.

I watched with mild, despairing accomplishment as Mason's smile fell, just like the snow breathed down from the mountain. Beneath my resolve, agony surfaced, bruising my chest. But I kept Mason's glare and forced myself to stare harder, deeper, until our Connection fluttered inside my skull.

Something flickered in Mason's face. A flurry of memories, soon crushed by an utter, complete abhorrence.

"Well, my dear, I believe it's time to take some *responsibility* for your actions." He turned to the mountain. "You took my children from me, Alira. Now, watch me take theirs."

Mason thrust his arm forwards, curled his first, and sharply retracted.

The centre of the mountain exploded. Eagle's Overlook succumbed quickly, collapsing with the rest of the mountain. Screams poisoned the air: parents shrieking, screaming as the high-pitched wails of children hurtled across the caldera. As the entire town crumbled with the mountain, the sounds of those dying children stabbed me, each screaming needle pushing into my heart, my stomach, and I felt sick. Sick with the reality—with the abomination occurring before my very eyes—and the sure, undeniable gag of spending my future—*any* future—with the *monster* that was Mason...

After all this time, I finally saw the truth.

He wasn't my lover. He was *never* my lover.

He was my fucking rapist.

Eagle's Eye completely crumbled in a cloud of dirt and carnage, taking Eagle's Overlook with it. The remains of that mountain entombed almost one hundred innocent children.

And Mason just *smiled.*

Through the deafening chorus of screams, engines roared. A flurry of black vans skidded onto the icy plateau and spilled armed men. Rebels, thugs—who knew the difference anymore? With rows of ammunition strapped around their chests and their faces smothered with black fabric, they jumped out of the van as a single entity. Bullets peppered the dusty air.

Half the crowd ducked, the other half ran towards the rubble, desperately clawing through the wreckage of an entire mountain.

Masonians charged towards the Rebels, their guns firing, their gleaming swords held in grubby hands. Behind us, charging down the slopes of the mountain, men and women donned skis and snipers, shooting at every Masonian they saw.

As Mason's violin shrieked, we locked diamond eyes. Numbness fluttered inside my skull.

I banked left and ran.

"Alira!" he screeched.

An open van door loomed, the Rebels too high on Masonian blood to notice me lunge into the driver's seat. The wheel was so rough and cold, the pedals stiff beneath my feet. I clipped my seatbelt just as Mason loomed in my peripheral vision. Muscle memory kickstarted as I thrust the van into gear, slammed my feet down, and skidded off across the plateau.

The van ached and grumbled beneath my touch, the unchained tyres screeching in defiance. We lurched and skidded across the ice and snow, following the path of two blinding white headlights.

In the side mirror, Masonians slaughtered *everyone*—man or woman. No children, for they had already been exterminated.

Like ants upon a mountain.

Sobs ached to burst. I swallowed them quickly and veered towards the southern edge of the caldera, where glaciers rose high into the mountains. A road lay ahead, clinging to the curving ledge of two glaciers. With Mason's convoy at my tail, I dove towards that icy road, twisting the wheel as the engine roared

The van lurched to the side. Wheels skidded. I frantically turned the wheel but the skid worsened.

The wheels lost their grip entirely. I fell.

The van rolled again and again as it tumbled down the mountainside. I plunged into an icy crevasse. Windows cracked and shattered, raining glass upon me. I lifted my hands, protecting my face as my coat's sleeves completely shredded. Eventually it shuddered to a creaking stop.

Ears ringing and head throbbing, I forced my eyes to open. Only the seatbelt held my upside-down body safely within its clutches. Unkempt hair tickled the roof of the van, dented and decorated with open metal scars. Ahead, the van's white headlights illuminated the glacial cave I had fallen into. Walls glowed blue beneath the white light, highlighting the network of glacial streams that trickled across gravel and stone.

Blood trickled from my nose and up between my eyes. No doubt it matched the angry red streaks staining my hands and forearms.

Voices echoed. Distant voices, bouncing off the crevasse's icy walls. I listened to the violin inside my head. Only hatred sang back.

I unclipped myself and fell from the seat, collapsing to the roof of the van with a loud, pained groan. Time was not on my side, I had to hurry. Fractures skipped across the front window, which I easily pushed away.

Cold air grasped me, cooling the wet blood. Above the gaggle of Masonians ogling at the wreckage, the aurora shined. It was so bright, as though powered by the souls of all those innocent children.

That same light illuminated a wide space between the icy walls, bordering a small stream. It led up, into the bowels of the glacier, but wolf droppings scattered the ground. But no bones, which meant the animals had to have found a way out. I peeked below the van, but the other side of the crevasse was far too small for me—let alone a wolf. So, the crevasse in front had to be the only way in or out.

Mason's sonorous voice echoed down. *Rope* and *climb* were clearly audible.

Please Gods, may there be a way out of here...

With a limping gait, I rushed into the crevasse.

* * *

THE AURORA RIPPLED upon a mess of stars. It welcomed me with open arms as I clambered from that icy cave. With a heaving groan, I limped further from the Masonians infesting the bowels of that glacier.

The aurora's light allowed the landscape to be viewed in remarkable detail: the sea of mountains tickling the stars, the pearly skin of lakes, the snow-capped tips of trees that merged into the horizon... All around me, this icy world shone, born from the bones of over two billion men, women, and children.

I stumbled on, quickening my pace. Masonians would soon spill from that glacial crevasse and there was no way to escape in my condition.

My condition...

Tears ached behind my eyes and I gazed into that aurora, imagining my Pa smiling down at me. I longed for the warmth of his arms, the tender reassurance he so effortlessly gave.

I wandered to the edge of an enormous, gentle slope. The smooth layer of snow could make a quick getaway, should I find something to slide upon.

I quickly searched my immediate surroundings. A few trees were dotted about the landscape, surrounding the odd fallen trunk. Remnants of an old avalanche, perhaps?

Painful memories emerged at the last avalanche I'd witnessed.

I limped towards one of those fallen trunks, withered and decayed by the elements. With bloody fingers, I tugged at the trunk's decrepit flesh one crack at a time, until it peeled away in one large piece that could easily embrace my bruised body.

I returned to the top of that slope, gazing down its untouched majesty. The beauty of Mason's brutal world gazed back, mocking me.

I thought of Eagle's Overlook. I imagined the faces of all those innocent children crushed beneath Mason's tyranny.

Ashworth wanted to end Mason's reign. He had used me in a sordid plot to ensure Mason's mortality, to wish for the day a Rebel might stick a sword through Mason's sour heart and end his cruelty forever.

And they still thought that. Mason, Campbell, the Free People...

They had no idea.

I gazed to the wondrous landscape and felt nothing but utter horror at what I'd done after my last conversation with Anya. My actions had spurred from a grieving, heated fire that burst my cells and boiled my blood, but now the sordid truth of what I'd done—*what the music had done*—was too shocking, too atrocious to ignore. Music sang across my memories, now so jeering, and I hated its sound. I hated its *relief*.

I remembered the way my fingers danced across the healing keys of a golden piano. I remembered the blood that coated those same fingers as I wandered, aimlessly, through a moonlit forest.

Such a small amount, I remember thinking. Unbeknownst to me, there was a reason for that.

Just before Mason's insanity obliterated Eagle's Overlook, that lonely attacker tried to shoot him. Everyone, including Mason himself, thought he'd missed.

But he didn't miss. I'd watched one stray bullet collide with an oblivious Mason's shoulder.

And I'd watched it bounce right off...

Like rain upon a window, Mason had once explained.

And there, as my hands caressed the abhorrent *miracle* growing inside my womb, I remembered Mason's *satisfaction* as Eagle's Overlook crumbled beneath his fist.

Beneath his *smile*.

How many more mountains would crumble now that he couldn't die?

Now that he was *immortal*.

Gazing at Mason's New World, a single, stunned tear trickled down my cheek.

What have I done?

27

The sun rose from beneath a field of mountains. A line of pale lilac teased the horizon, dulling the intensity of the aurora above. But still, it persisted as I wandered up the rocky incline at the edge of the Brüster Mountains. The remains of the Icelands lay ahead: huge, angular boulders rested upon a grey sea of utter calamity.

Leo's Landing was visible in the distance: a small pool of fiery light surrounded by trees. From this distance, the village looked too small and helpless to contain the merchandise Joe had been so certain still existed.

I pulled the hood even lower across my brow, hiding my eyes.

I gazed at the world beneath my toes. Everything seemed so small, up there in the mountains. So delicate and precious.

My gaze wandered to the Icelands, now nothing but chunks of rock and snow. I prayed to the Old Gods—for the first time in what felt like centuries.

Please, Odin, I begged inside my head. *Please may they forgive me...*

The violin screeched. I cried out, my voice echoing across the mountains, bouncing off the mounds of rock and ice until it found my ears again and again.

Knees collapsed beneath me, my strength failing. As Mason's *fear* screamed inside my head, I imagined the sight that must have donned his eyes.

I imagined the horde of Rebel soldiers, exhilarated grins upon their faces as they met the Destroyer of the Old World with their guns held high. I knew Campbell was amongst them with his sword unsheathed, for he had been waiting his entire life for such a moment.

My heart ached for Campbell. *I'm sorry*, I wanted to scream.

Emotions sang inside my head: hate, terror, fury, failure...

Clutching my skull, shrieking at each whip of the violin's strings, I listened as Mason's hate took centre stage, obviously gutting every Rebel in his path. The very world trembled beneath such fury and birds erupted from trees, squawking and squealing as the haunting howl of wolves rippled across all the New World forests.

But then the violin malformed, singing terrible ballads of defeat. Perhaps Mason's men were dying, maybe there were just too many Rebels.

Whatever the reason, Mason's fear was deafening. It was so odd to hear such despairing melodies, but there they were, screaming inside my head.

I imagined Mason's face falling, the sparkle in his eyes dimming with anticipated death and defeat. How strange it must have been for him, to consider death after all these years. Is that why he was so afraid? Did he envisage his fate in the afterlife, succumbing to an eternity of torture within Hel's fiery grip? Or perhaps, after all that time, he was simply afraid of failure.

Whatever the truth, Mason held little hope. He knew his long and wretched existence was about to come to a stark, painful end.

I imagined the bullets in his revolver running empty, the metal casings peppering the snow at his feet. He'd unsheathe his sword, watching the blade's mottled gleam with panicked breaths. His violin screeched with desperate accomplishment and I imagined him cutting down an attacking Rebel, then another, and then another.

Mason's music, riddled with defeat, spiked with a call of utter loathing and I imagined Campbell strolling up to him, his own sword unsheathed, a relieved grin permeating his mound of dense stubble. As the violin subdued into numb understanding, Mason knew his end had come.

What did Campbell do? Impossible to say. Perhaps he stuck his sword right though his heart. Or maybe he attempted to slice Mason's throat.

Maybe, after everything, he took a great, sweeping slice at Mason's neck, hoping to remove his head entirely.

Whatever happened, Mason's fate seemed inevitable...

Until Campbell's sword bounced off Mason's skin. Hard and solid.

Like diamond.

The Free People's Rebellion ended with the sound of silence, as Mason's utter, unmitigated shock wiped his music from inside my skull. It stayed silent for a while—an eternity, it seemed. Alone upon that mountaintop, I listened to the void with a crying heart.

Mason's music returned with more power than I thought possible. I cried and shrieked as it rejoiced. Mason's anger, his *exhilaration* wiped whatever fear, whatever failure was left and turned it into a raging, unstoppable power. A low rumbling filled the air, small rocks rolling down the mountainside.

As Mason's newfound, reenergised power loomed across the New World, I imagined the scene, somewhere far away. Of Mason, his safety now no longer a concern, marching to one Rebel and then the next, cutting them down one by one. Blood would spatter up his arm, his angry, *relieved* smile both wide and sinister, before he'd sliced through another, and then another. Rebels would eventually scatter, merging into the trees as they escaped Mason's immortal fury.

I prayed Campbell was one such survivor.

Nestled within the mountains, I listened to the fury as a sunrise bled over Mason's New World.

28

———

The ground still shook as I arrived in Leo's Landing.

A low rumble vibrated the air, animals shrieking and squealing. Dogs raced around the space, barking and yelping. Birds fluttered from trees, spilling the snow that soaked their branches. Rats scuttled across the road, crisscrossing their way between trembling huts. I steadied myself against one of those huts, pulling the hood low across my brow. There I remained, until the quaking ceased.

An air of normalcy came across the village, the inhabitants scurrying back into their homes and doors slamming firmly shut. A few lone dogs remained noisy, the echo of their barks resonating between the trees.

I exhaled a long breath, mist floating from my open lips. I took a limping step forward.

Nausea quickly rose. I fell to my knees, hunched over as I vomited up the remains of a rabbit I'd eaten some hours beforehand. Yellowed filth spewed into a deep, steaming hole.

I collapsed back, letting the cold air soothe burning cheeks, and wiped my mouth on my sleeve.

Mason's violin still sang. Exhilarated, angry, satisfied... A myriad of emotions as another Rebel town succumbed. That latest quake was the

275

second in the last twenty-four hours, the sixth in the past two days. He'd been busy.

That last one rattled my very bones. The epicentre must have been close. That meant Mason was close, too, for he wouldn't dare destroy a town unless he had personally scoured it, ensuring I was not hiding within a cellar. I quickened my pace down the road and tried not to panic. It would do nothing but make things worse, and I was running out of time.

I passed one door, then another, before I finally saw it.

A modest size for a hut. Its bright green door was loud and garish, and terribly recognisable. Joe had been right: I couldn't miss it.

I paused on the doorstep, the door's marred surface screaming indecision. I squeezed my eyes closed, fighting the growing sense of fear. This could go one of two ways and yet, I didn't have a choice. Whatever happened, I needed to remain hidden—now, more than ever.

Mason's curved knife weighed heavy in my hand. Ashworth's blood still stained the blade.

Don't think about it, girl.

I barged into the hut that reeked of smoke and weed. *"Don't move!"*

An elderly man thrust his hands up. He remained like a deer caught in headlights, the glints of firelight from his oily, silver hair the only movement upon his frame. He stood frozen at the end of a long table, smattered with unloaded guns, bullets, and bags of gems. Those jewels sparkled in the light from the fire, burning rather happily at the side of the hut. A roasting spit punctured what remained of a small rabbit and its rich odour stuck to the back of my throat. I swallowed another wave of nausea.

"Stand up, *now!*" I yelled, rounding the table. He immediately rose to his feet, bumping the table. Bullets clinked to the wooden floor.

"What do you want? Bullets? Drugs? I-I don't work for the Mulch Gang anymore, I can't—"

"Shut up!" I gathered the hessian sack tucked into my jeans and threw it down the table. "Fill that up."

He gathered it quickly, beads of perspiration pebbling his brow.

"I want all the gems, all the jewellery, and all the ammunition you have." I noticed the stack of guns upon the wall. "The hunting rifle—I'll have that too."

He did as instructed, spilling contents into the sack.

"Throw the bag down the table."

Again, the man obliged. The sack fell in a miserable, loud heap against the wood.

"Please," the man said, his aged skin quickly losing colour. "I-I've given you everything!"

"Not everything." I pushed the blanket from my brow. "You sell coloured lenses. I need them."

The man's face, now completely devoid of colour, switched from fear to pure, unmitigated panic.

"I don't know what you're talking about, I—"

"Thirteen years ago, you sold coloured lenses to Joe Matheson. I know this because he told me so, and he carved your fucking address into my brain. So..." I waved the knife doused in blood. "Are you going to help me?"

"Please, if Mason finds out then—"

"He'll kill you?" I narrowed dangerous eyes. "*I'll* kill you now if you prefer?"

"Okay... Okay..." The man showed defeated palms and edged to a stack of boxes by the fire. On my instruction, he placed a velvet box at my side that contained—sure enough—six pairs of coloured lenses, two of each colour: green, amber, and blue.

"Thank you," I said sincerely. "If Mason comes knocking, tell him I'm heading to the Woodlands."

I wasn't, of course, but I hoped it would keep Mason happy, perhaps sparing this poor man's life.

I'd already escaped the town before I hunched over, vomiting. Again.

"C'mon, give me a break, kiddo..." I grumbled, rubbing my aching belly.

After a while, I found a lonely cave, deep in the forest and hugging the base of a tall mountain. Yes, it would do nicely.

Soon, a fire's warmth thawed the frosted walls. I stared mindlessly into that fire, watching each burning ember race to the rocky ceiling. I couldn't afford to stay long, but I needed an hour or two to regain my strength. Then I would Roam to the next town, and then the next one, and the one after that. I would be a ghost, never staying in one place for too long. I couldn't risk Mason, or Svenja Svellec, finding me.

I horrible rush of unease, of *dread,* materialised at her name. Flashes of those golden teeth, the gleaming edge of a scalpel slicing at my nethers. I squeezed my eyes, determined to block out the images.

Breathe in... One... Two... Three....

My heartbeat slowed. No, I would be fine. I had supplies now, at least. Perhaps I could afford a proper meal—and something other than fucking rabbits.

I dragged the hessian sack to my side and examined my new hunting rifle. I practised my aim, nestling the butt deep into my shoulder. Old familiarity settled in my bones. Oh yes, a fine piece of kit.

I explored the rest of my stolen contents and picked out a single teardrop pendant, sparkling fervently in the firelight. Was it real? Probably, yet I doubted they all shared the same authenticity. I hoped a buying Trader or a Merchant wouldn't be too thorough in their examinations.

I refused to sell the purple necklace, dropped by the mourning Aristocrat who only wanted to save her children. Its weight held down my pockets, acting as a constant reminder of her fate—of all their fates.

But even then, I felt those musical claws whispering, breathing across my consciousness. *Go back to him, Alira,* it said. I squeezed the purple necklace until it almost burst my palm.

I inspected the lens box. Black velvet; highly luxurious.

The box clicked open. Expertly crafted lenses stared at me. So lifelike, so *real...*

I picked out the amber ones. These used to be my favourite, back when Joe originally presented them to me. That colour had donned my eyes for so many years, hiding them away from the world. Campbell liked them too.

I threw those amber lenses in the fire, watching the sparks burst upwards.

Green and blue lenses remained. Equally pretty. Equally unnatural. *Decisions, decisions...*

I almost threw up again as I inserted the green lenses. I blinked away the blurs, lines sharpening before the rocky veins of colour in the walls. What did I look like? Not Maya Doe, for sure.

Good.

I let the cold wall sink into the layers of dried sweat upon my back. I couldn't wait to have a shower, to douse myself in hot water, to cleanse myself of Ashworth's blood and the memories of those last few days.

Anya and Heidi flashed before me, as did the remains of Eagle's Overlook.

Tears threatened. I sniffed them back just as quickly. Plenty of time to crumble, later. I sniffed again and again and—

A sob broke free. Then another. Another.

Force them back, force them back!

But the dam had already broken, that pool of resolve spilling with the rest of my tears. In its wake, darkness. An empty hole inside my chest. A void, filled with nothing.

Empty. Utterly empty.

I let myself fall into that darkness. I explored it, allowed those fake green lenses to drop from my eyes and my limbs to curl around that painful pit inside me. Unhindered sobs shook the entire cave, rattling against the stone. I didn't care. I needed that release. I needed the world to know how much I missed Anya and Heidi. I needed the Old Gods to hear how Campbell had broken me, how Mason had *destroyed* me. I mourned for the those murdered in Eagle's Overlook, and those lost souls who ran with thugs and lapped up their promise of a *better life*.

I cried for Ashworth—not for his blood coating my hands, but for what he had done, and what he had tried to do.

Everything burned as I released it all—a torrent of grief and regret. A flood of poor decisions, desperate dreams, and stupid, idiotic deals. I hated myself for those deals. I hated the woman Campbell had once shaped, who Mason had later carved.

But most of all, I hated the music. Always singing inside my head, pulling and pushing my destiny—my *choices*.

Because the music was the reason I was in that cave. That music was the reason I had failed myself, failed everyone else. It was why I was alone.

Alone.

The truth startled me, stealing my breath.

Alone.

Yes, I was. Truly alone.

My hand found my belly and lingered. I remembered the child inside of me—the one I'd craved, the one the *music* had groomed me to create. To *save*.

I remembered a similar pain in a different life, where I'd sobbed in the cold corridors of Mason's Palace. Anya was there. She had knelt before me and placed a tender hand upon my stomach.

You are never *alone,* she'd said.

I wished I believed those words now. I wished Anya was with me, telling me that it was going to be okay, that I could *do this...*

But Anya would never speak again. I'd never hear her voice or feel her comforting warmth.

I was alone, in every sense of the word. With a bloated heart, I realised the babe inside my womb would not change that.

My hand still rubbed back and forth. Slowly. Leisurely.

I still had a purpose—it was the *only* thing I had left. The music inside my soul would ensure I'd birth this child, and I would obey it. Whatever the cost, I would obey.

Even if I resented myself for it.

"You can do this," I whispered, my throat like sandpaper.

Yes. Even on my own, even with this looming pit of regret and fear and loneliness, I would do this.

I could do this.

I had to.

29

WINTER

Smoke hung thick and heavy in the air as I wandered into Loki's Lost Longhouse. Away from the biting cold, the searing warmth from the central hearth was a sudden and welcoming reprieve. Delicious tingles raced up and down my arms as I waddled into the mounds of drunken revelry.

Men and women continued to laugh and chatter, the longhouse's rabble completely unaware of my presence. Waitresses zigzagged between the tables, large trays of mead in their hands. Some deposited drinks to waiting customers, other cleared plates of food from the tables. Delicious scents of roast lamb and root vegetables wafted up, interspersed with the heady tones of alcohol. I inhaled deep, craving a large gulp of mead, and hoped the residual fumes would calm my racing heart.

Gently parting the sea of merry people, I leant against the bar. The wood, though newly graffitied with runes of the Old Gods, was in remarkable condition. Very little scuffs or scratches marred its surface, nor did rings of moisture bleach its rich brown tones.

It made sense, really. Loki's Lost Longhouse, and the town of Gerta's Grotto where it resided, were only established recently. It was one of several towns built after the *Freefall*—or the Fall of the Free People. What was the name of the Rebel town that existed here, before Mason formed the chasm that swallowed it whole? I couldn't say. Yet Mason had made a solid effort to wipe all evidence of Rebellion cleanly away before commissioning this new town to be built, along with several others across the Snowlands.

The bartender finally caught my eye. I smiled as warmly as I could, though it still obviously appeared forced.

"Can I help you, love?"

"I..." I coughed, trying to clear the scratch from my throat. "I-I hear you have a telephone?"

"It'll cost you." He perused the weapons upon by back. A rifle and a shotgun proudly sat either side of my bulging rucksack. Next his eyes scanned my long leather coat, covering layers of woollen jumpers and scarves. "You've clearly got a lot of money on you, so I'd say you can afford it."

Too tired to argue, I delved into my pocket. Fingerless gloves appeared with a large handful of coin that I slammed on the bar. "Will this cover it?"

The bartender's eyes widened at his glimmering counter. "Absolutely," he crooned, sliding each gold coin into his palm. Caressing them to his chest, his eyes motioned to the corner of the longhouse, where a solitary table lay ready and waiting.

"Take a seat," he said. "I'll bring it over to you."

"Thanks." I edged away until I remembered, "Oh, what date it is?"

The bartender startled, unable to hide his frown. But as he stared at my large, bulbous belly, his confusion suddenly dropped.

He smirked and said, "It's the *Seventeenth Day of the Twelfth Month,* if that helps."

Eight months.

I pushed myself away from the bar. "Thanks."

Both hands supporting my belly's immense weight, I slowly wandered to the corner table, tucking myself into its warm seclusion. I audibly groaned as I released my shoulders from the guns and the rucksacks, my lower back sighing into the wooden chair's embrace. I'd been on the move for several days, determined to reach Gerta's Grotto within the week. Time kept sprinting away from me, emphasised by my huge belly.

Away from the chatter of drunken guests, I relaxed into the chair's hard contours. I gazed at my bump, like I so often did, and caressed its enormous curvature. The baby moved rather vigorously that evening and each little pulse drew a small smile upon my face, my scarred heart humming a beautiful melody.

I wondered what his eyes would look like. Would they sparkle like Mason's, or mine?

Hopefully mine.

The bartender plodded over with a large wooden box and dumped it on the table with a loud *clank.*

"You've paid upfront for ten minutes," he said with a clipped tone. "Any longer and it'll cost you double."

"I'll keep that in mind."

With a curt nod, he returned behind the bar and continued pouring mead to his drunk customers. I huffed as each golden stream entered the tankards neatly lined up upon the counter. As the entire longhouse buzzed with laughter and conversation, and handfuls of coin spilled from one palm to another, I couldn't help but wonder how much he'd made from this night alone, even without my contribution. Judging by the merry customers and empty tankards, it must have been a stupid amount. He could easily afford to give me more than ten minutes, but clearly extorting a pregnant woman wasn't below him.

With a heavy sigh, I opened the box. A mess of wires jumped out at me, unkindly hitting me with memories of Carter's Den. I hastily shook them away, for the longhouse was already choked with smoke and I didn't need echoes of Carter's scarred face smirking at my impending choices.

The handset's smooth skin cooled my palm through the thin cotton glove. That same chill rose up my arms, trickled down into both legs and caused my foot to twitch nervously against the floorboards. I delved into my pocket, picking out a scrunched piece of paper that cost me more than my leather coat, and spread it across the table's unblemished surface.

I chewed my lip for comfort as I dialled the number scrawled on the paper's creased, white skin. I scrunched it away quickly once the dial tone rang, unable to stomach the sight of it.

A soft, succulent voice hummed on the line. *"Good evening, this is Maelstrom's Switchboard Operator. Where would you like your call rerouted?"*

I pressed the side of my thumb against the corner of my eye, allowing the glove to soak up the tear before my green lenses dislodged.

"P-put..." My throat eroded my words before they had time to escape.

"*Hello?*" the woman asked again.

"P-put me through to Lord Mason."

"*And who should I say is calling?*"

That ominous chill refused to leave me. I shivered, despite the stuffy warmth. "Just tell him I...have information about Alira."

"*Of course.*" Her chirpy tone made me want to gag. "*One minute please.*"

The line clicked and a monotonous dial tone hummed. If I concentrated on it long enough, I'd forget the melodious notes of a violin, constantly swirling around my skull...

"*Yes?*" Mason's rich voice sang down the wire, caressing my ear like sheets of pure velvet. "*Who is this?*"

Sitting there, hearing his voice—feeling our son's delicate movements within me—my decision felt so weighted, so...*wrong.*

I needed to remember why I was there, why was doing this...

"Hi Mason," I said, weakly.

Silence, both in my head and at the other end of that phone. Two loud breaths steadily escaped his lips.

Gradually, his mellow music returned.

"*Alira...*" he said, carefully, as though he didn't quite believe his ears. "*This is a surprise.*"

I chuckled in sardonic agreement. "For us both."

"*I suppose it's pointless to ask where you are.*" His tone settled back into normalcy, control and power dripping from each enunciated syllable. "*However, I'd be grateful if you'd indulge me as to the welfare of my son.*"

Tears broke barriers of my eyelashes, trickling in slow streams. One of them slipped across the scabbed cut upon my cheekbone, cutting through the crust. I winced at the sting. My attacker had cut me deep those few nights ago, evidently.

Despite the assault of fearful, fresh memories, my smile came easily as I caressed my huge bump.

"He's fine." A small titter broke the barrier of my lips. "He's energetic today."

Mason's laugh rolled down the line like a softly breaking wave. "*Indeed. Well, I am immensely glad to hear that.*"

His violin morphed into something dark, and infinitely more sinister.

"*So,*" he growled. "*To what do I owe the pleasure of this call? I assume it is not simply to hear my voice?*"

A bitter huff escaped my throat, away from the handset, before I returned it to my ear.

"I'm here to discuss a deal with you." Trembling fingers massaged away the throbs lingering deep inside my temple. "I mean, the *possibility* of a deal with you."

"*Interesting,*" he purred. "*And what, dare I ask, are you proposing in this deal?*"

I took a moment to regain my breath. I needed to think how to structure the words, to layer them very, very carefully into the cake I'd use to barter my future.

"I love my son, you know I do. You know I'd do anything to keep him safe..."

My son stretched, pressing against the outer wall of my womb. I felt the shape of the strange protrusion through my jumper. A foot, I think.

"*I'm listening,*" Mason prompted.

"I... I can't protect myself anymore, Mason. I'm slow, lumbering. I-I can't run away f-from...from..."

Fear ballooned inside my chest, pushing more tears down my cheeks. I remembered the horror of that night. I remembered the hate, the *amusement* in those four grubby faces as they held down my writing limbs...

Mason carefully listened to the music, and the trickles of fear that must have quivered a piano's strings. "*Does this have anything to do with what happened two weeks ago?*"

My heart stuttered. *Two weeks?* Had it really been that long? The memories were so fresh, it could have been yesterday.

"I-I don't know what you're taking about."

"*No, of course you don't,*" Mason spat. "*After all, your music screams in that much terror simply for fun, doesn't it?*"

Tears drowned my words. I remained silent at Mason's triumphant little chuckle.

"*Regardless of what happened, you are trying—ever so eloquently—to say that you need my protection. Isn't that right?*"

"Yes," I breathed, barely audible.

"*Hm,*" Mason crooned, with an obvious grin. "*Well, that is interesting.*"

"I just want him to be safe," I said, and I meant it. The thought of losing him—especially now, when I could feel the subtle indents of tiny limbs against my flesh—would completely destroy me.

"*I know you do, and I like that about you, Alira. My son's protection lends to a mutual advantage, after all.*

"*But I trust you understand that I can't simply allow you to live freely in my abode. Despite how events played out, you were once a willing member of the Free People's Rebellion and certain...luxuries you enjoyed before may have to be...rethought.*"

My hand clenched around the handset, cramp spreading into my fingertips.

"What do you want?" I snarled.

Mason's violin quivered with anger, and hate, and the dribble of past betrayals.

"*I say, 'Jump'; you ask, 'How high?' Is that clear?*"

I chewed my scarred lip. "Yes," I replied.

"*You will work in my establishment with utmost respect and compliance. I bought you as a Slave, remember? I daresay it's time you pulled your weight in that particular duty, so if I tell you to spread your legs and enjoy me, you will do so without hesitation. Understood?*"

Another cold tear trickled down my cheek. Hate and disgust ballooned inside my belly, curling around my baby's limbs. "Yes," I forced myself to reply.

"*Excellent!*" Mason's violin completely disagreed with his buoyant tone. "*Oh, and one more thing, my dear...*"

I awaited the terms of my future with numb compliance.

"*I trust you understand that a Slave cannot, in any circumstance, legitimately raise my son.*"

Mason might as well have stabbed me through the chest with a rusty nail.

"What?" I breathed, then panic rose hot and blinding. "B-but you said that—"

"*I said that I'd give you and my son protection, that I'd allow you to live within my walls. Given past events, I'd say I'm being more than generous.*"

That rusty nail, its metallic skin so dirty and jagged, started to rotate, stringing out my pain one lingering second at a time.

"He's my *son*, Mason."

"I know, and I respect that. But your past choices lost me a lot of good, loyal men. I hold you personally responsible for the Icelands and—let's not forget, my dear—your half-arsed attempt at an abortion."

I remained cold, chewing on my tongue until I tasted the iron tang of blood. The truth of what happened that night sang nastily around my memories. I wanted to scream that truth to Mason, to punch him with the facts: Ashworth forced that pill down my throat, under the watchful eye of Svenja Svellec. Like I so often did, I thought about the layer of gold smearing the inside of my skull, calling to her soul. It echoed back to me, residing somewhere in the Fjordlands, far away.

"The deal I'm offering is incredibly generous," he said with a heavy sigh, as though I was akin to a nagging child. *"While you will not be my son's official mother, I appreciate that you'll always be his biological mother and, of course, you will still be a notable presence in his life."*

I looked at my bump, imagining the baby that lay snuggled within. I longed to hold him in my arms, to kiss that button nose...

"Can he still call me *Mama*?"

Mason took an awfully long time to reply.

"I think we're far past such honourable titles, don't you agree?"

My face scrunched around crushing despair, forcing tears to leak in hot, acidic streams. Sobs ached to burst, my entire future crumbling, just like Eagle's Overlook.

"Alira," Mason demanded down the handset, held limply in my hand.

Slowly, with great effort, I returned it to my ear. Mason heard my subdued sniffles and his tone grew gentle. *"You will see him grow up. I promise you that."*

I had known Mason long enough to know that such promises held little weight.

"Are you telling me the truth?"

"Perhaps, depending on how this conversation ends."

I gazed at the other people in the longhouse. All were laughing and drinking to merry excess. The once happy, warm atmosphere suddenly grew suffocating.

I sighed down the phone, hanging by the weight of my choices—both past and future.

"I can, however, give you another promise," Mason said, when he sensed my doubt. *"Should you decline this generous offer, I will hunt you until the end of time and I will find you—that I want to make excruciatingly clear."*

I swallowed against the painful ball in my throat.

"And when *I find you, Alira, you will never see our son again."*

That wasn't a lie. I believed that entirely.

"So," he continued with a lightening tone. *"Why don't you tell me where you are?"*

My tongue ached to curse him and all his *fucking* deals, but I quickly held it still between my teeth. My fingers delved into my pocket and, like they so often had done recently, caressed the purple diamond, still attached to its silver chain. Visions of the Icelands—of Eagle's Overlook—flashed in unison behind my eyelids, followed by the screams of so many innocent people.

I didn't want to do this. Far from it.

But then I felt the cut upon my cheek. I remembered the tight depress of fingers on my upper arms, holding me still as the knife waved with sick, teasing motions.

Dark, unsympathetic memories haunted my vision, not of *my* fate, but my son's. His entire existence had been condemned before he was even born, and he didn't deserve that. He deserved to live.

Music be damned. *I* needed him to live...

"Alira," Mason impatiently growled down the telephone.

"The longhouse, Gerta's Grotto," I said, and slammed the phone down with a hard rattle.

As Mason's violin rejoiced, I carefully considered the choice I had just made.

Perhaps Mason's protection would make all this worth it. Yes, I had to surrender my freedom, my very soul, but it meant I could cuddle my son close to my bosom. Mason knew that, and he knew me too well to think I'd do anything but.

He also knew how far I'd go to ensure the safety of my son. My body, my *compliance,* was a nice extra. Nothing more than a way to punish, to tighten the noose of control around my neck. Perhaps, after a while, I'd learn to enjoy it?

I felt sick, for the first time in months.

A couple of deep breaths and I quickly wiped my face, just as the bartender came to remove the telephone.

"Could I have a tankard of water?" I croaked, as he met my teary gaze. "Looks like I'll be here for a while."

* * *

THE LONGHOUSE GRADUALLY EMPTIED AS the hours lingered on. Caressing my huge bump, I sipped my tankard of stale water and observed the wandering mass of people. Some were more inebriated than others, stumbling against the bar or grasping their cackling friends for dear life. Others simply grew tired, or frisky, and wandered out into the snow alone or with potential partners.

I eyed the couples, noticing the affection gushing from their eyes and wondered if Mason and I once appeared that enamoured with each other. I couldn't remember anymore.

The necklace weighed ever so heavy in my hand. I squeezed it as tight as my aching muscles would allow, so constant reminders of my integrity scratched against my palm.

Deep inside, I knew I didn't have a choice. My son's life was too goddamned precious and I would not lose another one. I couldn't protect him anymore—the horrific events two weeks ago proved just that.

I'd underestimated how difficult this would be—the fatigue, the fear, the physical impediments... I desperately needed help. I could no longer do this on my own and yet, everyone wanted me dead. Who else could I turn to, if not Mason?

Campbell? *Svenja?*

Until my son was born, I was akin to a walking target. Mason's entire mortality rested on my son's birth and the vast majority of people in his *New World* wanted to destroy us. They had already broken me twice before. I would not survive a third time. Mason, as wretched as he was, was the only person who understood this, who could *protect* us.

This wasn't anything like that firelit cave where my son was conceived. I wasn't doing this for *my* future. I was doing this for my son's.

So why did *regret*, once again, come crunching the back of my skull?

The door barged open. In walked two Masonians, their blue coats speckled with snow, their heads kept warm by fur hats. Cold eyes perused the scene with intense precision.

They spotted me easily. After demanding a drink from the bar, they took their tankards to another table and silently watched me.

Evidently here on Mason's orders, just to keep a watchful eye until my transport arrived. Perhaps he was worried I'd run again.

The thought had occurred to me, too.

My face twisting, I took a long, loving stare towards my bump, trying to flush out the stench of regret. *I'm sorry I'm doing this to us, baby-boy, but we need help. I can't do this on my own anymore...*

Minutes wore on. My tankard of water had been completely emptied yet I kept it suspended in my hands, if only for comfort.

"Care for a refill?" the bartender asked. His face had developed a distinctly paler sheen since the Masonians' arrival. I forced a small smile and shook my head. He motioned to remove the tankard.

"I'll keep this, if you don't mind." I needed something to occupy my hands—and the tankard burned less than the necklace.

A little dismayed, the bartender took slow and careful steps back behind the bar.

For a while, nothing changed. Until the low hum of engines rattled into the longhouse. Breath caught in my throat. *This is it*, I kept thinking. My freedom was all used up, just like the last dribbles of water clinging to the bottom of the tankard.

I waited for the flood of Masonians to burst inside. More minutes ticked by and nothing happened.

One of my guarding Masonians, clearly impatient, stood to his feet and strolled towards the door with his tankard suspended in his hand.

The door burst open. A flurry of snow flew into the longhouse, along with masked intruders who aimed shortened shotguns. Bangs ricocheted.

Bodies fell with loud thumps. The bartender stumbled back against the bar with his palms up in surrender. Another bang splattered his head across the pristine wood.

I pressed my rifle into the crook of my shoulder, comforted by its weight, and convulsed my finger against the trigger. One intruder fell, then another. A Masonian convulsed as lead ripped his throat out.

Two more intruders flooded in. The last Masonian fell, his fur hat speckled with blood.

Intruders' eyes found me, panting, cowering into the corner of the longhouse.

I fired, but they'd already leapt behind fallen tables.

My rifle clip emptied. I startled, desperately digging for an extra box of ammunition.

The box rattled in my fingers. I gasped in panic, hurling the smoky air into my lungs as trembling fingers fought with the box.

I was too slow. An intruder gripped my rifle's metallic snout and ripped it clean from my fingertips.

Terror consumed me. I tried to scramble to my feet but my belly made me slow, my movements so lethargic despite my racing adrenaline.

I was easily plucked back, pulled by my hair to the wooden floorboards. I landed with a hard slam and sharp rods of pain rippled down my spine. I forced it aside and crawled across the bloody floorboards.

Intruders surrounded me. Four of them, their faces covered with black masks and their eyes obscured with glass goggles. And yet, despite their covered features, I detected the smirks painting their lips, their mutual satisfaction as one crouched before me.

"Hello again, sweetheart."

I recognised his voice. The husky, the sonorous tone was just as frightening now as it was two weeks ago, when those same thugs held me down, taunting me with a serrated knife.

Horrifying realisations dawned as he plucked that exact knife from his inside pocket.

"You left us too soon last time. We told you: One-Legged Jay wants that little baby out of you."

"No, no!" I screamed, protecting my precious bump with shaking hands. I

propelled myself back. Inhibited by my sheer weight, three intruders pounced upon my flailing limbs, like foxes on their prey.

Dripping with sick enthusiasm, the knife-wielder hopped above me, kneeling on either side of my hips, and stroked the cool blade against the scabbed cut upon my cheek.

"Shall I decorate your other cheek tonight, darlin'?"

"Don't hurt him! *Please!* Do anything you want to me but don't hurt my baby!"

The man leant close, revealing stained yellow teeth. "Oh, we're not going to hurt *him*, sweetheart," he said, as rancid breath fluttered across my features. "We just need to get him out of you. One-Legged Jay has a lot planned for Mason's son, after all."

All my fear, all my abhorrent nightmares suddenly reformed anew. They grew more wretched, more horrific, and I screamed as fingers dug into my flesh.

"Shh…" the man with the knife crooned, his hot breath warming the tears upon my cheeks. "Try not to make too much noise, hey?"

The knife descended.

A figure burst into the longhouse. A deafening *bang* erupted, ricocheting against the walls, rattling up into the rafters that held strings of rosemary and thyme.

My attacker's head burst open. Warm blood splattered my face. He fell to my side, lifeless, the knife still gripped within his fingers. Another bang and the man holding my left arm fell dead. The two other intruders jumped to their feet, releasing me, and I scrambled to my waiting box of ammunition.

The stranger threw their lean body behind an overturned table, surviving the bulk of the bullets before they returned the gesture. One more intruder fell to the ground.

I snapped my loaded rifle shut. No hesitation in my shot, just relief as the last intruder stumbled about, clawing at the bloody dot between his shoulder blades. He fell in a motionless heap.

My rifle found the surrendering palms of my heroic stranger, just peeking from the splintered table.

"Don't shoot!"

Air caught in my throat. I recognised that voice: the kind tone, the slight echo of immaturity... I'd laughed with that voice, heard its jokes and jibes...

No, that's impossible...

"Joe?" I whispered; the name so scandalous it barely seemed real.

Seafoam-green eyes peeked from behind the table. I took in the chocolate-brown hair, the gaunt face, the charismatic mouth that could always barter a good deal...

Joe Matheson stood, Campbell's black revolver still smoking in his hand.

Joe... I tried to say again, but the word caught in my throat. With trembling, weak limbs, I stumbled towards him and collapsed in his warm, embracing arms.

"Gods, it's good to see you," he whispered into my hair. With a gentle movement, he separated us, holding me at arm's length. I clutched those arms, desperate fingers grasping at his leather coat, terrified he'd disappear if I dared to let go.

"H-how are you here?" I breathed to the space between us. "I thought Carter's men killed you."

Joe's lips quirked into a smirk. "I played dead when I ran out of bullets. Lying in a pool of my own blood, I must've looked like shit because they didn't even check my pulse."

He waved Campbell's black revolver. "This thing's saved my life ever since."

"Oh my Gods..." I crushed him into me again, burying my face into the crook of his neck. To feel such unadulterated joy was so unusual, so unexpected that my limbs failed. Joe caught me before I tumbled.

"Take it steady," he said, righting a fallen chair and easing me down.

He rushed behind the blood-stained bar and picked out a glass bottle, full of water. I sipped it as Joe took residence in the opposite chair.

"How did you know I was here?" I asked, after the water washed away the shock.

Seafoam eyes dropped to my pregnant belly. "Truth be told, I didn't. I thought Mason found you, months ago."

"Not exactly," I muttered dryly. "So, why are you here then?"

"I was on the trail of the Jay Gang."

I cast my eyes to the corpses, staining the wooden floorboards. "They're gang members?"

"Yup, formed by Carter's stragglers, apparently. Run by some mystery man called One-Legged Jay. For the last few months, I've been trying to figure out what they're up to." Joe's cracked lips tilted up in sardonic amusement. "Given that most people want me dead, I originally hoped I'd be able to barter a deal with this new gang, maybe do some runs for them in return for some protection."

Joe took a sad stare around the room. "Of course, I'm beginning to rethink that plan."

I caressed my belly, trying to halt my incessant shivers. "Why do they want my baby?"

"I don't know," he said softly. "But from what I've seen, their motivations are vastly different from the Mulch Gang's, and even the Free People's."

"What d'you mean?"

"From what I've seen so far, they're not into drugs, trafficking, or even goddamn liberation. They cause carnage wherever they go but with no particular cause. Word is, they trashed Eagle's Overlook before Mason got there."

"That was them?" I remembered the raging bonfires, the look on poor Harald's face as they set his beloved inn alight... "I thought they were Rebels."

Joe sighed. "Probably a mixture of both. After the Icelands, I heard that many of the Rebels pledged loyalty to One-Legged Jay in the hopes of some retribution. Now, it's not just the Icelands, but Eagle's Overlook, Bear's Folly, and all the rest of them."

That made sense. An entire Territory had been wiped off the map and all residents of the New World felt the pain of cracking earth. Not forgetting Eagle's Overlook—one of the grandest towns in the New World—reduced to rubble around the limbs of screaming children. *And* the weeks following, when numerous Rebel towns easily succumbed beneath Mason's wrath.

Yes, I could understand their rage, their desire for revenge. That did not mean they could use my son in their sordid schemes.

"They found me two weeks ago," I whispered. "I was staying at the inn in Phantom's Bluff. I'd befriended the innkeeper there."

Gerrat—a lovely, kind man. Blue eyes spilled compassion and under-standing, his thick beard braided with wooden beads. Though he was obliv-ious to my identity, he took pity on a young, pregnant woman and always gave me a good price for a comfortable room in his inn.

Such a beautiful town. Just a selection of small shops, huts, and a central market choked with stalls and great big buckets of spiced wine, steaming in the cold air. Nestled at the towering edge of one of the tallest mountains in the Glasslands, it overlooked a field of winding glaciers. Their creaks and cracks echoed up the town, their very bodies illuminated with turquoise.

People busked along the main roads, others laughed and joked around blazing braziers. The people were kind in that town. The very air was just...*happy.*

Things felt a bit less lonely there.

I'd planned to give birth there, maybe even settle there. I had imagined my son and I hiking up the glaciers, only to return to a feather bed and a warm fire. We'd have listened to the bard and the music, then danced arm in arm until bedtime. *Please, just one more hour of dancing, Mama.* How wonderful such a life would have been.

But then the men in masks came. They killed Gerrat—just butchered him like an animal—and set his inn on fire. I fled, but in my pregnant state, I couldn't run fast. They had easily plucked from the snow, held me down as that serrated knife sliced my cheek.

Masonians had roared in just before the first cut in my belly. In the confu-sion, I escaped to the nearby forest, hiding within the trunks until my attackers grew tired of trying to catch me.

I remained in that forest for a long time, too scared to move. Shivering, hungry, exhausted... Squeezing the purple necklace in my fist as I considered my options. As I considered my newest *failure.*

The journey across the Glasslands—to the nearest settlement to Phan-tom's Bluff—was the hardest of my life, but I didn't have a choice. Those men were still looking for me, so I'd forced myself to keep going. On the fourth day of the hike, I'd bled a little. Crying and scared, I lay in a cave with limited supplies and willed my son to stay put—and healthy. *Please, Freya, may he be alright...*

The bleeding thankfully stopped after the second day and I forced myself to carry on. Then I spotted a polar bear wandering dangerously close to the cave, sniffing the air.

Alone with my thoughts, the flood of rumination threatened. What would've happened if the bleeding hadn't stopped? What if I'd gone into labour—unexpectedly and with no supplies—and given birth to a premature baby? What if he needed medical attention? What if *I* did?

What if that polar bear decided to investigate the smell of blood? How fast could a postpartum mother run when chased by snapping teeth?

So many questions. So many consequences.

Suddenly, an idea rooted. An ugly bush of thorns cut away my hope, growing over the decaying bed of lilies those weeks in Phantom's Bluff had once nurtured. But the idea kept growing, those thorns kept stabbing, and I finally accepted the dismal truth.

I needed help.

Once I'd accepted that, there was only one person in this entire World I could turn to.

Who could've guessed that Joe Matheson—of *all* people—would save me in Gerta's Grotto? If I were in brighter spirits, I would've burst out laughing at the absurdity of it all.

I barely had any friends left, so Joe's sudden appearance was akin to a miracle. How many more miracles did I have left? Maybe I'd already used up my allotted free miracles; I'd have to pay for the rest.

"I'm sorry, girl," Joe said, after I'd explained what happened in Phantom's Bluff.

My forced smile barely reached my nose. "They're going to keep coming after me, Joe. I have no idea why this *One-Legged Jay* wants my son, but I'll be damned to let him have him."

"Damn lucky I found you then, innit?" Joe chuckled, standing to tuck the revolver in his jeans. "C'mon, Masonians are perusing the area, so we better get moving."

"I'm staying here," I said weakly, unable to meet Joe's stunned frown.

"Well, that doesn't make sense. Masonians are on their way and..." Joe suddenly realised the situation he had stumbled upon. "Shittin' hell... You've given yourself up, haven't you?"

I licked the salt from my lips. "It's the only way I can save my son."

"No, it not!" Incensed, Joe fell back into the chair with a great huff. "Girl, why the fuck would you give yourself back to him?"

"Because where else am I going to go?" I replied softly.

Joe's face softened. With a heavy sigh, he leant forwards and clasped my hands within his. His heat was a welcome reprieve to the ice trickling up my fingers.

"Please think about this."

"I've spent the last two weeks *thinking about it*." I huffed bitterly to the space between us. "It's the only way."

Joe snapped his hands away, disgust spreading like a stain upon his face. "He doesn't deserve your cooperation, girl!"

"But I deserve to be *happy!*" Clear liquid dribbled from my eyes, doing little but paint pity on Joe's features.

"Do you honestly believe you'll be happy with him?"

I avoided his eye and stared at the chandelier of antlers. Soon the candles would die, as would the hearth, and we'd be surrounded by cold shadow.

But there, beneath the warm light, I knew—without a single doubt—that no future with Mason would ever be *happy*. He would continue to destroy, to maim and punish. And he would hurt me again, in the future. Mason's insatiable virility would never separate him from his destined *mate*, no matter how hard she begged. The deal I'd just agreed to merely screamed that fact.

I recalled the last deal I'd made with Mason, eight months previously. I remembered how eager—how *excited*—I was to run to his Masonian camp. My stomach lurched so hard at the memories, I thought I'd vomit right over Joe's scruffy boots. I hated the woman I was back then. I hated how devastated she was when Ashworth crushed her idiotic dreams of a *future*.

This time, I had no delusions: I knew the monster Mason was, and the mere thought of being under his roof made me squirm. No excitement, no eagerness. Just dread.

The exact same deal, made by two different women and for two very different reasons. I hoped history would remember that.

"No," I said. "Of course, I won't be *happy* with him, Joe. But at least my son will be safe."

"And in the hands of a tyrant," Joe stated, eyebrows raised.

Joe was right. Mason would carry our son in his arms. He'd even claim to *care* for him as he'd train his Firstborn to paint dancing lights in the sky, or to pull pretty flowers from the ground, or to turn the entire landscape into a pit of convulsing ruin.

Mason would ensure our son would be a Destroyer. *That* was Mason's destiny, that was why he wanted a son. Mason didn't want *his* World destroyed, he never had. But he wanted the next one to crumble. Someone must have taught Mason how to control his power— and how to destroy the Old World—and I'd bet on everything I had that it was William, his father. So, Mason would train *our* son in the same way, spurred on by Arabella's barbaric desperation that had done nothing but smear hate and anger upon his soul.

And yet again, Joe was right—I *had* given myself up knowing the consequences. Why? Because I was desperate and selfish. Because I wanted a son just as much as Mason did, and I would do anything to ensure his survival, as would the music inside my soul. Besides, I didn't owe anything to people of this World—not when they'd done all they could to hurt and maim us. That didn't make my decision right, but it helped ease the guilt inside my heart.

This was my future, my *destiny.* Sebastian had been right all along: I couldn't run from it. Not anymore. Not after Phantom's Bluff.

And as for those poor souls in the next World...

"I hate that I'm doing this," I whispered. "I fucking *hate* it..."

"Then why *are* you?"

I caressed my belly and a small sob burst free. "Because I want my son to live—and I know a large part of that is the music and my fucking destiny... But even if all of that was taken away... I'm still his mother, so is really so wrong of me? Is it so terrible that I want to hold him, to see him grow up?"

"Mason will never let you be his mother." Joe's words punched me in the stomach. "But you know that, don't you?"

I chewed the scar on my lip. "I don't have another option."

Joe licked his lips, chapped and rosy from the bitter outside air. "But what if there is? I'm hiding too—from Mason, Campbell, heck even One-Legged Jay once he finds out what I've done here. Just like you, I'm on the run so why don't you come with me? I can protect you, take some of the weight off your shoulders. Please, let me help you..."

I met those seafoam eyes, once so full of immaturity and betrayal, and saw the sheer...*righteousness* that suddenly sprang out.

"Why?" I asked. "Why would you do that?"

"Because I owe you..." Guilt flooded the air, thick and suffocating. "I started all of this, I put you on a path full of pain and suffering. After everything you've been through—everything *I* did to you and Campbell—I just want to make amends. Heck, I *want* you to be happy."

Another road opened to me, one not bordered with thorns, but a field of beckoning bluebells. A smile, small yet genuine, curled my lips. My bump was so large as I held it impossibly close.

"You'll be protecting Mason's son," I said—because I needed him to understand what he was offering. "He's destined to destroy the next World, *that's* why I'm the End of Everything. Aren't you at all worried that you'll be helping me raise a killer?"

"Aren't we all killers around here?" Joe sighed, squinting into the firelight, soaking in the bursts of orange light upon his skin. "I'm a dodgy bastard—my moral compass went haywire a long time ago. Besides, this kid's done nothing to me, nothing to anyone. To call him a killer before he's even born is a tad presumptuous, innit?"

A laugh broke the barrier of my resolve, spilling *relief* down my limbs. My heart, usually so heavy and burdened, rose high into my chest as the first trickles of *hope* reappeared.

"So, this is how it's going to be, huh?" I asked. "Two traitors, running from retribution?"

Sadness flicked upon Joe's face. He bowed his head, staring at the dried mud on his boots. Then he met my gaze.

"How about two old friends, just trying to survive."

My lips stretched with my wide, ecstatic grin. Relief continued to lift my heart, merging into the surviving candles that sent thick rushes of warmth down my arms. I took my metaphorical shears and cut down those dangerous thorns, one at a time.

I desperately needed help, and I thought Mason was the only person I could turn to. It took nearly two weeks of tears, blood, and crushing dread before I decided to call Mason. This decision took less than a nanosecond, and my heart had never felt so light.

"Yes," I whispered, unable to relax my cheeks. "I'd like that a lot…"

With a tender smile, Joe stood to his feet and offered me his hand. I allowed him to pull me up, relishing this dizzying rush of optimism.

My guns hanging from my shoulders, my rucksack slung across Joe's back, we escaped the death of that longhouse. I relished that icy air, breathing it deep inside my lungs, holding its fresh freedom inside my body.

I didn't look back to Loki's Lost Longhouse, where Mason and his convoy would soon be entering. In fact, the thought didn't even occur.

Regret didn't sneak upon my skin, like it so often did. My fate, my *future* was as clear as the wall of towering mountains and I was ready—oh, so ready—to dive deep into their majestic embrace.

Me and my son, climbing with Joe up the throat of the world.

The mere thought was exhilarating.

What would Mason do, when he discovered the longhouse empty? I doubt he'd be best pleased. Oh, if only to be a fly on the wall! To witness his face fall, his sickening arrogance drop to his pounding black boots. It would all be rather hilarious.

Whatever happened, I'd be far away, keeping my son warm until he was ready to pop out. I already anticipated my smile when *Mama* would first pass his lips.

As excitement teased existence, I leant into Joe's side. Unspoken thanks poured from beneath my leather coat.

With a tender smile, Joe passed his arm around my shoulders, holding me close as we walked towards those mountains.

30

I groaned into a makeshift bed of furs as another contraction hit. Sweaty hands clenched and fisted the blanket beneath me.

Gradually, as the wave of pain rolled away, I relaxed into the release.

Joe's concern arose from the other side of a rickety wooden door, "You hanging in there, girl?"

I agreed with a tiresome tone.

Slowly, I moved my sweaty, naked body across the fur blankets, already soaked in amniotic fluid. The interior of that wooden hut, so thick and hot, was choked with the heavy scent of organics and I needed some fresh air. I perched next to the open window, inhaling the iciness of the Glasslands' mountains. An aurora danced high above, caressing the landscape with pristine blue light. Behind that, billions of stars sparkled, more brightly than I'd ever seen before.

Mason's power was growing. His violin, full of anticipation, sang with glorious, exuberant melodies. How different to the screeching anger merely three weeks earlier, when he arrived at an empty longhouse. Despite the agony of that morning, I still smiled.

Cool fingers of wind parted my damp hair, skipping across my flushed skin. I closed my eyes, free of the contacts, and relished her touch. Freedom was so beautiful.

Another contraction grew like a curling ocean wave. I squeezed my eyes shut, my arms taut above cramping hands that gripped the window's wooden frame for dear life.

I barely had time to catch my breath before another wave of pain, and then another, and then another. The urge to *push* grew stronger, then irrepressible. I groaned loudly through the sickening pain, spreading my knees wide over those blankets.

As the aurora's light flickered across those mountains, I pushed my damn heart out.

Loud cries escaped my throat, my entire body searing yet in utter, bewildered awe. My hands caught the warm, slippery softness of new skin and I sobbed in astounded joy, carefully supporting the small being I was giving birth to.

Finally, a small baby's cries filled the stuffy room.

Exhaustion rose, pouring lead through my body. I collapsed back onto those furs and placed the warm, mewling being upon my tingling breasts. As I wiped the bits of mucus from his face, I examined him: the shape of his nose, the delicate rosiness of his skin, the dimples in his chin and around his eyes.

Something ballooned inside my chest: such a deep, powerful sense of love that I laughed, then cried, then laughed again.

My body, so sore and torn, rejuvenated. Flesh stitched back together, my abdominal muscles shrank and tightened. My hair, drooped across my shoulders, flared with glossy life. Power and strength—the likes of which no mortal should ever possess—prickled through my bones, exploring the body my son's birth had now preserved.

Immortality. The last price I would pay; the last gift the music would bestow.

I didn't care, for there was no greater gift than what was in my arms.

I cradled my new-born son, breathing him in, inhaling the scent of new life.

"Hello, Aleksander," I whispered in my native tongue.

As if my words had roused him from his slumber, eyes peeked open, as if adjusting to the flickering light. His eyes, like polished silver, stared back at me. His cries stopped as he saw my own eyes, as though he was utterly enraptured by each little twinkle, each sparkle.

As I continued to stare, a shape formed: a smooth, pristine ball of diamond that sparkled wildly. No emotion spilled from his soul, for there was no groove or crevasse to pool such a thing. My son's soul was untouched, unfolded. Utterly perfect.

For a moment, I was terrified that my son would see my own soul, to catch a glimpse of the emotions that had shaped it. But as I continued to gaze at his features—skimming my sight across *his* soul—I felt my own morph. The birth of my son was such a powerful, beautiful event that it embraced my soul, coating it in a burst of emotional protection that allowed him to safely explore its peculiar shape.

Something new fluttered inside my skull. Soft and delicate, like the sprinkle of snow upon my brain.

My son felt it too. A joyous bubble of laughter erupted from his throat, his small limbs wriggling.

Tears of joy seeped from my eyes as my son and I formed our Connection.

* * *

Sometime later, as I nursed my son under the watchful flicker of a fire, Joe Matheson stood in the doorway of the little wooden hut we had commandeered for the last few days. A rifle hung from a strap across his shoulder, his brown hair rippling in the cold breeze as he perused the scene below him.

Through heavy-lidded eyes, I watched the man I'd known almost my whole life. When had he morphed from that immature, treacherous Trader into our fearless protector? Clearly his own experiences had shaped his soul too.

"Any movement?" I asked, struggling to stay awake.

"Nah, I reckon we'll be safe here for another day or two." Joe stared up and blue light caressed his features. "Jeez, I've never seen that aurora so bright before."

"Mason's celebrating," I replied, listening inside my head. "You should hear how loud his music is."

My son wriggled against me. I gazed at him and that sprinkle of snow reappeared inside my skull.

I continued to cradle him, cocooning him within more blankets, warming him with my own heat. That delicate Connection resurfaced, informing me that he was now content. I grinned as he surrendered to his sleep, relishing the last of those cold prickles as they began to wane, then disappear entirely. But they'd return when my son would wake for his next feed. I couldn't wait.

Joe closed us off from the outside air, cocooning us in the warm light, and sat directly opposite. We both just stared at the baby in my arms.

"He looks like Mason," I stated.

Joe paused for a moment. "Does that bother you?"

"No." An elated smile worked my lips. "He has my eyes."

Joe stared at my baby again, gauging his mess of dimples. But I didn't need to see his silvery eyes to know that he'd inherited mine. I just knew.

I placed a loving kiss upon my son's forehead, my heart gushing as he snuggled deeper into my hold.

Watching him sleep so peacefully, I thought of the innocence of his soul. Totally unblemished, like fresh layers of snow.

How could Mason sire such a beautiful being? How could my son's pristine, spherical soul be born from his angular monstrosity?

I recalled Svenja's efforts to turn Arabella against Mason and the hate that shaped his soul as a result of that. Did Svenja know, I wonder? Did she understand that to end the Family's Line, she'd helped create the very monster she was so determined to destroy?

A Destroyer.

My son's gentle coos found my ears. How could this sweet, innocent being possibly kill countless? It seemed so ridiculous for Svenja, or even Mason, to think such a sordid thing. And yet, apparently, that was his destiny.

Yet, Arabella was proof that destinies—that *personalities*—could be irrevocably changed. Arabella ceased to be a Protector as soon as she threatened Mason's life. Given such a fact, was it too foolish to believe that I could raise my son to *protect* life instead of destroying it?

Perhaps, now that my son was born—now the music was no longer needed—it freed my mind up to those possibilities. Perhaps *I* could finally choose *my* destiny, to fully decide whether I'd live up to my infamous title.

Because yes, I felt free. Like my heart had lifted from a pond of sludge and finally been wiped clean. But it was more than joy, more than comfort and happiness and delight.

It was triumph. Triumph that I was there, cradling my son in the middle of the mountains and not shackled to a bed in Mason's new residence. It was the pure, shuddering relief that Joe had not been a minute too late, or those intruders a minute too early.

It was the unbreakable realisation that I'd lived the last two years bowing to the music's wishes, but no more. I'd felt those musical claws retract from my soul the moment my son cried his first breath, the moment my dormant immortality ignited. I closed my eyes, listening to the violin's song, and realised my unbreakable Connection with Mason was, in its own way, also an echo. Nothing but a reminder of the music that had taken such dark joy in ensuring the baby in my arms existed.

But, as that bright, silencing freedom coursed through my veins, I decided that I wouldn't allow myself to be the End of Everything. I wouldn't allow my son to grow up knowing what devastating power he possessed, or what he could do with it. After all these months—all those wretched decisions—my mind cleared. Like the dark fog that had consumed my head—my *heart*—had been finally blown away. Perhaps it was some renewed purpose now the music had unwrapped its own twisted agenda from my soul, allowing it to now be reshaped into something *I* wanted: No longer to birth Mason's son, but to *protect* him from his destiny. To protect him from the music, and the man who still relished its siren song.

After everything that had happened—all those experiences, events, and emotions—this was the *true* sound of silence. The only one that mattered.

"Mason can never find him, Joe," I said, as waves of exhaustion rolled over me. "I won't allow that, I-I *can't* allow that."

"Damn right." Joe smiled, and behind those intelligent, cheeky, *kind* eyes, I saw his sincerity—his absolute resolve. "We'll protect him. No matter what happens, we'll keep him hidden."

"Yes..." I stared down at my sleeping son. My gorgeous, sleeping son. "I won't let him find you, Alek. I promise."

THANK YOU FOR READING!

Have you signed up to my newsletter? You'll receive exclusive stories, a free map of the New World, and get first dibs on all my future releases. If I've (hopefully!) convinced you, scan the QR code below to sign up and receive your free PDF Map of the New World, created by the incredible Andrés Aguirre Jurado (@aaguirreart).

* * *

If you've enjoyed *The Sound of Silence*, please consider leaving a review on Amazon and/or Goodreads, as these are incredibly important for all authors, but especially for indie authors. Not only do reviews help more people find my books, but reviews also provide valuable feedback for me, too!

ALSO BY ESME CARMICHAEL

The Connection Series: Book 4

The Bonds of Blood

Welcome to the End of Everything. Try to escape your destiny.

<u>**Coming soon**</u>

ALSO BY ESME CARMICHAEL

The Connection Series: The New World Novellas

The Waltz of Wolves

Before The End of Everything, there was a Waltz of Wolves...

Campbell Anders wishes nothing more than to escape Maelstrom. Endlessly bullied by his cruel, Aristocratic family, Campbell's life is nothing short of miserable. But when the charmingly cocky Harrison Dagger is dragged into the Anders' family home, Campbell's life takes a dangerous, unexpected turn...

The Waltz of Wolves is a standalone prequel that will be released as 3 novellas. Part 1 can be read before or after *The End of Everything*.

Download *The Waltz of Wolves: Part 1*:

CONTENT WARNINGS

- Sustained threat
- Foul language
- Violence
- Blackmail
- Prostitution (implied, not described)
- Assault
- Torture
- Rape (as dubious consent/coercion)
- Genital mutilation (threat of)
- Grief
- Genocide
- Death (includes death of a child)
- Terminal illness
- Drug use
- Alcohol use
- Gaslighting
- Numbing
- Depression
- Terminal illness
- Suicide

- Paedophilia (mention only)
- Infanticide
- Slavery
- Pregnancy
- Pregnancy through rape
- Miscarriage
- Forced adoption (mention only)
- Abortion (including forced)
- Emotional manipulation
- Emotional abuse
- Abusive relationships
- Stockholm Syndrome
- Forced sterilisation (attempted)
- Anxiety
- Trauma
- Post Traumatic Stress Disorder

ABOUT THE AUTHOR

Esme Carmichael is a UK independent author and published her debut novel, *The End of Everything*, in January 2021. Most of her stories have vivid worlds, dark and dystopian themes, and characters you'll love-to-hate and hate-to-love.

Esme co-hosts the live-streamed Steam Queens podcast, is an ambassador for #TheWriterCommunity, works full time as an ocean scientist, and refuses to believe her TBR-pile is out of control.

facebook.com/esmecarmichaelauthor

instagram.com/esmecarmichael_author

goodreads.com/esmecarmichael

tiktok.com/@thebookishwriter

www.ingramcontent.com/pod-product-compliance
Lightning Source LLC
Chambersburg PA
CBHW051459030726
47592CB00006B/2004